THE HELENA CRYSTAL

Book Three
of
The Five Angels Trilogy

KIMBERLY M. RINGER

Kisy Kane
Publishing, LLC
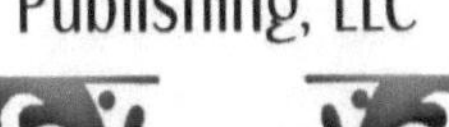

KIMBERLY M. RINGER
FANTASY AND PARANORMAL ROMANCE

DEDICATION

For My Little Human.

Boop Snoot.

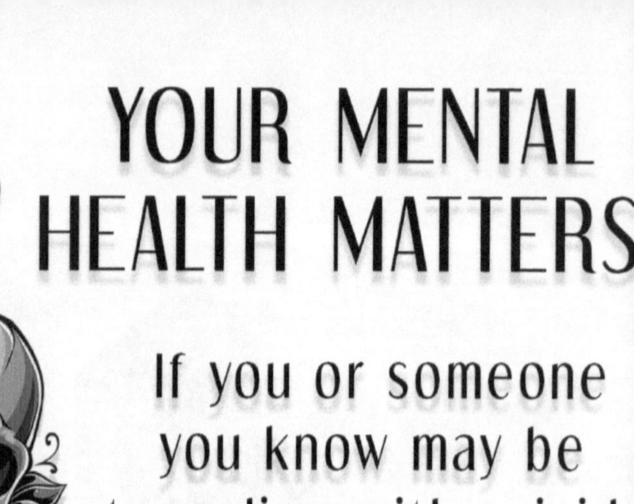

If you or someone you know may be struggling with suicidal thoughts, you can call the U.S. National Suicide Prevention Lifeline by simply dialing 988 or the full phone number: 800-273-TALK (8255) any time, day or night, or chat

Crisis Text Line also provides free, 24/7, confidential support via text message to people in crisis when they dial 741741.

Content Considerations

Family Death

On Page Death

Emotional Violence

Physical Violence

Politics

Religion

Profanity

Sexually Explicit Scenes

Torture

Skinning

Depression

War

Suicidal thoughts

Misogynistic Society

Narcissistic Persons

Magic System

Genocide

Bones

Sexual Assault (not MC's)

Manipulation

Skeletons

Destitute Society

Animal Death

Blood

Maps

NALSAR WORLD MAP
LANSKER FROZEN ISLANDS
CURTAILS OF THE NORTH
NALRIN
LANSKER SEA
VORTILE
CINDER
THE WHISPERING CHANNEL
OBSECURITIAN
SILTIC MARSH
THE GLEAMING OCEAN
ENCHANTED CANAL
SOUTHERN ISLES

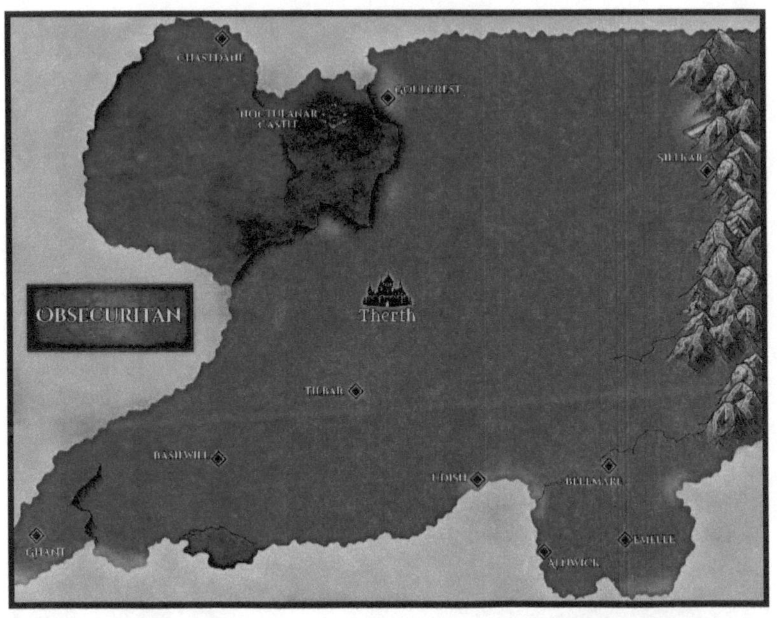
CHASEDALE
GOLECREST
HOCTULANAR
CASTLE
SILLKAR
OBSECURITAN
Therth
TILBAR
BASHWILL
TIDISH
BELLMARL
EMELLE
GHANT
ALDWICK

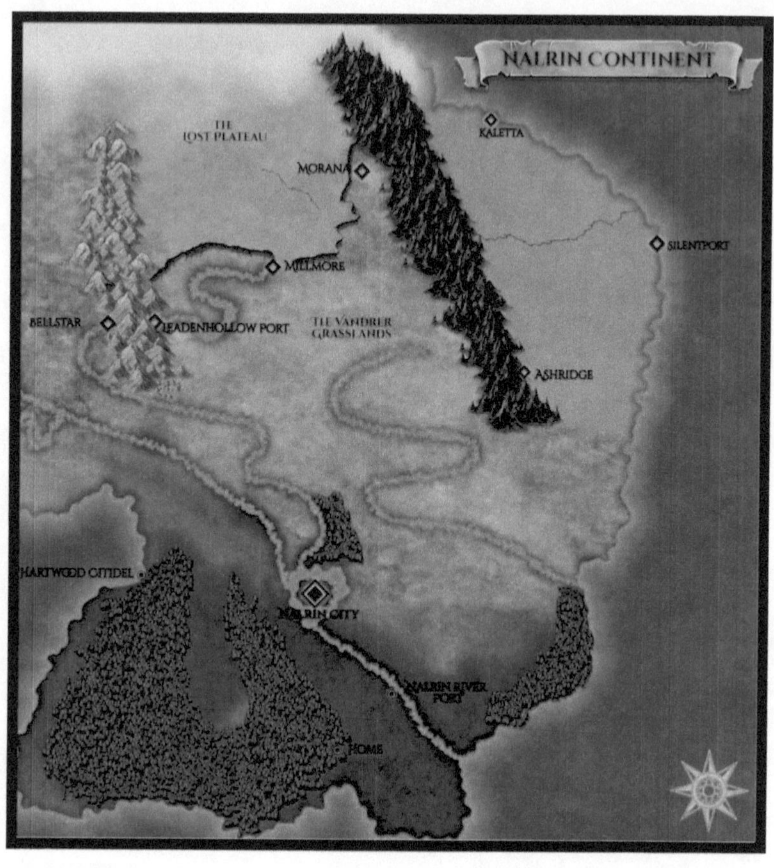

NALRIN CONTINENT
THE LOST PLATEAU
KALETTA
MORANA
SILENTPORT
MILLMORE
BELLSTAR
LEADENHOLLOW PORT
THE VANDRER GRASSLANDS
ASHRIDGE
HARTWOOD CITADEL
NALRIN CITY
NALRIN RIVER PORT
HOME

CONTENTS

1. Chapter 1   1

2. Chapter 2   6

3. Chapter 3   9

4. Chapter 4   15

5. Chapter 5   22

6. Chapter 6   34

7. Chapter 7   39

8. Chapter 8   44

9. Chapter 9   48

10. Chapter 10   53

11. Chapter 11   62

12. Chapter 12   67

13. Chapter 13   74

14. Chapter 14   82

15. Chapter 15   91

16. Chapter 16   99

17. Chapter 17   106

18. Chapter 18   111

19.	Chapter 19	116
20.	Chapter 20	124
21.	Chapter 21	129
22.	Chapter 22	135
23.	Chapter 23	144
24.	Chapter 24	147
25.	Chapter 25	154
26.	Chapter 26	159
27.	Chapter 27	163
28.	Chapter 28	167
29.	Chapter 29	173
30.	Chapter 30	182
31.	Chapter 31	190
32.	Chapter 32	196
33.	Chapter 33	203
34.	Chapter 34	209
35.	Chapter 35	214
36.	Chapter 36	219
37.	Chapter 37	225
38.	Chapter 38	231
39.	Chapter 39	237
40.	Chapter 40	242
41.	Chapter 41	246
42.	Chapter 42	249

43. Chapter 43 253

44. Chapter 44 257

45. Chapter 45 264

46. Chapter 46 269

47. Chapter 47 274

48. Chapter 48 280

49. Chapter 49 287

50. Chapter 50 289

51. Chapter 51 293

52. Chapter 52 295

53. Chapter 53 297

54. Chapter 54 302

55. Chapter 55 307

56. Chapter 56 309

57. Three Long Months Later 311

58. Epilogue 319

Song Inspirations 325

Jump 40 Years in the Future 326

Duchess' Crown 327

Other Books by K.M. Ringer 339

Ashes and Flame 340

The Ashstrike Sanctorum 341

Weekend Series 347

About the Author 350

CHAPTER 1

WE WERE FUCKED. SO royally fucked. Two months. It had been two fucking months since that day in Alnwick. Two months since I had shoved the pain of losing Lindy tight into my heart and forced myself not to think of it, even though her absence was staggeringly obvious. CJ had voiced on more than one occasion how I would have to face my grief eventually. The problem was that if I allowed myself to, especially while on the road, I wouldn't be able to function. Instead, when that door tried to crack open, I slammed it shut with a good hard kick, bolted it, and shoved a chair under the handle.

I had been cold and distant with him since our collision with Ansel in Alnwick. The second night after Alnwick, we stayed in a mining town called Emelle, and I opted to sleep on the floor rather than share the bed with him. He didn't deserve it. Sure, I was still mad as a snake that he had used his charge to keep me out of that fight, but I couldn't allow myself to have that comfort when she was...

I shook my head, blocking the thought.

After Emelle, we arrived in Bellmare, a small quiet town nestled in the forest just outside of the Gendril providence. I had actually liked Bellmare. Unless you were looking for it, you could have missed it completely. They had a strict curfew in place at night and rules for when and where you could be intoxicated. Being so close to the border left many dangers lurking in the night that did not fall under the laws of Gendril. When we met with Lord Dannet, he of course wanted to hear the whole story, just like every other Baron, Mayor, Lord, and Judge.

"Two years ago, Megan transported us to Nalrin." CJ had said, taking my hand. *I still had a hard time believing it had only been two years since I plopped the two of us into my grandmother's garden. So much had happened in such a short amount of time that, even as we retold the last two years, I found myself not wanting to believe the story myself.*

"That is when I found out that I wasn't human, but Sangra. About a year before I brought CJ and I here, my parents had died back in the Manusia. Only they hadn't. Instead, they came back here, tried to build the weapon of the Five Angels, where in the fight at Noctulanar Castle, my mother was killed." I took a *deep breath before continuing, "My father didn't take too kindly to that. Now, he has gone through the Ardith to purge all light from himself, and now controls pure darkness."*

"That is what flies through all of Obsecuritan. One of the Ash'bani, who was in Ghant, told us about Ansel and that he was destroying everything in his path. He has that darkness purely at his command." Owen said. "There is much more to it than that, but that is the short version."

"I see." Lord Dannet said, stroking his long brown and gray beard. "Is it true, Lady Megan, that you see the future?"

"It was." A pit in my stomach churned as I raised my head high. He cocked an eyebrow, insisting I continue, "I haven't had a vision since before we fought my parents at Noctulanar Castle."

His face was contemplative. "I spent about a week in a coma at the hospital after our fight in Noctulanar, but no one knew why. My visions have not come back. I don't know if they ever will."

"And you, sir, are an Angels Blessed Vernadali?" Lord Dannet said, turning to CJ, who nodded. "A human, turned Vernadali."

I squeezed CJ's hand, and he threaded his fingers through mine, clutching tightly. An Angels Blessed Vernadali. The all-mighty badass bodyguard.

"Yes, sir." CJ rubbed his thumb over my knuckles. "After we returned home, I went to the Curtails of the North and trained. A year later, I came home, married Lady Megan, and we received word during our honeymoon that Clarice's father, King Babak, was dying."

"Yes. Princess Clarice, or should I be calling you, Queen Clarice?"

"Clarice is fine, Lord Dannett." Clarice gave him a short bow. Darkness swam around her fingertips. She was still trying to sort out how all the power that had transferred from her father upon his death was going to be contained and controlled within her. She had said it could take months or years before it settled.

Lord Dannett raised his eyebrows at the short bow she gave him, then said hesitantly, "You should not bow to me. You are ruler of this land; I simply oversee this small territory."

"Lord Dannett, you oversee this territory, and I am only giving you the courtesy of your title," she said humbly.

He studied her for a long moment. While she held his gaze with that of a Queen, there was respect in the lines of her face. Lord Dannett broke eye contact first, then looked over at my family. "It was my understanding that there was another in your party. That is, if my Takeover is to be believed from the meeting last year in Nalrin City. Where is she?"

All sound vacated my head. I gripped CJ's hand tighter and felt that door wiggle and bang against the chair and bolts I had jammed it shut with. I could feel everyone's gaze on me, and I opened my mouth to say the words, but could not.

"Lindy Keller. She..." Jean tried to say, but there was a lump in her throat too.

"Lindy Keller was lost to the darkness that Ansel controls." Clarice said, pain lacing laced her voice.

"May the Angels grant her peace and serenity." Lord Dannett's head hung low. *"I am sorry for the deep-rooted loss you feel. What, if anything, may I do to help in your endeavors to stop Ansel?"*

That was two months ago. We had spent every day of the last two months telling that story over and over again, and it didn't stop the pain in my chest every time I heard someone else say that Lindy wasn't with us anymore. We had stopped at as many towns as we could to warn them about Ansel and what he controls. Most had believed us and issued evacuation, urging residents to head to the Seltic Marsh or Nalrin territories. The ones who didn't believe us, well, we could only hope that they wouldn't fall to Ansel as he made his way through the region.

Now with the gates of Therth so close, there was nothing I wanted more than to sleep in a comfortable bed, curl up next to CJ, and get a good night's rest. Like four days of solid sleep. I looked at CJ and let out a small sigh.

Only, there was just still so much to do, and so much to learn before we moved on to the next step. Apparently, only the Helena Crystal could stop Ansel, and that was if it even existed. Everyone we had asked about it told us the same thing. There hadn't been any new information provided, and I only felt this dark cloud closing in closer and closer around me.

The problem was that, if I found the Helena crystal and used her, there was the very real likelihood that I would have to give my life. No one had asked, but I couldn't allow my father to destroy everything I had come to love and cherish. If I had the ability to stop it, I would. I'm not scared at the prospect of dying. In fact, there was a part of me that welcomed it, but CJ... CJ would not let me be a martyr to the cause.

I turned to look at him as he sat astride his horse as we reached the gates. He turned to face me, concern, and a small encouraging smile on his face. I gave him one back as dread filled me. I saw his shoulders tighten, and I shook my head.

He moved his horse over and asked, "What?"

"Not now."

He narrowed his eyes at me and said, "Don't pull that shit. I hate all the emotions that I'm getting from you right now, and most of them are totally justified."

I nodded, my eyes flicking to Jean, Owen and Clarice, but he reached over and took my hand, pulling my attention back to him. His touch was soft and firm in my hand, and I just wanted to curl up in his chest right now.

"We are all hurting from losing Lindy. Angels," He tipped his head back and let out a heavy sigh. "It kills me just thinking about it. I have no idea how I'm going to tell Logan."

Logan.

Lindy and Logan had met and fallen in love over the last year. So much so that when we had come home early from the honeymoon, we found out that Logan had proposed to Lindy. They were so happy together. Lindy's bright smile as she looked to Logan flashed through my mind, and my voice was thick as I said, "Ceej."

He turned to face me, and a heavy shadow passed across his face. He squeezed my hand tightly before he muttered as if the oath itself would break the world, "If Ansel hurts a hair on your head, Megs, the Angels themselves won't be able to stop the hell I will rain down upon him."

"There is no guarantee any of us will get out of this," I whispered.

"Megan Isabel Mathewson," he growled at me, and I met his gaze. "Don't. We will make it through this. I don't care what I have to do to ensure it. We will have our forever."

Yes, CJ would save me and let the world burn.

CHAPTER 2

THE GATES TO THERTH Castle, Clarice's childhood home, opened with a groan that I felt reverberate into my lungs. I vaguely heard the guards demand to know who we were, and Clarice simply removed the hood from her cape without a word in response. Now that we were back in Therth, I could feel the door that was blocking out Lindy's loss push hard enough against the chair in place crack under the weight. I pushed back against it, desperately willing it to stay shut.

Someone has to be strong for them and I decided that it was my responsibility. It's the least I could do. They've known her longer, and they have the right to grieve. I closed my eyes and mentally pushed back on the door and blocked the pain that was behind it.

After the gates closed behind us, guards and stablemen appeared out of apparent thin air to take our horses. Lord Dannet of Bellmare wanted to do something as a thank you for the warning and gave us the horses to make the long trek back to Therth easier.

I sighed as I dismounted the chestnut gelding that had been my ride for the last six weeks. I told Lord Dannet that we would have the horses sent back to him. I tried to argue with him, but he wouldn't have it. Now that I stroked the gelding's head and his big brown eye met mine, I could feel the connection that we had made. I ran my fingers through his thick mane and the thought of leaving him, especially after losing Lindy, hurt. I bent down and put my forehead to his. I'd been just riding whichever horse the Council had made available to me, and it would be nice to have a horse of my own. I wanted to buy one once CJ and I got back after the honeymoon, but things had taken a left turn. I scratched the gelding's nose, and a small smile crossed my lips.

I sighed, lifted my head, and said, "So now that you're mine. What should I call you?"

The gelding just stared back at me, and I could swear I could see the contemplation in his big brown eye as it stared back at me. "Marcel?" He shook his head.

"George." Another shake of his head. I couldn't help but giggle. The blasted horse was answering me.

"Clifford?" I said with a smile, and he let out a huff.

"Kyrian." And an even larger huff burst from the gelding. I shook my head. "I love the name Kyrian. What's wrong with Kyrian?"

The gelding's eye looked off to the side as CJ wrapped an arm around my waist and gave me a quick kiss on the cheek.

"What are you doing?"

"Trying names for my new horse," I said, standing taller. "Lord Dannet said I could keep him. So, he deserves a name."

"You always named your pets."

"And what is wrong with that?" I said to him like he was crazy. "If they are part of our family, then they deserve a name."

"Okay. Okay. Well... then since he can't gallop in a straight line, I would call him Ziggy," he chuckled, and I sent a small spark of power at him, and he winced, but smiled brightly at me.

"Hey! Of course, he can run in a straight line. It's just your horse is so slow, we had to keep circling around you," I said in defense.

"Tucker isn't slow," CJ pouted.

I looked at CJ and raised my eyebrows. "And you were giving me a bad time about naming my horse, and you named yours, Tucker?"

"Well, like you said, our pets need names." CJ rolled his eyes and gave me another quick kiss on the temple. He stroked the gelding's neck, then looked at me and smiled.

"Ziggy." The gelding just looked at CJ, and I could swear he tipped his head at him.

I clipped his halter around his neck and slipped his bridle off. "Seriously? Ziggy? You want your name to be Ziggy?" He rubbed his bare head against my side, and the blasted horse was either agreeing to the name or he just wanted to scratch his face. Scratching his face was probably the more appropriate reason, but he was stuck with the name now. "Ziggy it is then."

Alexei, Clarice's Silnaree, ran up to the gates and had Clarice in his arms faster than I could have imagined. After a welcome that made me turn my head to give them privacy, Alexei asked, "Lindy?"

Slowly everyone looked at me, and when I opened my mouth to say something, my voice caught in my throat. I felt Ziggy rub his head against my arm and CJ squeeze my shoulders. That door was opening again, and I couldn't push it shut. I could see the bolts fly from the hinges, and the chair under the handle was cracking under the pressure. Tears fell from my eyes as the words spilled from my mouth. "Ansel killed her."

CHAPTER 3

HIGH WITCH DORITH AND Princess Erida, Clarice's sister, met us when we walked through the main doors of the Castle. I stopped in confusion when they bowed to Clarice.

"Queen Clarice. Welcome home." Dorith said.

I looked at Clarice. Her face was an emotionless stone except for a small twitch in the corner of her eye.

"I am *not* Queen." She said, dismissing them, and then sighed. "Though I suppose you have already planned the coronation?"

"We have. Once we heard you were in Kisling, we figured you would be home within a week. The coronation is scheduled for in eight days," Erida said with a graceful curtsy.

I eyed her closely, and I felt my power tingle at my skin. One move and I would roast her where she stood. She had been so vile and vicious to us the last time we were here, but as I studied her, and saw none of it. Her ember had softened. Her face was relaxed and there was no resentment in her voice. No trace of all that nastiness at all. Her voice was soft and fluid, like the dutiful servant of a Queen. My power retreated, and I blinked.

"Thank you, Erida," Clarice said with a short nod and then continued, "It has been a very long trip and we are tired. I'm sure there is much you wish to bring me up to date on, but we need to rest. I assume our things are still in our respective rooms. "

"Yes ma'am. Your things have been moved to the Reining Quarters. Everyone else's rooms have been undisturbed since you left. Morning meals will be served promptly at 8:oo, noon meals will be at your leisure, and evening meals will be in the Grand Hall one hour after sundown... if that is acceptable." A servant woman who had short jet-black hair, almond bright green eyes, and skin the color of fresh milk, said with gentle care. When she looked at each of us, a question crossed her face. "Shall I instruct Madam Lindy when she comes in?"

"Lindy... Lindy won't... be joining us any longer." Jean's voice cracked as Owen pulled her close to him. She, too, was holding the grief in as long as possible.

"Very well, Madam," she said with a small curtsy.

"Very well, Madam?!" I said snidely, a crack breaking through the air, as I felt a lump in my throat cut off the last words. "That is all you have to say? No question as to why she won't be with us? No question as to why someone who has been at our side since the very beginning will not be staying with us anymore?"

That inner door shattered into splinters. Tears swelled in my eyes, blurring my vision, and I fought hard to keep them contained. felt the heat radiating off my Maltal on my back, the electricity humming in my ears, and it bounced up and down my spine.

"Megs?" I thought I heard CJ say to me in warning. Someone grabbed my hand, hissed, and I had the fleeting thought that it had been CJ. I felt my power run through me, but there was nothing stopping the flood of grief that was rolling through the door that had burst open. Hot, blinding heat flashed through me, and then it was as if I had been dumped in the frozen waters of the Lansker Sea as the grief suddenly came crashing down on me.

A growing ice-cold hole seemed to spread across my chest, and I wrapped my arms around my stomach to stop it. Then I was gasping for air. I couldn't breathe.

Where did all the air go?

I gasped over and over again, trying to gulp down as much air as I could. My power bounced so hard around my insides, and I couldn't concentrate enough to control it.

"Megs." I heard CJ, but his voice was muffled by the humming in my ears. "Megan."

A rainbow of colors danced before me as my vision faded in and out.

Fresh air.

I needed fresh air.

I was suffocating.

I tried to turn to go back outside, but CJ's arms were tight against me. I threw my power against him, and he instantly let go, hissing a curse I couldn't make out.

Once I was outside, I saw everything in shades of blue and felt my power pulse wildly. I felt for the cocoon to pull it all back in, but it was nowhere in sight. There was nothing but the crackling of electricity within me, lightning strikes, and nothingness in my chest.

I tried once again to take a deep breath, but I couldn't.

My heart raced, and I took off running. I had to separate myself from everyone else. I had lost all control.

The edges of my vision were fading to black but crackled with electricity. I stumbled into the garden on the left side of the castle, collapsing to my knees as the darkness closed in around me.

I pushed back against that consuming grief, but it engulfed me. This time, it broke down the last of the walls I had built up to keep the pain and loss at bay. I grasped for any semblance of control over my power, but the electricity pulsed so violently that I threw my arms wide and my head back, releasing it in one huge burst.

Visions of Lindy flooded my mind.

Lindy. The girl who knew everything about The Five Angels.

Lindy. The girl who was my best friend.

Another burst of bright white lightning shot out from my fingers.

Lindy. The girl who loved so fiercely and who was so fiercely loyal.

Another burst.

Lindy. The girl who was going to officially become my sister-in-law and marry Logan.

I leaned forward on my hands and knees and took slow, deep breaths. Tears flowed down my face and dropped heavily into the dirt, where my fingers dug deep into the dirt.

This wasn't just about Lindy. This was about Matt. This was about me and CJ's lives being turned upside down. This was about Madame Winters, Colletta, and the lives of all the innocent people that were dying at the hands of my family. It was all on my shoulders. The loss I have had to endure in the last five years and now the responsibility to fix it all. All of it was lying on my shoulders. I couldn't fix it. I couldn't make all the pain go away.

"Megan?" CJ's voice weaved its way through all that pain. I whipped my head around to him and he froze. Clarice was standing just behind him.

I felt my hair rise from my shoulders, my eyes burn, and my vision shifting from shades of blue to shades of red. My body moved without a conscious decision as venomous rage, hot and molten, filled every vein in my body, feeding my power even more. It begged to let it out. It pushed painfully against my bones. Each nerve in my body was on fire with the need to release it, and I gladly obliged.

I huffed out air in burst after burst, and I heard the statues that filled the garden shatter. Concrete and marble sprayed in every direction.

I felt the ground slip out from underneath me as I opened my eyes to see my hands covered in that black tar that had overtaken Lindy.

My syths now in my hands, as tar covered skeletons tried to pull me into their grasp, they circled me as if looking for an opening. My power wrapped around my syths, and hands in threads. One of those skeletons reached for me but pulled back as if not daring to touch me.

They would not get to my family. They would not take anyone else from me. I grasped onto the pain of Lindy's death and used it as fuel. I felt a smile curl at my lips. I was going to cover the garden in the dust of their bones.

With each pulse of my power, concrete and marble flew through the air. With every slash of my blades, I took every one of those skeletons down. I felt a burst of dark power push against me and I flicked it back with my own. Sweat dripped down my back as I continued to lay waste to everything around me.

Another blast of dark power hit me, and I turned toward it, roaring at the source. With a few flicks of my wrist, I wrapped tendrils of electricity around that dark power. Darkness wrapped around my legs, slowly crawling up. Screaming, all I saw was the tar that had consumed Lindy, now crawling up my legs. I threw all my power into it, trying to burn it off. Trying to make it release from me, but it did no good. The smell of rotting flesh filled my senses and my eyes burned. When the blackness reached my waist, it stopped, and I saw three skeleton heads circling me in the black tar and shadows that covered the lower half of my body. It circled me again and again, alternating from terrifying roars and hysterical laughter.

What shred of reality was left slipped.

Everything slipped from me.

The ground, my power, my emotions, everything.

The only thought going through my head was that I was no better than my father. I might as well have killed Lindy myself. If it were not for me, she wouldn't have been there. My family wouldn't have been there. This should have stopped with Mom, Dad, Matt, and me.

I felt nothing but guilt and a new huge gaping hole filled with that guilt, and regret replaced the grief of losing Lindy. I released a blood-curdling scream at the same time that a hand clamped down on my shoulder. The blackness vanished with a pop, and

I felt nothing. One last bright burst of power, although not as strong this time, escaped as I fell to my knees sobbing.

Strong arms lifted me up from the ground. The spicy citrus smell of him wrapping around me like a blanket. I looked up into his eyes and said, "It was all my fault. It's my fault she died."

His steps faltered a moment, before lightning flashed bright in his eyes, and he said, "Go to sleep, Megan."

CHAPTER 4

I BLINKED AT THE sun shining through the window and groaned. Every muscle in my body screamed as I rolled over and stretched.

"Oh, thank the Angels, Megan." CJ's voice was strained and when I turned to look at him, he was climbing up onto the bed, and kissing me, my face between his hands. When he pulled back, he rested his forehead against mine and said, "I've been so worried."

"Wha..."

"You've been sleeping for two days, Megs." CJ sat back and took my hand in his, running his thumb over my wedding ring. There were shadows under his eyes, and I wondered if he had slept.

"What? Two days?" I looked out the window and back at him.

"We've all been worried sick."

I blinked, and then I remembered what I had done, and shame filled me. I curled up into a ball and pulled his arm with me.

He curled up behind me, holding me tight when he whispered, "I knew you were here. I could feel you, but after what happened... Megs... Don't go away like that again."

My heart hurt at the pleading in his voice, and when the shame washed over me again, and a sob burst from me, he just pulled me closer. "Shhh."

"I'm so sorry, Ceej." Another racked through me, and I held him tighter, as I just repeated, "I'm so sorry. I'm so, so sorry."

For two days after that, I refused to leave our room. Refused to speak to anyone. I only ate when CJ threatened to bind me to the bed and stuff food down my throat. So, I ate, but within minutes I felt sick to my stomach and threw it back up.

When Jean or Clarice tried to check on me, CJ would send them away and if he wasn't here, I just didn't answer the door. Owen came by sometime late yesterday afternoon. CJ let him in, and they sat and talked for a while, acting as if I wasn't here. I stood in the window watching as people cleaned up the damage I had caused to the garden the entire time he had been here.

Owen had asked CJ what I was feeling and what it felt like when I had my magical temper tantrum, for lack of a better phrase. I froze when he had asked and wasn't sure if I wanted to know what CJ felt. CJ just said he didn't want to talk about it. I felt horrible for putting him through that. The Vernadali bond gave him a front-row seat to how I was feeling. What's worse is that all I remembered was feeling full of rage and loss. It wasn't until after I woke up and CJ told me what had happened that I even knew I had destroyed the garden.

I felt bad about it, and I would have to apologize to Clarice for it. With the amount of money that I had in the Nalrin reserve, I could afford to pay to have the statues replaced. Where beautiful flowers once blossomed, there was nothing but the rake marks where they had cleaned up the mess I had made.

I sighed as I stared at the spot where I had lost all control. What they couldn't cover up were the lightning tendrils that forked from that spot throughout the garden. I saw one of the gardeners trying and frowned as one of the gardener's muted voice came through the window. "The marks won't come up," he said. "It's scorched into the ground. A permanent mark now set into the ground."

"But Queen Clarice—"

"She has already been informed." His eyes flicked up to my window and met mine. I turned and went to sit on the large four poster bed.

"Great. The hospital room in Nalrin, and now the Gate to the Underworld held marks of my temper," I whispered to myself as I climbed back under the blankets.

The worst part was that it didn't appear anyone was going to hold me responsible for my actions. Owen had even said that Clarice was glad for the clean slate in the garden. Jean just said that I was entitled to a breakdown after all I had been through.

Personally, I was embarrassed. I didn't understand why my body reacted so violently and delusionally. I've dealt with loss in my life. I lost my brother and then lost my parents, twice. Why had my mind failed me so wholly at the loss of Lindy?

I sighed heavily and could feel CJ's eyes on me, studying me closely. The why didn't matter when it came down to it. I just had to make sure I never did it again. I had to get my emotions under control. If I didn't, I might lose control of my power again, and who knows who I'd hurt?

Two more days passed, and when CJ returned from breakfast, I tried to talk to him about what occurred in that garden.

"Clarice tried to stop you," CJ said quietly.

I blinked at him and said, "Is that the darkness that I felt wrap around me?" I chewed on my thumb and slid down onto the floor.

He tipped his head to the side, and then asked carefully, "What did you see, Megs?"

My eyes flicked up to him and I felt my heart race. I consciously took a ragged deep breath and let it out slowly to calm myself, before saying, "The tar that consumed Lindy. It wrapped around my legs, and then I saw it circle my waist."

"Babe," he kneeled before me and ran his thumbs across the top of my knees. "That was just Clarice's power. She was hoping it would contain you so that you wouldn't hurt yourself."

"Is she okay?" My voice was small and broken. "I remember fighting against it. Trying to push it away from me."

"She was knocked backwards, but she is fine. Nothing but a couple of scraps."

"Promise me she is okay?" I begged, my eyes wide.

His hand lifted and caressed my cheek and wiped a tear away. "She's fine. Everyone is unharmed, worried about you, but unharmed."

I couldn't believe I had attacked her, and I leveled the garden the way I did. All that destruction, and it came from me.

Six days had now passed since I had that tantrum, and I still wasn't planning on leaving our room. CJ tried. Angels did he try. He baited me with studying to find out what we could about Helena and when that didn't work, he tried to lure me out with spar practice, offering to let me beat him to a pulp if I wanted.

"Why would I want to beat you up?" I mumbled.

"Retribution for using my Charge against you?" A small smile on his face.

"Will it bring Lindy back?" I played with a loose thread on the curtains by the window. I was staring out at the bare garden again. There was a lone crow picking at the ground where flowers once blossomed, searching for bugs.

"Megs." His voice was soft and full of the same sadness that filled me. "We all miss her."

"Do I not have the strongest power of any Sangra in modern history?" I said, my voice sounding dead, even to my own ears. "Everyone keeps telling me I do. What good does it do if I can't protect the ones I love or bring them back?"

"If you had the power to bring her back, would you really do it?" His eyes were filled with concern and caution. When I didn't answer, he loosed a breath. "Megan. What's dead should stay dead."

I looked at him for a moment, not sure how to respond to him. He was running his thumb absently over the tattoo of the three vertically alternating swords surrounded by a laurel with my name on it. It sat just inside of his forearm, branding him as my Vernadali. My ultimate protector.

"Babe." He said with a sigh as he came and leaned on the windowpane next to me. "We've been studying a lot in the Royal Library and... there are a lot of scripts that tell the stories of what has happened to those who have come back to the land of the living after they have died. It's not pretty."

My ears perked up a bit. "So, we could get Lindy back?"

He froze. His stare filled with fear, trepidation, and shock.

"Why not?"

"Why not?" His eyes practically bugged out in shock. It was as if he couldn't believe I was actually giving this serious consideration. "Megan. She was consumed by pure darkness. That is going to leave its mark. She would never be the same. She would be a tortured soul among the living. She would not be the Lindy she was when she died. She would not be the one that each one of us loved. Besides, she doesn't even have a body to come back to. What is physically left is under Ansel's control. Why are you even talking about this? She's gone."

"She didn't die a natural death. She should have died a natural death!" My voice rising, "She was *supposed* to marry Logan and have kids that grow old with ours and live. *Live* Ceej. She was supposed to live." I was screaming now, holding back tears.

I could feel my power rise from a depth within me, deeper than I had ever felt before. I stopped. I looked at him and said through gritted teeth, "Why can't she come back? We have to bring her back. We need Lindy back. *Logan* needs Lindy back." Taking a shuttering breath and then saying with an exhale, "I need Lindy back."

"What is dead should stay dead." He grabbed my hands and ignored the zapping of my power against his skin. "Megan. You want to know why we can't bring her back? I'll tell you. Those books tell of stories where the dead have come back and killed everyone they ever loved. They've possessed others. They've been a shell of their once selves. All those records in the library record murderous, violent, psychopathic rampages. Before you say it, they are not just stories. This is the Gateway to the Underworld. Every single time a person is brought back from the dead throughout a very long and extensive history, their reanimated life is recorded. Every single one is ragingly violent. Every. Single. One."

The realization and reality that bringing her back really wasn't an option made that hole in my chest grow again, and I closed my eyes to seal it away.

"I just want the pain to stop. I don't want to miss her anymore. It's just like losing Matt all over again. I love them and I just want to have them in my arms." My voice hitched as I fought back the lump in my throat.

CJ pulled me into his arms as I wrapped my arms around him. "I know, babe. I know."

I felt him hiccup and knew that he was crying if I dared to look up and meet his eyes. He was trying to be strong for me, even through his own pain. Not only for himself, but also for Logan. He held me tighter and kissed the top of my head, so I let myself surrender to his comfort and cried for the first time since I woke up.

CHAPTER 5

I WOKE UP THE following morning with CJ's arm wrapped tight against me and the room still bathed in darkness. I blinked and as I looked around, I realized I didn't feel so empty and hollow. The weight that had been lying so heavily on my chest was... lighter. My power... relatively calm. The pain of losing Lindy was still there, but it wasn't all consuming like it had been.

I just didn't feel like I was going to be crushed under the weight of it anymore. There had been a release in finally crying it out with CJ last night. I took a deep breath and CJ bolted awake.

"What's wrong?" he said, his charge flowing over me.

"Nothing." I sat up and looked at him. I took another deep breath as he studied me, and I sort of felt like me again. I didn't feel separated from myself. I cocked my head to the side as I realized that the depth of my power had shifted...

"The depth had shifted," I muttered under my breath. It was like that depth had made enough room for it all. My power sat calm, cool, and collected. No cocoon needed.

"Don't scare me like that." CJ flopped back on the bed, then looked at me. "Wait. What shifted?"

"My power. It feels calm. Calmer than it has in." I let out a long breath. "A very long time. I can't explain it. Don't ask me to."

I laid down and curled up next to him. We laid like that for a few minutes. His fingers made lazy circles on my hip, and I felt my insides swim and a smile cross my face. Yes, I was definitely feeling better if I was having fleeting thoughts of ravishing him. The blankets were bunched at his waist and his bare chest had a stream of light across it. I realized I was playing with the small hairs just below his bellybutton, and I smiled a little wider at the thought.

"Whatever just went through your head. Leave it there for a moment while I gather my wits." He said, trying to come out of his deep sleep. Then his head turned toward me as he smirked and pulled me on top of him. "You've been locked in this room since you woke up from your magical hissy fit and this morning you wake up with a smile on your face and that sparkle in your eyes has returned. Now, seriously, Megan. What is it?"

"Nothing. That's just it. I don't feel crushed by that weight anymore. And you and I know that wasn't just a little hissy fit. I watched them clean up the garden for two full days. That was after I had slept for two days. That is days of cleanup. I annihilated it."

"Don't worry about it. You heard what Owen said."

I let out a big sigh and looked toward the window. "I will tell Clarice I'll pay to have it replaced. I have more money than I know what to do with in the Nalrin reserve. Working for Julian has at least done that. Add that to what I have from Ansel and Symatha's estate back in the Manusia, and what they are paid in your Vernadali salary, and we could already retire wealthy back in the Manusia. Though, the price we have had to pay..."

"Hey. We all knew what we were signing up for, babe. Lindy knew what she was doing when she followed us." He said, rubbing his thumb across my forearm.

"Did she really have a choice?" I ran a finger over his chest muscles and could feel his body responding to my touch. The corner of my lips twitched up.

"We all did."

"I'm sorry, Ceej," I whispered, suddenly feeling very selfish for bringing him into all of this.

"What for?"

"I brought you into all of this. I should have sent you home. Sent you somewhere safe when all of this started. You know, like we did with Logan."

I felt his breath hitch under me as he let out a long breath. "Logan. "

Our eyes met and his were filled with the sadness of not only losing Lindy but telling Logan that she was gone. "I'll tell him," I said before he could say anything else.

"No. I should. He's my brother." I nodded and let him have this. It wasn't as if when we did finally show up in Nalrin that he wouldn't find out. If he didn't find out beforehand. "And you know damn well I wouldn't have let you send me off into a protected cell. We are in this together, Megan. Until the very end."

Before I could bite back a retort, there was a soft knock on the door.

"Come in." I regretfully moved off CJ and pulled the blankets up to give an appearance of modesty.

An olive-skinned girl who couldn't have been older than eight or nine walked in dressed in a dark blue sleeveless shift with delicate lace around the hemline. Her hands were neatly folded at her waist, where a white apron was tied. Her hair was black as night and her ice-blue eyes looked toward the bed, without meeting ours. "Vernadali CJ and Lady Megan," she said with a curtsy.

"Yes, Miss Caroline," CJ said with a tip of his head.

"Queen Clarice would like to know if you and Lady Megan would like to join her for breakfast this morning. She also wished me to let you know she understands if Lady

Megan would not be joining. However, Queen Clarice requires Vernadali CJ's presence this morning."

I turned to CJ and I saw the silent question in his eyes. I turned to the girl and said, "Let Clarice—"

"Queen Clarice," The girl said firmly.

I looked at CJ and he rolled his eyes. "Please let Queen Clarice know we both will join her for breakfast."

With a small curtsy, she backed out of the room.

I turned back to CJ and raised my eyebrows.

"The servants here are very... demanding upon titles. Clarice says that is one thing she wants to rid the place of when she has control over everything."

"Is she coming with us? Or now that she is the Gatekeeper to the Underworld, will she have to stay here?"

"I don't know. I think she is still trying to figure it out." He said, then reached over and kissed me on the cheek.

When his lips touched, I felt heat flow through my face, and I was sure I was blushing like a schoolgirl.

"Come on, let's get dressed. Shouldn't keep *Queen* Clarice waiting." He said in a mocking tone that made me laugh.

He turned and smiled brightly. "I've missed that."

"What?" I said as I reached for my pants to slip them on.

"Your laugh." The small smile on his lips undid me. This man could always make me feel better. He knew how to handle me. Over the last few days, he had proven that. He knew what I needed, and what I didn't. I was in awe of him all over again.

We walked hand in hand into the dining hall to find the long table in front of us full of various Lords and Barons, some of which we had met on the way back to Therth. There was one lone woman sitting at the table, just three chairs from where Clarice was sitting. My eyes were immediately drawn to Clarice. I could feel the power radiating off her. Her features had stayed sharper than they were originally. Her hair had returned to its original black, but still hung just below her chin. I liked the red on her, but the black was much more her style.

I giggled when I saw what she was wearing. CJ's hand gripped mine tighter for just a moment, before releasing it and placing his hand on the small of my back, his thumb rubbing back and forth on my spine. We stood there for a moment, and when I looked at CJ, he gave me a look as to warn me not to say anything. She was sitting in the most hideous dress I had ever seen. She looked pale and uncomfortable. I actually felt sorry for her sitting there.

When Clarice saw us, she jumped up and ran toward me. The guards moved as to protect her, but they halted with a sideways glance at them by Clarice. There was a scab on her check and a new scar was going to form on her forehead.

"Clarice—" I started to say, but she put her hand up.

"No apologies are needed." She said with a smile and when I tried again, she continued, "Seriously. No apologies."

Then I fully saw what she was wearing, and I tried unsuccessfully to hide a sneer. The dress she had on didn't look any better on her up close. I'm sure back in the late 1600s in the Manusia it would have been considered the best finery available, but nowadays? It had more layers in the skirt than I had blankets on my bed. There were so many straps and ties on the bodice, it must have taken an army just to get her into it. Not to mention the color almost matched her skin tone, which was saying something. The deep rich chocolate gown made her look... well, sick. "Clarice, what are you wea—"

"Megan." She cut me off and wrapped her arms tight around me. Then whispered in my ear, "Not a word. I can hardly breathe in this Angels forsaken thing. Underworld's beings, I have so many pearls on this dress that I feel like I just sprang from one of those oysters in the Manusia."

"You know you are Queen now, right? You can change the dress code." I whispered back with a smile on my lips.

She pulled back and said with a satisfied sigh, "Megan. Don't go away like that again. You've had us all so worried."

"Clarice. I've just been upstairs," I said with a light laugh, trying to make it sound like it wasn't a big deal.

"But you wouldn't talk to any of us. I was about to send a message to Julian to send some doctors immediately. I was..."

Her voice hitched, and then she pulled me into a tight embrace again.

"Where are Jean and Owen?" I asked.

"In the library. They are searching for information on Helena," she whispered before pulling away and leading me up to the head of the table.

"Please bring Vernadali CJ and Lady Megan something to break their fast and we will start," she instructed the servants and then she stood at the head of the table with us sitting on either side of her. Once everyone had taken their places, and the guards were sure that I would not hurt their precious Queen, Clarice said, "Many of you are wondering why you've been called here, and we will get to that shortly. First, eat."

A plate of three small Bloussootos, a cured meat and cheese filled pastry, a glass of Gendril wine and two small Leemos sausages were placed in front of me. I didn't much like Leemos sausages. They're a little too gamey for me, but I didn't have the heart to say thing. However, the Gendril wine reminded me of a syrah back in the Manusia, only it was blue.

When everyone had finished their breakfast and the servants carried away our dishes, Clarice looked at me and sighed. She slowly stood and addressed the table. "You have been called here not for my coronation, though you are welcome to attend should you wish, but because of the darkness flowing through the lower providences."

There was a murmur that filled the room from the dignitaries I didn't know, but when Clarice continued, everyone fell silent. "My family and I have visited a few of your towns and villages on our way back from Alnwick and have heard this story. Some of you may have even seen the devastation on your travels here and know what I speak is the truth." She met a few older Lord's eyes.

"Ansel Keller has completed the Ardith and has emerged from the Underworld," she paused as gasps and murmuring crossed the room.

"My lady, the Ash'bani only go to The Five Angels to purge themselves of the darkness." A pudgy, pockmarked, burly man sitting four seats down said in a mocking tone.

"Historically, Ash'bani have only gone to The Five Angels, yes. I can see how you would have made such an assumption. However, this is not what happened. Ansel Keller has traveled to the Underworld and has purged himself of all light and now can control pure darkness. The Ja'Nee are under his control, and the darkness he spreads through your towns and villages will consume all those who it touches, allowing him complete control over them."

The room was silent as the various attendees looked at each other in confusion. It was a full three minutes before the Lord of Basilwill spoke. "Basilwill was consumed two weeks ago. There were only a handful of us who escaped. I lost my wife and two sons to the darkness he controls."

"Tilbar, as well, my Lady," another man says toward the end of the table.

"And Sillkar," the only woman at the table says.

"Sillkar?" I say in shock. "But that is along the northern pass to the Seltic Marsh." She nodded her head slowly, staring at the middle of the table. "Clarice, he's moving north. He's working his way back to Nalrin and reaching for every large town along the way. He said he was building an army. It's an army we cannot fight without *her*.e's " My voice heavy with meaning.

How is he able to move so damned quickly? Then an image of when we awoke along the northern edge to Gendril flashed through my mind. "Could he ride the mounts the Ja'Nee were riding toward Noctulanar? But that wouldn't make sense either, because that was months ago, and we saw him in Alnwick after that." I was thinking out loud more than anything.

"Lord Bernat." Clarice said to a thin older man with a long gray beard. His eyes turned to Clarice and I was shocked at the sadness that lay within them. "What are you thinking?"

"I was just wondering what mounts Lady Megan was referring to, the clouds of darkness or the Nocturnes?"

Clarice looks at me. She couldn't describe them. She was... otherwise disposed. She gave me a quick nod, and I turned my attention to Lord Bernat. "The beasts were not cloud like. They were more like giant ravens."

"Nocturnes. They are only from myth. Well, that is what I thought until I saw them fly over Goulcrest just over two months ago."

"I'm sorry, my geography of the region is... well, lacking obviously. Where is Goulcrest?" I asked.

"To the northeast of here, my lady. Just along the Noctulanar border."

I shifted my eyes to CJ, and he gave me a quick nod as he realized exactly what I was thinking. It was just over two months ago we were on that ledge and saw Ja'Nee heading toward Noctulanar Castle. I sighed, sitting back in my chair. As the three of us looked at each other, questions burst from many in the room, expecting Clarice to answer.

"Queen Clarice, if Ansel has a way of moving across the continent so easily, how are we to protect ourselves from his onslaught?" one asked.

"Is it true that the Gate to the Underworld has been shut?" another asked.

"What are we to do if he shows up to our door?" asked another.

And so it began. The three of us just looking at each other, as the people of Obsecuritan were left helpless. There was nothing we could do to save them from my father. There were no answers for us to give them. None that would leave them satisfied. The only thing we could do was to find Helena and stop him as soon as possible to minimize the death that he would bring upon the people of this continent. We couldn't save everyone. People are going to die and there is nothing we could do to stop it.

Except... I let out a long, deep breath and said, "Helena."

The man sitting next to me stopped halfway through whatever it was he was saying and looked at me. I just stared at the table, but my eyes shot up in shock when I heard CJ echo that single name that meant my destruction.

"Helena." He knew the price, just as I did, but he said it anyway. He knew she might be the only thing that could stop this madness. He would fight the cost, but he knew.

When our eyes met, there were tears in his eyes. Then Clarice spoke, silencing the entire room. "She is our only hope."

She looked at both of us and sighed. "Helena."

"Helena." The three of us say again in unison. The chatter and shouts from up and down the table stopped as every head turned to us in shock.

The lone woman at the table said, "She is but a myth. She does not exist."

Clarice's face became unreadable. "She is our only hope. As much as I hate to bring you this news, the Obsecuritan people are on their own until we can find Helena."

"We are on our own? You are just going to let the rest of us die while you go on a wild goose chase? How do we know you will not just give up and walk away from this?" Lord Sabum said. His town had been hit hard when Ansel rolled through. We had been too late when we came to Udish five weeks ago. "Besides, legend says it's in the control of the Fairies of Cinder. They won't just hand over a weapon of that magnitude, even if it exists. "

"I have been in contact with Head Julian and he is in negotiations with their Queen. This is no longer just about Nalrin or the lands here in Obsecuritan. This is now about saving the whole world of Nalsar. Regardless of race, gender, stature, or family connections, Ansel must be stopped. The price my family alone has..." Her eyes flickered to me for the briefest of moments, "and will pay is just as much as yours will."

A very thin, tall man who was sitting in the very last seat at the end of the table stood slowly, so we could see him. He was so well hidden behind the large man in front of him I hadn't noticed that it's Ash'bani.

"Ma'lady, I have a question."

Clarice nodded for him to continue.

"It is rumored that the Fairies have the Helena Crystal. It is also rumored among my people that due to the spell Helena cast, the only way for it to be effective again... there must be a bloodline to the one to be destroyed. That the reason it has never been used again is that any of that race within distance of the spell cast will be killed. This would mean..." He looked up and made eye contact with Clarice. I knew what he was going to say, and I could feel CJ's eyes on me, but I couldn't bring myself to look at him. "That if Ansel has another brother, a daughter, or son, that person would have to not only sacrifice themselves but also murder a complete race. Is that something you are going to condone here?"

"The plan is to lead him away from all Ash'bani, so that no other Ash'bani other than those who fight at his side, which I haven't seen any of, would be sacrificed." I said slowly, raising my eyes to meet his. "We... Queen Clarice would never condone the slaughter of an entire race. She is a gentle, kind monarch who wants nothing more than the best for her people. I can guarantee you it troubles her much to not be able to protect her people until Ansel is stopped."

"There is no one to cast the spell though, Lady Megan." He says with sad, pleading eyes. "He murdered his own brother in his trial, his sister died when she was young,— "

"He had a sister?!" I blurted before I fully registered what he had said.

"Yes ma'am. She was run through at twelve by a sword."

I shook my head. He had a sister. Of course he did.

"Megs." I heard CJ say as he came around to my side, resting his hand on my shoulder.

"Continue, please," Clarice ordered.

"His parents faded long ago. There is no record of him ever having a son or daughter. So, I ask again, who is to cast the spell?"

Before I could say anything, Clarice saved me. "Lady Megan is his daughter."

Half of the men at the table jumped to their feet and drew their swords. The guards in the room snapped to attention and surrounded Clarice.

"Enough! She has agreed… Lady Megan is very determined to stop her father," she bellowed loud enough to fill the room.

When the room did not settle, there was a heaviness that filled the air, and I felt the temperature drop low enough that I could see my breath as I exhaled.

When the men did not stand down, I climbed up onto the table. "My name is Megan Isabel Matthewson, formerly the daughter of Ansel Keller."

Not one of them made to sheath their swords, so with a wave of my hand, I flung their swords to the wall behind them. They wouldn't be able to remove them from the wall until I walked out of this room. I could feel my power at my fingertips but didn't look down. I didn't have the patience for this.

"My name is Megan Isabel Matthewson. I am the biological daughter of Ansel Keller. I vow to locate Helena and use her against my father. Yes, that means I have agreed to sacrifice my life so that you bickering little shits can live. Do you think for one moment that I wouldn't want to return to the way things were before? Do you have any idea what I am giving up so that you can live?"

I felt my power buzzing against my skin, took a deep breath and concentrated on centering myself before I opened my eyes and stared each of them down.

"No one is asking you to give yourself up for this," one of the Lords down the table said, but didn't look up at me.

"No one had to. He has to be stopped. I don't see any other options other than finding the Helena Crystal. So yes, I do have to give up my *life* just because my father… my father broke the laws of this world, the Council punished him, too damn harshly in my fucking opinion, but it isn't like that matters and now he wants to bring this world to rubble. I am giving up my life, not because of something I have done, but because a man who just happens to have his blood run through my veins is bent to destroy a world. Apparently, the sins of the father rule over the spawn. Now you have the fucking balls to raise your sword at me?"

"Megan," CJ said sternly as he grabbed my hand. CJ was fully charged up now, and I had to wonder if it was to protect me, or to protect everyone else in the room. I squeezed his hand hard and knew that threads of that electricity had threaded itself over his hand and wrist as well. What scared me, though, was that I could feel my power coming from deep in that new well that had opened up inside me. A well I could not currently feel the bottom of.

"I'll talk to you later, Clarice. Oh, and don't let them dress you in that dress again. It washes you out and makes you look a lot older than you are. Burn it in a million tiny fires." I saw her smile just a little as I left the room.

CHAPTER 6

CJ SPENT THE NEXT hour just walking me around the grounds, and when we reached the garden I destroyed, I stopped and stared. It looked so much more barren at this level. The smell of freshly overturned dirt filled my senses to the point I could taste it.

"What happened here?" I asked.

"Oh, there was this really beautiful woman who kinda lost her shit, then spent the next week either sleeping or ignoring everyone and stayed locked up in her room. Oh, and she worried the crap out of everyone who loves and cares for her," he said it sarcastically, but every word was true.

I gave him a pointed look. "I know that, smartass. What I want to know is what happened from your perspective."

CJ looked at me and a shadow of something that I couldn't pinpoint crossed his face. He hid it so well, I almost didn't see it. He looked out over the garden for a moment before he spoke softly and seriously, "No, you don't."

"Yes. I do," I said firmly, making him face me. His gaze met mine. They were sad but stern. "Babe, you didn't let the Charge take over. You didn't come out to stop me. You stopped me in the woods with that damn thing, but you didn't stop me here? I want to know why?"

He stared at me for a long minute before running his hands over his face and through his hair, holding onto his neck before finally dropping them and saying, "Megs, I've seen you fight. I've fought with you. I've seen you spar against every one of our family members, hold your own against Mickel, and yet, I've never seen you move like that. You moved with such ferocity and speed that I wondered if you even saw what you were really attacking." CJ let out a big sigh. "It was more than that, though."

"The bond made you feel everything that I was feeling." I said in understanding.

"My heart broke for you. Yes, we are all feeling the loss of Lindy, but there was so much loss, sadness, anger, and emptiness flowing through you. Then I felt something shift in you. I can't even explain what I felt. What was worse was that I kept expecting to have the Charge take over, and it didn't. It was almost as if it knew to stay back. That scared me even more. I couldn't move. How am I supposed to protect you from that? When even the Vernadali Charge doesn't take over? It's supposed to take over in every situation. It is supposed to keep you from harming yourself, to keep you from getting harmed. It just sat there like it didn't even exist. I failed you." His voice cracked ever so slightly at the end and I realized he was blaming himself.

"Look at me." I took a hold of his chin, forcing him to do so. "You haven't failed me, Cory James. You never have."

His hand reached up and ran his thumb across my cheek. "I'm your Vernadali. I'm supposed to save you from all harm. That is my job. Furthermore, it's my job as your husband. I'm supposed to protect you, Megs. Make you happy at all costs."

"Ceej, you couldn't protect me from this. You couldn't protect Lindy from Ansel. You can't protect me from the pain of that loss. You did everything you possibly could," I said as calmly as

I could, then realized I needed to tell him the one thing I hadn't told him yet about that day. The pit. That endless pit. "I need to tell you something about that day."

"Why does that scare me, Megs?"

"Because it scares the ever living shit out of me." I paused, looked up at the sky and took a deep breath. When I let it out, it came in a quick huff. "I told you earlier that my power finally felt calm, but different. That I couldn't explain it."

He nodded but waited for me to continue.

"In Alnwick, when we fought my father, I felt my power sputtering out. I felt the end of it. I felt when I was going to have to fight with my own hands. I knew I could not hold him any longer, not because he was stronger, but because I didn't have enough power to fight him. Fight him Ceej. Not win, just to fight him. I knew I didn't have enough power to do it. That cemented the need for us to find Helena. Now... The other day, I felt the floor where my power ended crumble beneath me."

He was silent for a minute, as if he was waiting for me to go on. When I didn't, he said, "Why is that a problem? If you have more inside you, isn't that a good thing? I mean, we might hold our own against him should we face him again."

"Ceej, I can't see the bottom of the pit. I no longer know how far down the pit goes. Let alone how to control it. I don't know if there is more, or if I just have a deeper pit to hold what I already did. I don't need the cocoon anymore. It might have just made more room for it to sit within me."

"So, we practice. Maybe Witch Dorith can help you."

"But what if I hurt someone?"

"You aren't going to hurt anyone."

"That is bullshit, Ceej, and you know it. Clarice can tell me all she wants not to apologize for what happened, but I know the scars that will form on her face are from her trying to stop me."

This time, he had the smarts to stay quiet.

"Not to mention that you even said that you couldn't bring yourself to move. Even with all your Vernadali training, that damn Vernadali Charge, and the need to protect me at all costs, you said you couldn't bring yourself to move." His mouth opened to say something, but I continued. "Don't get me wrong, I'm glad you didn't. I could have hurt you, and I would have never forgiven myself, but it doesn't change the fact that there was something in you that made you stay where you were. Something inside you knew that there was something seriously wrong, and that you had to stay away from it."

"I don't know what you want me to say, Megan." He turned away from me, balling and unballing his fists.

"I don't want you to say what you think I need to hear. Be honest with me. Tell me exactly how it is. Tell me that everything here scares the fucking shit out of you, because I know it does. Tell me you didn't know what to do that day because neither of us have ever experienced anything like it. They can't possibly train you for that. I want to hear you say that you will stand by me no matter the outcome of this. That if I am standing in the middle of my father's army with Helena in my hands and have the chance to stop all of it, that you won't stop me. That you will let me do what I need to do." My voice broke as I fought back the tears. That, that was really what this was all about. I needed him to let me do what I needed to in order to save Nalsar.

"Megs," he said, choking on the words as he turned back toward me. His eyes filled with a fear and hurt that I couldn't put into words, studied me for a long moment before he continued. "I realize Helena may be the only way to stop your father and I agree we need to find her. However, I'm not giving up on you. I have waited since we were kids for you to be mine, even though it took me growing up and pulling my head out of my ass to realize it. I just want us to live long, happy lives. Have a bunch of children and then see them have their own children."

"It sounds great when you say it like that, but it isn't the reality we live in," I said, barely above a whisper. "The point is, I'm going to have to die."

"*My* point, Megan Isabel Matthewson, is that I'm not giving up on our life together. I realize that I may have to grow old without you, but I'd really rather not. I'm not sure I could live past your last heartbeat, so I will always be searching for that loophole."

He reached up and cupped my face with both hands. "Up until that last moment. Until you finish uttering whatever words, you will need to say to rip your father from this world, I'm going to be looking for that Angel's be damned loophole to get you out safely. I won't give up on you. I won't give up on us. I won't give up on finding a way for you to live. "

CHAPTER 7

"Jean?" I said.

I looked up from the book I was reading. I had been spending every moment I could over the last few days in Therth's library combing through what we could find on Helena. Clarice had told us the short version of how High Witch Helena Rowland stood on the highest mountain in the land of the Cinder Fairies and cast a spell; a spell that was to heal the damage to the world, but also to take away the darkest of darkness. Legend said that she scaled the mountain alone, while the Cinder Fairies held off her lover, the one who was causing so much destruction across the world, at the foot of the mountain. When she reached the top, she cast the spell, and it worked. Her lover shriveled to dust, and the land touched by his evil had healed. When she didn't return, the Cinder Fairies scaled the mountain to retrieve her. What they found was Helena siting at the peak with a crystal in each hand; one red and the other black.

In magic, especially magic that powerful, nature must find a balance. She had defeated her lover and healed the damaged lands, but it was such a massive, world-altering spell, that when nature went into balance, it split her soul into two crystals, one red and one black, and left her body with no resident.

Legend also said that when her soul split, all that was good in Helena Rowland went into the black crystal, which the Fairies named Helena, the Crystal of Pureness. Any darkness in her was captured in a vibrant red ruby that the Cinder Fairies immediately shattered for fear it could return evil to the lands. The ruby bled for 13 days. For 13 days, the Royal Guard of the Cinder High Queen stood guard as it bled into the ground. When it stopped bleeding, it screeched and disintegrated into dust, every particle absorbing into the ground.

We had found nothing much different from that story in everything we had read, which was frustrating. The one thing we could verify was that when they took an inventory of who all died that day, they found that in a town nearby which had been full of Chiklaree, the same race as Helena Rowland's lover, the townspeople had been turned to stone. The stone had melted away in the next rain. Every inhabitant of the town, every man, woman, and child had been destroyed.

"Jean!"

She looked up, startled.

I pointed to the book I was reading. "I might have a lead to finding where the Cinder Fairies may be hiding her. I would love to tell you if you would just pull your nose from your book."

Jean smiled and looked a little sheepish, but when I didn't say anything, she rolled her eyes. "So, get on with it."

"The Cinder Fairies didn't keep Helena in Cinder. They thought it too much of a threat so hid it in the..." my heart dropped as I read from the page.

"Where?" Jean and Owen, who had come around the corner to listen, said in unison.

"The tallest mountain at the edge of the Lost Plateau in a forgotten temple."

"Well, at least we don't have to spend four and a half months on a boat to the Cinder Plains, only be turned around to Nalrin," Owen said way too casually.

"But the Lost Plateau, Owen," Jean said, despair in her voice.

"Not to mention that the grasslands between Nalrin and the Plateau are not super easy to navigate," Jean said.

"Is it too much to hope that the Cinder Fairy Queen moves it every so often? I mean, if its location has been recorded, doesn't that lead to the chance that it could be found? Something this powerful... would need to be locked up. At least heavily guarded, right? Even the Mirror of Remembrance was deep in the Nalrin Library."

"I would think so. I guess we will have to see what Julian says." Jean said.

"Julian? What does he have to do with it?"

"Well, A, he is head of the dimension, remember?" Jean said.

"Right."

"And B, he's been talking with the Fairy Queen to get information since we first realized this might be the only way to stop Ansel."

"Why do I keep forgetting that?" I said, shaking my head.

"You have a lot on your mind." Owen tried to comfort me, but it wasn't working.

"But if I don't remember details, how am I going to do this?" I leaned back in my chair, resting my head on the worn black leather, and sighed.

"Or Julian can send us to rendezvous with the High Queen's consort and meet him on Vox Isle in three weeks," CJ said as he strode into the room. He gave me a wink that made my breath catch. I could swear I saw a flash in his eyes before he turned to the others and said, "Julian sent word and we are to be at Vox port in three weeks. They will wait no longer."

"Clarice's coronation is tonight. We will have to leave first thing in the morning to get there on time," Jean said.

"Do we know if Clarice is going to go with, or does she need to stay here?"

"We don't know," Owen said sadly. "I want her to go with, but... Gatekeeper to the Underworld. It's... it's a terrible burden."

"And a burden I must carry until the day I die. I can't change it," Clarice said, coming into the room with her hands on her hips. "I really wish I could. I don't want this responsibility and never did. It was just one of many reasons I left, but there is literally nothing I can do to change it, except to cease existing, but I would really rather that not be the case."

"Clarice. I didn't mean..." Owen said before he trailed off.

"I know Owen. I also didn't want you guys to know any of this because I didn't want you to change how you treated me. All I had wanted was to be treated like a normal, everyday person. When you allowed me to live with you and become part of your family... they were the happiest decades of my life," she sighed. "But to answer everyone's question. I have already planned for Erida and Dorith to handle all of my duties, so I will accompany you to Vox Isle and beyond. That is, if you still want me," she trailed off at the end in a way that broke my heart.

"Of course, we want you to go. We just didn't know if you would be able to." I stood up and took her arm in mine. I secured the book by tucking it under the other and headed back to our rooms.

"Well, the gate is closed, and I don't want it open until we can stop Ansel. Don't want to risk anything else escaping that he could control. My father died trying to close it. I may not have liked the man, but I will not let his death be shamed by letting that become a possibility. Dorith and Erida can handle everything else. They have been for quite a while, anyway."

"Question," Owen asked, and we stopped just shy of the door, turning to look at him. "Witch Dorith mentioned it has to be a blood diamond to close the gate. Okay, so two questions. The first is, could you reopen it without a blood diamond?"

"I'm Gatekeeper to the Underworld. Of course, I can open it. That's easy. I'm assuming the second question is whether I'll be able to close the gate without another blood diamond? Since two of my blood are now in the Underworld?"

"Well, yes." He said, eyes wide, and nodding.

She sighed heavily. "A blood diamond doesn't have to be blood. It is stronger, and the casting will be smoother if it's four beings are connected by blood, but as long as the Gatekeeper is at the head of the diamond, and the other three open their power to the mercy of the Gatekeeper, yes, we could close it again if needed. The blood connection just makes pulling the power from the others easier. It's... much more complicated, if not."

"So, if we opened the gate today, you, Jean, Megan, and I could close the gate again?" Owen asked. I blinked at him, then looked at Clarice. I hadn't even thought about that.

Her face was tight, but she said, "Yes, but I couldn't ask that of you. I... I am not settled in my powers yet, and I fear I would kill you by taking every drop of your power to complete the spell."

The room was quiet for a long time before Owen chuckled, and ran his hand through his hair, "Well then. Let's *not* do that."

I felt Clarice relax under my arm and huff out a laugh. "Yeah, let's not do that."

"Alright, since Clarice won't be killing us today, and she has a coronation tonight, let's go see which dress Erida picked for your coronation because I'll be damned if you are going to wear anything like that *other* dress you had on."

"Megs, I have a couple of meetings to attend. I'll see you back at our room, okay?" CJ said, but there was a twinkle in his eye that warmed me in all the right spots.

I nodded and turned back to Clarice. "Dress time?"

"Why does this scare me?" Clarice said as we headed toward the Reining Quarters.

CHAPTER 8

"You have to be kidding me," I said when we walked through the entry into the dressing hall where Erida had her coronation dress on the mannequin. "Seriously Clarice. This is a fucking joke, right?"

"It's my grandmother's," Clarice said, trying to hide the smile from her face with Erida standing right there.

"And I'm sure it looked wonderful on... HER," I said, trying to be respectful.

Erida stepped forward and said, "It is traditional to wear a dress that your ancestor wore."

"I'm sure it is. And that is all fine and dandy, but don't you think your new Queen should look exceptional on her coronation day and not... washed out and cold?" I said seriously. "The brown fabric is the same color as her skin. No one could tell where her skin begins and where the dress ends. Is there anything in that closet that isn't skin toned? You are two for two right now. She needs something to make her pop."

"It's-" Erida started to say before I interrupted.

"Tradition. I heard you the first time and got the memo, Erida. However, Clarice is going to look awful in this dress." I held up my hand to stop her from talking. The frustration on her face was only masked by her astonishment that I was even talking to her this way.

"I realize your customs and traditions are different here. I completely understand the need for you to respect those who came before you, and you shall, through the ceremony. That all being said, where I come from, royalty is supposed to look elegant, traditional, and amazing. Clarice will not look amazing in that dress," I continued as I pointed at the dress on the mannequin. "I may not know a lot about fashion, but Lindy taught me a thing or two about color. Clarice. Needs. To. Be. Dazzling."

"Clarice, you are Queen. What do you think?" Erida was trying to defer to Clarice to get her way. I crossed my arms and raised an eyebrow at her. I downright dared her to cross me on this. Gatekeeper or not, if she was going to be crowned the fucking Queen she was, she was going to look amazing doing it.

Clarice looked at me and I couldn't tell if she was scared or just assessing my behavior. "I... I don't know. Megan has never been this passionate about clothes before. Even for her own wedding, the only thing she really put her foot down on was *her* dress and the bridesmaids' shoes. She basically let Lindy and Jean pick everything else. They organized the entire event. Megan gave them a general direction and would only really speak up when there was something she really didn't agree with. So Erida, I am deferring to her judgment."

Erida shook her head and laughed. "Okay," she turned to me and lifted a finger. "But I have final say. We have to meet tradition."

I put my hands up in surrender. "Deal."

And so it began. Erida and I went through the lines and lines of dresses that lined the dressing room until I saw a white and ice blue sleeveless dress with silver trimmings hung loosely on a hanger.

"Erida. Put this on the mannequin." With a wave of her hand, it replaced the original dress Clarice was going to wear. The underdress was ice blue with silver embellishments. There was a white corset that pointed below the breasts that was attached to a white overskirt that left the ice blue under dress showing in the front. Three silver chains hung around the shoulders from a jeweled neck piece. When Erida looked from the dress to Clarice, her eyes widened.

I stood there, confident in my choice, and crossed my arms. Erida looked from Clarice to the dress and then to me. Her mouth widened, and then she jumped and clapped and said, "Clarice, this is perfect. You are going to be stunning!"

Clarice just looked at us, dumbfounded.

The dress was perfect. The white and ice blue satin was going to set her skin off perfectly. There was a slight train, and as I ran my fingers over the bodice, I felt the boning and sighed.

"Well, Clarice, you will only be in it for a little while, but you probably will have problems breathing. "

"Why?" Clarice asked.

"The corset is boned and lined with more velvet, so you're going to be really hot." I smiled as a thought came to me. "Though, I also believe that Erida will probably cinch down the corset as much as possible, so ya, you won't be able to breathe much, but it's only for a couple hours. You'll survive."

"I grew up in corsets. It's nothing new for me, Megan. And yes, Erida will enjoy strapping me in. It will be her way of getting me back for all the ones I probably cinched too tight when we were girls growing up," she said, smiling at Erida, who was grinning back with satisfaction. Then Clarice tilted her head and her smile faltered. "Erida, you wanted this. All of this. I expected you to be more..."

"Hostile?" She said with a laugh.

"Not hostile, exactly, but difficult." Clarice said honestly. "Really difficult, actually. You were so vicious when we first arrived. Before Father died. What changed?"

Erida seemed to expect the question. She took a deep breath and said, "Clarice.... You always got the best tutors. The best of everything and I wanted what was given to you," she stopped, glanced at me, then took a step toward Clarice. Her eyes were shining, and it looked like she might cry, but there was a shadow of shame on her face. As if she knew what she betrayed, she shook her head, wiping it all from her and with resolve continued, "When Father died, and I saw what came out of the gate... it terrified me. You just did what needed to be done. You did not hesitate. You fought. All while I just sat there... frozen."

She clung to the skirts of her dress as she tried to keep her composure. When she could speak again, she threw her hands to her sides, looked up with pride in her eyes before continuing. "Then you, the first daughter of a man who just died, pushed aside all that pain and did what no one else in that room did. You strode upstairs and wiped out all the Ja'Nee so naturally. Everyone bowed to that power, and I knew the power had *chosen* you. I do not have the resolve to do what you do. That power chose you. You walk up to danger and face it. I don't have the fortitude to do that. The power and crown are going to the right person. I bow to you sister, my Queen."

"You are stronger than you know, Erida. When the time comes, you will see that. I have no doubt," Clarice said as she pulled Erida into a tight hug.

I was so glad to see them reconcile, and it was such a personal moment that I excused myself to let Erida help Clarice get ready.

CHAPTER 9

"LADY MEGAN, VERNADALI CJ, your seats are here," the attendant dressed in a dark blue sleeved jerkin, breeches, cream tights and black square-toed shoes, said curtly to us when we entered the massive hall.

Not much had changed since we were here last time. The only difference was the ice blue and white fabric, which matched Clarice's dress, wrapped loosely around the black pillars that lined either side of the room. The ceiling peak had the same ice blue and white fabric bunched into an elaborate knot before flowing down around the rest of the room. My shoes clicked on the white marble floors as we walked up the aisle to the front row. As we made our way toward the front, I looked at the people we passed. There were a few faces I recognized, mostly Lords and Ladies of Obsecuritan, but it was strange to be met with glares and nods of respect.

"Please be seated and do not move until the conclusion of the ceremony," the attendant said, indicating the first couple of seats in the front row. I gave CJ a look, and he basically gave me a look back that made me keep my mouth shut.

"How am I supposed to sit when I can barely breathe standing in this dress? Did I really have to wear this damn corset?" Dark green and black with about three layers of skirts with tight sleeves to the elbow that belled open to the wrists, the dress was beautiful, but the most uncomfortable thing I had ever worn. I tried to wear something less extravagant, but when Erida saw what I had chosen, she left and came back with three 'more appropriate' dresses and told me to choose one of them. As part of the family, we were required to dress the royalty part, and considering I had changed what Clarice was wearing, she was going to ensure that I was properly dressed.

"According to Erida, yes. Now sit," CJ said in that husky commanding tone. "Besides, if you stop complaining, and maybe if you're *really* good, I'll take it off for you later." Heat flooded my face, already picturing exactly how he would remove it.

"Hopefully quick and in shreds," I growled in anticipation. "Maybe pick up where we left off earlier?"

He let out a shuddering breath and said, "Those lips did a fine job, babe." Then he leaned closer and whispered into my ear, "So behave, and I'll prove to you once again just what mine can do."

"Yes, sir." My voice was thick, and I sat with my hands in my lap. I clenched my legs together tight at the thought of all the talents I knew his tongue had.

To distract myself, I looked around the nearly packed hall and saw that most of the Lords from the meeting earlier had stayed. Lord Basilwill, Lord Bernat, and even the Lady of Yurry had stayed. I let out a little laugh.

"What is it?" CJ asked.

"I was just thinking. At first, I was surprised that so many from the Council meeting this morning had stayed, but then I thought, would they dare to miss the coronation of their Queen?"

"Well, it's more than just the coronation," Owen said, leaning forward so we could see him sitting beside Jean. "Remember, we live so long that this isn't something that happens every sixty or seventy years. The Gatekeeper to the Underworld is someone who reigns for hundreds of years."

"Hundreds..." I breathed.

"Clarice could rule over Obsecuritan and be the Gatekeeper to the Underworld for seven hundred plus years." Owen whispered.

"But, Sangra don't..."

"Live that long?" Owen's eyebrows shooting up to his forehead. "They don't, but she is Gatekeeper of the Underworld. The Angel of Death affords more than just extra power to keep the Underworld in check."

Before I could ask anymore, the Herald struck the marble with the staff three times on the ground to bring everyone to attention.

"The Council of Obsecuritan calls forth the Coronation of the House of Heros, first daughter to King Babbak, Clarice Gwyn." He raised his hands to the back of the room where Clarice was standing in the dress we had chosen earlier, and a white cape adorned with silver embroidery. She was holding a swirling black and silver glass ball in her left hand and a silver scepter with an obsidian black jewel at the end of the other.

Alexei, Clarice's Silnaree, stepped forward and walked with her step by step up the aisle. When they reached the Herald, they each bowed.

"Clarice Gwyn, are you or are you not the rightful heir to the House of Heros?"

"I, Clarice Gwyn, have inherited the key to the Gate of the Underworld by death and virtue of my father, King Babbak of the House of Heros."

"Alexei Stragis, Silnaree of Clarice Gwyn, as bound by the Gatekeepers' darkness of King Babbak, do you wish to advance to the House of Heros and hereby be crowned Grand Duke of Heros?"

I looked at Jean, confused. "They marry them in the process?" I whispered quietly.

"Yes. The coronation cannot continue unless she is married. Stupid old traditions," she whispered, barely loud enough for me to hear. "I thought you knew that."

I shook my head and looked back to where Clarice and Alexei were standing.

"Yes," Alexei said, smiling brightly at Clarice.

"Clarice Gwyn of the House of Heros, do you wish to advance the House of Heros and hereby be crowned Empress?"

A murmur echoed through the hall as a gasp left my lips. Empress? They wanted to elevate Clarice to Empress?

"Empress?" Clarice asked carefully.

Jean leaned into my ear and whispered, "There hasn't been an Empress since the time of the 1,000 Years War. They said they didn't want someone with those powers."

I nodded. "She would literally outrank everyone in Nalsar except Julian." I breathed the words in awe. I felt CJ's hand on my back, and when I looked at him, he smirked at me.

At that same moment, the Lords and Ladies of Obsecuritan rose and spoke as one. "The Lords Council convened and by unanimous vote has determined that Clarice Gwyn of the House of Heros qualifies for the title of Empress. The Council hereby elevates the guardian of the Gate to the Underworld to Empress."

CJ didn't seem phased by the proclamation and as his smirk grew, I hissed, "Did you know about this?"

CJ stood, a wicked gleam now in his eye. "The Vernadali confirm such assent."

When he sat back down, he whispered against my ear so lightly, no one else could have heard him, "They can't do it without a Vernadali present for the vote." He looked like he had been caught with his hand in the cookie jar.

"And you didn't tell us?" Jean said, somehow hearing him and swatting him upside the back of his head.

"Couldn't. I just had to stand there and look pretty," he said as I glared at him.

The Herald stamped the staff on the cold marble floor to bring everyone back to attention and repeated, "Clarice Gwyn of the House of Heros, do you wish to advance the House of Heros and hereby be crowned Empress?"

Clarice hesitated for only a moment, staring at CJ. Oh yes, there would be words between the two of them. She narrowed her eyes at him once more and said clearly, "Yes."

"State your vows."

Clarice turned toward the hall and, with her head held high, spoke clearly to all those who were in attendance.

"Here do I swear, by mouth and marriage, by light and dark and by right of birth, to uphold the natural laws of the Underworld and the secrets it holds within;

I shall champion for change and safety within all of Obsecuritan;

I shall be loyal to the populace of the land and not the power within;

I shall listen to our estates and to protect same;

I shall strike and spare, to punish and reward in all matters;

In peace or war until the Underworld claims my soul and I depart these lands;

So say I,... Empress Clarice Gwyn of the House of Heros."

"Empress Clarice and Grand Duke Alexei, please kneel." They kneeled, and each received a simple crown upon their heads; both black as night and looking like a splash of water.

They rose and faced the hall as the Herald shouted for all to hear, "I present to you, Empress Clarice and Grand Duke Alexei."

Tears filled my eyes, and a lump solidified my throat as I swelled with pride and happiness for Clarice. I smiled brightly as the hall erupted in cheers of "Long live Empress Clarice and may the Angels bless you with many heirs."

CHAPTER 10

A WEEK AFTER CLARICE'S wedding and coronation, we finally reached the Port of Singta, a dirty, smelly, and crime ridden town with cobblestone pathways and brick and clay buildings. I couldn't wait to get on board that ship, Angels above. The smell was horrible. I pulled my scarf up over my nose, but it did little good.

The general store we passed said it sold fresh meat. Fresh a month ago, maybe, with no preserving. That's not even to mention the smell of the bodies that probably hadn't washed in months, and the piles of feces that were... well, everywhere. I'd never been a neat freak or germaphobe, but this had to be the most unsanitary place I had seen since arriving in Nalsar. It was the only ship that would stop at Vox Isle on the whole of the north-west coast of the continent for another three months, so here I was in this filth-ridden town.

As we rounded the corner, the ship taking us to Vox Isle came into view. A full-rigged ship, dark black wood with white and green accents, was a beautiful sight. Clarice dismounted and glared at her four guards that her new husband wouldn't allow her to travel without. After she spoke to a man who I presumed was the captain, she came back and said, "Dismount. We can take the horses onboard."

"What?" Owen asked. "I thought they don't allow livestock on non-cargo ships."

Clarice laughed. "Being Queen... I mean Empress has its perks."

As I loaded Ziggy onto the ship, I finally relaxed. We were on our way to a real, tangible lead. Even if the Queen's Consort did nothing but verify what we found at the Therth library, it would lead us to the end of all of this.

I groaned at what that meant, though. The Lost Plateau. Underworld beings. The stories I've heard. People have lost their minds wandering the expanse. I shuttered as I remembered Clarice explaining to me how dark clouds that hung over the plateau and turned day to night.

Ziggy nudged my hip, bringing me back. I smiled and rubbed his muzzle. "Demanding little thing, aren't you?" I fed him the carrot I had in my back pocket and went to remove his tack and took my time brushing him down. CJ brushed Tucker down beside me and at one point tried to say something, but then held back and went back to brushing. Brushing Ziggy was a soothing and repetitive motion that allowed me to clear my head, even just for a few minutes.

I was just finishing up when CJ leaned up against the post to watch me. "What?" I asked.

"Nothing. Was just thinking that you look so content, and I haven't seen that... well, in a while," he said, smiling slightly. It was a smile that made my stomach quiver and my cheeks warm.

"Oh, really?" I said, tossing the brush in the bucket next to him. I reached up and put my arms around his neck as he pulled me closer.

"Yup," he said, pulling me in for a kiss.

"Oh, Angels. Get a room!" Owen said as they walked down the aisle.

I smiled against CJ's lips, jumped and wrapped my legs around his hips, his hands instantly going to my ass and giving it a firm squeeze. "What if I don't want to?" I said over my shoulder.

"Seriously, Megan?" Jean said.

"Fine," I said with a sigh and put my feet back on the floor. CJ's hands didn't move for a long moment before I said, "You guys are no fun."

"Well, as your aunt, I can say I don't need to see that," Jean said.

"And as your friend, I don't need to see it, either," Clarice laughed.

"Are we really that bad?" I said sheepishly, my cheeks flooding in embarrassment.

"No. You aren't. We are just giving you a bad time," Clarice said. "It is actually quite nice to see you two act normal, instead of two people with the weight of the world on your shoulders."

I smiled at CJ, who just shrugged. Only, there was a twinkle in his eye that said I was in for a workout once we were alone.

"Well, if everyone is done giving us a bad time, I believe we are required to be topside. Wish I could stay below deck with the horses. At least the smell doesn't make my stomach flip down here," I said, feeling that weight slowly press on me again. I was so tired. "Maybe it will smell better once we get out on the open ocean. I plan on ravishing my husband in our room and sleeping. In that order. Multiple times."

As if on cue, the bell ran, startling the horses, telling everyone to get on deck. After calming Ziggy and the other horses down, we made our way through the stalls. I grabbed CJ's hand as I got this hollow feeling. I hated not knowing what lay ahead of us. I still hadn't had a vision, and the longer I went without them, the more I missed them. Not having them was so damned frustrating. They had always been a part of my life. Now, not having one for so long, well, it was becoming more and more clear, I may have relied on them too heavily.

"I'm dying," I said as I put my head over the edge of the boat yet again. "No. I've died and I'm paying for... well, for something that I did in my life to piss off the universe. It's the only explanation." Four days. Four days of not being able to keep anything down. Not to mention the violent headaches. They hadn't been this bad since before King Babback died.

"You aren't dying. You are just seasick, though I did not peg you for being one to be this sensitive to the movement. I thought maybe CJ, but not you." Clarice laughed as the contents of my stomach were once again forcibly projected over the edge of the railing. "Look. There is Vox Isle. You will be able to get your feet on land in just a few minutes. Come on, let's go get Ziggy ready."

"Okay but keep a bucket handy." I said, not daring to look up to where Clarice was pointing.

We headed down the stairs to where the horses were kept, and it actually helped to prep Ziggy for departure. I don't know if it was the fact we weren't up on the deck anymore, or if Ziggy just provided me enough of a distraction. CJ had tried every distraction technique possible over the last couple of weeks. I enjoyed most of them immensely, but I still had headaches, issues keeping food down, and just being tired and worn out from all of it.

CJ brought our bags down from our room and secured it to the saddle, then helped me into the saddle. His hand stayed on my leg and when I looked down at him, I tried to reassure him I was fine, but he just said, "Like you would tell me if you weren't."

"True, but you know me better than anyone, anywhere. Plus, with that bond, you know exactly how I'm feeling," I said a little too sharply and winced. "I'm sorry Ceej. I just need off this blasted boat."

CJ looked at me with a questioning look, opened his mouth to ask something, but shut it again.

"What is it?"

"Megs. You have been feeling off for... how long?" He asked quietly. I looked at him, but then he continued, "You are lethargic. Can't keep food down."

I just looked at him. He raised his eyebrows at me and then looked at my stomach and cocked his head to the side.

Realization at what he was asking hit me hard and fast. "No." I whispered. "I don't think so, at least. I'm fine. Just need off this boat," I said, trying to hide it. I had been feeling worn out for a while, if I was being honest. I was feeling *really* off, actually. More so since my little magical hissy fit in Therth, but pregnant? Angels. Now would not be good timing for a kid. Yes. I want his kids, but now? I couldn't even think about it.

"I know, but you can't lie to me. I know you're feeling weak. If that isn't the reason, then what's going on?" he whispered, watching for anyone else around us who could overhear.

"I don't know. I'll be fine. I'm seasick or just tired from, well, everything," I said, forcing myself to smile. "Can we just go back to the resort for a month?"

An evil teasing smile crossed CJ's lips, as he slid his hand up my thigh, but before he could say anything, Clarice and her guards showed up. "I'm going to get Tucker ready." He said, kissing my hand.

"Everything okay between you two?"

"Of course. I'm just tired and CJ worries. It's in his job description," I said, laughing.

"Literally in his job description," she said, joining me in laughter.

Vox Isle was a surprisingly barren place. Red rocks and plateaus jutted out all over the landscape, creating a beautiful skyline in the setting sun. Sunlight danced in a rainbow of colors across the tops and onto the streets.

"Queen Clarice," said a man in a military uniform with deep blue and gold wings that he kept tucked tight behind him. I studied the black double-breasted jacket with gold embroidery on it, trying to sort out how it was put on. There were slits in the back for the wings, but his wings looked too big to fit through the small openings. "I was instructed to give this to you the second you arrived."

One of the guards that accompanied us dismounted and took the note from him. "It is Empress Clarice," he said, almost snarling the words to the man.

"Kuntz," Clarice said in warning.

The guard nodded slightly as he ripped open the message, and after reading it, handed it to Clarice. "I advise against it, Empress. It deviates from our plans, which puts you in jeopardy."

Clarice read it over, laughed, and said, "Really, Kuntz? It only suggests that since we arrived so late in the day, that we take a night to rest before we meet with the envoy from Cinder." She turned to the man in the military uniform and said, "We will meet your master at the specified place and time tomorrow. Ask him to please not be late, for we wish to be on the next ship set for the Nalrin continent."

His head snapped up, and a sneer crossed his lips. "You dare give instructions to the Consort of the Cinder Queen?"

Clarice was off her horse and standing before him before I could blink. "I dare ask for the Consort to the Cinder Queen to be respectful of Empress Clarice of the House of Heros timetable," she said in a gentle, commanding tone.

I stared at her in shock.

Clarice. Just. Pulled. Rank.

Clarice. The one who didn't even want us to know that she was a Princess just pulled rank on another house.

"Remember, Empress. His Highness is here as a favor to you and yours," he said sternly.

"No. His Highness Thegas is here because his Queen is tied up in a civil war among her people and cannot chance traveling due to mutiny in her own house," she said firmly. He sputtered something about wanting to know how she knew so much about what was going on in Cinder, but she continued, "Now, His Highness has been kind enough to offer us a good night's sleep, and we would like to accept his kind offer. We shall see him tomorrow." Clarice turned her back on him and made to mount her house.

"Excuse me... Empress," he said, his voice less sure of himself. When she looked back at him, he continued. "How do you know of the Cinder's High Court? Word has been sealed. Even I cannot utter the words. The Court's language is bound."

"I am the Gatekeeper of the Underworld. The shadows of the dead advise me of things that do not make it out of Courts," she said sadly. "Many have died. Needlessly. I only hope that your Queen can instill confidence and peace soon."

I could do nothing but blink. So much had just happened in such a short conversation that I was having a hard time processing it all. I looked at CJ, then Jean, and then Owen. They all were looking at Clarice, as if they had just met her. The poise with which she handled herself was impressive. Not to mention the information she had given with respect and tact and the new abilities she just said she had. What else was she not telling us?

No one spoke as we made our way to the inn. Not a word was spoken until we were in our room.

"Clarice, why don't the guards head downstairs and get some food and beers? Have them open a tab under my name," I said when everyone had secured their beds.

"Lady Megan. We are not to leave the Empress," one of the guards said.

"And we need to have a *family* discussion that I'd really rather not have the guards overhear. Please leave," I said, trying to stay calm. My heart was pounding, electricity filling the air. I was on the verge of losing my shit. Very quickly. Again.

"You cannot and will not give us orders, Lady Megan," the head guard said.

"Yes. Yes, she can. From this point forward, you are hereby ordered to accept any order from Lady Megan, Lady Jean, Sir Owen or Vernadali CJ, as if they left my own lips. Now, please. We have much to discuss. You heard Lady Megan. Go and refresh yourselves," Clarice ordered.

When the last guard was out of the room, CJ asked. "What the actual fucking hell, Clarice?" He spoke with such ferocity, it even shocked me.

"CJ," she placated.

"No seriously, Clarice. I've had to wrap my head around a lot the last couple of years. Megan actually loving me for me and wanting me here. Megan being this super powerful being, her parents not really being dead, trying to kill me, and now trying to destroy a whole world. You being the fucking Empress to an entire continent *and* Gatekeeper of the Angels' damned Underworld. Not to mention the fact that I am Angel blessed to be some super powerful bodyguard for my wife, which I think I have all taken in great stride. Thank you very much. I've learned and adapted. Now, you can talk to dead people? Of course, the dead talk to people. Why not?!"

He took a minute to compose himself after his outburst and to settle down enough that he wouldn't yell at her again. All the while, no one else said a word. When he calmed, he said, "I don't know why, Clarice, but this one bothers me on a whole new level. The dead actually talk to you? What is this? I see dead people?"

I tried not to giggle at his movie reference, but I couldn't help it. "Megan, don't."

"What? I'm not the one using movie references to get a point across. It's not like any of them will understand that line." I tried to control my laughter. I don't know why I thought it was so funny, but I just couldn't stop giggling.

"Clarice, what else aren't you telling us?" Owen said.

"A great deal. I want to, but there are things that even I do not know I can do yet. My father never told me about this. Mostly because I declined the position and took off, but not the point. It takes years for everything to settle in. My father had once said it took him ten years before he settled into his Gatekeeper powers."

"So civil war in Cinder, huh?" Jean muttered.

Clarice nodded. "What I'm hearing is not pretty. A third of the High Court has been murdered in their sleep, mostly on the Queen's side. Apparently, Lord Deezasil wants his daughter to ascend to the throne, and most of who have died are those ahead of her in the line of succession. You cannot say a word. If this were to get out, it could throw the economic balance of the world in jeopardy. The Cinder Queen is taking a great chance in sending her Consort out of Cinder to even talk to us. I'm not sure why she did it when—"

"Megan? What's wrong?" CJ said, interrupting Clarice as my vision faded to black.

CHAPTER 11

I COULD FEEL MYSELF coming out of a deep sleep, but I couldn't come fully awake. Am I still dreaming? There were faint voices far off in the distance, but I wasn't sure who they were.

"Lindy?" I said as her face filled my vision. "Lindy! I miss you so, so much."

"You have to wake up, Megan." Her voice was strong, demanding, and... not right.

"Wait. How?" I stammered.

"NOW!" Lindy screamed in my face, and I jolted awake. The room spun, and I laid back down.

"Lady Megan?" a lilting musical voice said. There were light footsteps, with a faint flapping and light breeze, before I felt thin, quick fingers on either side of my face. Then they are gone. "Give her a minute. She's coming back. Her pulse is steady."

"Lindy?" I mumbled as I tried to push through the haze. I opened my eyes, but the lights were too bright, and my head felt like a million jackhammers had been running nonstop for days inside my head. I blinked and rubbed my eyes as I tried to force them open again.

"What did you do, Ceej? Hit me with a baseball bat?"

"That is what you get for making fun of my movie references," he said with a small laugh, but he asked more seriously, "How are you feeling?"

"Like you hit me over the head with a baseball bat." I tried to sit up, but the room spun again, and I put my head back down. "What's wrong with me?"

Suddenly, there were eyes that were oversized black caverns hovering over me. There were no irises, but what looked like fine vines twirling in the blackness filled the eyes. I reached for my syths, but CJ grabbed my hands. "Easy, Megs. Friendly."

With a calm, lilting voice, the thing in front of me said, "Lady Megan. I am Physician Sonol. I am a physician in female specialties accompanying the Consort of the Queen of Cinder. I have an affinity to examine the body without invasion."

"So x-ray vision." I croaked. My throat was dry, and I indeed felt like CJ had smacked me over the head with a baseball bat.

"I am sorry what?" he asked, standing back up straight, where I saw rust-colored wings with black and white laced throughout, spread out behind him.

"Never mind," I said as I heard CJ snort beside me. "What's wrong with me?"

"Well, first you are extremely dehydrated, but that is no surprise considering that you were so ill on the boat. What concerns me is the dark sickening spell that was cast upon you. Who would have done such a thing?" Physician Sonol looked horrified at the notation.

"I'm sorry what?" Nothing he was saying was making sense. I looked around the room and then felt my stomach drop when I didn't see Lindy there. She was so real.

"Someone cast a sickening spell on you. I broke it. You are welcome, but those are incredibly difficult to cast." His long, thin hand and spindly fingers flipped around in the air like he was casually swatting a fly. "This particular one was laced with a pure darkness that Cinder's have not seen since the 1,000 Years

Wars. Frankly, you are lucky that I was here to break it for you," he said, standing a little straighter with pride.

I eyed CJ, then Clarice, who said, "How long do you suspect she's had it on her?"

"A year? Give or take a few months? It grows stronger the longer it is in place." Physician Sonol stood up straighter, pulled his shoulders back, and his wings fluttered just the littlest bit. "I am considered one of the best, but much longer, and I may not have been able to break it. As it is, it took most of the night."

"That would mean..." CJ looked at me and I could see him doing the calculations. I nodded.

"That would be about the time we went to Noctulanar Castle," Jean said.

"Maybe Penny cast it on her when we were in the Nalrin Library." Owen's voice was hesitant, but thoughtful.

"There has to be a propensity of darkness already in the person, but it would need to be amplified with pain, hurt, or some other strong emotion to take root," Physician Sonol said.

"Ansel." Jean, Owen and Clarice said in unison.

"Probably right after your Mom died," CJ said softly. "And Ansel is Ash'bani. Do you think that would do it?"

"If this Ansel had not gone through the purging ceremony—"

"He hadn't, at that time." I forced myself to sit up.

"Couple that with the pain of losing his mate," he said contemplatively. Mate, because Cinder Fairies only have mates. Not husbands or wives. There were only mates, whether chosen or biologically. "If he cast it while he was still at Noctulanar Castle, he could have harnessed the dark energy from there. Did you have any pain or sickness when you returned from Noctulanar?"

I looked at CJ, realization slamming into me like a brick wall. "Seriously?" I could not believe that it could be the answer that had baffled us all.

"Well, the doctors didn't know what happened." His voice was hard. "Doesn't answer why after your parents faked their death, unless there was something else there, but..."

"What?" Physician Sonol said attentively.

"When we still lived in the Manusia, Ansel and Symatha, her parents faked their deaths, and she was in a coma for a while afterwards. We thought it was because of the blast at the house, but they couldn't find any physical reason for it," CJ said.

"When Symatha, my mom, died at Noctulanar, I... I faded in and out of consciousness before I fell into another coma. But when they tried to wake me up, it took... well, other measures to bring me out."

Physician Sonol just blinked a few times, those swirls in his eyes freezing, then moving faster, before he said, "That could have been the catalyst. There may have already been a connection from the first time. He could have grabbed that thread, but would have had to start it pretty quickly, though. The emotions would have had to be fresh in order for it to stick that well. And the closer he is to the person he is casting it on, would make it more likely to take."

"So, the pull I felt around the time of the wedding, and what we thought was the Darkness that had fed on me at Noctulanar, wasn't King Babak calling Clarice home?" I asked.

"Wait. Not only was this your father who cast the spell, so there was a blood tie. He is Ash'bani and hadn't gone through the Ardith yet, but the darkness at Noctulanar fed on your blood?" His eyes were wide in shock as I nodded. "Why would you allow that? Noctulanar darkness is one of the sources of pure darkness."

"But I thought pure darkness could only come from the Gate, which is in Therth." I took a sip of water from a cup that CJ was handing me. The coolness felt so good on my sandpaper throat.

Clarice took a deep breath. "No, Megan. There are places in this world that pure darkness can leak out if it's called. Noctulanar is one of those locations. History for another time. It isn't usually a problem with a full-strength Gatekeeper, but my father was sick. I'm still... settling into my new role, so..."

"All the stars aligned, as they say." CJ sighed. Clarice and Physician Sonol just nodded.

"But Megan's okay now, right?" Jean said. Worry lacing her voice and I just looked at her and smiled.

"I'm feeling better, a little tired, maybe, but better." I felt down to my power, which sat calmly within me.

"As I said, she's a little dehydrated. She needs sleep and lots of water," he looked pointedly at me at the last bit. "I will be here until His Highness leaves and returns home. Call me if you need anything."

"Thank you."

"Please tell His Highness that we look forward to meeting with him this afternoon." Clarice said, every bit the Empress again. "And thank you again for everything you have done for Lady Megan."

CJ met Physician Sonol at the door and asked a few questions, and when he shook his head, there was a mixture of disappointment and relief on his face. My heart hurt at the look on his face, and tears pricked at my eyes. Physician Sonol bowed, tucking his wings in tight, before backing out of the room.

"I'm sorry Ceej," I pushed to CJ.

He came over and kissed me. Then bent down to whisper in my ear, "You have nothing to be sorry about, babes. It's okay. The thought of kids with you brings me tons of joy, but right now?"

"I know." I pushed to him.

"I just wanted to make sure before we continue on. It could change how we proceed. We can talk more about it more in private," he whispered. "I love you."

CHAPTER 12

AFTER I GOT A couple hours of sleep, CJ holding me tight the entire time, we made our way to our meeting with the Consort to the Queen. I couldn't get Lindy out of my mind. The entire time I slept, I dreamed of her. Why Lindy? Why was it Lindy yelling for me to wake up?

Once again, CJ asked me how I was feeling. As if the last twenty times he asked in the last hour were not enough.

"CJ, for the last time. I feel fine."

"Here, have some more water. You need to keep your strength up." He tried to hand me the canteen for the fourth time in five blocks.

"Cory James, if I drink one more drop of water this morning, I might as well float to the damned meeting. Trust me. I'm fine."

"Well, you didn't tell me how bad you were before the boat. I should have pushed the matter. I could feel something was off, but you said you were okay, so I dropped it. I should have pushed it." He pulled me to a stop and held my hands tight. I really didn't want to have it again.

"You want to have this conversation again right here and now?" I pulled my hands from his and crossed my arms across my chest and raised my eyebrow at him. When he just narrowed his eyes at me, I continued, "Look. I thought it was just from all the non-stop traveling we have been doing. Not to mention the magical hissy fit I had. I could easily explain the fatigue away with just those two things alone." I said with a finality that surprised even me. "Now that I know it wasn't just seasickness, I'm eager to get on our way. I seriously need the distraction. That is, if that is okay with you, Vernadali CJ."

My family just stood there, staring at us. I could have sworn I saw Jean's mouth drop open, and Owen reached over and lifted it up to close it for her.

CJ and I stared at each other for another long moment before he sighed and said, "I worry. Both as husband and Vernadali, for the record." He gave me an adorable, apologetic smirk before saying, "You are right, of course. I'm sorry. Let's get this meeting over with."

The sun overhead bounced off of the red plateaus casting a bit of an eerie light to shine down upon a surprisingly empty street. The buildings were red brick on three sides, with floor to ceiling glass on the street side. Inside, you could see races from all over the Nalsar dimension, watching as we walked down the street.

I felt a bit on display and wondered if Clarice's guards had purposefully cleared the streets as a security precaution. I missed the days we could walk down the street without a million heads turning. Even when I was working in Nalrin, a head would turn occasionally, but now it was like the Megan show. I felt everyone's eyes were on me. Even my own family's.

A block later, we stopped in front of the one building that did not have an all-glass front. After a quick discussion with the guards, we were led inside and instructed that His Highness Thegas was upstairs waiting for us.

At the base of a spiral staircase, Clarice stopped, tipped her head to the side, and I swear I saw her eyes haze over. I put my hand on her elbow and asked, "Clarice. Everything okay?"

When she didn't answer, I sent my power out, but I couldn't see anything past the open areas. All the rooms in this building were spell blocked. Clarice shook her head and looked at me. Her voice was huskier as she said, "Something is off."

A Cinder guard with black and teal wings said, "The rooms were swept two hours ago. Every room has been locked since then, and only His Highness' guards have been allowed in the building since then. Now please follow me." He gestured to the spiral staircase, and led us up to the fourth floor, opened the door, and froze.

There was a sharp, tart smell that filled the room, and I let out a gush of air in shock. What we saw before us could only be described as grizzly, at best. I looked around and felt all the color drain from my face. There was thick blue blood everywhere, which explained the tart smell.

His Highness Thegas was bound at the ankles with his hands stretched behind his back, wings torn to shreds, and a bright blue line crossed his throat. The thick blue blood had flowed freely from the cut, which meant he had been killed within the last thirty minutes. The sheer horror on his face was hard to look at. Sadly, he was the one who died the least brutally.

There were two other Cinder fairies in the room in various stages of torture before they succumbed to death. Fingernails partially pulled off their fingers, long careful cuts up and down their arms and legs, not to mention the way their eyes had been sewed open. Then there were the markings on the edge of the wings that had been sawed off. Angels they had cut very, very slowly, all to entice the most pain.

I heard Jean gag and throw up behind me, but I couldn't stop looking around the room. The sheer brutality against the two, but then the quick death they gave the Queens Consort just seemed so out of place. Blood pooled under each of them, but the splatters on the walls were only around the other two. "Something isn't right about this."

"Other than His Highness Thegas being murdered, and his attendants being tortured," the guard snapped.

"I mean no disrespect. I did not have the pleasure of knowing His Highness or anything about him, but tell me, what do you see here?"

"The brutal slaying against our court," he growled through clenched, serrated teeth.

"I don't disagree. However, look past that. His attendants were tortured. His Highness wasn't. He was only bound and killed. Whomever did this, wanted His Highness Thegas to see what they were doing, and to watch. Why?"

"Only?" the guard turned toward me, clenching his fist, and leaning toward me, wings fanning out behind him. Faster than I would have thought possible, CJ was standing between us, with his hand on the guard's throat, holding him back from me.

"Lady Megan was not disrespecting your royal family. She was trying to explain to you that this was not just a random act. Something is off about this," he said calmly, then with meaning said, "Now back off, and if you move towards her again, I will kill you where you stand. Are we clear?"

The guard sputtered a moment, then nodded his head. CJ let him go and took a couple of steps back.

Clarice was standing in the middle of the room, eyes covered in that gray mist again, and focused on something we couldn't see.

"Clarice?" I asked, putting my hand on her elbow.

"Shhh," she said with a horrified expression on her face.

Guards were pouring in. They tried to restrain us until the guard who led us in told them he was the first to walk in and they were already dead.

"What if they came in over the night and did this?" one said.

"Not possible. I spoke with His Highness not three hours ago." said another. "His Highness hasn't passed to the Underworld more than thirty minutes ago, by the state of the blood in this room."

Clarice whipped her head around and, with eyes as black as pits, said, "Will you please silence yourselves so I can hear them?"

The look on her face and the sound of her voice ensured that for the next ten minutes, you could hear nothing but the blood dripping onto the floor. When she turned back around, her eyes had returned to normal. "Anyone who does not have the highest clearance in Cinder or Nalrin must leave now."

Two Cinder fairy guards stayed, stating that since the death of the two personal guards, who had been acting as attendants of His Highness, they had been elevated in clearance. I reached my hand out to CJ and, as he intertwined his fingers with mine, we moved to leave the room.

"And where do you think you two are going?" Jean said.

"We don't have clearance and are respecting the wishes of Empress Clarice," CJ said with respect.

"Stay. As you know, Vernadali receive the clearance of their Charge. Megan has a higher clearance than anyone in Nalrin except maybe Julian himself." Owen tilted his head as if he couldn't believe he just had to say that.

"I do?" I said, shocked.

"Honey, how do you think you could do all that you have done?" Jean said.

"Favors? Begging? His being nice? Umm, because no one can resist Megan's good looks?" CJ said.

"You can be so damn naïve, and plain stupid," Jean said, leading me back into the room. "You do full background checks for council placements, and you think you don't have clearance for this?"

"That is for work only. Not for something like this," I said mumbling. Clarice and Jean just rolled their eyes.

When the door shut, Clarice told everyone that His Highness Thegas was killed as a message to the Queen. "You were right that there is something off about the way the murders were executed, Megan. They want the Queen of Cinder to step down immediately. This was a power play for the crown."

She gave them some details that I did not understand, but the Cinder guards did and when she was done, the Cinder guards bowed in respect and moved His Highness onto the bed in order to prepare him to be transported back home.

"I hate to be disrespectful, but do you know if His Highness had anything physical to give us or was everything to be verbal?" I asked softly.

One of the guards looked at me for a moment, his eyes and wings originally swimming in bright oranges, now swimming in dark red, making his eyes look like vast pits of lava. "There was a box he was going to give the Empress."

He searched the consort's body for a key, muttering apologies to the dead, and when he found it, he walked across the room and kneeled in a pool of blood to unlock a trunk. After removing a couple of false bottoms, he pulled a box from under an elegantly embroidered cloth. He carried the dark blue box etched with "Queen Clarice" in elegant silver lettering on the top to Clarice and bowed as he handed her the box.

"My apologies for it stating Queen, Empress. We did not receive word that your status had been elevated until you arrived on Vox." He bowed and handed it to Clarice.

"None needed," she said, taking the box and running her hand over the top like a precious gift. "Please give your Queen our condolences and our hope she can restore peace within her house."

As he bowed again and we turned to leave, I stopped, turned toward the two guards who had such a heavy duty ahead of them, and said, "And thank her for her help in our venture. She has paid a great price for it." They nodded and cut down the two guards who had needlessly lost their life.

There were guards posted outside of every room now. They led us to a room on the ground floor that was encased in iron. When the door was shut, Jean and Owen went to work on casting incantations to ensure our privacy. Clarice broke open the seal to the box and opened it slowly and carefully.

The only items inside were a black oval medallion etched with what almost looked like an eye, with flowing lines that reminded me of the Cinder Fairies' eyes. Clarice picked it up gently, cocked her head to the side, and slowly handed it to me. She turned back to the box and stared at the only other item in the box. A lone sheet of paper only about five inches square.

She seemed to take that sheet of paper with a reverence and carefulness I didn't understand. Slowly, she lightly touched the lettering, which was slightly raised on the paper.

"Clarice?" Owen asked.

"Sorry." Clarice shook her head. "It isn't every day the Queen of the Cinder Fairies writes a letter. Let alone one of this magnitude."

"Queen Clarice," Clarice started. "There is danger in which you seek. I know the struggles you face and the death you will endure."

"Wait, how does she know that?" CJ asked. "Who else's death are we having to endure?" His eyes swept over our family, and when they landed on mine, there was a fear that he was trying very hard to keep hidden from me in them.

"She has been in contact with Julian. It's also rumored that the Cinder Queen is omniscient. It is why there is such a battle for her throne. Unfortunately, it hasn't protected her," Clarice said before starting over and ignoring anything else CJ was trying to say.

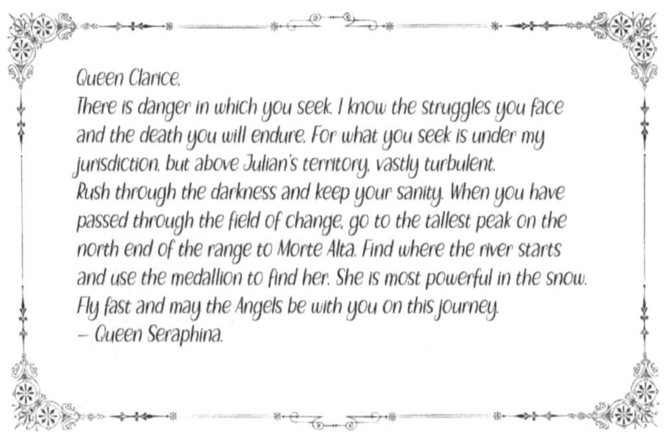

CHAPTER 13

"WELL, THAT'S NOT CRYPTIC." CJ said, running his hand through his hair and tipping his head back to look at the ceiling.

"It would have to be. What if this ended up in someone else's hands?" Owen said, laughing.

I took the note from Clarice and read it over a few times before speaking. "I think this confirms we have to go through the Lost Plateau."

"How?" Jean asked.

"She says that we have to go above Julian's territory, which the Lost Plateau is the only territory on the Nalrin continent that isn't strictly under Julian's jurisdiction. While it is part of the Nalrin continent, it technically isn't under Julian's Nalrin jurisdiction. It's under King Krunl's, who 380 years ago gave the land to the Cinder Fairies for their use. The Cinder Fairies, however, have allowed King Krunl's family continued guardianship of the territory. Not to mention it says to rush through darkness and keep your sanity. Where else is known for people losing their minds in the vastness?"

"The Slumbering Expanse." Owen's voice was heavy with a meaning I didn't understand, but Jean looked at him sadly.

"But the Slumbering Expanse is south of Julian's jurisdiction, and closer to Cinder than anything else," Clarice said, reflecting on the note from the Queen. "What I don't understand is the field of change."

"Did you expect it all to make sense?" I tried to lighten the mood. "Look, she mentions that we have to go to the tallest peak on the north end of the mountain range, right? So, we can minimize the time we have to spend in the Lost Plateau by either going through Vandrer Grasslands or taking the river through the Grasslands."

"Dragon Fjord isn't an option. It goes through the Grasslands sure, but between the rapids and waterfalls, it doesn't allow for transportation," Clarice said.

"Theoretically, we could go up to Ashridge and through the Black Mountains, but that could take longer than just going through the Plateau. Depending on where Ansel is, we may need to go around and through the Midstrada Mountains. It would be the long way, but..." Jean looked at the rest of us before she continued, "We need to know more."

"Don't you think we should have more to go on before we go somewhere like the Lost Plateau?" CJ said.

"We have moved on less," I muttered and then sighed. "Remember going through the portal to meet up with the High Witch of Alnwick?"

"And look what that cost us," Owen said, just barely above a whisper.

"Megs..." CJ noted how I had flinched, and just reached over and took my hand, squeezing it softly.

"Owen is right. We lost Lindy when we didn't have all the information we probably could have had." My mind raced through the clues the Cinder Queen had given us. "Let's head back to the hotel."

"And do what?" Jean said all the fight had been drained from her. Her shoulders were sagging and everything about her said she was just defeated. "This was our best shot at getting some answers on where to go next, and all we got were more riddles. Everything has been a riddle since this all started."

I watched each of them. Each of their faces was so full of defeat. They were so tired. Tired of the running. Tired of the puzzles. Tired of the stress. Tired of everything. This wasn't their fight. They shouldn't have to continue this journey. Losing Lindy didn't just break me. It broke them, too. I could see it in the way Jean looked at Owen. The way Clarice had looked at Alexei back in Therth. The way CJ looked at me.

"Go back to the hotel and get a good night's sleep. We'll catch the boat to Nalrin in the morning," I said as I walked out the door.

CJ found me sitting on the beach as the sun was setting just beyond the horizon. He didn't say anything, but just sat down next to me and kicked his boots off. Sinking his toes into the sand, he sighed contently as he leaned back and just watched the water. It reminded me so much of some of our days back in the Manusia. Maybe that's what he was thinking too, because he didn't even try to talk to me, touch me, or anything. He just let me sit there.

He sat there for an hour just listening to the waves, wiggling his toes in the sand, before he said, "It's getting late. Do you want me to get you something to eat and bring it back here or to the hotel?"

I turned to face him. His eyes were soft and full of concern, but he didn't push anything. "Why aren't you asking me why I ran off? Why I didn't go back to the hotel? Why I came here and have been sitting here for hours by myself? Why didn't you give me the third degree the second you sat down? How did you know I wasn't on that last ship to Nalrin without everyone? And why are you so fucking amazing that you just sat here for over an hour, and the first words aren't condemning or judging me, but ensuring that I get something to eat?"

There was a short chuckle from him before he shook his head. "I'm not hassling you about it, because I know you are already beating yourself up for everything that has happened. I'm making sure you eat because I'm your husband and my number one concern is you and your well-being. I'm fucking amazing, because I have you. I think answers all that." I gave him a pointed look, but he just sat there smiling.

"Ceej," I said, drawing out his name in reprimand.

Sighing, he said, "I checked with the harbormaster. He said the ship to Nalrin left with only a few people on it, and none matched your description." He let out a long breath and shrugged. "Besides, Ziggy and your stuff are still at the hotel."

"I could have left all of it, knowing you would have brought it back for me. You wouldn't leave Ziggy behind."

"True," he said, smiling. "Besides, that Vernadali charge you *hate* so much? It told me you were still within reach. I was pretty sure you hadn't left the island without me."

"I thought about it." I couldn't look at him. "I thought about getting on that boat to the Nalrin continent tonight, even though it wasn't going anywhere near Nalrin City, and just heading straight for Morte Alta. That way I couldn't endanger any of you anymore." Saying the words as I looked out over the ocean made my stomach roll. I didn't think I could do this on my own, but would it be so bad to try if it kept them safe? I could feel the tears about to fall.

"That doesn't surprise me." He reached over and took my hand, interlacing his fingers with mine. "You know I would have found you, right?" he said, forcing me to look at him.

"I wouldn't want you to. I don't want to lose you like we did Lindy. I couldn't bear you not existing anymore, Cory James Mathewson. I can't live with you in this world."

"I know, but I don't want to lose you, either. Damn it, Megan. I don't know how many times I have to say it. I'm not giving up on us. Yes, the odds are seriously stacked against us both making it out of this, but I can't accept it. I won't."

"Jean looks like she has. Owen probably isn't far behind her, and Clarice has a whole territory to protect. She could do that so much easier from Therth."

"Even if Clarice goes back to Therth. Even if Owen and Jean go home. You and I will finish this. Together." His eyes flashed and I jumped back a bit. He didn't... did he?

"What?" He said, looking around for what had made me jump. "What is it?"

"Did you just do the Vernadali Charge thing on me?" I tried to stifle the anger building in me.

"No, Megs, I promised I wouldn't do it unless it was imperative."

"Your eyes did the flashy lighting thing when you said that," I said cautiously.

"I swear. If it happened, I am sorry. It wasn't meant to be."

I looked at him for a long time and didn't see any sign of him lying, so I just nodded.

We sat until the light had fully left the sky, and there was nothing but stars. "Lay with me? Just to gaze at the stars?" I asked.

He pulled me close, leaned back to lie down, and I curled up next to him, laying my head on his arm that wrapped back around me.

"How many times did we do this back in the Manusia without neither of us making a move?" CJ asked, a smile in his voice.

"I've been in love with you for as long as I can remember. Just because it took us graduating high school to realize it doesn't mean shit. So, for the sake of this discussion, I'm going to say, every time?" I poked him in the ribs.

He twitched and said, "Angels, we were stupid. We could have been together for so long." He stared at the stars a moment longer before he said, "I'm sorry. I'm so sorry I didn't pull my head out of my ass earlier so we could have more time. All of our friends back in the Manusia have known we loved each other for years. I can't tell you how many times James begged me to ask you out. He told me you would have said yes, but I don't know. I was stupid, and I'm sorry."

"Becca and Amber kept telling me the same. We can't go back and change the past. We can only move forward. My life has taught me that." I sighed contently and snuggled in closer. "It would have been nice to have more time with you like this, but if this is all the Angels have allowed, then I don't want to spend it mad or fighting with you."

"Agreed," CJ said, wrapping his arm around me tighter. His thumb rubbed against my hip, and I felt a soothing calm spread across me that even wiped away the headache I didn't realize I had. I smiled.

"What?"

"I keep forgetting you can do that?"

"What?"

"Soothe the pain away."

"What hurts? Did you punch a wall on the way here?" he said, only half joking. I had done that on so many occasions to keep from getting into a fistfight growing up.

"I hadn't realized I had a headache until you soothed it away."

He kissed the top of my head and we laid there a while longer, watching the stars and listening to the waves crash on the beach.

"Ceej?" I said, barely above a whisper.

"Yeah." He rolled toward me, and we were now facing each other.

"Nothing would make me happier than to carry and bear your children. You know that, right?" We had done nothing to prevent pregnancy, and it wasn't something I had even thought about until he suggested that I could have been.

He was so shocked by the statement that he just put a hand on my cheek and pulled me close to kiss me. Forehead to forehead, he breathed, "I know."

"I don't want you to think that me not wanting to be pregnant now is because I don't want your children. I do. Angels save me.

I would be fucking honored to be the mother of your children. I just... until all of this is over... I want to carry them safely, and nothing we are doing is safe. I also want to bring our kids into a better world, one where my father isn't destroying everything." I had to tell him. The look on his face when Physician Sonol said I wasn't pregnant broke my heart. "Fuck, right now we don't know if we will even make it out of this. How can we bring a child into this world with so much destruction going on? We can't have a kid in tow with what we are doing."

"Megan." My name was a caress on my skin. "I know. I guess I just let my thoughts get away from me. When I had allowed myself to think that there was a possibility you were carrying our child, it made me so proud and honored. You will carry my children someday, and if for some reason we can't have our own biological kids, we will adopt. You are going to be an amazing mother." He kissed me softly, then said, "When Physician Sonol said that you weren't, I was disappointed, but yea, I was relieved at the same time. For the very same reasons."

"Same page?" I asked.

"Same page, babe." He kissed me again, and smiled against my lips. "Not going to stop me from worshiping you every chance I get though."

That sent a heat through me that made me shiver.

"It's getting cold, and we only have a few hours until we need to be up and moving in the morning. Let's head back to the hotel. Before we leave in the morning, we can stop by the apothecary and get the contraceptive. It's good for three months, right?"

"Yeah." As we stood, I pulled him to face me again and asked, "Are you sure?"

"Yes. Once we get through this whole thing with your father, we will talk about kids. Until then, it's just not safe." He kissed me and led me into town.

The whole way back, CJ just held my hand. There wasn't much to say, and I wasn't sure whether to be comforted or worried about that. When we got back to the hotel, I didn't make eye contact with anyone and climbed straight into bed. CJ climbed in with me and held me tight throughout the night.

CHAPTER 14

I PACED AS THE ferry that was taking us from the western coast of Nalrin to Nalrin City prepared to enter Nalrin Bay. CJ watched me carefully ever since Jean and I had that huge fight on the ship from Vox Isle. I was wound up tight. What's worse is I couldn't even lie about how I was feeling with CJ. I tried to fake it, and everyone had called me out on my bullshit. Owen and Clarice were giving me space, while Jean wouldn't even make eye contact with me.

"Megan, you have to stop pacing and calm the hell down." CJ placated.

I stopped and glared at him. "Didn't anyone ever tell you the best way to piss a woman off is to tell her to calm down?"

He cringed and went to find a spot where no one else was sitting, crossed his arms, and continued to watch me. I sat down next to him, leaned my head back on the wood walls, and sighed. Sure, Jean and I had both said things I knew we shouldn't have said. Okay, mainly me, and I would apologize for them later, but I just couldn't let it go.

We had just finished eating and decided to stretch our legs up on the deck when she leaned against the rail and sighed. I leaned my hip against the railing next to her and asked, "You okay?"

"Just trying to sort it all out."

"Jean, I understand why you are feeling so defeated. We just have to press on." She had been quiet for hours after we left the Isle and absolutely refused to make eye contact with anyone until dinner. When she joined us for a stretch of the legs, I knew I had to take a moment to talk to her. She wasn't usually the quiet one.

"I'm not sure *we* have to," she had finally said quietly through her teeth.

"And what is that supposed to mean?"

"Do you really need me and Owen?" She still refused to make eye contact. "I mean, we are just a liability to you, aren't we? We just get in your way, or are we just an army to protect you?"

"Where is this coming from?" I asked, taken aback. I never thought of them as a liability or my own personal army. "You are not meat shields, and you aren't a liability to me either. I never would have made it this far if it weren't for all of you. You are part of my family. I would do anything to protect you. Hell, I'm even going to die to do just that."

"Well, we aren't *all* here, are we?" she spat.

Even though I knew they blamed me for her death, it still felt like I had been punched in the gut. "You're blaming me for Lindy's death."

"We wouldn't have been there for your father to kill her if you weren't leading the charge."

"Seriously?" Rage burst for me so quickly that there was no chance of holding it back. I felt the wood groan under my power as it burst from me, and then recoil deep within. IT RECOILED. "Weren't you already working with Julian on the uprising before I dropped into your life?"

"That is beside the point. We were dealing with the uprising, not directly going after your parents," she spat. "We took off after your parents because we wanted to protect you."

"You didn't have to take this journey with me. You trained me the best you could. You could have gone back home after Clarice's father died. I'm sorry my fucked-up family has ruined your life so damn much. Oh wait, you are part of that fucked up family."

"This is Ansel and Symatha's fault, this is not mine." Her fists were balled up. I felt a small shove from her power, and I could feel mine respond at my fingertips.

I felt CJ's Charge wrap around me like a blanket, instantly cooling my power as I let out a slow breath before saying, "Yes. She was your sister, and therefore, part of the family." Her face had a shadow pass over it, but then she steeled her features as she turned fully to face me for the first time, but before she could say anything I continued, "But you were never really part of the family after Grandpa died, were you? Why didn't you come with Grandma when she came to visit me?"

"That would have worked. Symatha would have allowed me to see you, right?" she said sarcastically.

"Grandma took me on all kinds of trips. You could have gone with her. There were opportunities, *Aunt* Jean. You've been to the Manusia a dozen times in my lifetime. Admit it. I just wasn't on your priority list. Your other family was much more important to you. You loved them more than your own sister, more than your own sister's kids. Just because you and Symatha weren't close doesn't mean that Matt and I wouldn't have liked to have a good, loving relationship with you." My voice cracked, and I fought the tears. "Do you have any idea how hard it was to see all our friends with families get together? None of that existed for us. You knew I existed, even if you didn't know Matt did. You knew *I* existed. We didn't know *you* existed. You could have fixed that. *You* could have had a relationship with us, even after we grew up and became adults."

"That isn't fair, Megan." She looked as if I had smacked her with a fish.

"It doesn't make it untrue."

"Maybe not, but that doesn't mean I haven't been trying to make it up to you since the day you arrived."

"Maybe, and I appreciate everything you have done, Jean. I really do. I don't want you to die. I don't know if I can recover from losing another family member at this point, and I really need your help. That being said, if you are only here out of guilt, then maybe you should go back home." Frustration billowed out of me, but I took a deep breath and said, "At least you would be safe."

I meant it too. She could go home. At least I knew she wouldn't be in Ansel's path.

She looked at me silently for a moment longer before getting up and heading to her cabin.

I knew I had hurt her, but I couldn't find it in myself to apologize for it. Should I have laid my voice to it? Probably not. That being said, it still didn't make any of it untrue. Even now, as I remembered that conversation, I felt guilty for hurting her, but part of me felt lighter for voicing what I had buried. I tried to let the rocking of the ferry calm my nerves, but it slowed to a stop.

"Megan," CJ said in a hurry, bringing me out of the memory. "You have to see this."

"What?" I said instantly on my feet as CJ grabbed my hand and led me to the railing on the north side.

The homes on the bank. You could smell the burned flesh mixed with...

"Oh Angels!" I said in horror. "Ansel can't be this far north already? Can he?"

"When we were in Therth for the coronation, we had reports he was in Noctulanar, then we made the stop in Vox Isle, so yeah, he could. We are the ones who were crawling north."

"Those poor people." The whole village was nothing but timber, tar, and smoke. They hadn't had a chance.

"Megan, the Captain." He pointed to a tall burly man walking toward us.

In a drawn-out drawl that reminded me of someone from deep in the south, he said. "I have 'structions not to 'pproach

Nalrin docks. Seems the city be' attacked, and they not be allowin' any persons through."

"The city?" I asked. "But there are precautions. The city is walled off. Surely they could fend off any attack... unless."

I turned to CJ, who finished it for me. "He just poured over the walls and... it's citizens. There would be no way for the Nalrin Guard or Vernadali to stop him."

My stomach dropped. CJ's eyes met mine before they flicked toward the city. I knew what he was thinking. Logan. Logan was still in Nalrin.

"We have to gain access to the city." CJ commanded every bit the protective Vernadali.

"I cannot be goin' any further into the ba."

"Captain. I understand that you have instructions, but I need to get to the City Center," I said, trying to look and sound important.

"Ma'am. If I take you to da Nalrin Docks, I be losen' my vocation," the captain's voice quivered slightly when he said that. It made me wonder who depended on him to put food on the table. A roof over their head. Does he have a family? Where do they live? Surely not here on the boat. Though maybe.

"I will guarantee that you will not. Nalrin Head Julian and I work... closely and he will take my recommendation." I hated to pull any assumed rank. I sounded like I was better than him, but I wasn't. Still, I stood there trying to act the part.

He studied me for a moment. "Who are yas'?"

"This is Vernadali Cory James Mathewson. I am his Charge, Lady Megan Mathewson. We are traveling with Empress Clarice and two of her companions, Lady Jean and Sir Owen. There are also a few of the Therth Guard."

"Oh, Angels." The Captain's face drained of all color. He spoke slowly at first, but then started talking faster and faster. "I be sorry, Lady Megan. If I had known, I would have set ya' up in me' private quarters."

"Captain, it's alright. We don't normally want special treatment. However, in this case, it is imperative that we get to the City Center," I said.

"Yes, ma'am. I mean Lady Megan. I be getting' ya to da' Nalrin Docks, where ya' can take da' trains, if they be running." He bowed deeply and then took long deliberate steps toward the wheelhouse.

It took three hours to get through the barricade that was set up in the bay, and another hour to get docked and unloaded. It was eerily quiet, with no one in the stables. We boarded the horses ourselves and headed toward the main terminal but stopped when the smell of torched flesh and tar filled my nostrils. I prayed to the Angels that it wasn't coming from inside.

All hope vanished when we walked into the main terminal, and I just stared. Gone were the beautiful statues. Gone were the people hustling and bustling to get to their next train or to the right boat to continue on their journey. Gone were the smooth floors and smooth ceilings.

Instead, the smell of smoldering wood and tar was heavy in the air, and my heart sank into the pit of my stomach. Tar, concrete, marble, wood, and general devastation were everywhere. There were marks and divots in the stone flooring and along the wall that looked like.... I bent down and put my hand to them.

"Fingernails," I said, barely above a whisper. I felt sick to my stomach and had to breathe through my mouth to keep from heaving all over the floor.

"What?" Owen said, half paying attention as he rubbed circles on Jean's back. She was currently bent over, hands on her knees and trying to not throw up. I turned to look at Clarice's guards, who were standing arms limp at their sides, and slowly scanning the entire area.

"Look for survivors," one of them said.

"You won't find any," I mumbled. "The marks in the floor are finger lines. People dug their fingers into the floor and walls trying to crawl away from the tar as it grabbed them." I felt my power stirring deep within me at the thought of what the people in here must have gone through. Having seen it firsthand, I felt the electricity bounce up my spine and to my fingers. I rolled my neck, willing it to settle.

I looked down and my fingers were sizzling with the force of the electricity circling my fingers. I took a couple of deep breaths to center myself.

I am not in danger. I am okay.

I am not in danger. I am not dying.

I do not need to protect myself right at this moment.

"Megan," CJ said in a warning tone. I turned to him as he reached out and took my hand, calming me instantly. I gave him an appreciative smile. He squeezed my hand in response.

"Let's see if there are any trains running." Owen said, heading in that direction. I pulled myself from that spot and tried not to think about what had occurred here on such a grand scale.

The tar played with them. It didn't just consume them. It tortured them. I pushed to them without realizing I had done so.

"It appears that way." Owen said, his voice full of sadness for the loss of life here.

I made myself move and headed toward where the trains would have been. When we turned the corner, we found they were in no better condition. The ones that were there had their cars partially on the tracks, partially off. Some were disconnected from each other and one was even on its side against the far wall.

"Guess the train isn't an option." CJ said, laughing a little.

"What's so funny?" Jean said, a little too snarky.

"Nothing, but if you can't laugh at the small things, the big things will crush you," he said seriously. "So, things like that train on its side, it looks like it's sleeping against the wall... Never mind."

My stomach dropped. All this destruction. Would Logan even have had a chance? What about Julian and all the other friends I've made while working in the center? Was anyone still alive in all of Nalrin City?

"We need the horses," I said, not much louder than a whisper as I scanned all the trains. I could feel the panic rising in my chest at the thought of Logan. "I'll put the enchantment on them. Should cut the ride down to about six, seven hours if the tracks are clear? If we are lucky, we might get there before dark."

"The horses are going to have to step carefully over the tracks, though. We can't take it at a full gallop." CJ ran his hand through his hair, but his eyes were focused in the direction of the city center. I knew his mind had gone to where we would hopefully see Logan again.

"Wait," Clarice said. "Look. The line that goes to the City Center is only partially off the tracks. If we can move it, we can get there."

"I know we are a powerful bunch, but seriously? They are made of solid rock! It would take a crane to move them." CJ said.

"Or someone who is the most powerful Sangra in all of history." Jean said, looking at me.

"You have to be kidding," I whispered. "I'm nowhere strong enough to move something like that."

"Maybe not alone, but you might be with the help of Owen, Jean, and someone who harnesses the power of the Underworld." Clarice wiggled her fingers as dark power flitted through her fingers.

"You're serious, aren't you?"

"Very much so. I'm sure in a few years I could do it myself, but I don't know my depth yet. I don't know how to control it all. I'm actively holding back because I don't have control, and I won't for a long time, Megan."

"Can you try?" I whined.

"What if I try and just shatter the car? Then we are faced with the prospect of having to move a car from one track to another, instead of just moving this one fully onto the rail system."

"It's worth a try, Megs," CJ said next to me as I continued to stare in disbelief at Clarice.

"Alright," I huffed. Then I wondered if this was happening when she was a few years into her power, if she could just toss Ansel into the deepest burning pits of the Underworld and let the Angels and Gods play with him as they wished. "The horses are the backup plan. How do we do this?"

CHAPTER 15

OVER THE NEXT HALF hour, Clarice worked with me to teach me the movements and incantation needed to move heavy objects. How was I supposed to move a multi-ton, solid stone train car? I don't know, but she had faith I could do it.

"If we can get the train on the tracks, can we even get them up to the center?" I said through gritted teeth as I practiced on some smaller pieces.

"Owen can," Jean said as she panted through the pieces she was working on.

Owen let out a dramatic huff as his rock lifted, and he moved it a foot before it fell to the ground. "That will be the easy part in all of this. Clarice, remind me to kick your ass later."

Clarice let out a light chuckle as I re-concentrated on the stone before me. I was getting more and more frustrated by the minute at the lack of action.

A couple hours later, I flopped down on the ground, my head in my hands, and said, "This isn't working. We are wasting time. Let's just get on the horses and head up."

"This will work," Clarice said, but when I glared at her, she backed off and looked at CJ.

"Come on, babe, let's see if we can find some water or a snack." He grabbed my hand and hauled me up, pulling me out of the rail room and over to the cafeteria area.

The cafeteria looked just like the rest of the depot. Tar claw marks, and nothing but a vast, empty feeling. It took some rummaging around, but we found the back storeroom with supplies. CJ threw a bag of protein chews at me, and said, "Eat."

I narrowed my eyes at him, and he just shook his head and continued with a, "You aren't going to make any progress if you don't have any fuel in you. We will take more back to the others as well. You also needed a break."

"Ceej, Logan."

"I know." He leaned back on the wall and tipped his head back and repeated. "I know."

"It's like Schrodinger's cat. Logan's neither dead nor alive right now, and it's killing me." I popped a couple of the chews in my mouth, and actually sighed as they melted down my throat. I looked down at the packaging and smiled at him. "These are my favorite ones too."

He smirked at me. "I know. I had to dig to the bottom of the box to find them."

I twisted the cap to the water and chugged most of the bottle down. CJ did the same, and when I reached for a box to fill for the others, he grabbed me around the waist, and swung me against the wall, his hands tight on my hips.

When my eyes met his, he leaned in and rested his forehead on mine. "Why is it I want to just fuck you at every inappropriate time? I want nothing more than to bury myself deep within you and just make it all go away. Just for a little while. Put a blissful look on that face of yours."

Every fiber in me responded to his husky tone, and I hadn't even realized that I had wrapped my legs around his waist, until I felt him hard against me, and I felt my nipples harden.

"Ceej," I breathed, and I didn't know if it was a warning or if I was begging, but he pulled my legs off him, and pulled my jeans down, bent me over the counter, and the next thing I knew he was filling me in one long stroke. I only had half a conscious thought to throw the silence incantation and close the door to the room.

He dragged out, and then pushed himself back into me, unbearably slow, as I moaned. There was a small huff of a laugh as he ground himself against me.

"Angels, Megan, I pushed back up against him, lifting my chest to look over my shoulder, and the look of ecstasy on his face was all I needed right now. He reached up and threaded his hand through my ponytail, and I felt every ounce of me clench around him at the movement. He let out a giggle, and as he picked up the pace, and pounded into me over and over.

I was already getting close, and I felt him twitch within me. "Please—" I said, but he cut me off by slamming into me harder and faster. There wasn't a coherent thought in my head, only the pleasure he was giving me. It didn't take more than a couple of minutes of him pounding into me before I was screaming his name in release. A few more strokes, and CJ was following me over the edge.

He fell forward to lie on my back a moment, before I felt him slowly retreat from me.

"Let me get something to clean us up. Then you have work to do, babes." I smiled as he placed a small kiss on my shoulder.

After we did indeed clean up, we grabbed water and snacks for everyone and headed back out. Before we left the room though, I turned to him and said, "Thank you for getting me out of my own head."

A smirk lifted the left side of his lips as he said, "I wasn't lying when I said I want to be buried in you at the most inopportune times."

Before I waved the incantation off, CJ leaned in and kissed me, and let his lips linger a little longer before backing away. I smiled at him and opened the door to find Owen standing there, smirking. I crunched my face, knowing we had been caught.

"You think I couldn't have waved that incantation off?" Owen snickered and crossed his arms. I just looked at him, but he said, "You are allowed to have your moments, and I didn't really want to hear it."

Trying to change the subject, I raised the box, and said, "We found snacks!"

He just tipped his head back and laughed.

Another two hours passed before Jean and Owen were able to successfully move the boulder. I growled in frustration. That's when my boulder budged.

I froze.

"Megs?" CJ said, but with a huge smile on his face.

"It moved?" I stared at it.

"It did." Pride laced in his voice.

So, I tried again and again. Nothing I did made that damn boulder move. I centered myself and tried to dig as deep into myself to make the damn boulder move. Still, the damn thing would do nothing but sit there and taunt me.

It took another hour of them coaching me through it before I could move it again. Each time it got easier, and when I was able to get it to just hover, even for a few seconds, we moved on to the train car.

There we stood. All five of us, staring down a solid stone train car with its front off the rails, and back half on, half off. I was shaking my legs and arms out like I was readying for a prize fight. My power was controlled, but for the first time in a long while, I had butterflies in my stomach.

"So how are we doing this?" Jean said seriously as she stared at the mass of solid stone in front of us.

"On three," Owen said with a note in his voice that made me realize he thought this was as much as an impossible feat as roping the moon.

"Okay." Clarice calmly. "One... Two... Three!"

I focused all my power on that mass of rubble. I swooped my arms down low, crossed my arms across my chest, fisted my hands and brought my arms to my sides, hands at my ribcage, when I felt my power vault from deep within and out through my fingers as I pushed out. Not electricity, but just power.

The train car lifted from the ground and then Clarice said, "Now slowly..." she eyed me carefully before continuing, "lower your hands down." When I did, the train carefully re-aligned onto the tracks.

Silence.

I just stood there staring at the train car. I... I couldn't believe it. How did we just do that? Back in the Manusia, that would have taken a massive crane to get the car back on the tracks. I jumped back as a buzzing filled the room, and a whoosh of air blew across us and the car slowly hovered over the tracks.

My jaw dropped. It really worked.

Oh. My. Angels. It really worked.

"Well, at least Ansel didn't break the systems," Owen said, breaking the silence. "We can thank the Angels for that small mercy."

"Is no one seriously going to comment on the fact that we just moved a MULTI-TON STONE TRAIN CAR without touching it?" I said, astonished. When I looked around, though, CJ and Jean were both still staring at the car in amazement.

"We did it." Jean's voice was low and disbelieving. "Clarice, how did you even know we could do it?"

"I didn't. I had faith that either we could do it with Megan's help, or we would be riding the horses up. Honestly, I was really hoping that we would be able to, because I have saddle butt,"

Clarice said, rubbing the inside of her thighs. "Yes, I know we've been on a boat the last few days, but... my legs need a rest."

Seriously? She was going on hope? Hope that we... I couldn't even finish the thought.

CJ came over and put his finger under my chin and closed my mouth. Then he turned my face toward him and softly kissed me. In a whisper no one else could hear, he said, "You are one amazing creature, Megan Isabel Matthewson."

Then CJ picked me up like I weighed nothing and carried me to the train car for our ride to the City Center. "Come on everyone. I need to find Logan."

"And Julian," Jean and Owen said in unison.

"How about we see if anyone survived?" Clarice said sadly. It made me wonder what the dead were saying to her as I noticed her eyes already turning the misty gray. She slowly climbed on board and went to sit at the back of the train.

Owen took to the controls and got us moving toward the center, Jean sitting just behind him. I turned to CJ. "I'll be right back."

I sat down next to Clarice and just took her hand. It was ice cold. I looked at her and her eyes had gone completely misty gray again.

"Clarice?" I whispered. If she had sat back here to be alone, I didn't want everyone else to start crowding her. Her head turned toward me, but she just put a finger up to her lips and made the quietest "shhh" sound I had ever heard.

I watched her tilt her head back and forth, listening to whatever the dead were saying for about forty minutes before her eyes returned to normal. Once she registered who I was, her eyes filled with tears, and she threw her arms around my shoulders and cried.

I suppose even the Empress of the Underworld had a right to cry. She had been through so much in the last year. The weight of all of it must be brutal, and I hadn't seen her falter. Not once. She had to be one of the strongest people I had ever met.

Slowly, the sobs turned to tears, and eventually, even the tears dried up. We were entering the third wall when she finally said,

"He did not absorb everyone like he did with Lindy. He murdered most everyone who was in that station. It was a bloodbath."

"What?" I said, not fully registering the words. I had suspected that they were tortured, but to have it confirmed.

"He did not just let the tar move through the buildings, absorbing everyone. He murdered most everyone in the station., she said, her voice hoarse from the crying. She looked at CJ and Jean, who had joined us now.

"He... just killed everyone?" I said, confused. "But why? Why not just take them for his army?"

"Megan, he tortured them for hours before they died. THEN he let the tar feed on their corpses," she said, unable to even believe her own words.

I thought back to the finger marks in the stone, which now seemed so much worse than what I had thought had happened before. How could he do such a thing?

"Megan, the ones he absorbed," she said, horror in her voice, "They do not talk. I tried to reach out to them. There is nothing there. There are wives hunting for their husbands, husbands looking for their children, and they cannot find them. It is as if they were sucked into a great abyss."

"Lindy?" I asked, not being able to fathom that kind of death. A nothingness?

"Since I realized I could do this, I have been trying to find her spirit in the Underworld. She's not there," she said, unable to look me in the eye. "I found her parents. I found a multitude of her relatives who said they had heard she died, and have been searching for her themselves, but... they have not been able to find her either."

I looked at Jean, whose face was contorted in a mix of grief and confusion. She couldn't believe what Clarice was saying. "She's just... gone?"

My eyes met CJ's, as he whispered, mortification in his voice, "What exactly is that tar doing?"

No one had an answer, and we just sat in silence until Owen, who had stayed unusually quiet, announced we were finally entering the center city walls. We broke through the wall and when the car came to a stop; the doors opened slowly with a groan. Walking through the eerily silent checkpoint room sent chills skittering over my skin.

"This is just wrong," Owen said quietly. His words carried through and bounced back against the walls as if he had screamed at them.

We made our way through what at one time would have been the bag check area, which was surprisingly undamaged. If Ansel didn't make it here, then where was everyone? Did they make it to the Downs?

Our boots echoed in the room like thunder against my ears. I couldn't help but feel as if we should have been tiptoeing through the hall. We all jumped, and CJ pulled me behind him when a monkey jumped down from one of the higher windows. Letting out a little snort when he realized what had scared him.

"My mighty Vernadali protector. Protecting me from all the monkeys," I whispered in his ear. He rolled his eyes and gave me a quick kiss on the cheek as we moved toward the main doors.

As we got closer, I thought I heard feet shuffling. I eyed CJ and pulled my syths out, seeing the others do the same. We slowly opened the blacked-out doors and stepped out into the courtyard where the Nalrin Guard and what I assumed was every Vernadali stationed in Nalrin stood before us with weapons drawn.

CHAPTER 16

CJ AND I IMMEDIATELY slid our syths back into our belts and put our hands up. I scanned the crowd looking for Logan but didn't see him. The courtyard was battered, and bits of tar hung on the top of the wall to the left of us. I eyed Owen, who took a sideways glance at Jean before they too slid theirs back into place. Clarice took a moment longer before stowing her whips away. She was eyeing people in the crowd with a particular interest that I couldn't place.

"Name, Vocation, and Identification Number," the black-haired guard in the front row said.

I opened my mouth to speak, but CJ blurted out, "Vernadali Cory James Mathewson, 34685A1, escorting Lady Megan, Sir Owen, Lady Jean and Empress Clarice. Is Logan Mathewson alive?"

Every Vernadali snapped to attention and re-sheathed their weapons. The Nalrin Guards, however, were a bit slower to respond to the classification CJ had just announced. It wasn't until a familiar voice rang out, "Guard, step down. Angels 1 Ranking. Remember it. Honor it." That they obeyed.

"Remi?" I said, a little surprised, but relieved.

"Well, it is not Julian," he said, smiling as he stepped out from behind the first row of Vernadali, who hadn't moved.

Remi and CJ clasped forearms and clutched a fist to their chest in greeting as I looked through the crowd for Logan and Mickel. As I scanned the crowd of people, I realized only the Guard and Vernadali were in the courtyard.

"Remi, where are the civilians? Did any of them make it?" My voice laced with concern.

"A few. Most of the outer two walls did not make it. Once we heard what happened at the docks, we opened all the gates to the center to allow everyone in. We didn't check identification cards until we had secured the wall. The inner walls have fewer access points, and much of the lower class fell to whatever it is that Ansel has at his beck and call." His voice was lined with sadness. He looked up at me and continued with a pleading look, "What is it he controls, Megan?"

"Maybe we need to talk in private. Did Julian, Logan, and Mickel make it?" I asked.

"They did," Remi said, relief flooding through CJ and I. Remi turned to CJ and smiled. "Julian is with Mickel and Logan, who have not left his side. Logan keeps saying that if he lived and Julian died, then this guy here would pummel him into the ground."

"Well, considering what we've been dealing with, he might get a bye on that one," CJ said heavily, running his hand through his hair.

"A bye?" Remi asked.

"Sorry Manusia term. In football, when you get a week off during the season, it's called a bye." CJ said, smiling. "Man, I miss football. Megs, I love your family and everything, but what I wouldn't give for a calm Sunday eating buffalo wings on my parents' couch with Logan watching a Packers game."

I couldn't help but laugh. I'd seen that scene play out so many times over the years and it would be nice to have just one day off to relax and watch a game, but sadly, that wasn't an option. "Yeah, maybe next year, babe," I said, elbowing him.

Clarice stepped forward and smiled at Remi who beamed back, "Clarice... oh, I am sorry, Empress Clarice now. It is so good to see you."

Many of the Nalrin Guard behind Remi immediately bowed as Clarice was introduced.

"You too, Remi. I hope your family is staying safe," she said with a kindness that would make anyone feel at ease. The sound of her voice carried through the courtyard, and I could see even the Vernadali relax a little.

"Most of the Vernadali families have been moved to the Curtails of the North for their protection. Last I heard, the isle was on full lockdown. We tried to send Logan and Julian there, but Julian refused to leave, and by extension, so did Logan," Remi said.

"We should gather any of the Heads that are in the Center and update them on what we know. It's not much, but we need to know what happened here as well," Clarice said then as she scanned the crowd she said, "And any glamor or illusion that anyone has on, doesn't work on me, so I know that half of that Guard standing toward the back are really civilians."

Remi smiled. "Of course, it doesn't, Empress, however, we did not know who was stepping through those doors, and these civilians all volunteered to help fight. Most of them lost everyone else they cared for or feel like they have to do something to keep from going crazy." He waved his hand and the last few rows of people at the back of the courtyard faded from Nalrin Guard to just your average people. They were dirty, sweaty, and you could see the sadness in their eyes.

"Golch. Ronski." Remi said as two of the Nalrin guard stepped forward. "Please gather the dignitaries who are still here into the Council Chamber."

"Actually, have them meet us in Down D-4," I said before they could leave.

"Down D-4?" one of the guards said.

I looked at Remi, who gave me an apologetic look. "They don't have the clearance. They don't know where that is."

"Who does? It is going to be the most secure location to discuss these matters." I breathed, frustration lining my voice. "That's where they all should be now, anyway. So that the dignitaries aren't in jeopardy." I noted the wince Remi let show and sighed. "Where are they now?"

"In their respective residences." His voice was low, and careful, as if he knew I was about to rip his head off.

I blinked. "Excuse me?" There are emergency procedures should there be an attack on the city. Why were the dignitaries still in their residences? They should have been moved to the D level immediately. "Remi—"

"Megan, I was in the Center when Ansel hit the docks. In fact, most of the high-ranking Guard were on the docks. Mickel is the highest Guard left in the city. He tried to get Julian to mobilize, but he couldn't get him to move," He said, and let out a long breath. "Golch. Ronski. Go tell Mickel that they are here and that we will wait for them and the dignitaries in the Council Chamber."

Golch and Ronski bowed and ran off toward the Government buildings.

Owen looked at me, confusion written all over his face. "Down D-4? What is D-4?"

I sighed as we started heading for the governmental buildings.

"I'm not supposed to say anything, but I will say, there are more levels to the city than most know for security reasons. The Downs are one of those locations. It's only supposed to be used when the City is under siege, which it was," I said, anger and frustration boiling up within me. "And they didn't follow the emergency plan, which makes me nervous in itself. Why wouldn't they? I mean, they knew what was going on at the docks. They had to know that with the ease that Ansel was able to go through the Docks and first wall, that he would be at the center in no time."

"Wait," Jean said. "How do you know about this D level in the first place? Owen and I have Grade 2 clearance. We didn't even know about it."

"Remember, my vocation is to do all the background checks for any new dignitaries, which gives me Grade 1. Part of the job description is that I have to tell them where they should go in case of an attack on the city, along with the highest ranking Vernadali within the city. Obviously, no one listened to that part of the speech. Which reminds me, Remi, where is Vernadali Sanchez? Why are you running the Vernadali and Guard?" I said, switching gears. We were getting closer to the government buildings now, and I hadn't seen a single other person other than those who had met us at the security gates. For a city where there are usually lots of people buzzing and running around, it was the eeriest feeling.

"And here she didn't think she had clearance to be in the room with the Consort. Yet here she is running the city right now," Jean said under her breath. I gave her a look, and she said, "Well?"

Remi interrupted and answered my previous questions. "Mickel is the highest-ranking Guard in the City, and he is guarding Julian and Logan." It wasn't really an answer.

"Remi?" I said, drawing out his name. "What aren't you telling me?"

Clarice is the one who spoke in a dark monotone voice, "Vernadali. Those are the ones that spoke in one voice?"

"What?" We all said in unison.

"On the train on the way up from the docks, there were these voices. They spoke in unison. It was as if they were all tied to one thing. That would make sense if they were all Vernadali."

"What were they saying?" Remi asked, pulling us to a stop.

"It wasn't in the common tongue, so I don't know if I heard it right, but it sounded like, Missi sumus a tenebris ad tuendum ab angeli... Perg... something. I'm sorry I can't remember the rest," She said.

"Pergemus ad mortem tueri lucem." CJ and Remi said together.

I looked at both of them, waiting to have them explain, but instead they just stood there looking at each other. For as long as I have known CJ, I can only recall twice the level of sadness that crossed his face. Once when his great grandfather died, and the other when we first re-told of Lindy's death. I reached over, took his hand, and squeezed it. He squeezed back but didn't look at me.

"What does that mean?" Owen asked.

CJ's voice was distant as he said, "Roughly translated, it means: From the Angels we are sent to protect from the dark. To the death we will march to protect the light. It's our motto."

"I thought your motto was "Protect until Death"?" I asked, glancing down to his forearm.

"That is the abbreviated version," CJ said, squeezing my hand and pulling me closer as we walked. I could feel his Charge flow over me like a protective web. Normally, that would drive me crazy, but right now, it comforted me on a different level.

"There were at least eighteen Vernadali, possibly more, at the docks when Ansel attacked." Remi said as he climbed over a piece of stone in the street. "Megan, you asked me why I'm running the Vernadali. That is why. I am the highest ranking Vernadali in Nalrin right now. Save your husband. Vernadali Sanchez. Vernadali Jackson. Vernadali Chevlok. Vernadali Peters. All of them. They were all heading to the Curtails of the North to meet with other security factions to see what they could do to help in the fight against your father. The worst part is not only did they die, but we don't even have anything to put on the pyre to send them to the Angels."

CJ's hand clenched tighter in mine, if that was even possible, as we started across the reflecting ponds I had spent so much time admiring during my time here. Today they were still as glass, chunks of tar floating throughout, and the sound of our feet shuffling across the bridge just sounded wrong.

"How did anyone survive?" I said in disbelief. The tops of the roofs were chipped, broken, and laying in the courtyard. There were windows blown out, which had sprayed the glass in every direction. There was even a couch laying near the entrance to the Council Building. It vaguely reminded me of the one that was in my residence. I looked over to the Residence building to my left, and it was in the same state of disarray. The Main Government Building was strangely in much better condition. What wards had they used to protect it that they couldn't use in the other buildings?

"I'm not the person to answer that for you, Megan," Remi said, a bit defeated. Then there was something that flashed through his eyes, but I couldn't make out what it was. He just opened the door to the Council Building and led us down the hall in silence.

CHAPTER 17

As we entered the nearly empty room, I hoped it was empty due to the Heads not being in Nalrin at the time of the attack and not loss of life.

"Cory! Megan!" a voice bellowed. I instantly relaxed, and CJ sped up. Logan jumped over the banister, arm in a sling, and hugged CJ tight. What happened to his arm? Why didn't the physicians heal it? When I caught up with them, I gave him a huge bear hug. My heart sank when he released me, and he asked the one question I had been dreading.

"Where's Lindy?" he asked, hopefully looking around us to Clarice, Owen, and Jean. When he turned back toward me, I instantly felt the tears well and a lump stuck in my throat. The only thing I could do was shake my head.

"I'm sorry Loog," CJ said as he pulled Logan close. Logan's breath rushed out of him and the pain in his eyes, the shuddering of loss that swept through his body, was one I knew all too well. I felt the tears bridge over and stream down my face. My power pulsed in response to the mutual pain we were feeling but froze in my throat.

Julian, who I sometimes forget is only four feet tall, came to stand near us and asked softly but firmly, "How?"

"The tar," Owen said. "In Alnwick."

Logan snorted through his tears and muttered something that sounded much like, "I'm going to kill that fucking asshole." I didn't blame him. There was a secret part of me that was glad that I was the only one alive who could kill him.

"Alnwick? Why were you that far south?" Julian asked, looking at me and graciously ignoring Logan.

I tried to answer him, but when I opened my mouth to speak, no sound came out. My power was binding my voice. That frustrated me beyond reason, but it helped to keep me from having another breakdown the likes of what CJ liked to call the *"Great Magical Temper Tantrum of Therth"*. I certainly didn't want to go through a power break like that again. Just the thought of losing control of my power still scared me. I looked back at Owen, who was waiting to see if I would answer, but I silently told him, "*You tell him. I probably wouldn't be able to get through it anyways.*" He nodded in understanding.

"King Babbak had a nurse of sorts in Witch Dorith. After his death," he said, looking sideways to Clarice, who stood stoic the only way an Empress could. "Witch Dorith thought we might be able to find more answers regarding Helena with the High Witch of Alnwick. She had some special ties to the Cinder Fairies and thought that she might have some information that wouldn't be written anywhere. She opened the portal to Alnwick. We went through and walked into a town that looked much like the docks did when we arrived earlier today."

"Ansel's thing he is controlling," Julian said, not in question, but instead in confirmation.

"Yes. We call it the tar. We haven't found a better way to describe it. It is pure darkness under his control, but we can explain that once the other Heads have arrived," Owen said, trying to keep us from getting off track. He looked back at me and asked, "You sure you want me to tell him everything?"

I just nodded, still feeling my vocal cords unable to produce sound.

"We ran through the town, looking for any survivors that we might be able to help, and we were able to help a few, but when we faced Ansel..." He paused, looked at each of us, and then, with his head hung a little lower, he continued, "Julian, for all the power that this family controls... Angels, for all the power that just Megan and Clarice control... when Megan tried to delay him so Lindy, Clarice, Jean and I could get a head start, he flicked it off like it was nothing."

"We ran. Buildings broke apart where he flung his power at us," Jean said, but then her voice hitched. There were about twenty other dignitaries that had joined the room since we started. Remi, who had been staying very quiet through all of this, slowly closed and locked the door when Jean stopped talking. Telling this part of the story wasn't easy for any of us.

It was Clarice, in all her grace, who then told the hardest part. Her voice was dark and full of sadness, but holding her head high, she said, "We took shelter in the stables on the outside of town. Any hope of us being able to stop him without Helena had vanished. We knew that given his ancestral line, he could not be easily killed to begin with, but now, with pure darkness under his control, Helena *is* the only way. When Ansel came around the corner at the end of the street, he left the only exit through the stable on the opposite side. Most of us made it across before Ansel was at the stables. Megan and Lindy were the last to try to come through. For some reason, they stopped. I couldn't hear what they were saying, but I saw Megan try to push Lindy through the door, just before the tar took hold of Lindy's leg and... consumed her."

I looked up at Clarice, and the tears in her eyes were bright. Logan let out a sobbing cry. My heart cracked and the ball in my throat tightened. I wanted nothing more than to comfort him. "From there, I am not sure how we were able to hold him off long enough just to get out of there, but when we had the chance, we ran."

Clarice met my eyes, and I silently told her, "*We were able to get out of there because of you! Don't be modest. And thank you for leaving out the gruesome part of her death.*" She gave me a quick nod.

The room was dead silent. Julian looked at each of us as if assessing the truth of the statements. Tears ran down our cheeks, and I just stared at Logan. The various Heads, of which there are about forty of them now in the room, had various facial expressions that ranged from disbelief to sadness to horror. It was the Head of the Blug Mountains, a 20-foot-tall ogre looking creature that spoke first. "I had received reports of creatures being consumed by what Ansel Keller has under his control, but I didn't believe it until about a week ago, when I saw it for myself.... I am sorry that your friend, and loved one, died in this manner."

"I, too, have received similar reports from the Seltic Cities," a ragged man said from a few rows back.

"Joshua, surely he hasn't been to the Seltic Cities?" Owen said in disbelief. I couldn't believe it either. The Seltic Cities were along the Slumbering Expanse Coast, and it seemed so far out of the way from the path we thought Ansel had been taking.

"He has. He blew through Seltic West about three months ago?" he said. "Seltic North and East were damaged, but most of those cities were destroyed by creatures just taking advantage of the confusion."

He had spread his net far. He didn't go north in one group but had sent the darkness out on its own. How was he able to control it out of his presence? The lump in my throat was losing its grasp and I couldn't help but think about how similar our two worlds are. Even here, bad people take advantage of a bad situation to do bad things.

"Has anyone else heard anything?" Julian said finally.

A few dignitaries had heard nothing from home, and I could tell from the way they shifted in their seats that they were probably wondering if that wasn't because everything was okay back home, but more because the town or territory didn't have anyone left to send word.

"Vernadali CJ, could you please escort your brother to my office, or to Lady Megan's residence, where he may grieve in private?" Julian whispered.

CJ looked to me, obviously torn between his duty to me as my Vernadali, and his duty to his brother.

"Go," I said softly. "Be with Logan. He needs you. We can tell them anything they want to know. Besides, I have a few questions for them as well. We will meet you back at my residence."

CJ's eyes softened as he pulled me close and kissed me. It was soft and sweet, and it completely caught me off guard. Part of me couldn't believe that he was kissing me in front of what was left of the Council. The other parts of me wanted to never let him go so that we could keep each other safe for the rest of our lives. However long that was.

"Thank you," he whispered against my lips.

I nodded as he walked out of the room with Logan. I was proud of those two boys. Logan had just found out that his fiancé had died, yet even through his tears and grief, he walked out on his own.

CHAPTER 18

Once Remi had re-secured the door, Julian turned to me and asked, "What questions do you have for us, Lady Megan?"

Well, the formalities are upon us. Where to start?

"First Head Tokog mentioned that he saw what the tar did. What exactly happened here, Julian? And why were the emergency protocols not followed?" I said.

"First, emergency protocols were not followed, because other than myself, the only ones who knew each aspect of them were at the Docks at the time of the attack. When I tried to set them into place, the garrisons of the Guard who were out in the open were wiped out immediately. We simply didn't have the resources."

"You still could have put the Heads into the Downs," I said as hissing through my teeth. There is a reason we have these secure areas and for the pain of ensuring that they are properly maintained, they damn well be used when needed. "How many times did you tell me to drill it into each and every one of their heads when I gave them emergency briefings?" I said, pointing toward the dignitaries.

"The Downs are sealed off. We couldn't get there," Julian said, trying to calm me down. "We found a dozen or more of the Nalrin Guard buried in the rubble, one with a detonator switch. Not sure where he got it since we don't make them here in Nalsar. The only thing we can think of is that Ansel set it up for him to use. Who must have brought it over from the Manusia. Mickel has and is interrogating the rest of the Guard as we speak to ensure that we don't have any more traitors."

"Mickel," I said with relief, glad to hear he was doing something productive. Julian nodded.

"Second, as to what happened, we only know so much. The attack started on the neighboring towns, but we thought we were safe, being on the island and all," Julian said with a glint of humor in his voice, "We will not be making that mistake again."

"Julian," I said admonishingly. There were murmurers throughout the Council room and Jean elbowed me.

He gave me an apologetic look and continued, "It is the truth. We thought we would not be reached. We thought ourselves safe. When he attacked the docks, we opened all the gates to allow as many to the center as possible. Here we could surely hold him off. This city was built for fortification. We didn't think that one man would be able to get past the Docks and then the next few walls. Only we were very, very wrong. The tar, as you call it, had skeleton creatures within it, pulling people into the tar, and from what was described to me, those people didn't just die. They were consumed."

I cringed and looked away. The image of Lindy being consumed by the tar and then roaring loudly at me was still firmly etched into my head.

"When he reached the center wall, the tar carried him over and set him down in the courtyard outside like it was nothing. There were many lives lost that day throughout the city," he said somberly.

"How did you survive?" Clarice asked.

"We... we aren't sure. When Ansel stood outside of the main buildings here, he seemed to toy with us. I stood outside in the courtyard, shattering windows, breaking off chunks of the buildings. It was almost as if he relished the sound of people's screams. The tar sat just on the other side of the reflecting ponds, bubbling as faint screams could be heard throughout the city. It was not a sound I will be able to forget anytime soon," he said, shaking his head. I noticed that some of the dignitaries had their heads hung low and were quietly crying. "Then Ansel started twitching. With each twitch, the tar lessened. As the twitching increased, Ansel screamed in pain, and fell to his knees, grasping his head. Just as quickly as it started, the tar picked him up, and they slithered from the city."

I crunched my eyebrows together. "How long ago was that?" I asked.

"Eight days ago." Julian said.

"You have to be fucking killing me. That can't..."

"Megan, what are you thinking?" Jean asked.

"It's been what, eight, nine days since we were on Vox Isle?" I said, still not sure if it was even possible. They nodded. "And the timing would be about right for when the spell he put on me was broken. Right?"

"What spell?" Julian asked hesitantly.

"A possibility, I suppose," Jean said before turning to Clarice. "Thoughts?"

"Why are you asking me?" Clarice said, surprised. "I didn't even know she had had that spell on her."

"What spell?!" Julian said a little more forcefully.

"Apparently, there was a spell put on me back when we were at Noctulanar, right after Symatha died. It would seem that before we left Noctulanar Castle, that good ol' Dad put a weakening spell on me bound by the darkness of Noctulanar and pain of losing Symatha," I said, trying to explain it the best I could. I didn't fully understand it myself. "When we were on Vox Isle meeting the Consort to the Cinder Queen, his physician came and... well, it's a bit of a long story, but one of his physicians saw me, found it, and broke it. That was about eight or nine days ago. I was just wondering if maybe by breaking that spell, if that weakened him at all and caused him to retreat."

"Are you okay?" Julian asked, a bit concerned. He wasn't normally this emotional in public with us, but considering what had occurred, I guess I shouldn't be surprised he was shoving protocol to the wind.

"I'm fine. I'm feeling stronger than I have in a long time." I gave him a reassuring smile. "It's also one theory of why I haven't had any visions since Noctulanar. And before you ask, no I haven't had any yet, but it's only been a week."

"And did you meet with the Cinder Fairies Consort?" One of the dignitaries asked from the front row.

"In a manner of speaking. Unfortunately, before we arrived at the meeting, he, along with some of his company, were brutally murdered," I said sadly. "However, we were able to retrieve the information we required."

"And why did you need to meet with the Consort to the Queen of Cinder?" another dignitary a few seats down asked.

"Lady Megan and her family were meeting them to obtain information as to where to find Helena, The Crystal of Pureness," Julian said firmly.

There were gasps and murmuring throughout the room. I took a deep breath and closed my eyes, knowing exactly where this conversation was going.

"Helena, The Crystal of Pureness?!" The dignitary from the Sapphire Burrows said in a disbelieving tone. "She's just a legend."

Yup. Same story, different day.

"Look. I'm going to cut to all the usual statements about this. Legend is true. It's the only way we have found to stop my father. Yes, I have to kill him with it. Yes, the likelihood I will die is... well certain." I was very thankful CJ wasn't in the room at the moment. I really didn't want to have that conversation again in front of a bunch of dignitaries.

"No, I am not planning on wiping out the whole of the Ash'bani race," I said, making sure to make eye contact with

Titus, the Ash'bani Head, and he gave me a small nod, but other than that, I was unable to read his expression.

"Yes, I realize there are going to be casualties, but if I don't do this, he will not only destroy Nalrin, Obsecuritan, and the Seltic Marsh, but he will go to the Southern Isles, the Lansker Frozen Isles, and Cinder to wipe everyone out. He will destroy all of Nalsar. Then, what is to stop him from going to other worlds and doing the same? I'm sure Manusia would be next on his list because someone cut him off on the highway ten years ago."

The entire Council chamber, for the second time since they all arrived, was deathly quiet. I took another deep breath to calm myself. It wasn't until I was done ranting that I noticed the faint blue haze over my hands. Once again, I lost my temper with the Council. Julian's eyebrows were raised slightly at me.

"I've told you I'm not cut out for politics," I said, folding my arms across my chest. "This is, what, the third time I've stood in front of the Council, and the third time I've snapped at them?"

A slow, smirking smile crossed his lips as he shrugged and said, "You do fine." There were a few huffs from the dignitaries, but I rolled my eyes.

"Julian, do you have anything else for us?" Owen said with pride in his voice. He looked over at me and smiled slightly, nodded, and looked back at Julian.

"Not for now." Julian said, his mouth tight. "It is getting late and we should all get some sleep. Everyone report back here at 11:00 morningside. Megan, may I talk to you for a moment?"

"Actually, Julian, I would really appreciate if the lecture could wait until tomorrow morning. I would like to go see my brother-in-law. However, when you see Mickel, send him to my residence, please. I'd like to see him." I stood straight and met his gaze with each word. Julian nodded, a small fatherly smile on his lips. I turned on my heel and walked out of the room.

CHAPTER 19

JUST BEFORE I TURNED the corner to where my residence was, I heard voices whispering down the hall. I peeked around the corner and saw the two guards in front of my residence whispering to each other. I leaned back against the cold, dark wooden walls and tried to listen to what they were saying.

"I've been stationed outside this room for months. Thought it a nice, easy station until *he* showed up. Now she's back and we find out she can't even keep her own family safe?" one of the guards said.

"Doesn't make our chances good at all. Why we don't just run to another dimension and leave this one to him is beyond me. Head Julian is too close to her. Just lets her do whatever she wants. 'gardless of the consequences to the rest of us," the second guard, whose voice was deeper than the firsts, said. Damn fucking cowards. I'd like to see them do what we are, but no, he just wants a nice cushy job like guarding an empty room.

"Fucking cowards," I muttered as electricity surged from me and hit the closet next to me. I looked through the door and there were a few brooms smoking. Whoops.

"I asked Head Renald that exact thing the other day and he said that the Council is just too scared of both Head Julian and Lady Megan." the other guard said and lowered his voice a little lower before continuing, "It is rumored she has more raw power in her than any other Sangra in history."

The deeper voiced guard whistled in amazement and then said, "If that's true, combine that with what I've heard Empress Clarice can do, and I can see why the Council, including Head Julian, wouldn't want to get on their bad side. What an asset she would be in any war."

"Hey Megan. What you doing?" Clarice said, making me jump in surprise.

"Shhhh," I said, holding my finger up to quiet her. Then silently told her, *"I'm listening in on the guards' gossip."*

Clarice nodded and leaned up against the wall next to me.

"Empress Clarice? Of Therth? The one running around with Lady Megan?" the other guard said in surprise. "I thought King Babbak still reigned there?"

"No. He died. Rumor has it that even though Empress Clarice renounced the throne and walked away from her Silnarre, she couldn't stand for Princess Erida to take over. So, she hired a witch and had King Babbak killed before he could transfer and properly train Princess Erida."

Oh No. They did not just... My head snapped toward Clarice and I could see her getting angrier by the moment. I grabbed her hand, and it was ice cold. Her power weaved between our fingers, in thin, smokey tendrils. I was so used to the blue of mine. It weirded me out a little, seeing her magic come across so dark. Yes, I knew everyone's could be a different color, but black had such an inherent bad connection. I knew it was because she was now the Gatekeeper to the Underworld, but... I guess it shouldn't surprise me that others believe the worst in her because of it.

"Well, if she is as powerful as what I've been hearing, it wouldn't surprise me," the deeper voiced guard started in again, "I heard 'dat when they returned from somewhere south of Therth that she destroyed King Babbak and Princess Erida's favorite garden, just out of spite. There's even been a rumor she is working with Ansel Keller," deeper voiced guard said.

Clarice and I rolled our eyes. "Yeah, if I am working with Ansel, why have I not killed you already? Oh, that is because I am too busy eating the cute fuzzy bunnies for fun, too."

I stifled a laugh and said, "Besides the fact that I'm the one who blew up the garden." I trusted Clarice completely. I peeked back around the corner just as Mickel opened the door to my residence and said, "If you two *ladies* are done gossiping..." he said with a snide smile before continuing, "Maybe you would like to apologize for those comments to Lady Megan and Empress Clarice."

"Damn it, Mickel!" I said, stepping out from around the corner. "Sometimes I really hate how in tune you are to me." Ever since he became my bodyguard, he had become hyper-aware of my presence. Most of the time, it didn't bother me. It was part of his job. I respected that, but it was also really annoying sometimes. This was one of them.

"CJ warned me you were outside," Mickel said, smiling.

The guards turned redder than tomatoes and stammered over their words. Rolling my eyes, I just said, "I don't need or want your apologies. Not like you would mean them, anyway. Now if you don't mind, I have a brother-in-law who I would like to talk to as he just lost his fiancé. But it isn't like that would matter to you or anything, right? You're just worried about your own hides. You even said you thought this would be a nice, easy post for you."

They were beat red, and I could tell they wanted to deny it, but wisely, they stayed quiet. I was ornery, and maybe I was looking for a fight, but I just continued, "Mickel, can you have these two replaced with someone more loyal? Someone who I believe would actually help protect my family should we be under attack." Then I turned to them, put my hand on my hip and said, "Because that *is* what your job requires. You realize that, right? As part of the Nalrin Guard, you would actually need to put your lives in danger to protect others."

I turned and walked into my residence, with Clarice right behind me. Just as she walked past them, jumped toward them, and yelled, "Boo!"

The guards about jumped out of their skins. Mickel was laughing hysterically and now turned to them and said, "Please send Vernadali Remi to me and explain to *him* why I am releasing you of duty."

When Mickel closed the door, I closed my eyes and took a deep breath. A large hand fell onto my shoulder, and I knew who it was without accessing any of my power. "Mickel, if you are about to tell me that I shouldn't have acted the way I did, then you can jump off the balcony."

Before I realized what was happening, I was wrapped up in his arms, where he held me tight. "Megan. I was so scared for you guys. I should have been there for you. I shouldn't have let you talk me into coming back here and watching over Logan. Not that it was a hard job. He followed all the rules and has actually done really well here. I'm highly impressed."

I pulled back from him and furrowed my brow. "You impressed? That's not possible."

"Seriously. He's been the easiest assignment I've had in ages," he said, smiling. "He's been really successful here. He has genuinely earned a lot of high-ranking official's respect. For a long time, he wouldn't even admit that he knew you or CJ. Refused to give his last name. Didn't want the association. He didn't say he didn't know you two, but he just dodged the question. He tried very hard to make a name for himself based on merit, and not connections. Obviously, people knew he had to be connected somehow since I was his bodyguard, but once I knew he was going to follow all the rules set in place for him here, unlike someone else I know, I backed off and was just a shadow in the wind."

"Where is he?" I said, a lump tight in my throat. Between my heart aching for him and Mickel vouching for him like that, the way he handled himself in the last few months has made me proud of him on a whole new level.

"He fell asleep a few minutes ago. CJ jumped in the shower." Mickel said. "Where are Jean and Owen? I heard they made it back alright."

"I'm sure they will be along shortly. They haven't really had much time alone for a while," I said. "Probably went to one of the guest quarters for the night."

He nodded his head. "How are you holding up?" he said, dropping his arms and crossing them across his chest. All bodyguard again.

"Mickel, you are going to give me whiplash," I said, laughing a little. Out of the corner of my eye, I saw Clarice lay down on the couch and throw a pillow over her face. I gestured for Mickel to follow me out onto the balcony, and I closed the double french doors as CJ stepped out of the bathroom, towel around his waist. I may have let myself appreciate that view longer than necessary, but oh, how a bath sounded good right now. I pulled myself from that thought and quietly said, "Mickel... you don't believe anything the guards were saying about Clarice, do you?"

"No," Mickel said seriously. "Megan, you know better than most, that we hear a lot of rumors around here. There are going to be those who don't believe everything that the Council says is truth. It's a government. It's not inherently trusted. So, when they hear these rumors, the Council doesn't necessarily come out and make a statement against them, or even have any information as to what is true or what isn't, well..."

"They believe what they want to believe," I said, sighing in resignation.

"They believe what they want to believe."

"The problem is that it's not like we can give the Council constant updates on what is happening. What if those correspondences were intercepted by my father?" I said, almost pleading with him to understand.

"Megan, you don't have to explain yourself to me. I am one of the few people in this city that completely understands. I've lived with your family. I've known Jean and Owen almost the entirety of my life. If there is a more loyal person to this family within this dimension, I would have you introduce me to that person."

"Mickel. I do not question your dedication or loyalty to us," I said, putting my hand on his forearm to comfort him. He looked visibly upset that we might question it. "Really. I wasn't questioning you at all. I was just saying, I'm not sure what people think I should be doing? I'm doing the best I possibly can, but I can't do everything. I know I'm an outsider. I know that the only family history I have is through either Jean, who has worked for the Council as an Enforcer for several years, or the one who is trying to destroy the world."

I could feel the tears well again in my eyes, and I didn't know if they were out of frustration or just feeling overwhelmed. "I don't really have any right to demand their respect, their confidence, or anything."

Mickel's eyes softened as he said, "Maybe not, but for all the rumors that are going around that aren't true, there are a lot that are telling of your bravery. When the news reached us, you crossed the southern territories to warn them that Ansel was destroying everything in his path, you should have heard the talk around here. There were people talking in the halls about how brave and noble Lady Megan is."

His smile faltered when he thought about his next words. "Right now, people feel defeated. They have just experienced a horrible tragedy and lived through a battle in a war they shouldn't have lived through. There is no morale around here. We don't feel protected anymore. We had been living under the impression that no one could hurt us here in the center. It was the belief that no one would ever get past the first two walls at most, let alone over the wall to the CENTER of the city. There was this sense of feeling untouchable and all of that was all blown down in a single afternoon."

When he put it like that, "I'm sorry, Mickel. I'm just having a pity party. Pity Party for one," I said, pointing to myself.

"A pity party? Is that another one of those Meganisims?"

"No. It's a phrase used in Manusia where someone is just feeling really sorry for themselves." I sometimes forgot that we weren't all from Manusia. Things sure were simpler back then. I laughed a little, remembering how my biggest headache there was the traffic from work.

"What's so funny?" Jean said, coming through the door out onto the balcony.

"I was just remembering how back in the Manusia, my biggest headache was the traffic trying to get home from work," I said. "How things have changed. Not all for the bad, but they sure have changed."

"Okay, then," Jean said, not knowing exactly what to say to that.

"Yeah. Anyways, what happened after I left?" I asked.

"Other than you leaving Julian fuming, but entertained? Which Owen and I find hilarious, by the way." Jean was beaming from ear to ear.

"Other than me leaving Julian fuming?" I said, knowing that I was in for one hell of an ass chewing later for that.

"Well, the Council pelted us with questions. We answered some and declined to answer others. When we declined, we explained it was on the basis of keeping our direction and full plans secret as to help ensure our success. That only made a few of the Heads even more upset, but we held our ground. Most of what we discussed was what had happened in Obsecuritan and what we saw at the docks. Then Owen and I secured one of the guest rooms until we left."

"I'm sorry I just bailed on you. I left you to deal with that on your own, and I'm sorry."

"It's okay. You put your family first, which I am proud of you for. The Council can sit there and deal with it." Jean chuckled with amusement.

"Still, I'm sorry. I know that Mickel would like to talk to you, and I really want to relax for a few minutes. So, I'm going to go take a bath. Then maybe go to bed. Yes. Bed sounds great. Mickel, can you make sure everyone has a comfortable place to sleep tonight?"

He nodded. "As you command, Lady Megan."

THE HELENA CRYSTAL

I rolled my eyes and headed toward a steamy solace and said over my shoulder, "You're still on Logan duty!"

I heard a heavy sigh as I closed the door behind me.

CHAPTER 20

THE NEXT MORNING, LOGAN and I sat on the couch while we waited for the others to get cleaned up. The healers had come and finished healing his arm before most of the family was up. His stomach had growled loudly. The Physician scolded him for not eating properly, and after talking, we weren't sure when the last time we had sat down for a meal. It seemed we shoved something down our throats whenever we could. So, we agreed to head down to the dining hall to eat like a normal family.

Now though, sitting there with him, I didn't know how to comfort him. I just looked at him.

"I'm still in shock, Megs," Logan said with his elbows on his knees as he stared at his hands. He took a couple of deep shuddering breaths and said, "All I know is that it feels like someone ripped a hole through my chest."

I took one of his hands in mine and squeezed it. "I know. There is this... pit in my stomach that is just a hollow void. There is no entrance. No exit. Just a vast void."

"CJ said that you held it together for a bit until... you didn't," he said quietly after a moment. I felt more than heard CJ stop moving behind us. "He said that you were able to carry on for a while, but that it all crashed on you at once."

I nodded and said through a sigh, "I didn't... haven't... handled my grief well."

Logan looked at me. His eyes held so much sadness and pain in them, but there was concern for me as well. "Logan. Don't worry about me. CJ can handle me. Worry about yourself. Allow yourself time to grieve. Allow yourself to feel everything and nothing right now. Lindy deserves nothing more than to have you acknowledge what an amazing being she was."

"The world out there just keeps going. Your father, Ansel," he said when he noted the look on my face, "just keeps destroying. How can the world move on when such a bright light has been extinguished?"

"I don't know." My voice was barely above a whisper.

"Loog," CJ said, coming to crouch down in front of him. "We are all here for you."

"I guess I need to process all of this before I can start grieving." A lump was hard in his throat. "One thing I know for sure. I want Ansel dead."

CJ and I eyed each other. Logan looked between us and after a long look at CJ, who wouldn't meet his eyes, and who kept staring at me, said, "What? What aren't you telling me?"

"A lot." I said, trying to sound nonchalant about it.

"Megan." His words were so laced with pain that I couldn't bear to look at him. I glanced at CJ and the pain in his eyes cracked that door of pain open again. I mentally kicked it shut so loud I think I even saw CJ wince at it.

"I can't tell him. Not yet, Ceej," I pushed toward him. *"Not just after he lost Lindy."*

Logan stood up with so much force, CJ had to bounce backwards to keep from being pushed over.

"No more secrets," he growled. "No more silent conversations within this family."

My eyes were wide, but CJ said, "Logan."

"Don't *Logan* me," he said, looking between us. "Just tell me what it is. Rip off the band-aid so I can just heal all at once."

"I will die by the time this is over," I said, my voice quiet, but it echoed through the room like a cannon had gone off. I could feel the rest of the family come and stand by the doorway behind us. Each of their embers burning bright, regardless of the pain we were all in.

"What?" Logan whispered horrified, as I looked at CJ, whose hands were balled up in fists.

"Not if I have my way," CJ said just as quietly and came to put his arm around my waist. "But there is a way to stop him. According to legend, there is a way to stop Ansel, but it very well may cost Megan her life to do it."

"Bullshit." Logan spat as he stared at us. Then looked back to the rest of the family, who didn't say a word. I wasn't sure they were even breathing. "Tell me." Logan said.

And so CJ did. He told him the whole undiluted truth of Helena, and what the cost of stopping Ansel will be. He told him about Vox Isle, the slaying of the Cinder Fairy's Consort, and how we were now going to head north to Morte Alta to find Helena.

When CJ was finished, Logan's eyes flicked between CJ and me. "I'm assuming you are looking for a loophole." CJ nodded. "AND, I'm also assuming you are all planning on leaving in the next couple of days?"

"Tomorrow morning." We had discussed it last night after Logan crashed out, deciding that it did no good to sit around Nalrin. There wasn't going to be anything here to help us. No more additional knowledge to be found. We knew where we had to go, and every day that passed was another day that Ansel was growing in power.

"I'm going with you," he said, crossing his arms.

"The fuck you are!" I shouted at him.

"You are not going to cloister me up in a tower while you fight the dragons, Megan," Logan said. "You sent me here to keep me safe. You sent me to Nalrin so that when Lindy... when this whole mess was done, I would know the culture, the way of life here, so that Lindy and I could have a life here. Well, Lindy isn't here anymore, is she? There is no reason to keep me locked up."

"Logan," CJ said, but snapped his mouth shut when he saw the look on Logan's face. I, however, stared him down. A million reasons ran through my head for why he shouldn't go.

"Lady Megan." Mickel's voice said from behind me. "Logan has been training with the Vernadali. Not only has he been an excellent study, he has been basically going through physical bootcamp with them. With that training along with everything that he has had through his life in the Manusia..."

"Mickel. Please. Shut. The. Underworld. Up," CJ said through gritted teeth. Then he turned to Logan. "You think *I'm* going to allow you to go with us?

"Allow?" Logan said. "Who...? You are not Dad."

"Damn fucking straight, I'm not. I'm your brother. I... I can't lose you too, Loog," CJ said, his voice thick and cracking. They stared at each other for a long moment before CJ took a deep breath and said, "I can't lose you, Logan."

Logan's eyes softened and showed every ounce of pain he felt. "I can't just stay here, Cor. I can't just sit back and do nothing. I don't want to die. I don't want any of you to die." A quick glance at me made me wonder if he, too, was thinking of what kind of loophole there might be that could save me.

Logan turned to his brother and stared him down. "I couldn't face Mom and Dad, knowing I left you guys to do all the hard work. I... I couldn't, can't, face Lindy in the afterlife, knowing I did nothing to help you guys along the way. I can't face her knowing that she died helping you stop Ansel, and I just sat on my ass doing nothing."

When no one said anything, he turned to me, eyes pleading. "Megan, please."

I turned toward my family, looking each of them in the eye. Jean's face was streaked with tears, Clarice's throat bobbed up and down, and even Owen had tears in his eyes. Mickel, damn him, stood there like an immovable wall. He simply nodded, almost imperceptibly. We all understood what he meant.

Letting out a huge breath. *"How would you feel if we made you sit on the sidelines right now?"* I pushed to CJ.

That made CJ flinch. So, I looked at Logan and said, "Okay."

Logan's shoulders sagged in relief. "Thank you."

"I swear to the Angels, though, Logan Francis Matthewson, if you die? I will resurrect your ass just so I can kill you again," I said, pointing a finger at him. CJ chuckled a bit at that, and I cut him a look.

Hands up in supplication, CJ said, "I was just thinking Clarice may have to leave that door open for a while. I will be right behind you, and I think Mom and Dad will be in that line as well."

Sighing. I flopped back down on the couch, leaning my head back on the cushion, "So, I guess that means you are going, too, Mickel?"

"I believe you gave me orders to protect him." Mickel said carefully. "I assume the same conditions apply to me?"

It was Jean who spoke up. "Oh yeah! And I'll be in that line, repeatedly."

Owen agreed with her, "And I'll make sure that when it's my turn, it's painful." Clarice chuckled darkly. I don't think I even want to know what was going through her head.

"We are so royally fucked," I said wearily about the same time I heard Logan's stomach growl.

"Food?" Logan said, rubbing his stomach and looking sheepish.

"Food." I chuckled.

CHAPTER 21

As WE MADE OUR way down to the dining hall, we could hear people's discussions turn to whispers. When we walked into the large open hall, the first thing I noticed was that they had replaced the long wooden tables with round ones that had ten matching wooden stools with royal blue cushions. A feeling of unease fell over me as we made our way to the counter to get some food. It was how people's conversations stopped as we walked by. As if we were a wave that flowed through the room, drowning out all sound.

Not to mention the worn, beaten, and defeated looks on everyone's faces. Even the children who sat at the tables looked like they hadn't slept in days or had done nothing but cry since my father had attacked the city. There wasn't a person I saw who didn't have bags under their eyes. Very few actually ate the food on their plates, even though there were adults trying to get the children to eat.

CJ grabbed my hand, and while I could feel his charge on full alert, I was instantly calmed by his touch.

I grabbed food from the counter without thinking of what I was putting on my plate, placed my hand on the sensor, without looking to see how much it cost, and headed toward an empty table in the corner. When we were all seated, we just sat there staring at each other over our plates. I had lost my appetite, and saw Logan, someone who could and has, eaten someone out of house and home, just sit there mindlessly moving his food around his plate with his fork.

The hall was slowly filled with whispers again, when a girl walked up to me. She couldn't have been older than three or four and was dressed in clothes that would have had her living within the third ring, but now were torn and dirty. "Lady Megan?"

"Yes?" I said, my voice sounding too loud for the room.

"Are you going to save us from bad man?" she said as her voice trembled a little. Her eyes were hopeful, but you could see the redness in them from where she had been crying.

I turned around on my stool, bent down to look her eye to eye, and took a deep breath before saying, "What's your name, sweety?"

"Kelelis," she said, looking down at her feet.

"Kelelis, I am going to do everything I can to stop the bad man. It will not be easy, though. Do you have any brothers or sisters?" The whole hall was listening carefully to our conversation, and I didn't like it. I even saw CJ move his chair closer, and Mickel had put his utensils down, paying very close attention to the room.

"I have Reggie, he this many," she said holding up six fingers, "and Momma had Baby Toryal before bad man come. She's really little. Poppa says Kelelis no play with her like Reggie. He says I break Baby Toryal."

I couldn't help but smile. So simplistic, but so adorable at the same time. A tall blonde-haired man came to stand behind her and she grabbed onto his leg. "Well, Kelelis, I will do what I can to stop the bad man, okay? Can you do me a favor, though?"

She nodded her head and put her thumb in her mouth. It was such an innocent gesture. "I know that your brother Reggie is going to be very brave for you, but then, who is going to be brave for your Baby Toryal?"

She looked up at her father, and he smiled down at her. Kelelis stood up straighter and pulled her thumb from her mouth before saying, "I can be brave for Baby Toryal."

I smiled at her. "Alright then. I know I won't have to worry about her with such a brave little girl looking after her."

"Kelelis, can you go sit with Reggie and Grandma? I would like to speak to Lady Megan," her father said in a sweet, calming voice. I stood up but felt CJ shift in his seat and stand behind me.

"Sure, Poppa," she said as she skipped around the tables until she climbed back up onto one of the stools where a gray-haired lady and little brown-headed boy were sitting.

"Lady Megan," Kelelis's father said, bowing. When he stood up, he continued with a calm but yet weathered voice, "I do appreciate you giving my daughter hope and trying to make her feel important in the chaos that is our world."

I nodded, knowing that this is going to be the nicest thing he has to say to me.

"However, the children are not the only ones who are scared," he said before lowering his voice, "My wife gave birth to my daughter just a day before *your* father came over the wall and then took her from me."

A lump lodged deep in my throat, and I was barely able to manage an "I'm so sorry", before I saw the flash of steel in his hand. Automatically, I tried to put a wall up between us, but I wasn't fast enough.

CJ and Remi, who I didn't even realize was in the room, tackled him to the ground, and Mickel was there a split second later, binding him.

Somewhere in the distance I heard a little voice scream, "Poppa!" Clarice was standing next to me, hands ready to defend, and I wasn't sure if the room darkened or if it was my vision. Owen and Jean were still trying to figure out what exactly had happened.

I just stood there, holding my hands over the handle to the syth that was buried to the hilt in my lower stomach. What? I looked down and saw blood oozing out of my fingers, but I didn't feel anything. I didn't feel what was so often described as that hot, searing pain. I didn't want to bend over in agony. I didn't feel anything, but wet. It was as if I was watching it on TV.

Did someone seriously just stab me?

Anger and fear flowed through me like a raging river.

I looked up and stared at the sight before us. Someone had just stabbed me and now there were dozens of people with their weapons out in *my* direction. "You think killing me is going to make things any better?" I screamed at them. I could feel the tears well in my eyes. Why do they always blame me? This, this... isn't my fault.

"You want to kill me because of something that I didn't do? I am *not* the one who has been ruining the countryside, taking your lands, taking your crops, or your families. I'm not the one who came over that wall and took your friends, neighbors, lovers... mothers, fathers, or children. That person is not ME. I just happen to have some of the same blood run through me. What you all don't understand is that it is also that same blood that is the only thing that can stop him. Killing me? That only condemns you all to the Underworld."

"Megs..." CJ said, relinquishing the man to Remi and standing before me.

"Lady Megan," Mickel said as he put his hand on my shoulder.

"Don't Lady Megan me, Mickel," I said through gritted teeth, and his hand was instantly gone. A moment later, I saw him run out of the room, full sprint.

"Megs..." CJ said.

"DON'T!" I spit as I looked out over the crowds of people in the hall. The tears of frustration were flowing freely now. "I am so fucking tired of having to explain myself all the time. I know people are dying. I know that your loved ones are being taken from you. My own family has not been spared that tragedy, either."

At these words, some of the citizens of Nalrin put their weapons away. "Lady Lindy Keller was lost to the same tar that came over those walls at the control of my father, Ansel Keller." I took a step forward and slipped a little on the floor. CJ reached out and caught me as I looked down and saw blood dripping on the tile. For a brief moment, I wondered why I was still standing there. In a swift motion, CJ swung my legs from underneath me and picked me up.

"We miss her immensely," I said before he too was running me out of the room.

And still I felt nothing. He carried me as if I weighed nothing more than a pillow he was bringing to bed. I looked up at him and could swear I saw lightning flashing in his eyes, just as it did when he had used his charge against me to keep me out of the fight after Lindy had died.

When we busted through a set of doors, we were met with one of the physicians that had helped try to figure out why I wasn't having any visions.

"I really wish my visions would come back," I said against CJ's chest.

"What?" CJ said, Mickel standing just behind him.

The physician looked at me questioningly and then said, "Mickel, what did you two give her to stop the pain?"

"Nothing." Mickel and CJ said in unison.

He put me down on the gurney, and put his hands to my face, before saying, "She's in shock... and her temperature is dropping. We need to get her inside." He looked down at the syth still in my side, "Thank you for not pulling that out. It is low enough it may have just damaged her intestines, but we won't know for sure until we get her under the machines."

CJ held my hand, and I grabbed onto it tight when they tried to tell him he needed to wait outside.

"I am her Vernadali. I will not be parted from her side." I thought I heard the physicians tell Owen, Jean, Clarice, and

Logan that they needed to wait outside, and it was only when Mickel told them to stay that they agreed.

The last thing I remembered was Logan saying, "I can't lose her, too."

CHAPTER 22

WHEN I WOKE UP two days ago, the nurse came in, checked my vitals, and said they had kept me sedated in the physician's ward for three days. Three days. I lost three fucking days. Then the nurse said that I had to stay in bed, and if it hadn't been for CJ, I may have zapped her right then and there. Of course, I've complained to each of them ever since, and Owen told me that was the exact reason they had kept me sedated.

My side. ANGELS!

Someone had stabbed me.

It was healing quickly, and that in itself was a testament to the medical advancements of this dimension. Sure, I was sore, but not even Nalrin's advanced medicine could keep me from that.

Last night, CJ had sat on the side of the bed running his thumb across the back of my hand. Then he told me how he watched them operate on me, "Once I realized you weren't going to die on me, I tried to be patient and I realized how amazing it was to watch the doctors work."

135

He got really animated as he said, "They had you under this massive machine, but as they slowly, and I do mean slowly, pulled the syth out of your side, the machine sent small, concentrated waves to the injured area. Between the healing magic and those waves, it closed the wound enough to keep you from bleeding out. I wonder if they recorded it. It was so cool. Your body was projected, like a hologram just above you, so every physician in the room could make sure everything was being done correctly."

I had to admit, it was adorable to see him like that. He was excited about something. I hadn't seen that kind of excitement from him since we were back in the Manusia.

After he told me all about it, we just continued to talk and that in itself was comforting. We weren't talking about anything in particular. We just talked. It was like it used to be back in the Manusia. At some point, he had climbed in next to me in the bed and I was snuggled up next to him as best I could. We had been staring at each other for a long while when his eyebrow cocked up and he smirked.

"What?" I whispered as I moved a lock of hair away from his face. It had grown out again since he had come back from the Curtails of the North.

"Just thinking about us."

"What do you mean?"

"How far we have come in just a few years. The experiences we have had," then he dropped his voice got gravelly as he said, "The amazing sex we have together."

My toes curled at that. "I miss that."

"It's only been a few days," he said, smirking.

"Too long," I said, running my finger along his jaw and across his lip. "I would love to just be locked in a room with you for days. Never having to get dressed. Just fucking each other's brains out the entire time."

"Fuck," CJ said in a drawn-out frustrated whisper. "Remind me to get that set up, and soon."

I just reached over and smiled at him. We laid like that for a while, forehead to forehead, when I thought about just how little time it had been since we got married. "Is it really only October?" I asked.

"Yea. October 28th." His eyebrows furrowed together. "Why?"

"How is it that it has been only four months since we got married? I mean, a little less than that, but still." I asked, sighing. "We had a honeymoon, met Clarice's Dad, fought Ansel, lost Lindy..."

"Had a magical hissy fit," he said, smiling and flicking my nose as I glared at him.

"That doesn't even begin to cover everything." I giggled. "We've also seen one of the family become Empress. Empress, Ceej. Clarice is a fucking EMPRESS. Then we removed a curse we didn't even know existed off me, come back to Nalrin, only to see it has been attacked, and then I went and got myself stabbed."

"First of all, you didn't get yourself stabbed. By the way, he's been put in a holding cell and will be tried for an assault on a government official." I rolled my eyes, but then he smiled brightly. "There has been a lot, but you know what they say. The first year of marriage is the hardest."

"Asshole." I smiled back at him.

Then he lifted himself up onto his elbow and kissed me.

"I love you, Megs," he whispered against my lips, as he ran a thumb across my cheek. Then, in a low, commanding tone that made my toes curl again, he said, "You are to heal. You need to do so quickly, so that when you are no longer hooked up to all these machines, I will be able to worship you properly... and extensively."

"Mmhum." I agreed as I felt that hot pulse between my legs. For newlyweds, we have not had nearly enough alone time together. I wanted nothing more than to pull him over me and have my way with him, but as our luck would have it, the nurse came in.

"What in the name of the Angels!" she yelled. "Vernadali CJ, I must respectfully request that you not mount Lady Megan while she is healing."

I blushed, but then said, "He wasn't. He was just snuggling and kissing me."

She tried not to smile, but then pushed CJ out of the room. "You can see her in the morning. She needs her rest."

The nurse fussed over me for a while, and when she finally left, she turned down the lights and demanded I try to get some sleep.

Three and a half months, almost four months. That's all we've been married for. I really wanted to get some alone time with my new husband. I pressed my legs together a little harder to stop that throbbing and tried to think of all that laid ahead of us.

Morte Alta. Jean had said it could take a few months to go the distance, but it would largely depend on how long it took for us to get through the Lost Plateau. The Lost Plateau was much like the Manusia's Bermuda Triangle. We could get lost in there, and there was telling how much time we would lose, while we were on this scavenger hunt. Ansel could level most of the continent in the time it would take us to get to Morte Alta and find him to destroy him... if we found Helena there, and it didn't lead us somewhere else.

Sighing, I closed my eyes and made myself clear my head to sleep.

The next afternoon, Jean came to visit and told me how she and Owen had been talking to Julian to see if we could use the dragons again but were not having much success. I had just woken up from a medically assisted nap, because I did not, in fact, get much sleep overnight. Unfortunately, this made me a bit groggy when she first started talking. According to Julian, the dragons would lose all sense of direction in the Lost Plateau, and therefore, we could just fly in circles for days without realizing it. I vaguely remembered telling her, "So it's okay for us to go through there, but not his precious creatures. Jerk."

Jean had raised her eyebrows in a questioning shock before saying, "Did you just call Julian a jerk?"

I just rolled my eyes. Jerk was the kindest descriptor I had in that very moment.

"While entertaining, you know he is upset about how you treated him in that Council meeting," she said.

"I bet. How many people have ever called him out in public?" I smiled a bit sheepishly. "I know I shouldn't have done it, but..."

"But you were tired," Jean said as she came to sit on the edge of the bed.

"I'm so tired, Jean. I'm tired of fighting. I'm tired of death. I'm tired of the politics. I'm tired of the bullshit."

She nodded, and before I could ask her what she really wanted to talk to me about, she said, "Megan, I want to apologize for that fight we had on the boat. You are strong headed. You are determined. You say what is on your mind. I don't mean to say that you didn't hit a nerve with me with everything you said, because you did, but you hit that nerve because it was the truth."

"I'm not sorry I said those things, Jean, but I am sorry for *how* I said them," I said, playing with my fingers. "I do wish that you had tried to see Matt and I when we were kids, and I am still a little bitter about it, but I don't love you any less. I just really wish we could have known you earlier. Wish you could have known Matt."

She smiled sweetly before saying, "Me too. Me too."

Just then, the nurse who had kicked CJ out last night came in and told Jean that I needed to rest and that she could come back later.

"We will be back after dinner to talk about what our next steps will be, okay?" Jean said as the nurse was shooing her out of the room.

"Okay," I said as I leaned back in the hospital bed and sighed. There was so much that needed to be done, and I was just stuck here until they thought I wouldn't hurt myself. The wound was scabbed over and tender, but I was only sore, bored, and eager to get out of here.

"Lady Megan?" Physician Reynolds said as she came into the room a few minutes later.

"I'm here," I said, sighing, "Where else would I be?"

"You know we are keeping you here to ensure that you don't hurt yourself."

"So I've been told."

"Well, let me have a look," she said, bringing her tablet over my abdomen. A hologram showing where Kelelis's father had plunged his syth into my side appeared at eye level. It looked much like the hologram they had shown me of my brain when we were trying to sort out why I hadn't had any visions.

The hologram showed some thin lines where they were still healing, but otherwise, everything looked good as far as I could tell. She turned off the hologram, then said, "I need to look at the exterior please."

I lifted my gown up so she could see it, and after she poked and prodded me some more, before she continued. "Well, you seem to be healing exceptionally well. I wouldn't expect anything less from someone who has been wearing the Golden Medallion of Sa Ra."

My hand instantly went to my neck, where the medallion still sat. It had been there for so long, I hadn't given it a second thought until she mentioned it. "I... I don't know what you're talking about." I stammered.

She gave me a knowing look. "Really?"

"Really," I said a little more confidently and tried to sit up fully in the bed. I winced slightly but tried hard not to show it.

"You need to work on your lying technique, Lady Megan," she said with a smirk, then patted my leg. "Don't worry, your secret is safe. I know the Council would confiscate it in a split second if they knew you had the real thing."

"How do you know it isn't a replica?"

"I walked in on Lady Jean and Empress Clarice, chanting to the Angel of Healing while you were still sedated," she said quietly as my eyes shot upwards. "They stopped immediately, but when I examined your wound, it had healed faster than it should have."

"Nalrin has the best medicine around. CJ even told me how you used concentrated waves to stimulate the healing process. You are just that good at your vocation."

"That is true, but even at that, you shouldn't be as healing as fast as you are, Lady Megan," she put the tablet down on the table next to my bed and pulled the chair up to the bed. Taking a deep breath she said, "Lady Megan, I know you have an Angel's Blessed Vernadali, and I have no doubt that the Angels have blessed you as well, but if the Angels were going to heal you, they would do so fully. I may not be the best physician in the ward, but I am still a physician, and as such I would like to think, not a stupid woman."

"I don't mean to insult your intelligence, Physician Reynolds." I really wasn't, but I had to deny it.

She patted my hand and then changed the subject. "How do you feel?"

"Other than sore when I move, I feel fine. Bored, but fine," I said as cheerfully as I could. "Any chance I could get out of here?"

"Possibly, but there are restrictions," she said, crossing her arms and letting the corner of her lip rise in amusement. I raised an eyebrow at her, and she continued, "No training. No stress. Most importantly, no hard riding for a couple of weeks."

"A couple weeks!" I said, astonished. "Certainly, you are not serious."

"I am very serious. The jostling and movement of riding could strain the muscle and cause more damage. It would do best to—"

"I can't sit around for another two weeks." I interrupted, grinding my teeth. "Seriously, I can't be that hurt, if his royal hinny hasn't even deigned to show his face in the Physician's Ward."

"If you know of some way to heal faster, then I'm all ears," she said knowingly. Her eyes flicked to my neck, then back up. I glared at her. She had me and she knew it. "I'll release you tomorrow if your condition approves."

"Bu—"

"Lady Megan. If your condition improves tomorrow, then I will release you. We can then discuss the limitations at that time, as they *will* depend on how you are healing." She picked up her tablet and said, "I'll make you my first patient. So, just in case you have a miraculous recovery, I can release you and you can be on your way to... save us all."

She winked, but her voice had trailed off so sadly. She turned and started to walk out of the room. I couldn't help but say, "Who did you lose when Ansel came through the city?"

She stopped but didn't turn around. She kept her voice low and away from me, but her voice hitched when she said, "My sister, my 14-year-old daughter, my 8-year-old son, and my husband of 45 years. My 10-year-old daughter was at her aunt's residence here in the center when he attacked, thank the Angels. My sister protected her, but your father took her, too."

I was stunned. Her entire family had just about been obliterated. Sadness washed over me for the loss this woman has endured. "I'm... I'm so sorry."

"It is not your fault." She put a hand on the wall, as if she was trying to gain strength from its stability, before she said with as much professionalism as she could conjure, "Lady Megan, I will be here first thing in the morning. I hope you have a powerful night of healing ahead of you so that you can stop this monster."

I watched her turn the corner and I couldn't help but stare at the spot she had been standing. There was a woman who had lost so very much and yet, she didn't seem to hate me for it. Why? Why wouldn't she when so many did? Don't get me wrong. While her reaction was what I have wanted from everyone else, the reasons I am laying in this bed said otherwise. Society seemed to want to blame me, and then there was this lone woman, who not a month ago lost so much, yet she didn't hate me for it. She renewed the hope that has slowly been disintegrating within me.

CJ rushed in just as I felt the tears fall down my cheeks.

"Megs. What's wrong?"

I couldn't look at him yet. I just stared at the door where she stood and let the feeling of hope fill every vein in my body. Finally, I closed my eyes, smiled, and looked at him.

I reached up and grasped onto the pendant at my neck. "Get Owen, Jean and Clarice. We need to use... we need to get me healed."

"I don't understand. That's what you are doing here. You are healing," he said with his brows furrowed. Then he noticed I was holding my necklace and understanding crossed his face.

"Physician Reynolds said if I make a significant improvement by the time she comes in the morning, she will release me."

"We won't be able to get on the road right away," he said, a smile slowly crossing his face in understanding. "Though if you seem to be healed, then she won't have a choice but to release you with no limitations."

"Correct," I said, as Clarice walked through the door.

"I'll go get Owen and Jean," CJ said, then turned to Clarice. "Wait here. We have work to do."

CHAPTER 23

CJ HELD MY HAND all night while they chanted. By morning, I was a little sore and tired, but when Physician Reynolds came in, she was met with me sitting up in bed, legs crossed, hands in my lap, and smiling. My family, however, stood on either side of me, arms crossed over their chest. She paused for only half a step before regaining her composure.

"Good morning," she said cheerfully, a wicked gleam in her eye. "Megan, you look like you feel better."

"Feel great. Good night sleep will do wonders for the healing process." I smirked at her.

"Well, let's see how you look." She brought out the scanner and studied the projection. She glanced at me a few times while looking at it, then said, "All right, let's look at how the incision is healing."

I lifted my shirt and moved my shorts down to show a faint pink scar where the glue and faint scabs had been yesterday. She huffed out a breath in amazement and ran her very cold fingers over the scar. "It's incredible." Her eyes flicked to me, then back at the scar. "How did you get the suture glue out... No. Don't tell me."

She stepped back, made a few notes, and then looked at me. "Do a couple of sit-ups for me."

I did, and there was a small smirk on her face as I winced at the last couple.

"Sit on your knees," she instructed, and I did so. "Now I want you to sit with your feet under you, but off to the side."

"So, like a frog?" I asked.

"I don't know what a frog is," she said, but then showed me. "Like this."

"A frog sit." CJ chuckled under his breath, rolling his eyes. I was trying very, very hard not to laugh as I got into position.

"Okay. Now pull yourself up to stand on your knees, without using your hands. Do the motion 8 times in a row... without wincing, and I'll release you this morning." She instructed, but then added with a smirk, "No limitations."

I eyed her and moved to sit on my knees. CJ moved closer, and she put a hand on his chest to hold him back. When he looked at her in shock, she met it with one of her own that told me she may know a bit too much about how our family works before turning back to me. She cocked an eyebrow that said, "*You want to leave? Do it without injuring yourself.*"

"And what does having her do these movements tell you?" Owen asked, confusion all over his face.

Taking a deep breath, I started the motion and said, "She wants to make sure I can ride a horse."

Down and up.

Down and up.

Down and up.

Oh, the muscles were fatigued, and they were tired, but I continued. "And that I won't hurt myself doing so."

The last two I had to concentrate on not showing any emotion, but as I turned to her after the last one, she gave me another one of those cocked eyebrows. In total Megan defiance, I just stared her down and did five more quick reps, just to show her I was okay. CJ smirked and let out a small chuckle at the defiance he felt through that Vernadali bond. Physician Reynolds shook her head and flat out laughed.

CJ came over to me and, as he gave me a quick kiss on the top of my head, whispered, "Snarky shit."

I gave him a wicked smile and looked back at Physician Reynolds. "Was that sufficient for you, or are there more motions you'd like for me to demonstrate?"

A slow, knowing smile crossed her face. "Okay, Lady Megan. I'll release you, but please try to be careful. Take breaks when you can. If you can take a boat, take a boat. At least for the next week. I'm sure you will be fully healed by then." Then, with a wink and a smile, she walked out of the room.

CHAPTER 24

CJ AND I HAD just finished loading the horses onto the boat that was going to take us up the Calenola River when Logan came and gave us our room assignments. The blue and white, six deck river boat had a massive paddlewheel in the back, and over two hundred rooms for guests. I sighed as I looked at what would be our home for the two-and-a-half-week river trip to Bellstar at the base of the Midstrada Mountains.

"Seriously?" I groaned as I looked at the assignment. "The President's Suite?"

"Mickel and I will be sharing a room in one of the luxury suites across the hallway next to Owen and Jean. Clarice will be in the other President Suite next door to you," he said, smirking.

"We would be just fine in one of the standard rooms," I said, turning to brush down Ziggy. It was obvious Julian not only arranged for the horses to be onboard, but also the room assignments. Ziggy rubbed his head on my hip again as I secured the halter and tied him to the railing. I patted his neck and leaned against him.

"Not gonna lie, Megan," Logan said. "This is all a fucking shit show, but at least we get to travel comfortably."

"You remember that when we are going through the Midstrada Pass, Grasslands and Plateau," CJ told his brother. Tucker, CJ's horse, appeared to stomp the ground and huff in agreement.

"Your stuff has already been put in your rooms, and the Captain said we will depart in about twenty minutes," Logan said as he made his way to the mare that was assigned to him. He looked over and slipped her a small carrot. He had really gotten attached to her, and I decided right there that if we lived through this, I would buy her from the Council for him.

We finished settling the horses and headed up the balcony to meet with the others. Nalrin had wasted no time repairing the docks. I wasn't sure it could be brought back to its full glory, and honestly didn't think it should. This was war, and it should leave its mark on the world so that we learn from it. Making everything the way it was before, or erasing it completely, was not the answer. How can you learn not to do something again if you remove it from history?

Mickel met us on the main deck, but his eyes scanned every person he walked by, every alcove, everything. Sure, I noted all the entrances, exits, and escape routes by instinct now, but he was taking it over the top. By the time we got to the fifth deck where our rooms were, I had had enough.

"Mickel, what's going on? Why are you so jumpy?" I asked quietly.

"I don't like these types of boats. Too many levels," he said, almost growling.

"You know the Vernadali already swept the entire boat, and vetted every single person on this thing, right?"

"Not the point. It's just... I don't like crowded places. It puts me on high alert, that's all," he said, rolling his shoulders. "I'll settle down in a few days."

We stood on the balcony watching the docks, and while I recognized some of the faces of those boarding the boat, I couldn't place them. I noticed Mickel's eyes narrow a few times, and he looked like he was trying to puzzle something out. Twenty minutes later, the last of the passengers boarded, the ramp was hauled off, and the Captain came over the speaker system.

"Thank you all for boarding the Nalrin Marie. We will leave shortly, so please make sure to stow your items carefully, as there will be wet weather on this trip. Dinner will be served in approximately three hours and will cease service two hours thereafter. As a reminder, the fifth deck of the Nalrin Marie will be strictly off limits." We looked at each other and only then did I notice that we were the only ones standing out on the balcony.

"Angels, save me," Mickel said as he turned and stomped down the row. When Mickel reached the stairwell, he took the stairs two at a time. As the Captain continued with his various announcements, the entire boat heard as Mickel barged into that room, and the speaker went quiet.

Five minutes later, Mickel and the Captain met us on that balcony. "Tell them." Mickel said with a voice I had rarely heard him use.

"Empress Clarice," he said, bowing. She responded by crossing her arms and rolling her eyes. He looked straight at me. "Lady Megan, I am under orders from Head Julian that you and your family are not be disturbed during the trip. Therefore, all guests who were originally scheduled for this level have been rescheduled for another departure date and time. The level below is comprised of only the Nalrin Guard brought on as protection for your family, and half of the other levels are as well. In fact, nearly half of the persons on this boat are here by order of Head Julian and Vernadali Remi."

"Remi?" I said, turning to CJ.

"He's been promoted to oversee the Vernadali in Nalrin," CJ said, a touch of pride in his voice. "Took them long enough."

"Apparently there are so few Vernadali left, that there were none left to spare." Mickel said, glaring at the Captain, but I saw

CJ flinch slightly. I grabbed his hand and felt his charge wash over me. I eyed him, and he backed it off slightly.

"They cannot accompany us the entire trip," I said firmly.

"They are *apparently* under orders to accompany us up the river, over the Midstrada Pass." Mickel paused, not wanting to give our entire trip away. "And on the next leg of the journey. They do not know the path we are to take, but they are supposed to follow or accompany us."

I eyed him carefully, but it was Jean who said, "They won't be able to make the final stretches with us. That would be... difficult to do."

"And you knew nothing of this, Mickel." CJ said, his eyes narrowing.

"No," Mickel said. His voice was holding back the anger that I could tell was simmering under that tense exterior. "Julian did not inform me of this little addition to our trip. Likely because he knew I would have strongly objected to it. We won't be able to keep our movements hidden with this large of a group following behind us."

"How do you know all of this, Captain?" Owen asked carefully.

"I was ordered to attend the briefing with the Nalrin Guard this morning, who are now stationed on this boat. There will be additional military resources meeting you in the North. There is also a battalion in the North that is being mobilized and is supposed to meet you in Millmore," he said, meeting Owen's eye. So, he knew more than he was saying for sure, especially if he knew we were going all the way to Millmore.

"Why?" Owen said in an uneasy tone. "Why were you ordered to attend such a private briefing, and know so much about our plans? Mickel didn't even know about it. We didn't even know about it."

The Captain had the good sense to look a little nervous before he spoke. "I was a Captain in the Nalrin Sea Armada. I therefore have Class C1 clearance, and while I realize that your family has higher clearance, I am the only Captain who works this river, who knows how to handle the mobilization of this many troops, and who knows how to keep the mobilization quiet. We are doing so as quietly as we can, so that your father-"

"He is not my father," I said through my teeth. "While his blood may run through my veins, I will not lay claim to him."

Nodding, the Captain continued, "So that Ansel does not know your movements for as long as possible. There are already rumors you are heading north. There are also rumors that after Ansel left Nalrin, he headed northwest. Head Julian believes that... Ansel will likely try to stop you or meet up with you somewhere in the Grasslands. While it will not be a secret for long, Head Julian wants to delay that knowledge for as long as possible, and have you protected."

I crossed my arms and just stared him down. CJ's hand was on the small of my back and I felt his thumb move to lend me comfort. Julian was a serious thorn in my side sometimes. Yes, the help was needed, but I not only had two very powerful Sangra in Owen and Jean, the highest ranking Nalrin Guard, an Angel's Blessed Vernadali, and if that wasn't enough, I have the freaking EMPRESS OF THE UNDERWORLD with me. Having an army will not increase our odds of winning. It's just going to be more souls to feed the tar.

"Having a mini army behind us will not help with stealth," CJ mumbled, but then said, "And the reason no one else is staying on this level or that this level is strictly off limits doesn't seem strange to the other passengers?"

"Vernadali CJ, we have made it known that there are repairs being made, and that, for everyone's safety, they are not to enter this level. It was noted on all their tickets, told to them as they checked in, and they were once again reminded in the announcements," the Captain said.

"What is your name, Captain?" CJ asked.

"Captain Morrow. Everyone just calls me Captain."

My mind was spinning at all that had happened in the last thirty-eight hours. Angels, Julian had mobilized an entire company of the Nalrin Guard to go with us. I couldn't even think about the strategy that had gone into making that happen. Vernadali and Nalrin Guard alike were now stationed on this boat, and Julian was sending even more to met us up north. I couldn't wrap my head around it.

I turned and leaned against the railing, looking out at the countryside slowly passing by. While this wasn't the fastest way north, it was the least conspicuous and faster than going on horseback.

I blocked everything out and watched the coastline go by, trying to clear my mind. We were passing the Turlel Forest, and while the forest was beautiful, there wasn't much to see. CJ had stood there behind me, resting his hands on either side of me on the railing, letting me think. I'm sure that charge told him how anxious I was. I really tried not to think of all the ways this could go so very, very wrong. What if we couldn't find Helena? What if Ansel cut us off? What if every one of my family members died? How many of my family members would I have left?

When he gave me a couple of soft kisses on my neck and shoulder, heat and power ran through my body in a rush. I tried very hard not to let my body take over, and concentrated on taking a deep breath, to center my power.

'Ceej.'

I felt a small huff of a laugh against my neck, as he kissed that spot just behind my ear. I tried not to lengthen my neck to allow him more access. My family was standing right here, and I was not going to make out with him in front of them. They already gave us enough shit.

I turned toward CJ and leaned against the railing. He was trying to distract me, and it was working, but my stomach was still a ball of knots.

We watched each other for a long moment before he sighed and kissed my forehead. Slowly, I wrapped my arms around his waist, and he pulled me closer to him. As he did, he rested his chin on my head and whispered how it was all going to be alright. I still didn't like how it gave him insight into my feelings. He shouldn't have to sort out his feelings and mine all at the same time. I couldn't imagine how he was even doing it.

However, it was nice to have comfort when I needed it, even if I didn't show it.

I took a deep breath and let the smell of him wash over me. That scent that was just pure CJ, and my shoulders relaxed. Gods, it felt good to be in his arms. I couldn't wait to get him to our room.

As if he could read my mind, he ran his hand slowly up and down my back in that way he knew would drive me crazy. The soft, simple touches sent my power sparking under my skin, firing right to that spot between my legs. The heat that trailed those simple touches, dear Angels, save me. Heat flooded me, and I felt him smile against my head.

"No fair," I pushed toward him, feeling the evidence of his train of thought, as I pulled myself closer to him. His hand slid down to grab my ass, pulling me closer. I pushed a small moan at him in response.

A small huff and broader smile against my head that time.

"Megan's tired," CJ said, taking my hand and turning us toward our rooms. "I'm going to take her to our room and make her relax. Maybe even get her to take a nap."

CHAPTER 25

Once we rounded the corner, we all but flew down the hall. He backed up to the door. There was a small audible electronic click, and the door was open.

I hadn't even had a chance to look at the room that would be our home for the foreseeable future, before his lips were on mine. I threw my arms around his shoulders, and I wrapped my legs around his waist. He took maybe four or five steps before he leaned forward, and we landed on the large fourposter bed.

He instantly started stripping me of my weapons. When I lifted my hips, allowing him the ability to take off my syth belt, he pushed against me, and I felt the full hardness of him. Moaning, I reached down to help him with his belt, but he grabbed my hands and stopped.

"Don't you even think about it." His voice was husky and demanding as I looked at him, and a smirk crossed his face. Then, in a movement so quick, I didn't register it until he was done, he had my hands above my head and attached to the headboard with a silk sash that seemed to come from nowhere.

I raised my eyebrows at him, and he just said, "Now, are you going to be good? The doctor did tell you not to exert yourself. So... you are going to sit back, enjoy and relax."

"Ceej," I begged. He had one of his syths out and was slowly cutting the shirt off me, grinding his hips against me. Breathless, I said, "I'm fine."

"Mmmhm. That you are," he hummed. "And I am going to worship every inch of you." His syth quickly cut away my bra, and before it had landed on the bed next to me, he had my nipple in his mouth. My back arched and the feel of his hands on my breasts made that electricity zap anywhere we were touching.

I tried to move my hands to pull him closer, but they were still tied above me. I wrapped my legs around him again and raised my hips, begging him for more. I wanted him now. I wanted all of him.

A soft chuckle came from him as he raised his head with a smirk. "Oh, no my dear." His breath was a light caress across my skin as he moved south. My eyes rolled back as I concentrated on the feel of him.

"I told you while you were in the Physicians Ward to heal so that I could worship every inch of this body, and I plan on doing just that." He hovered over the light scar from that very visit, and his eyes snapped to mine as he kissed it.

Slowly, he ran his tongue along the line of my pants as he undid them. Slow, deliberate movements. He lowered them and when they were at my ankles, I kicked them off. He sat up, slipped his shirt off, and softly kissed his way up from just above my knee.

I pulled at the restraints above my head, and he stared at me. "Don't you dare."

I cocked an eyebrow. "I could get out."

"I know," he said as he kissed the top of my mound, then growled, "But I like the look of you like this. All laid out like my personal meal."

Dear Angels. What was it about that gravelly voice of his that undid me? I was completely weak against it. Before I could utter any sort of retort, his tongue ran slowly and deliberately up the center of me, stopping just before that bundle of nerves. A whimpering moan came out of me.

Slowly, he repeated the motion and moved back down, circling my entrance. I tried to raise my hips in response, but his hands had a firm hold on me. His tongue dove into me and then was circling my clit. I looked down and his eyes were watching me.

A small smirk. A gentle blow across that clit, and a shot of electricity went straight up my spine as he clamped down on me.

I couldn't take it anymore and moved my hips as much as he would allow. His hand slowly slid around and as he continued to lick and suck on that bundle of nerve, two fingers slid deep inside me, another finger teasing my ass. Inside I was a raging electrical storm. I could almost smell the material burning around my wrists.

"Ceej," I said, panting, but he didn't stop. Instead, he put three fingers in me, pumping. I matched those movements. CJ moved one of those fingers to my ass and slid it in at the same time two entered me again. A quick flick of his tongue and I was dangling off the edge.

"Underworld's being, Cory James." I was lost. The only thing I knew was CJ and the intense pleasure he was giving me. Nothing else in this world mattered. My whole world was centered around him.

"Cum for me, Megan," CJ demanded softly, then latched onto my clit and dove back in like it was the last meal he would ever have. I moaned and ground against him. I splintered into a thousand pieces and vaguely heard something shatter across the room. He continued until the orgasm slowly subsided, and I felt my legs jerk as he laid one last long lick down my center and flicked my clit.

I opened my eyes to him, smirking between my legs. Slowly, he stood and undid his pants, sliding them down. I pulled at the restraints to touch him and grunted in frustration. That smirk grew wider as my mouth watered watching him spring free. I licked my lips and reached for him with my feet.

He stepped back and said, "Oh no. No touching." Then he took himself in his hand and stroked. For all that was holy. The look of him as I looked between my legs and saw him stroking himself. I almost bit through my lip at that. His eyes centered on me and traveled up my body, drinking in every bit of it. The heat in his eyes as they met mine was one that would torch a forest in seconds.

"Tease," I groaned.

"Am I now?" He took one step. Just one step as he pumped his own cock.

"Mmhum," I licked my lips again, not able to take my eyes off him.

Slowly, he moved closer and crawled to hover above me. I could feel his hardness against me, and I tried to move, but he held my hips in place. CJ moved against me, and again, I tried to move, but he held firm. A soft kiss and nip to my collarbone as he did it again, had my back arching and my head rolled back.

CJ nibbled up my neck, and then looked me deep in the eyes as he plunged into me hard and fast. The feeling of being instantly filled with him had me biting down on his shoulder to keep from screaming. His moan was guttural and needy.

He didn't move another muscle as he made me look at him. One of his hands wrapped around my wrists, which were still bound above my head. He pulled out ever so slowly, just to the head of him, and plunged in again. He kept my gaze as he repeated the motion over and over again. The slow intensity of it, the look in his eyes, the pure desire, Angels!

"Beauty be the sin," CJ swore as he captured my lips with his, and then pounded into me. Each stroke was purposeful and full of need. I met him stroke for stroke, needing every inch of him.

"Megs," he said, deep and throaty. He moved a hand to my cheek and kissed me again as he slowed. He nipped at my lip, before nibbling down my throat until he reached my breast and sucked a nipple into his mouth. I gasped and wrapped my legs tightly around his waist, thrusting upward into him.

I was hovering over that edge again, and I could feel him twitch in anticipation within me. "Fuck me, Ceej. Fuck me hard." I begged, my voice barely above a whisper.

His eyes again roamed down my body between us. I could almost feel the heat of that gaze, as he looked between us where we were joined. He rocked slowly, and at my whimper, said, "Your wish is my command."

He bit down hard on my nipple and slammed into me. Again and again, he pounded into me. The sounds of our pleasure filled the room. I pulled on the restraints, and when he bit into my shoulder, a moan escaped me that sent my power rolling out in waves. I heard more shattering glass in the distance, and when his eyes met mine again, I saw lightning strike in his eyes as we careened over that edge together.

CHAPTER 26

"WHY DON'T WE JUST skirt the Plateau and take the Grasslands around to Morana?" I asked as we studied the map before us on the large table. We were four days from Bellstar, and the captain had allowed us to turn one of the unoccupied rooms on the fifth level into a strategy room. He also provided a large map of the continent with all the towns listed, big or small. We needed to see where we could reload on supplies, and what the terrain looked like.

We decided to take the river all the way up to Bellstar, cut through the Midstrada Mountains and catch another river boat in Leadenhollow Port up to Millmore. There apparently, we would meet up with the Nalrin soldiers from further up North. The question was whether or not to cut through the Lost Plateau straight to Morana or skirt around the Plateau and go through the Vandrer Grasslands.

"It's a crap shoot at this point," Logan said, running his hands over his head, much the same way CJ did. It made me smile, but

I hadn't stopped worrying about him being here. There was so much that could go wrong, and I would never forgive myself if something happened to him. CJ and I had discussed it at length last night, and he assured me I had made the right call, even though he hadn't agreed with it.

"We go through the Lost Plateau, and we chance getting lost for months in there," Mickel said, pulling me from my thoughts.

"But if we go around through the Vandrer Grasslands, and Ansel is heading north, there is the chance that we walk ourselves right up to his door," Logan said, leaning against the table.

"There are just too many variables." I sighed and looked to CJ, who was studying the north end of the map. "Maybe there will be more information on where Ansel is and where he is headed, by the time we get to either Leadenhollow Port or Millmore."

Out of the corner of my eye, I saw Mickel clenched his jaw.

"Say it, Mickel," I growled.

"If Julian has mobilized as many as the Captain has said, then it's likely Ansel is heading straight for Millmore. Since that is where the Northern battalion is supposed to meet us, there is no way that information doesn't get to Ansel. The way he is moving across the Continent... He is getting his information somehow. We just don't know how," he said before taking another deep breath. "Something tells me, though, that Julian is pulling everyone out. He will keep Nalrin City protected, but he will call for volunteers. Anyone able and willing to go will be ordered north."

"Because it's us?" I asked. "Or..."

Without looking up from the map, he said sadly, but with anger coating each of his words, "Because it is exactly what I would do. Because I know Julian has already called for aid from Obsecuritan, who doesn't have the manpower because of the rampage Ansel has already wrought there. He has also called for aid from Cinder, but we know they won't answer because of what is happening there. The Lansker Frozen Islands might answer, but it could take them months to get to Nalrin, let alone then make the trip to Millmore or Morana. Finally, because it *will* take everything this dimension has to stop Ansel, and right now, with the way morale is, no one knows if it will be enough."

"It won't take everything the dimension has. It will only take me," I muttered, just above a whisper. I could feel everyone's stares on me. So, I took a deep breath and said, "Help isn't coming. There are no other answers. We all know and have accepted that Helena is the only way. So we go to Morte Alta, ensure Ansel is within whatever that range is going to be, and I use her."

"We will be in Bellstar in four days." Logan said, purposely ignoring my statements. "Maybe they will know something."

"For now, we wait to decide on what path to take from Millmore," CJ said, bracing both hands on the table before us. "If even *we* don't know what direction we're going, it won't give any of Ansel's spies the ability to tip him off."

"Anyone know where Owen and Jean are?" I asked.

"They were up late last night talking to the guard. They may have had a little too much to drink and are probably recovering in bed." Mickel said, a smile playing about his lips at whatever he remembered of last night.

"And before you ask about Clarice, she was working on some Empress duties. Whatever that means. Honestly, I don't really want to know." Logan said with a knowing smile.

"Don't let her hear you say that. She might zap your ass," I said.

"Best action I will have gotten in months," Logan said, smiling, but there was that flicker of pain that crossed his face when he said it. He was trying. He really was trying to get back to whatever his new normal was going to be. I had tried to talk to him about it the other day, but he just waved me off. He said he was working through it and helping us helped him. It gave him direction.

When my eyes met CJ's, he smirked, and the heat in his eyes made my blood boil. *"Don't you dare,"* I pushed to him. I may have pinched my legs closed a bit.

He cocked an eyebrow as to say, 'What? I can't look at you?'

"You know damn well what you are doing."

He just looked me up and down and smirked in a way that said, 'Yea, I do.'

"Gods! Will you two stop?" Logan said, throwing a pen at CJ.

"What?" CJ said, acting all innocent.

"I have heard you two going at it just about every day on this boat. While I have to say I am impressed by your stamina, Cor, please keep it to your room!" He whined.

"Hard to do when your wife looks like that," CJ said, jerking his head toward me.

"We usually keep it to the room," I said nonchalantly.

"Excuse me?" Logan said, and when I looked up, Mickel's eyes were big as saucers.

"There was the utility closet a few doors down." CJ said, shooting me a look that conveyed how much he loved each and every little thing we had done in there. I smirked at the memory of him breaking a shelf as I sucked him off.

Logan just stood there and sputtered. It was such a brotherly conversation, I couldn't do anything but laugh. Mickel shook his head, smiling.

"What is it, Mickel? Go ahead, say it. Might as well. Logan certainly isn't holding back." I said.

"Well, Logan didn't have to live with you back at the house for long, and he doesn't know just how often Lindy used the silence incantation on their room," He smirked.

"What?" Logan said. "And why are you not using it here?"

I just shrugged, "It doesn't work over water... The movement of the water is too fluid. The casting won't stick."

"Are you fucking kidding me?" Logan said, but there was no bite to it. He just strode out the door as CJ and Mickel laughed.

CHAPTER 27

I FOUND MYSELF SEEING but not seeing. I was moving automatically. Brushing down Ziggy in preparation for the deboarding in Bellstar was soothing. It was quiet down here. No one was watching me or wondering if I was going to fall apart again. It was just me and the horses.

Tucker bumped his head against my hip in demand for a treat. "CJ is supposed to be the only one giving you treats. I only brought a carrot down for Ziggy." A huff and a nudge from Ziggy as well.

"You are demanding little things," I said, breaking the carrot I did have, in half, and laying my palms flat for them to take them.

"So, you are sneaking Tucker treats?" CJ teased, coming around the corner.

"Well, if you came down here more often and gave them to him, maybe he wouldn't have to beg from me," I said hotly.

"My little demon," He said, flicking me on the nose.

"Again, will you two please stop!" Logan said, but when I looked over Ziggy's back to where he was heading to his mare, Duchess, he was smiling.

"Anyway," CJ said as he smacked my ass just for good measure. "It will be nice to get off the boat. I'm getting antsy. There is only so much planning we can do before we just have to move."

I finished brushing Ziggy down and went to retrieve the rest of his tack. I threw the blanket over his back and then the saddle as there was an extra little rock from the boat and I had to adjust them a little bit more. I reached down and grabbed the cinch and threaded the strap through, humming quietly to myself. Ziggy huffed as I tapped his stomach a few times with my knee.

"Ziggy baby," I said to him. "It's only a saddle. Do you not want to get out of here?" When he huffed again, I murmured, "Then quite bloating your stomach. Stupid horse."

CJ chuckled behind me as he threw his saddle on Tucker. Heading back to the tack rack, I grabbed Ziggy's breastplate, which had a dragonfly at the juncture, and his bridle. Hooking the breastplate in place, I threw the reins over his neck and slid the halter off, securing it only around the neck.

Ziggy looked at me then, and then I wasn't seeing Ziggy, but me, wrapped in CJ's arms, black surrounding us.

Distantly, I heard a soft whiny, and then there were arms around my waist holding me up.

"Logan. Get Ziggy." CJ's voice said next to my ear. "Megan?" I started breathing really fast and subconsciously grabbed for CJ's arms.

Blackness surrounded us, but we were in... in a bubble? There was screaming and sizzling in my ears. White-hot light created a barrier between us and the blackness that swirled with red and skeletons. Realization hit me and panic bloomed in my chest. It was the tar that was Ansel's tar surrounding CJ and I. Then, the me I was watching, tipped her head to the side, and reached out as to touch it. Just before she did, the image cleared, and I was staring at CJ's face again.

"Breathe," CJ ordered. He held me as we sat on the ground. Slowly, he raised his hand to my face. "You here, babe?"

I blinked.

"Babe," he said a little more forcefully.

I blinked again. "Yeah. I'm here." I put my hand on his and grabbed it tight.

"What..." he blinked as realization hit him. "What did you see?"

My eyes opened wider in fear, and I shook my head as it all flooded back. My hands started shaking, and when CJ pulled me up from the ground, so that I could sit on my own, he took my face in his hands and put his forehead to mine.

"Megan. No more secrets." He whispered. "No matter what it is. There is nothing worse than what you already plan on doing. So, you have to tell me what you saw."

I shut my eyes, seeing nothing but it surrounding us. "It is worse." I croaked.

"Megan Isabel. Look at me," he demanded.

I slowly opened my eyes again, and he said again, "What did you see?"

"The tar."

"Okay." His voice was solid, but the word was drawn out like he was trying to understand but didn't.

"It was all around us. We were surrounded by it. You and me. In a bubble of some sorts, just completely surrounded by it," I pushed to him, not daring even to whisper the words as if that would prevent them from becoming real. *"There was sizzling, and screaming from all directions, and we were completely surrounded by it."*

CJ nodded, looked behind him to make sure that Logan wasn't within earshot and said, "Now breathe. You have to stop shaking, and that means you have to calm down enough to do that. Breathe."

In and out.

In and out.

Again and again, he did the movements with me until I stopped shaking.

One last deep breath, and I pushed, *"Why couldn't the first vision I see after breaking that curse from Ansel be of us sitting and eating dinner, or something mundane?"*

CJ huffed a laugh. "Megs, you never do things easy. Why would your visions be any different?" He reached up and ran his thumb along my cheek.

"What do you think?"

"I have no fucking clue." He said with a small giggle. "As Logan said, this is all a shit show. I'm not sure I even want to figure out any visions you may or may not get."

"The fact that I am seeing again is interesting, though," I mumbled.

He ran his hand through his hair and said, "We've been away from Vox for what, almost two months now? Who knows? Maybe that brain of yours has just healed enough to start tapping into your power again."

He stood, then reached down and helped me up.

"You good, Megs?" Logan said, holding Ziggy and Tucker.

I nodded and thanked him for keeping Ziggy calm for me, then went back to getting him ready to disembark.

I heard Logan ask CJ what happened, but CJ just waved him off, telling him I was just tired and dehydrated. It was the look on CJ's face that told him to drop it, even though he knew it was a bullshit statement.

CHAPTER 28

BELLSTAR WAS OPULENT AND full of entitlement. We sent word to meet with the Governor of the Territory, but he only deigned to speak to us when it was announced that Clarice was among the party. Ziggy had pulled on the reins and tried to rear up at the stables outside the Governor's office, and it took a lot of coddling before he would settle down. I really didn't like it here, either, and I had hardly spoken to anyone yet. I broke the tip off one of the carrots from my pack as I slid it to him as a bribe, promising him another carrot if he behaved.

As we walked in, I held onto CJ's hand tight, and were met by the Governor's assistant dressed in fine silks with dainty patterns swirling along the bottom edges. All the women in the room bowed at the hip, head down, and the men stood like they owned everything.

"Empress Clarice," a man with dark brown hair and wide almond-shaped eyes said. His skin was dry, and so yellow, he looked like someone who had a major case of jaundice. Everyone in this Angels forsaken town did.

Clarice just nodded, and I looked around, trying to look as bored as possible.

"Please come this way. His lordship is waiting in the gallery," he said and cursed a woman who was coming in with refreshments because she didn't move out of his way quick enough.

I turned to her and asked if she was alright.

"Yes, Lady," She said, refusing to meet my eyes, and when I bent lower to meet her eyes, they were black and blue. Both of them. Another bruise was still green against her cheek.

"Megan," CJ said quickly, feeling my temper rise.

"Who. Did. This?" I demanded of the girl.

Her eyes flicked to the assistant, then said, her voice soft and lilting in all the wrong places, "No, no one, Lady. I am a clumsy peasant."

I looked around and through the curtains of hair. I could see she was not the only one who had bruises in various stages of healing. My power surged to my fingers, and I glared at the Governor who had just walked in with his host of assistants.

Clarice was at my side in an instant. "Megan. If we push the issue, he will assassinate each one of them, just for being in this room and allowing the damage to be seen."

I took a few deep breaths, and I could almost see the smug satisfaction on his face as I did so. I knew Clarice saw it, too. I felt every muscle in her body go tense, and she quirked an eyebrow. Owen and CJ had moved their hands into easy reach of their syths, and Jean followed suit as Logan looked around at the woman in the room. He was noting the bruises as well.

"Governor, I would appreciate it if all your attendants would leave so that my family and yourself could have a private word, or two," she said, every ounce the Empress.

"We know, Logan." I pushed to him. His eyes flashed to mine, and I could see him restraining himself. I knew he didn't just see them, but his high school sweetheart, Rebecca, who

was constantly abused by her father at home. Logan had done everything right, but it couldn't save her. *"They are not Rebecca."*

"You are dismissed," he said, waving his hand and the woman flittered out on silent feet.

"Your men, too," she said sweetly in a way that did not leave room for argument.

"Who do you think you are, to tell a man where he can be?" one of his attendants said.

Wrong move. Clarice turned into that Gatekeeper of the Underworld. He was instantly covered in her dark power, and the room went silent. "I am Empress Clarice. I am Gatekeeper of the Underworld. I can say and do as I please. However, if you do not wish to leave, then don't."

She threw her hands out, and all eight attendants in that room were bound to the wall in Clarice's power. I glanced at her, and her eyes were black fire, her hair flitted in the wake of her power coming off her.

"How dare you treat my people this way?" the Governor said, jumping to his feet.

"How dare we?" Logan snapped, and I put my hand on his chest to stop him.

"Let me make something crystal fucking clear, Governor." My hands were bright with the electricity that weaved between my fingers as I brought them within inches of his throat. "One. You are going to tell us what you know of Ansel's movements."

"Nothing. I have heard rumors of him moving north through the Grasslands, but he has not touched my territory," he blurted, not daring to breathe too hard.

"Two. You will enact a law that states if a man ever lays a hand on a woman, in any faucet of disrespect, they will be executed on sight. You will not harm another woman in your or any other house," I said through my clenched teeth.

His eyes flared. "They are my property."

"Beings are not property," Logan growled. "Females are *not property.*"

"Finally, if I find out that any female is treated as beneath a male in any way, shape or form, your life is forfeit. Do I make myself clear?" I ground out, but when he didn't answer me, I fed my power a little more, and it crackled and sizzled as I brought my hand toward that spot between his legs. A large wet stain spread across the front of his pants, and I smirked.

"Understood," he said, and I pushed him back with my power so hard into the chair, it slid five feet backwards.

I turned on my heels, walked past Clarice, whose eyes had gone to gray mist again. What were the dead telling her? I couldn't stand to be here another minute, but just as I was about to walk out the door, Clarice said, "One additional condition. If you think to kill a single one of the women here, I will end you personally."

"I don't know what you are talking about," he said, trying to stand with any sort of dignity.

"As Gatekeeper to the Underworld, the dead tell me things. Be thankful that I don't kill you on the spot for what they tell me now." Her power pulsed as she said, "You want to rethink your answer?"

"I have never hurt or killed a woman in my house." The Governor said as he stood with that dark stain in front of him. There was something in the tone of his voice that screamed false.

"Rohanda Gadial." Her voice was harsh, and the power that fed through those two words was a promise of death. I felt it push against my bones, and I had the urge to kneel before her in supplication.

"I do not know who that is," he said, scanning the room.

"Are you to tell me that Rohanda Gadial wasn't brutally raped and then strung up by your bedsheets as you masturbated and released on her while she struggled for her last breaths?"

Mickel, CJ, Owen, and Logan's head whipped around to stare him down. The rage I saw on those boys' faces was not something I ever want to see again. I knew Logan was seeing Rebecca's father in that moment, and everything he wanted to do to avenge her death.

"What did you say?" Owen said, struggling for any sort of control. I so rarely saw his power manifest in a physical form, that the rainbow of colors gathering on his skin made me freeze in my place. Jean had just become a pillar of stone. She did not move from her spot, and every ounce of color had drained from her body.

"Clarice, could you say that again?" I asked carefully. I could not possibly have heard her right. Clarice would not, could not, make something like that up. She did not have it in her to make that up. I looked to Jean, whose face met mine, then we looked back at Clarice.

"Six months ago, the fine Governor Bronzewood here thought to have a party. Rohanda Gadial was one of the servants in this house. The Governor and two of his men..." She turned her head to the right to a couple who now also had dark stains across the front of their outfits, "thought to take Rohanda back to the Governor's Suite and rape her brutally. While I will not go into details of her assault, I will say they shoved more than their cocks in to her. That alone would have killed her. When they were finished with her, they strung her up on the rafters of the suite, by the Governor's own bedsheet, stood on the credenza, and masturbated until they finished on her. All while she struggled to breathe and eventually died. They let her hang like that for hours before they threw her body into the streets." Clarice enunciated each of those last words carefully, with a pulse of black mist off her hands.

Jean turned and vomited into a plant, and Logan soon followed. I was very glad that I had not eaten, but my stomach flipped and rolled all the same.

"Saefelae Stillcrag. Aubrey Gichir. Kelly Hagiul. Kilefae Graythorne." The names spilled from her lips as her head twitched. My visual swam, and all color leached from each of the boys' faces.

"Stop! I can't hear anymore!" Clarice yelled, clamping her hands over her ears.

I went to her and took her hands in mine, and said, "Clarice, we are here."

Her eyes opened, and they were living black flame. Tears streamed down her face, and I released her hands. With a flick of her wrist, there was a crack that went through the room as each one of those men's heads rolled off to the sides. She released them, sending them crashing to the floor.

It was Owen who spoke. "Mickel, please take Megan and Jean from the room. We will meet you in the Governor's office upstairs in a few hours. CJ, Logan, it is your decision whether you wish to stay."

I looked at CJ and his eyes were blazing at the Governor. *"Ceej?"* I pushed to him.

"Megan, please go with Mickel," he said firmly. I nodded. If I knew my husband. He would make whatever was going to happen last a very, very long time.

As Mickel took Jean's arm, I pushed to Ceej. *"Just make sure you and Logan can sleep at night with what you do in here. But if you torture him, kindly remove his dick and force it back to him for dinner."*

"Gladly." I heard CJ say through gritted teeth, not even pretending to lower his voice.

CHAPTER 29

MICKEL LED US TO the Governor's office, and once inside, Mickel put his fist through a wall. I looked at Jean and her eyes were big.

"Mickel!" Jean admonished.

He turned toward us, rage billowing off him. "I know exactly why Owen had me bring you two here. Don't think for one second I don't know what is occurring in there, and that I don't want to be there with them tearing him to pieces."

I just nodded and scanned the office, looking to distract myself. The utter opulence of the room was insane. The walls were slabs of white marble interspersed with gold pillars. The chairs and other furniture were a rich, plush deep green velvet. I walked up to the desk, which was made of shangwood, the hardest wood on the continent. The rich browns and pinks that weaved through the wood gave it a beautiful decorative touch. I shuffled through some papers on his desk, and after a few minutes, noticed the slight rise in the marble and sighed.

"Finally." I said, pushing the button just behind the desk disguised as decoration. I waited a minute before Julian's face showed on the LightCall.

"Governor, I really don't have time-" he started to say, before he froze. "Megan?"

There was a shrieking scream that filled the halls, and with a wave of Jean's hand, she silenced all sound from the room.

"I hope Owen amplifies those screams so that every male in this territory hears them," Mickel grumbled.

"Megan. What is going on in Bellstar?" Julian said.

"Julian, we are... relieving Bellstar of its current regime. Please send what Nalrin Guard you can spare immediately, along with a new representative, to oversee the restructuring of laws and social injustices in the territory," I said, using whatever professional voice I could muster at that point.

Julian looked at me for a moment and said, "Megan. What are you doing?"

"I told you. I am relieving Bellstar of its current regime. I will leave fifty of the Nalrin Guard, from the battalion that you stowed away on our river boat, here to keep order, while a new representative can oversee the adjustments that need to be made," I said, my fingernails digging into my palms.

"Megan. What is going on in Bellstar?" Julian said carefully, but more sternly.

So, I told him. When I was done, he was ghost white. He blinked, swallowed, and blinked again.

"Excuse me for a moment." Julian said as the screen went white and I waited two whole minutes before his face filled it again. Some of the color had returned to his face, but I suspected that he too had just lost whatever he had eaten last.

Taking a deep breath, he looked at me again and asked, "Who is in the room with you?"

"Mickel and Jean," I said, still using that professionality.

"And the others?"

I looked at Mickel and Jean. Professionality be damned. "They are indisposed at the moment."

"Megan," Julian said disapprovingly.

I just stared at him.

"What exactly are they doing at the moment?"

"Proving a point." When he narrowed his eyes, vehemently I added, "What needs to be done, Julian. Do not ask me for details. You can claim you don't know what happened to the Council. Plausible deniability, as they say."

He rubbed his hands over his face. "This is going to be a political problem, isn't it?"

"Probably, and I don't care." I shrugged, because I really didn't care if this was a political nightmare. "What they allow to happen here, and think that it's okay to do, is wrong. I understand cultural differences. I understand some cultures do not abide by my viewpoints. However, basic consideration for another's well-being is not something I am going to waiver on. Male, Female, Fairy, Human, Gukan, Ash'bani. No one gets to treat another being the way they treat females here. No being is property. No one deserves to be brutally raped and then ejaculated on as they struggle for their last breath. From the look on Clarice's face, that was only *one* of the stories she was told."

Mickel and Jean looked at each other, then back at me with a small sort of pride on their faces. Jean still looked a little green, and she held her lower stomach tighter.

"I agree, Megan." Julian said, trying to calm me down. "It is one of many reasons why the punishments for such acts are so strong here. I'm just thinking of the political fallout."

"I've told you from the beginning-"

"That politics aren't your thing," he said with a mischievous tilt to his lips, "I know."

"Yet, you still give me political power." I smirked back at him. "So, who is really at fault at here?"

"Governor Bronzewood. There is no doubt about that." Julian said sternly. "I have a few potential options for his replacement, but it will take a couple of days to decide, and then they have to get there."

"I can't stick around that long, Julian."

"No. Of course not," he said, thinking.

"As I said, I will leave fifty of the guard here. I don't think they will have much resistance. We could maybe lock down the town. It will make it easier for the Guard to keep things under wraps while you sort things out. Word will get around what happened to the Assistants and I'm sure many already can tell what is happening to the *fine* Governor now. Word will get out."

Julian just looked at me for a long moment. There was reprimand, stress, distress, and a hint of pride in his face. Finally, he said, "Stay safe, Megan."

I nodded, and the call was disconnected.

"Well, that went better than I expected," I said, leaning back in the chair.

"Glad it was you who called Julian. The rest of us would have been eaten alive." Mickel said, uncrossing his arms and sitting on the couch opposite the desk. He put his elbows on his knees and jerked his head to Jean to come and sit down.

She was still white as a ghost. When she came to sit down, Mickel pulled her close and held her as she wept.

An hour had passed before I cracked the door open and took half a step outside the threshold beyond the silencing incantation. Broken, cracking screams filled my ears. He had blown out his vocal chords. Good.

I walked out to the balcony and saw blood everywhere. They had very slowly skinned him alive. I saw him pass out, but with a wave of her hand, Clarice brought him back from his escape. She wasn't going to let him just go unconscious as they did this. The boys helped in whatever way they could. CJ had taken my suggestion literally, and the Governor no longer had that portion of his body anymore. There was a part of me that smiled at that.

CJ, sensing me on the balcony, turned his head. There was hate and rage in those eyes, the like I had never seen.

"You okay?" I pushed.

He nodded and jerked his head back toward the office. He didn't want me to see this.

"I need to," I pushed.

He sighed, but then I looked at Logan. He had one of CJ's syths in his hand and was slowly cutting a section of the inside of his leg right next to the main artery. The look on Logan's face was not one I would easily forget. There was so much rage, heartache, but yet a calmness about him. I studied him for a long moment and wondered if this was something he had dreamed of doing to Rebecca's father for so long, that it was almost cathartic for him.

The Governor's head was between Owen's hands now, and the rainbow of colors that bounced between his palms had me wondering what exactly Owen was doing. After watching for a moment longer, I decided I didn't want to know.

I could tell that CJ hadn't taken his gaze off mine, and when I looked at him again, I gave him a feral smile, turned, and went back into the Governor's office, and shut the door.

Owen was working through a rage that stemmed from something else, and Clarice, well, I suspected she was as well. I knew CJ would dump it in a bucket in his brain and leave it there. I was very concerned about Logan, though. Logan was the one who would bring it back to remember on repeat.

I closed the door, and said, "We should stay in here until they come to us."

Mickel gave me a knowing look and Jean finally said, "Megan. Please do not think me weak for not being able to handle this."

"Why would I?" I asked. "Even Logan threw up. Hell, rage still fills me at what that woman went through, and I'm sure Clarice heard many more accounts. What I saw them doing? He deserves it. Do I do think we may have crossed a line here? Yeah, but do I think relieving him of his manhood and feeding it back to him is still appropriate? Abso-fucking-lutly!"

Jean and Mickel looked at each other shocked, and then Jean said, "Damn, Megan. That's harsh, even for you."

"Morally gray, bordering on dark gray," I said, gesturing to myself. "I cannot allow a person to treat another being like that. I was serious when I told Julian I didn't care about race or gender. The basic right of any being should be the right of safety. That is not something that should be questioned. Ever. Every person should have the right to feel safe. To walk down the street and not wonder if they are going to be beaten because of their race, skin color, sexual orientation, or how they dress."

"It's a fight in every dimension." Jean said.

"I know. I didn't lie when I told Julian that I understand there are cultural differences in how beings are treated," I said quietly. "Still, don't feel bad about throwing up. If there had been anything in my stomach, I likely would have lost it as well. May have lost it again, at what I saw them doing out there."

Jean looked at Mickel with pleading eyes. Mickel took a deep breath and said, "It's not that. A long time ago, when we were much younger, Jean, Owen, and I were on a mission on an island to the northeast of here. Jean and Owen were captured. It took days to find where they were being held. When I finally got to Jean, she had been,—" His throat bobbed.

"Gang raped," she said quietly when Mickel couldn't finish his sentence.

"Brutally. So, I can envision exactly what that asshole had done to that servant. Once I got Jean out and got her somewhere safe, I went back for Owen. By the time I finally reached him, he was scheduled for execution the next morning and he had given up. He didn't think we would come for him." Mickel said softly, staring at the floor. "But I hauled his ass out of there, met up with Jean, and made a straight haul back to Nalrin."

"Once the Physicians in Nalrin could look at me, I was told the damage done to my insides from those events left me barren. It's why Owen and I never had kids," she said, looking up at me with tears in her eyes.

There was nothing I could say to that. 'I'm sorry' didn't feel like the right words, and I didn't think they were what she wanted to hear, anyway. She met my eyes, and I hoped that mine conveyed what I was feeling for her. Not pity per se, but a sadness and anger at her having to go through that and the aftermath of the trauma.

We sat in silence after that for another hour and a half. I pulled my syth out and played with it in my hands until there was a soft knock on the door. My power jumped to my fingers and flowed down my syth. I opened the door. Clarice was standing there covered in blood, but her face was clear.

"It's over," she said, then sighed. "We should probably contact Julian and ask him to send a new representation for the territory."

"Already done," I said, looking behind her for the boys.

"They are… cleaning up," she said carefully and put her hand on my arm.

"I'll go help." Mickel said and stalked out of the room before anyone could object.

Clarice came in and crouched in front of Jean. She looked her over, and then just pulled her into a tight hug.

Another forty-five minutes went by before the boys came into the office. They had obviously gone to change clothes.

"Took a shower too, huh?" I asked CJ as I pulled him close. He wrapped his arms around me, and I could feel his heartbeat slow to a more regular beat.

"Spit bathed it in the bathroom and changed clothes," he said. "I, I didn't want you to see me covered in that much blood."

"I saw what you were doing. I know how much there was." I held him close. He just nodded, but I could tell he was struggling with what had occurred.

I looked over at Owen and Logan, and they looked like they had done the same thing. Trying to lighten the mood, I said, "Look a bit like a Carrie prom?"

A smile from CJ and Logan who said, "Yeah. I know I will remember that experience for the rest of my life, but is it wrong that I enjoyed it? I know that it was wrong to take it that far. I know I saw her father. I know that everything we just did was ethically wrong. I know that we all dug into our own rage to do what we did, but…"

Owen was just standing there, watching Jean. She hadn't so much as turned around when they came in. Slowly, he walked over there, and they had a whispered conversation. Then Jean threw her arms around him.

"As I told CJ when I walked out of that room, just make sure you can live with yourself afterwards."

Logan nodded and said stood up a bit straighter, "I can. I may go to the Underworlds deepest depths for what I did, but I can."

"And you?" I pushed to CJ. He nodded his head and gave me a quick kiss on the top of mine.

"Okay then. Now that we all know, we will sleep fine tonight, the deepest depths of the Underworld aside," I said as Clarice's eyes had a bit of that black flame in them again, "Where is Mickel?"

"He helped us clean up downstairs and then said he needed to give the Guard some orders."

"Alright," I said, then caught them up on my discussion with Julian and while they all agreed they wanted to be a fly on the wall for that discussion, they understood why I did it immediately.

The LightCall bell chimed, and I went to answer it.

"Bellstar's New Management. How may I assist you today?" I answered in my best customer service voice. CJ and Logan bellowed out in laughter, and it was such a pure sound that I couldn't help but smile.

"Megan," Julian chastised.

"What?"

Julian sighed dramatically and leveled a look at me before launching in. "Ava Satgier was already halfway there, heading to a vacation spot in the ice. She will be there in a week. Tell the Guard you are keeping in Bellstar, and to just hold tight."

I paused before saying anything. "Julian, is it a good idea to send a female to run the territory, all things considering?"

It was Owen who said, "Ava's husband is Nolas Stagier." The name rang a bell, but I couldn't place it.

"The people of Bellstar will not challenge her nor him. He will be there in a month to solidify things, but the people of the region know of the Stagiers. She can handle them." Julian said.

"Okay. Story for another time, then." I said, "Thank you, Julian."

He nodded, and with a voice that was full of concern, said, "Come home safe, Megan. I also received word your package will arrive in Leavenhollow Port. Safe travels." Before the line went black.

Mickel had organized the fifty Nalrin Guard to stay in Bellstar and advised them that the Stagiers would be there within the month. It didn't take much to get the townspeople to abide by a strict lockdown until further notice. Word had spread fast. Mickel gave declarations regarding the treatment of woman in the town, and that the Governor was no longer in control.

The next morning, we loaded our belongings on the horses, and with the remaining fifty Nalrin Guard, we turned our back on Bellstar and headed over the Midstrada Mountains.

CHAPTER 30

THE PASS OVER THE Midstrada Mountains was wide and well-traveled, allowing us to make better time than I thought we were going to with the herd of guards behind us. It was a two-day trip over the pass, and we were planning on stopping in Houndmire, at the summit, overnight. I thought I smelled something burning, but didn't see any smoke for miles, and thought maybe I was imagining it. Only it kept getting worse the closer we got to the summit. We were maybe a mile from the town when I once again got a whiff of burned tar. I turned wide-eyed to CJ just as his nostrils flared with recognition, and horror crossed his face.

"*Stay with me,*" I pushed toward him. Putting my heels to Ziggy, we took off toward the town. I had forgotten how fast Ziggy could be when I let him open up. If it hadn't been for the horror I knew I would find in Houndmire, I would have whooped with excitement. CJ caught up to me and I met his eyes, which were filled with an exhilaration I hadn't seen from him in a long time. I looked behind me and saw the others galloping behind us.

"Come on, Ziggy," I said and put my heels to his side again. Ziggy burst up the gentle slope, and when I could see the archway to town, I had to cover my nose and pull him to a stop. The town was half destroyed by the same tar that had taken Alnwick and many others along the way.

"Fuck," CJ said, letting the word draw out as he looked around.

"Ceej, do you see what I see?" I scanned the town, and it just didn't make sense. "Ansel picked and chose which buildings to go after. The Bakery. The Bookstore. The Confectionery. The General Store. The Apothecary. All gone."

"But he left the news printer, government building, stables, and hotel?" CJ's face cleared in realization. "He left everything they would need to get the word out about him being here."

I dismounted and walked Ziggy over to the stables and was met with a hardy stout man with a long bushy beard. His brown hair was shaved along the sides, and long braids ran across the top in two rows. "Ma'Lady. What can I do ya fir?" he said with a deep voice.

"How many horses can you stable?" I jerked my head to the back of the building. There were a few large carts with supplies in them, and eight horses stabled inside.

"We be a main pass here, ma'lady," he scratched his beard and thought. "How many ye get? I got a pasture out back."

"There are about fifty Nalrin Guard who will be here soon, plus my family." I smiled sweetly when his eyes widened. "About sixty?"

"As I said ma'lady. I got a pasture out back if you don't mind them in there. Can put the soldiers out there too, iffin they no mind roughing it ta'night." he said, then jerked his chin to the hotel. "Candy's only got 'bout ten rooms. Few'a damaged when that came throa.'"

"Much appreciated, sir." I paid him for his services.

My family arrived about then, and I told them about the arrangement's I made with the stable keeper and Mickel said he would let the Commander's know when they arrived.

"I'll go over to the hotel and get us a few rooms for the night," Owen said and headed toward the hotel, Jean's hand tight in his. My heart hurt for them. So many memories had been dredged up in the last day.

"I'll work on unpacking our packs, then," Logan said carefully. "Help me, Cor?"

"Yeah. Sure," CJ said, but he hesitated for a moment, looking at me.

"Spend some with him. He is faking it well," I pushed to him, and Clarice looped her arm through mine at the elbow and I said, "Great. It gives me some Clarice time."

"What do the dead say?" I asked her carefully. Her eyes have had that glazed look since she went through the archway.

"Nothing," she said, "That is what is so disconcerting. You would think that I would hear something. *Someone* would have died after he left, but there is nothing. It's totally silent. Not to mention if I've counted the dates right, today is Hailsim. So, I should hear the dead."

"Hailsim? Why does that sound familiar?"

Clarice looked at me and smiled. "We crammed your head full of all sorts of things. I don't expect you to remember everything."

"Thanks, but what is Hailsim?"

"Back in Therth and throughout Obsecuritan, when the weather starts to get colder and everything starts to go from light grays to dark gray and black?" I nodded at her. "The spirits come out from the Underworld for one night and dance. Before you ask, no, you won't be able to communicate with Lindy if she is there, but you *might*, emphasis on the might Megan, get to dance with her in the gardens. Again, if she ends up in the Underworld. Next year, we will work it out."

"If I live through this," I said under my breath, but wrinkled my nose. "Wish I could at least get somewhat used to the smell, though."

"Burning flesh," she sighed. "There are bits of tar still here and there, so it won't leave until they can dispose of it. Not sure how they are going to do that, though."

The courtyard was a large open space, and in the dead center was a well with a bucket hanging. There were remnants of the tar around the base of it, but it didn't seem to touch the well itself. We stood there studying it for a moment, when Clarice said, "What he destroyed in this town versus what he didn't, seems random at first, but it isn't."

"CJ said the same thing. Said that Ansel left what they would need to spread word of where he was." I took a deep breath and then stared down the well. "At least we know he has come north. He's moving so fast, though. So much faster than we are. The question is, did he continue north across the mountain, or is he heading for Millmore? Will he be at the port?"

"He's erratic. There are times that his movements are clearly methodical, and then he goes and does something like randomly hit a pass-through town?" Clarice said. "I wish I knew how he was moving. It hadn't been long when he was in Nalrin, and from the looks of it, it's only been a few days since he hit here. Where is he going next? Is it Ansel, or does he have others who are executing his orders?"

I bent down and looked at the tar that was at the base of the well, and it didn't look the same. It almost looked like normal tar. I picked up a stick and poked at it. Clarice watched with interest as I poked it again, and it just squished under the pressure. She sent a wave of her power at it, and it just disappeared.

I blinked and looked at her. "It's not Ansel's tar." Clarice mumbled. "It just evaporated. It didn't scream. It didn't fight back."

"Are you sure? Maybe because he isn't here to control it, there is no substance, so it would dissipate."

"No." Her eyes were wide. "When we were at Nalrin, Julian and I went out to study some of the pieces. I was trying to see if there was a weakness to it. To see if there was something I could pull from the Underworld to stop it. And before you give me any lecture, I know what I'm saying, and I would have discussed it with everyone first."

I still gave her a look, and she smiled before continuing. "If my power could manipulate it, then maybe I could save someone when we come up against him. When I tried to use my power against it, it screamed, and it echoed into the ether of the Underworld. Every ounce of my being rebelled against the material. I couldn't destroy it with any known spell or method of my power."

Her eyes looked at where there was another batch of tar on the well and flung a burst of her power toward it. It vanished like it was nothing more than dust in the wind.

"Yet, this just poofs?"

She simply nodded. "I sent my power out in a wave over the courtyard, willing it all to vanish, and it just rose like ashes and vanished into the air."

"Someone attacked the village and staged it to look like Ansel had done it? But why?"

"Someone could be working with Ansel."

I shook my head. "We have seen no evidence anywhere, or from anyone, that he is working with someone else, or that someone is helping him out. I have no doubt there are beings feeding him information, but..."

"I understand."

I turned and leaned on the edge of the well and let my thoughts wander into the dark. At first, I thought it was just that it was very, very deep, but something flickered in it. It was distant, and yet not. There was a large open cathedral room, a shimmer, and a black crystal in a box, and a piece of paper with my name on it.

"Megan?" I heard distantly.

Shimmer.

I felt the edge of the well under my hands and I held on tight. The world tilted, pressure on my arm and there were strong arms around me.

"Megan," someone commanded.

I stood on a cliff's edge. CJ next to me, talking. A large expanse of grass, and a block of black moving toward us. The other me looked down to a small town at the base of the mountain before it faded out to Clarice's face.

"Megan. Look at me." Clarice's hands were on both sides of my face, as she tried to get me to come back.

I blinked and blinked again. CJ was holding me from behind. I blinked again and shook my head.

"I'm okay," I said, trying to free my arms from CJ's grip. "Really, Ceej. I'm okay. I'm here."

"What the Underworld, Megan." Clarice's voice was fueled by panic. "One second we are talking, the next you start tipping forward into the well. I caught your arm to keep you from going all the way over, but CJ got there... Angels, Megan. Why didn't you tell us your visions had come back?" she said as she realized what had happened.

"I've only had one other one since Vox." I rubbed my temples. "It didn't have to do with anyone else, so I didn't say anything."

I felt CJ tense behind me. *"Don't say a fucking word. They don't need to know,"* I pushed to him.

Clarice eyed me. "I call bullshit on that one, considering how CJ just reacted. Who else was there with you when you had it?"

"CJ, Logan and I were getting the horses ready to disembark at Bellstar," I said, keeping my voice down.

"You had a vision two days ago, and you didn't tell anyone." Clarice said, eerily calm. I made myself look at her, and there was fury on her face. "Two days ago, Megan."

"Yes. Yes, I did." I met her eyes. "And you know what? It sucked. Just as much as this one. And I didn't tell you about it because it didn't have anyone else in it. It was mine to sort out, not the family."

"Megan." CJ was trying to calm me, but I was having none of it.

"No, Ceej. They don't need to know."

"Need to know what?" Logan said as he and Mickel walked up.

Clarice turned on him and he jumped back, eyes wide, his arms going up to protect himself. "You knew?"

"Knew what?" Logan was completely confused.

"You knew Megan started having visions again?" Her anger simmering down a bit.

"She had one, yeah." Logan said. "She didn't tell you?"

"No." Mickel and Clarice said in unison.

CJ helped me to my feet, and his eyes were filled with nothing but concern and weariness. I felt tears well up in my eyes before I pushed to him. *"I'm not telling them about what I saw. I will not tell them how we die. I will not tell them that this might all be a false hope. I will not tell them."*

He nodded, but then said, "She had a vision when we were prepping the horses. What she saw was for her and I, and we will keep it that way. Get. Over. It." He looked at each of them with each word.

"But," I said, trying to placate the protectors in front of me. "They are not like they used to be. They used to be all fuzzy openings and smooth transitions, and I could see things play out exactly how they were going to happen. They aren't like that now, at least these two were not like that. I was outside of myself. Watching me from somewhere above. I was watching CJ and I do these things, and there was no conversation. There was no sound."

"Oh." Clarice tipped her head to the side as she processed everything that was said and not said.

"Look, I get you want to know what might happen, but these are not anything to help us." I said and when Clarice lightly glared at me, "Don't look at me like that. We don't ask you what all your super gatekeeper powers can do. Yes, I know you are still learning and sorting them out yourself. I know. I don't hound you for it, because it is yours to deal with. You know we are here for you if you want it, but we also know that you want to sort it yourself."

She smiled. "I'm sorry."

"It's fine. I mean, in the last year alone, we've been under a bit of stress, if you think about it," I said, shrugging like it was nothing at all.

"A bit of stress?" Logan blurted, astonished. "You call planning a wedding, getting married, helping your friend through her father's death, watching that friend not only become the most powerful, badass bitch there is but also become Empress of the Underworld, get married herself, watch your other best friend die, have to tell your brother-in-law that the love of his life was murdered by your father, and go on a quest for a *maybe* relic in the rare hope that it could kill said father... a bit of stress?"

All of us just looked at Logan.

"Yes," CJ said beside me. "Sounds like a normal year around here."

Logan looked at his brother as the rest of us just shrugged and agreed with him. "Well, fuck. I may need to start taking Dad's high blood pressure meds."

"Come on, let's get inside. I'm hungry," Mickel said, heading toward the hotel with fancy faded painting above the porch that said, "*Candy's*".

CHAPTER 31

THAT NIGHT, WE SHARED a room with Logan and stayed up talking like we had when we were kids. It was around two in the morning when we finally laid down and got some sleep. Now, the sun was just barely appearing in the sky, and CJ pulled me close. I moaned softly at the movement and heard Logan say, "Shut up, Megan."

My eyes flew open, and I was awake like someone had dumped cold water on me. Logan was pulling a syth out of the belt under his bed, and CJ had his in his hand at my waist. Completely charged up, I pushed, *"What is it?"*

CJ's voice was barely a whisper, but still seemed too loud. "What do you hear?"

I strained, but I didn't hear anything. I shook my head and looked at Logan. He raised an eyebrow at me, and I listened again.

I heard nothing. Absolutely, nothing. No birds, no sounds of servants working in the kitchen downstairs, not the sound of others moving, not even the sound of the horses across the courtyard. I moved to get up and look outside, but CJ's arm was tight around me. I stroked my hand against it in silent request, and he loosened it, but felt his charge wrap around me.

I crouched and, as quietly as possible, moved toward the window. At first, I didn't see anything unusual, but when I looked over toward the stables, it wasn't the pasture behind that caught my eye, but a swarm of flapping black heading straight for town. Memory flashes of CJ hovering over me on a shale cliff edge, and Clarice...

"Clarice!" I pushed to both CJ and Logan.

Not caring how much noise I made, I pulled a syth from my belt that was hanging over the edge of the bed and ran toward her room. Barging in, I saw her laying on the bed, encompassed in her power, staring at the ceiling.

"Clarice," I pushed to her, and there was a dark pulse of power against my mind. *"Fuck off. Listen to me. Breathe and look at me."*

She blinked.

I sighed in relief and then said, "There are Nocturnes headed straight for us. I need your help. We need you."

"Megan?" Clarice whispered, then her head cocked to the side. A sly smile crossed her face, and there was a wave of her dark power that pulsed three times in rapid succession before she sat straight up. She looked at me for a moment, her eyes slowly clearing.

"I hate nightmares." She rubbed her eyes before knitting her eyebrows together, and felt CJ and Logan embers behind me, syths in hand.

Her eyes went distant, then her head whipped around to look at the window, seeing the Nocturnes heading toward us. "Get everyone to stay inside." She threw some pants on, slid her feet into her shoes before rifling through her pack to pull a hair tie out. Clarice was a blur of motion as she braided her hair, stormed out the door and stalked downstairs.

As she emerged from the hallway, the Commanders were instantly at attention. Without so much as a glance at them, she barked orders for all the soldiers to remain perfectly still until released by her. Shouts rang out to men with the horses, and within moments, every soldier on that field was sitting on their knees and not moving. A soft, deep orange glow covered the pasture, and you could no longer hear or see the army stationed there.

She strode for the center of that courtyard and stopped next to the well and watching the Nocturnes hover above that field. Her ember pulsed, and a soft dust–like blackness burst from her and when it cleared, a black crown sat on her head, much like the one placed there during her coronation. The woman standing there was not my friend, but the Empress of Obsecuritan and Gatekeeper of the Underworld. I felt her power pulse against my bones, and I smirked, looking up to the largest of the Nocturnes.

A barked sound came from the largest of the Nocturnes as it swooped down and circled the Courtyard. It was so much more gruesome up close; the body of a raven, with hoofed feet and a snout nose, it was covered in feathers that were ratted and half plucked. It crashed down in front of her and stood there snarling. Clarice didn't flinch an inch.

"I command you to return to the Underworld," Clarice ordered.

The Nocturne's head twitched side to side, and then somehow clearly said, "You do not command us, Princess. The dark one pulls our darkness to battle and glory."

Clarice's power pulsed as she said again, "I command you to return to the Underworld."

Its head cocked to the side again, but I saw the strain on the ones in the sky as they fought the order. "Darkness commands us. Not you, Princess of the House of Heros."

"I am the darkness. I am Empress Clarice of the House of Heros. I am Gatekeeper to the Underworld and Commander of all darkness that reigns within." I didn't recognize that voice as coming from Clarice, but I felt it in my bones. The ground shuddered underneath us as the well opened up and became a pit of swirling black. Her hands balled into fists, as she said, "I command you to return to the Underworld."

"You do not control us, Empress of the House of Heros," it said again, but twitched slightly.

"Yeah, yeah, yeah," I said, stepping forward as Clarice pulled more of her power to the surface. "We heard you the first time. Since you deny the truth before your very eyes, who do you think rules over you?"

"The Dark One. He came to us with pure dark in his soul. He came and released us to fight and take over this world." The Nocturne cocked its head to the other side as it studied me. "You are pieces of him."

"Who else did he release from the Underworld?" I commanded. Clarice was almost vibrating with her power now. I could feel the pull against my bones. It called for total submission.

"Us and all Ja'Nee." His voice was full of delight. "We are to take and consume all we want. Pick the very marrow from your bones—" His voice was cut off as Clarice's power pulled at him. His eyes widened.

"You talk too much," Clarice said, wind now circling the area just as it had that day in Therth. "Now, I am going to say this one last time. I command you back to the Underworld."

When they made no movement, there was a heavy weight that settled over the town, forcing me to my knees. I felt CJ's charge hit me like a wave and dissipate against Clarice's power. Nocturnes plummeted from the sky and crashed into the courtyard.

Clarice was speaking in that tone that demanded obedience again, but I didn't hear the words. There was only that void. That command to return to the Underworld. It was if there were ropes wrapped around my bones as those commands were said. I fought against it, digging my heels in, and rejecting the command to jump into that the well.

I stared at the void, and I could swear I could hear it call to me. It sang of no pain, love, happiness, and freedom from of the responsibilities of this world. Freedom from the weight of this world. I stared into it.

The command to return to the Underworld pushed and pushed harder against my bones. Every cell in my body responded to it. It was a musical hypnotizing song against my very essence.

You wouldn't have to die.

You could live in the Underworld.

Free from the responsibilities of saving Nalsar.

Free from the pitying looks of your family, who know you will have to die, anyway.

You could end it now.

Come.

Come into my dark embrace.

Come into my comforting embrace

Come into my warmth.

I shall hold you and protect you.

I felt my body move to comply, but there was another surge of command, but not from Clarice. It came from behind me. Slowly, so very slowly, I turned my head toward that command to see an ember filled with lightning surge toward me.

A more forceful pull against my bones and I moved toward the darkness again but froze. Unable to move.

Lightning surrounded me, burned brightly, and tackled me to the ground, pinning me to that spot.

I thrashed and froze again as that lightning hit my chest.

Lips on mine.

Another strike to the chest.

Warmth filled me. Pure loving warmth broke through that dark song in my head, releasing the pressure against my bones. I blinked and looked up to where CJ was pinning me to the ground. I blinked again.

Distantly, I heard Clarice, in that powerful Empress voice, give commands in a language almost older than time itself. A wall of power barreled into us and floated harmlessly over the top of CJ and his lightning ember above me. Familiar and calm. My power had put us in a protective bubble.

"Clarice!" I panicked and swung my head around to look at her.

"Don't you fucking dare to move, Megan Isabel Mathewson." CJ's voice was fierce, and the pure command in it only allowed enough movement for breath to flow in and out of my lungs. I gave him a side glance, and his eyes were a rage of thunderstorms.

I growled at him in frustration. The only way I knew how to convey my anger at him using that charge order on me.

"Growl all you fucking want. Now shut up and do not move," CJ said. "There will be plenty of time for that argument, and trust me, there *will* be yelling."

I looked back toward Clarice and saw Nocturnes split between heeding her command to return and ignoring it, choosing to surge toward her in attack instead. Clarice dealt with them easily by wrapping them in her power and flinging them into the void.

When it was down to just her and the largest, he snarled, "The Dark One will find you. He makes his way—" then his head fell to the ground as Clarice flung the rest of his body into the void.

As it closed, she took a few deep breaths, pulled her power back into herself. Slowly, she turned toward us and, with tears flowing down her face, said, "I'm sorry, CJ."

Her power popped away, and she crumbled to the ground.

CHAPTER 32

"I CAN'T BELIEVE YOU did that, Ceej," I growled at him for the hundredth time, since we got back to our room. Logan had made himself scarce by just staying downstairs and having a drink with Mickel as I stormed upstairs, CJ close on my heels. We spent a long time just staring at each other before either of us spoke.

"Megan Isabel," He had said carefully.

"Don't you even go there, Cory James Mathewson." I threw a string of my power at him. CJ let out a pained grunt behind me, and I heard him miss a step behind me. I couldn't help the small smile that crossed my lips. I hope it stung like a bitch.

"I don't know what Clarice was doing, or why you were so affected by it, but you were about to jump into a black swirling void that appeared over the well!"

"You don't know what it was like," I muttered as I pulled my syth out and twirled it in my hands. I needed something to do with my hands. Sitting here idle was not working for me. There were so many emotions bouncing around in my head I had to keep moving, doing anything other than just sit in a room with a man I both loved with every part of me, and wanted shred to pieces in rage right now.

"Don't you forget, Megan, *I know* how it felt." His words came through his teeth in frustration. "Don't you forget I have that ability, too."

I rolled my eyes and tightened my grip on my syth, desperately trying to convince myself not to slit his throat in that moment. "How can I? I'm constantly checking my fucking emotions, because I know you can feel them. I don't want you to worry or freak out any more than you already do."

"Worry? Worry?" He stood and threw his hands up in the air. "Worry was the farthest thing from my mind today, Megs. I felt every ounce of your fear, relief, and *want* to go into that void."

My eyes snapped to his as I realized just how much he was in tune to every aspect of my emotions. No one should know how much I wanted to disappear into that blackness.

"How dare you," CJ said, taking a step toward me with a single finger extended in my direction.

A second later, I had him pushed against the wall, forearm across the upper portion of his chest, and my syth at his throat. His gaze hadn't softened, and anger now flared in his eyes.

"How dare I? How dare I *what*, Ceej? How dare I want the pain, stress, and constant fear to be over? How dare I want to have a day where the weight of the world isn't literally on my fucking shoulders? How dare I want a moment of fucking peace?"

The door swung open, and I threw my syth at whoever it was that had come in.

"Oh, fuck!" was all I heard, as I turned to see Logan against the doorjamb and my syth sticking from the door a few inches from his face.

"What in the fuck do you want, Logan?" I spit out through my clenched teeth, glaring at my brother-in-law.

"Well, um, if you are done ripping my brother to pieces..." His eyes flicked to CJ, and then back at me, "or if you're at a place where you can please pause for a moment, Clarice is asking to speak to you."

That released my anger like a popped balloon. I released CJ with a shove and stomped out of the room, pausing at the door just long enough to pull my syth out of the wood. As I stepped into the hallway, I heard Logan. "Dude. What did you do?"

"I saved her fucking life."

"I have a headache," Clarice said, sitting on the edge of the bed with her head in her hands. Jean rubbed her back and Owen got up to get something for her to take. She had been sleeping for the last three and a half hours, and during that time, CJ and I had indeed had that screaming match. When we heard Clarice was stirring, we set it aside for the moment, and came to check in on her.

Leaning into the furthest corner from everyone else, arms crossed, I stared CJ down from across the room. Mickel stood guard at the door, and Logan was sitting cross-legged on the bed opposite Clarice. Not taking my eyes off CJ, because I was indeed still extraordinarily pissed that he had used that charge on me, I asked Clarice, "How are you able to use so much of your power far away from Therth?"

"I was wondering the same thing, actually." Jean said in a calm, soothing voice. "You had once told us that the further you were from Therth, the weaker your powers were."

"That was not a weak display of power." Logan said, half in awe, half in fear.

Owen walked in and handed her the pain meds and a cup of water. She threw the pills back and downed the water in a quick motion. "It's different now," she whispered. Clarice was refusing to look in my direction and went back to rubbing her temples.

"Explain," I demanded.

Her eyes snapped up to mine, and I refused to avert my eyes. Clarice narrowed her eyes at me before saying, "It's different because now I'm Empress. I have total control of the darkness of the Underworld, so I could easily tap into that power, to do what I just did out there today. So, *I* can ensure that any creatures that are not supposed to be in this world are sent back. Like. I. Did. Today."

"Megan, don't take it out on Clarice," Mickel said. "If it were not for her, we would all be dead right now."

It was CJ that Clarice looked to next, and I met his eyes again. "I am sorry, CJ," Clarice said.

"Why do you keep apologizing to me? What could you have possibly done that you feel you need to ask for my forgiveness for?" CJ said with a long breath, pulling his eyes from mine to look at her. "Please, just tell me what happened out there?"

"The Ash'bani blood in my veins responded to her command," I said when Clarice looked at me, guilt all over her face. "The darkness in that Ash'bani blood responded to her command to return to the Underworld. Right?"

She nodded. "That or the darkness from when Noctulanar fed on your blood, but your Ash'bani heritage is more likely the culprit."

"Why didn't any of the rest of us feel it though?" Owen asked.

"Sangra and humans don't have the same sort of darkness that those born in Obsecuritan do. That darkness is pulled straight from the Underworld." Shaking her head, she continued, "Megan, if I thought you would have felt the command, or it would have been that strong, I would not have pulled that power while you were in that courtyard."

"Luckily, she has an Angel's Blessed Vernadali to save her ass." Logan's voice was laced with pride for his brother.

The room went stone cold silent. I could feel CJ's eyes on me. I could feel everyone's eyes on me, but I stared at a spot on the wall, unable to look at any of them.

Logan's eyes darted around the room. "What did I say?"

"Do any of you know what it is like to be under that kind of restraint?" I whispered, staring at a spot on the wall. No one answered, so I continued. "You have your mind, but your body suddenly is not your own. It acts as if there is someone else controlling it, because there is. As he laid on top of me out there, commanding me not to move, I couldn't even turn my head or open mouth to yell at him. I could barely move enough to allow my chest to rise and fall. I was a physical puppet."

"Megan, I fucked up. I'm sorry. I didn't realize," Logan said in a way that made my heart crack.

My eyes shifted back to CJ. I could tell he understood. "Not being able to do something of my own accord? To not even be able to twitch my fingers? To not even be able to acknowledge more than in grunts, what I knew was happening to me?" I croaked as tears fell. I even saw Clarice flinch slightly at that.

His throat bobbed. "Megs," He swallowed hard again. "I can't apologize for using it today."

"I know," I said, through the ball of knots in my throat.

I could see the others looking between us. Mickel opened his mouth to say something, but Owen elbowed him and gave him a short shake of the head.

"Megan, if you could have seen how I saw you out there. If you could have felt what I felt from you today." CJ's throat bobbed again as he struggled to control his emotions. "I won't apologize for using what power I have to save your *life*." My eyes narrowed just slightly, before he said through gritted teeth, "You moved to go into that void, and there was no way I was going to stand by and all that to happen. So, I say again, I will not apologize for using my Vernadali power to save your fucking life."

"Wait. What do you mean, what you *felt* from her today?" Logan asked his brother carefully.

CJ swallowed, and I saw a tear slowly fall down his cheek. It was Mickel who answered, "Vernadali, when they receive their assignment, have an emotional bond created with their Charge. It is to help in protecting them. So even if they are separated, the

Vernadali will know if their Charge is in danger and can come help them. Only, with CJ…"

"It's so much stronger," Logan said understanding, then a moment later, "Because of their relationship or because he is Angels Blessed?"

"*THAT* Logan is the great question of the ages," Mickel said, "One of which we will probably never know the answer."

"I'll go down and pay for another night," I said, looking out the window. "We've lost half a day, and we need all the daylight we can get tomorrow. That side of the mountain is too dangerous without daylight. The boat won't leave until we get there, but I don't want to stop halfway down the pass tonight. I'd rather let Clarice regain her strength before we head out."

No one said anything as I headed out the door. I indeed paid for another night and sent a message to Julian through the messenger's office that we were staying another night, and to ensure any forces that were meeting with us in Millmore were informed of the delay. I stood at the counter and sent one more message out before handing it to the steward, whose eyes narrowed before saying, "Are you sure, Lady Megan?"

I nodded, and he turned to send the message. Once all of the tabs had been paid in town, I walked out to an outcropping overlooking the hills that spread north. Finding a flat spot, I sat there staring out over the hills and valleys in the Midstrada Mountains.

I pulled out the medallion from the Cinder Fairies and played with it in my hand. My time on this plane was coming to an end, and I had a job to do before going to the Underworld. I had almost given into the void today. If it hadn't been for CJ, I very well may have given up and let myself fall into its comfort.

If I had, would Ansel's reign be quick and deadly, or long and torturous? How could I have considered going into that void without destroying him first?

I looked out toward the Black Mountains and felt my power stir within me. I brought my legs up under me to sit cross-legged and sighed. Looking out in that direction, I felt the medallion warm in my hand. My hand wrapped around it tightly, and said into the wind, "I swear to protect the world of Nalrin and give myself to destroy Ansel Keller."

CJ came up behind me, but he stayed back, leaning against a tufa about twenty feet behind me. He let me sit there the rest of the day. It wasn't until I started shivering well after the sun went down that he came over and scooped me up.

He never said a word, but when I curled up against his chest, he kissed the top of my head before carrying me off to bed.

CHAPTER 33

THE NEXT AFTERNOON, WE stood on the ridge before winding the last corner into Leadenhollow Port. I scanned the sight before me and huffed out a shocked laugh. There had to be at least three hundred soldiers dressed in solid black loading a boat at the docks. Clarice chirped at her horse and took off.

"Who's following her?" I asked, half rolling my eyes and looking at Owen.

Owen smirked at me, and off he went.

"And we aren't all following why?" CJ said.

"Because I know it's Alexei." I shrugged.

"WHAT?" Jean and Mickel said at the same time.

"Before we left Therth, he asked me to send word where we were going. If we knew where to find Helena, then he would bring soldiers to meet us. When we left Vox, I sent a message to Alexei telling him to meet us in Leadenhollow or Millmore."

"How did he know for sure where to meet us?" CJ said, at the same time as Logan asked, "We have talked strategy through all of this. What if we completely changed directions?"

"I sent a message to Leadenhollow yesterday afternoon, letting Alexei know that we would be here today. I also let him know we were delayed, but everyone was fine."

"Clarice is going to kill you for this, you know," Jean said, laughing.

"I know." I smiled back at her and blatantly ignored the boys. "She's edgy without him."

CJ gave me a knowing look but smiled.

"Since they got married, she has been more edgy. I thought it was just because of everything that has happened. Having to absorb all that extra power from the Underworld..." Jean said, staring off out to where Clarice was barreling down on Alexei.

"Oh, I'm positive it is exactly because of that," I said, "but in Therth, if he was in the room? She was... smoother. Calmer. I can't explain it."

Logan and Mickel chirped at the horses, and they took off ahead to meet up with them. I pulled Ziggy to a stop, and without saying anything, Jean and CJ did the same.

"What aren't you saying, Megan?" Jean said, half turning in her saddle to face me.

"I have CJ. You have Owen. We are Mickel and Logan's family. Clarice is family, but it's different from how Mickel and Logan are," I said sadly. "Alexei is her other half. She's already sacrificed so much in life trying to do the right thing. To get away from all that power, and she still ended up with it. *They* have sacrificed so much. I don't think I could be at peace if something happened to her, and they don't get just a little more time together."

They just stared at me, slack jawed.

"And when were you going to tell us... when were you going to tell *Clarice* that Alexei was going to break her one order to him?" Jean said.

"Now?" I said, putting a smile on my face and shrugging.

Jean shook her head and laughed. Truly laughed. I hadn't seen her do that since before, Bellstar.

"Jean?" I asked. "Are you okay? I know the last few days have dredged up a lot."

"Yeah," she said, a small bit of that spark in her eye dimming. "It's been a long time since I allowed myself to think of Savanora. Owen and I talked all night, the first night in Houndmire. It was nice to get the extra night to catch up on sleep. Thanks for asking."

"You're okay though?" I asked.

"Yeah," Jean said, then nodded ahead of us. Clarice was standing there, hands on her hips, staring me down.

I pushed Ziggy forward and just before we reached her, I hopped down and yelled, "Surprise!"

"I gave him one order Megan Isabel Mathewson. ONE FUCKING ORDER. Stay in Therth and keep it and Obsecuritan safe," she screamed at me, but didn't show an ounce of her power. Jean and CJ winced slightly, but I just smiled at her as she stood there hands on her hips, feet hip width apart.

"And he and I talked. He said he wanted to help fight. I said we didn't know where we were going. He got cranky. Begged. All kinds of other undignified Grand Dukey things," I said a bit on the whiney side, "and then I told him I would send word when we knew what direction we were heading, which I did when we left Vox. Julian confirmed Alexei would likely meet us here when we were in Bellstar. Then I verified that we would be here today by sending a message to Alexei yesterday afternoon."

"One. Fucking. Order," she said again, but her irritation was waning.

"Ohhhh, my big scary Empress." Alexei said, coming up next to her and giving her a kiss on the cheek. She gave him a sidelong glance, and her face went soft.

"Asshat," she said, returning the kiss on his cheek. He just shrugged at her empty insult.

"Well, you ditched your guard in Nalrin, so, I had to come and take their place." He beamed at her. She just glared at him again.

"Hi, Megan." Alexei said, turning to me. "Vernadali CJ, Lady Jean."

"Hi, Alexei," I gestured behind him. "You brought friends I see."

We started heading toward the docks as he said, "Since I was breaking her one order to me, wait, what was that again? I don't think we have been reminded of what exactly that was?" He put a finger on his chin in fake contemplation. Clarice glared at him, but Jean and CJ chuckled. "Oh right. Keep Therth safe. Easily done when most of the danger is up here. I had to leave the majority of the armies down in Obsecuritan. The southern continent has been in a bit of a riot since Ansel went through decimating it. Rebuilding is... is going to take a while."

"The Seltic Marsh is on the verge of Civil War, apparently." Clarice said. "They don't have supplies and they are coming over the mountains to see what they can get from Obsecuritan. There just isn't enough to go around."

Alexei led us down to one of the mid-sized riverboats that had the entire entrance level set up for horse stabling. "Lady Megan, I am Captain Parro. The second and third levels will house the Nalrin Guard and a few of the Obsecuritan company. We are securing another river boat for the rest of the Obsecuritan company to follow. We should have you in Millmore in three to four days though. There might be some bad weather the closer that might slow us down as we get to the Plateau. Sometimes, we have to stop to let it pass or risk grounding the boat."

"Thank you, Captain Parro. Where are our rooms? I'm ready for a bath."

"Your family is stationed in the owner's quarters on the fourth level. You are welcome to choose any room you want."

"I want the room furthest from CJ and Megan!" Logan said quickly, only half joking.

"You can't handle just a few days?" Jean said, turning to face him with her hand on her hip.

Logan's eyes were wide. "No. I can't take it anymore. That is my brother, and a woman I have known the entirety of my life. I don't have one family memory where Megan isn't there.

While she is only technically related to me by marriage, Megan is more of a sister to me than anything, so yeah." He turned to the Captain. "Seriously, the room furthest from them," he said, pointing to us.

Captain Parro was really trying to not laugh, but said, "Yes, Sir Logan." Then called one of the attendants to show Logan where he could hole up. "There are enough rooms on that level that you all can have your own private areas."

After Logan left, I said, "Remind me to put itching powder in his clothes."

"Lady Megan, is now the time for me to mention that this particular boat has been known for its Sexual Fantasy River Cruises?" he said with a smirk, looking toward Logan. "Every room on this boat has specialized spell-enhanced sound cancellation enchantments on them. Make as much noise as you wish. Someone could stand outside your door, and they wouldn't hear you."

I lost it at that point and had tears streaming down my face in hysterics.

"Seriously?" CJ and Owen said through their laughter.

"I am very serious. If he, or anyone on this boat, goes looking in the closets, they will find an... assortment of pleasure items."

"Oh, we are going to have fun tonight," Clarice said, winking at Alexei. I smirked at CJ, whose mind I knew was already in fantasy land.

"Yes, Empress. Your wish is my will, Empress," Alexei said, bowing low, but there was a slight smirk to his face that said, they very well may enjoy the evening, and not getting much sleep.

"Sexual Pleasure River Cruise, huh?" I asked. "Don't suppose that is a coincidence, is it? That we just happen to be taking this *particular* boat, while Ansel tries to sort out where we are heading."

"Did you think that *The Temptation* was just a wanderlust name for the boat?" He winked. "Seriously, we run one cruise a week. Each is catered to a different specialty. *The Watery Desire,* the other boat we are clearing for the rest of the Obsecuritan soldiers, runs same sex cruises exclusively."

CJ had his hand around my waist in a way that said if he didn't get me back to a room soon, then we were not going to make it there.

"Don't you worry, babe," I pushed to him, and he discreetly had me walk in front of him as Captain Parro led us toward the owner's quarters. I may have added a little extra swish to my hips. When we stopped, he may have *accidentally* bumped into me from behind, making sure I knew full well what he was planning when we got to that room.

When we got to the fourth deck, the attendant who had escorted Logan motioned to which room was his, and the Captain led the rest of us toward the front of the ship. Each hallway was color coded, and I smirked when Clarice and Alexei took a room down a red hallway. Owen and Jean took one down the yellow hall, and the look on Owen's face when they reached the second door made me chuckle softly. Finally, Mickel took one of the rooms along the railing that had its entrance in a purple hall, stating he still wanted to be close enough to us to ensure a semblance of security.

Captain Parro took us all the way to the front, leading us to a discrete door along the breezeway. "This is one of the nicest rooms on the boat. It has a private balcony with sound canceling incantations, so even though you are outside, it's still quiet. I will have your things delivered in the entryway by morning. We will leave once the horses are secured down on the base deck. Enjoy your evening."

Captain Parro had opened the exterior door to a small entryway that had a second entrance door. The entry acted much like a mud room. Just enough room to slip your shoes off and put a few things down. I looked back to Captain Parro as CJ worked to open the second door, and he was whistling as he strode down the breezeway with his hands in his pockets.

CHAPTER 34

CJ WAS STILL OPENING the door to the main cabin when I turned, already discarding my syth belt, jacket, and boots on the side rail. The door shut, and I started removing his clothes so fast that his shirt ripped as it went over his head. Once it was gone, he had me backed up against a wall and kissed me hard.

"Ceej," I pushed to him, and he only growled in response. He kicked off his boots, and when our pants hit the floor, it was a matter of moments before he was kissing me against the wall again. I raked my nails over his back, and he pushed against me, the full length of him pushing against my stomach. I reached down and palmed him and the moan that came from him, I swear, could have rattled the walls.

"Megs, I need you. Now," he said, but before he could pick me up, I moved out of the way and pushed him back against the wall.

"I know, and you are just going to have to be patient," I said, smirking, running my nails up his cock. He pulled me close, and I ground against him. He loosened his grip just slightly, and before he could do anything else, I dropped to my knees and ran my tongue along the underside of him. His salty taste ran through me, and there was a pulse that burst between my legs so violently, I was surprised it wasn't auditory.

"Ah shit," CJ moaned, catching himself on the chair and dressing table as his knees buckled.

I took his balls into my mouth as I gently fingered the head of him and groaned. His breath was quick and harsh. Slowly, I licked my way up him, taking my time. When I got to the head, my tongue swirled, and I let a little of that pre-cum trail from him to my mouth as I looked up at him.

"Fuck, Megan. You are so fucking—" His words were cut off as I took him wholly into my mouth and swallowed every inch of him. I knew he wasn't going to last long.

There was so much need in his eyes, I knew this was only going to be round one.

I slowly sucked and licked him and when he popped from my mouth, I whispered, "Fuck my face, Ceej."

The look in his eyes was one of surprise at this offer. I took another long lick up and down his length and flicked my tongue over the tip. The growl that emanated from him as I took him back down my throat was pure animalistic. He brushed my hair from my face, as I pulled back, swirling the head of him, right before I took him back into my mouth, moaning.

"Please." I begged him, and then there was a wicked gleam in his eye.

"When my beautiful, sexy wife asks so nicely, how can a husband refuse?" he said, taking my hair in his hands and thrusting forward. He paused only for a moment, and pulsed in and out at first, before driving down my throat in long, hard thrusts.

I moaned and my name rumbled loud through the space. He looked down and bit his lower lip as he picked up the pace. I swallowed every inch of him. My mouth and eyes were watering, but the feel of him sliding down my throat had me on the edge of coming myself. I reached down and pumped two fingers in and out of myself while grinding against the bundle of nerves.

He noticed, and said, "Flick that clit, baby." I obeyed, and I felt him twitching. He grabbed my hair harder as I moaned in delight at the feel of him.

"Angel's above," he said to the space. His hands gripped each side of my face as he fucked my throat hard and fast. A few moments later, he slid deep down into me as he released. Holding himself there, and I swallowed every drop.

"Megan." He said in blissful reverence, as I licked him clean.

He lifted me up and simply turned me to sit on the dresser next to us. I wrapped my legs around him, and he kissed me gently.

"You have always given the best blowjobs I have ever had," He said breathlessly, and I met his eyes, "but I never thought the sound of you begging me to..."

I brought my hand to his face and made him look at me. "Ceej. I never want you to get bored with our sex life. Whether we have days or eons. I never want you to be bored."

"How could I possibly ever get bored with you?" CJ said, astonished I would even insinuate it.

"Ceej, we have only really been together for two and a half years. While I certainly enjoy our sex life, if we have only a few days, or the life spans of a Sangra, I want to make sure you never bore of the bedroom," I said carefully. "So, just tell me what you want. If it is something I'm not comfortable with, I'll let you know. If you want to bring other men or women into the bedroom. Let's do it. If you want other people, wax, bondage, fire play, let's talk. Tell me what your wildest sexual fantasies are, and we will make them come true."

"Megs," he breathed. His eyes were wide as he studied my face. "You *are* being serious right now."

"I am." I let a little of that heat I felt for him shine through my eyes before I reiterated, "What are your most basic, or wildest, or curious sexual fantasies? Whether you have already thought of it, or you think about something you want to try in fifty years, should we live that long, tell me. We will make them happen."

"I refuse to do anything you don't feel comfortable with," he said sternly.

"And I won't do anything I'm not comfortable with. If it's something that I know nothing about, I'll research it. Find out about it, how to do whatever it is safely. Start at the beginning and see where our lines are."

"Do you know if you have a line?" he asked carefully.

I thought for a moment, and said, "I'm sure I do. I know choking will be off the table, at least for now, considering Derek, but I just don't know where any other line is. What about you?"

"I don't think I'd be comfortable choking either. I know Becca loves the rough life. She liked to brag, so did James, for that matter, so don't give me that look," he said when he saw the look on my face.

"I didn't think Becca would like it rough, but if it made her happy and they were safe about it, then..." I shrugged. He studied me with another long look, like he was trying to puzzle something out in my eyes.

"I have never had a partner who has offered anything like this. I'm sure there is a line, but I have no idea where it is." His hands tightened on my hips, and I pulled him closer, giving him a quick kiss. "Anyone I've ever been with before you has been pretty mainstream, or light role playing, light dominance."

"Which you do well, by the way. I would like to explore that side a little more. That time out on that ledge. It uncoiled something in me." I chewed on my bottom lip, suddenly finding myself sort of nervous. "I'd kind of like to try wax... maybe work our way up to some fire play if we can do it safely."

He blushed and smirked at that memory of us on the ledge. "There's been handcuffs, some spanking, but in the world of kink, it's pretty lightweight. Fire play, huh?" He smirked, reached up, and ran a thumb over my cheek. There was a fiery intrigue at that suggestion. "I don't know the first thing about how to do that safely, so we will have to look into it. If anything becomes too much though babes, you really have to tell me. I refuse to do anything you don't consent to, or you become overwhelmed by."

"So, we set up rules. We find out what works and what doesn't. Sort out a safe word, so if in the middle of anything, we are not good, no judgment for an instant stop."

"Mushu."

I raised my eyebrows at him and laughed. In my best Eddie Murphy Mushu voice, I said, "Dishonor on you-"

"Dishonor on your cow!" he finished for me.

"I don't know. Maybe. I might just start laughing and never get the words out. We could do something simple, too. Just use the light system. Red, yellow, green."

CJ just studied me for a long moment before finding whatever it was that he was looking for in my eyes. "You have given this a lot of thought, haven't you? Is this what you really want?"

I nodded. "I don't want us to get bored. The same thing every time. Some couples are okay with that. I have always wanted variety in my life. I don't want you to resent anything in our relationship, either. We are young Ceej. Let us see where we land."

"How did I end up with such a perfect partner?" he said, kissing me. "Can that offer be a two-way street? Let me know what you want, and I'll make it happen."

I nodded and before I could say anything else, he said, "Now, what *I* want is to hear is you moaning my name as you come repeatedly over the next few days. I do not plan to leave this room. No scheming, no Ansel, no Helena. The next few days are you, me, and this cabin. Food can be delivered."

With that, he kissed me and pulled my hips to the edge of the dresser. Kissed down my neck, nipped my shoulder and said, "And Since you just had your snack, I think I'll have mine. I believe I'll start... right here," he dragged a single finger down the center of me.

"Angels be!" I said, tipping my head back as he got to work.

CHAPTER 35

HE MADE GOOD ON that promise to stay in that cabin. For three days, we did not leave that room. Food and drink were delivered, and we fed each other, showered together, and made it a second honeymoon. Messages arrived from our family, but we just said we would deal with things when we got to Millmore. We were taking a few days off. The weather had been horrible, and we gained another night off, or so we thought.

It was the night before we were expected to land in Millmore that Mickel pounded on the door, demanding that we get dressed and let him in. I grabbed the sheet off the bed, because, well, I had indeed not gotten dressed in three days, and went to the door.

"What do you want, Mickel?" I ground out at him when I flung the door open.

To his credit, he didn't even flinch. "I need to talk to you and CJ." Then, even though I was only wrapped in that sheet, he picked me up and carried me to the bed. When he saw CJ, he just rolled his eyes and said, "CJ, seriously, please get some clothes on."

"What is it?" I said, getting up and grabbing a shirt and sliding it on quickly, before reaching for a pair of underwear and jeans. "Turn around a moment and talk while I get dressed."

Rolling his eyes again, he turned to face the wall, and said, "Owen and I had a LightCall with Julian yesterday. We tried to get you to join us, but when Logan returned, he said he wouldn't be returning to your room."

"What?" CJ said, coming from around the corner putting a t-shirt on. I gave him a once over and my eyes may have lingered just a bit longer on those abs of his. "I only told him that if he disturbed time with my wife again, he was going to lose his favorite part."

"*That* is what you threatened him with?" Mickel said. CJ just smirked and shrugged a shoulder. Our favorite guard let out a deep sigh. "Anyway, as I said. We had a LightCall with Julian yesterday. There is an entire battalion that just checked in at Millmore. They are supposed to accompany us to Morana, set up camp, and wait while we take the three-day hike up the mountains to Morte Alta and back."

"*That's* not inconspicuous," I said, plopping on the bed and sitting with my legs crossed. My ass stung a little from the spankings he gave me this morning, and I tried my best not to wince. "Adding all those soldiers to the Nalrin Guard and Obsecuritan soldiers already with us, it makes a statement. Mickel, you can turn around."

"It does." Mickel said.

"Any reports on where Ansel is?" I asked, playing with my fingers, and refusing to look up. It had been so nice to just check out for a few days. No worrying about who in my family would live through this. No, making literal life and death decisions. No, having to wonder how much longer until I would have Helena, and no wondering how long I would have her until I had to die myself.

Mickel didn't say anything. CJ came over and rubbed my back in small, soothing circles. "Just say it, Mickel." CJ said, a bit of frustration in his voice.

"Julian said that…" There was an audible gulp from him, and I popped my head up. The look on his face made my heart race. "He was at the base of the Black Mountains… and he…" Mickel snapped to attention, taking on the posture and demeanor he had when he was first assigned to me. It was if that was the only way to get through his next words, said, "Lady Megan, Vernadali CJ. Ansel Keller completely annihilated Ashridge. There is not one of the 800,000 souls who lived in that city alive. No word on whether the Grand Duke and Grand Duchess were present or not. They were last reported to be in Savanora on holiday, but Head Julian is still waiting to have official word. Ansel has set up camp in Ashridge for now, and it appears he plans to make his way north through the Black Mountains and the Vandrer Grasslands."

CJ slowly turned to look at me as I stared at Mickel. His eyes were full of tears. "Mickel, look at me."

Slowly, he relaxed and drew his eyes from the spot on the wall to mine. "Everyone?" I asked carefully. My mind was racing.

Mickel nodded just once in confirmation

"He… he knows." I whispered.

A slow nod from Mickel.

"He knows." I repeated. It was the only thought I could process. I felt CJ's charge surge through the room, and Mickel winced slightly as it hit him.

"Sorry," CJ said distantly.

"Megan," Mickel said carefully. "We need a game plan for when we hit Millmore tomorrow."

"He knows." I whispered again.

CJ rested his hand on the back of my neck and ran his thumb softly back and forth. "Mickel. Get everyone together. Just give us thirty minutes. Where should we meet you?" he said every ounce a Vernadali.

"Next level down. We turned one of the rooms into a Command Center last night. Go to the fourth door on the right, down the second hall. Thirty minutes should work. Will give the others a chance to meet us there," Mickel said, paused and then said to CJ. "Jean, Owen, and I have been working with Logan, and been working on keeping his sword skills up. The boy took to a sword like he had been holding one his entire life."

"Thank you."

Mickel nodded and without another word walked out and gently closed the door.

CJ turned me to look him eye to eye. My heart was racing, and my chest felt like an iron band was around hit.

"He knows."

My eyes were wide, and I could feel my legs and fingers twitch. Small tingles of electricity jumped between my fingers, and I pushed to CJ again. *"He knows."*

"Breathe," he said firmly.

I took a deep, shuddering breath and held it. Not moving my eyes from his, he reached up. and gently, in a steady rhythm, tapped on my chest. My eyes were locked on CJ's as I gave him a small nod and let out a long breath.

"Again." As he continued the steady tapping on my chest.

It took ten minutes of repeating that exercise to make the shaking stop and slow my heart rate down. He sat down on his heels and looked me in the eye.

"Ceej, he knows I'm going after Helena and where she is. Or at least suspects some part of it," I said, trying to keep the panic rising again and concentrating on the feel of my hands in his.

"It appears that way," he murmured. "It doesn't change anything, not really. So, he knows where we are headed and that we have found something that can stop him. It doesn't mean he will succeed. It doesn't mean that this war is over. It doesn't mean that we give up. On any of it."

"It means we have to hurry. We have to get to Helena as quickly as possible. We can't afford any more delays," I said, pushing my fears aside.

CJ's quick nod was the only response. I knew he was still trying to find that loophole, but he was doing what I needed him to do. I took another deep breath and it out slowly. "Well, let's finish getting dressed and see what the others think."

CHAPTER 36

TWENTY MINUTES LATER, WE were standing in a room with a large dining table, with the map the previous Captain had given us. This time, Alexei and Commander Kaiwan joined our family. Little figurines laid upon the map as indicators for where various forces across Nalsar were stationed.

Mickel, apparently, had more than one LightCall with Julian if he was able to get this much detailed information.

"Should we call for more soldiers to meet us further up north?" Logan asked.

"Do we even know where we are going?" Commander Kaiwan of the Nalrin Guard asked.

"Morana," I said, pointing to a small town that sat at the edge of the Lost Plateau but nestled up next to the Black Mountains.

"Do we know that Ansel will head in that direction? If so, will he go through the Grasslands or will he go through the mountains?" Owen asked.

"Will he try to cut us off or meet us in Morana?" Jean asked as soon as Owen finished.

CJ's hand found mine, giving it a tight squeeze as he felt the tension go through my body.

"The people of Ashridge, were they consumed by the tar, or did he just kill everyone and ransack the town? Does he have a physical army or is it just the Ja'Nee and the tar?" I asked.

"There have been no reports other than him having that substance with him and the Ja'Nee. A lot of Ja'Nee," Clarice said, Alexei standing directly behind her, his eyes studying the map.

Well, at least we weren't other being we were against. Having to go against other species would make this a lot harder. The Ja'Nee were not beings with conscious thought. They were pure darkness made and created for destruction only. They barely held a physical form.

"How long do you think it will take to get to Morana if we skirt the Lost Plateau and go around via the grasslands?" CJ asked.

"An army of this size? A month? Maybe a little longer?" Mickel said. Alexi looked to Commander Kaiwan, who nodded in agreement.

"And if we go through the Plateau?" I asked carefully, staring at the dead space on the map.

"Lady Megan, you can't mean to traverse the Lost Plateau?" Commander Kaiwan blurted.

I snapped my head up and glared at him. "I am weighing my options. If Ansel knows why we are heading to Morana, then I need to get there first, do what I need to do, and then hopefully stop him before he wipes out the entire dimension. Unfortunately, Ashridge is already lost, as well as most of Obsecuritan, not to mention what he did to Nalrin and any other number of settlements along the way. So, yes, I am weighing my options. That includes going through the Lost fucking Plateau."

"So, I'll ask again since you doubted my wife," CJ said with a tone that was not to be debated. "How long will it to take us to get through the Plateau?"

It was Jean who said, "If we don't get lost? If we don't have too many setbacks? Three, Four weeks? Not to mention we don't know how many soldiers will make it through there."

"What are we realistically looking at if we go through the Plateau? Mirages? Illusions? Mind tricks? Complete loss of direction? What sort of beasts are we looking at? I've read the books. I want to know what we are realistically looking at," I demanded.

No one answered me.

"Facts. I need them now. You want instructions on how to proceed? We need facts," I ordered. Pride shown in Jean and Clarice's face as I made demands on the group.

"Much of it is theory, but there have been confirmed reports of creatures living in the sea of sand. There are, of course, mirages. There have also been strange reports from the bogland, but I don't know of anyone who entered it and came back in one piece, so we don't know what is really out there. There have been people who enter, and they emerge months later, only to say they got disoriented and didn't know which direction to go. They were mentally and emotionally broken by the time they came out, so again, much of it is theory," Jean said.

There were many discussions now bouncing around the room, but I just stared at the map. My eyes flicked to Ashridge, then to Millmore, to Morana, and back to Ashridge. I slowly gazed across the Plateau. It was a straight shot across the Plateau, but we couldn't afford to take a month to go around either. There was the possibility, though, of cutting a week or two if we went through there though. Looking back at where Ashridge was, I cocked my head to the side.

"If he goes through the Grassland, he will have to come back around the lower mountains," I pushed to CJ. His focus went to that portion of the map, then back to Morana, then back to Ashridge, and then back to us. His eyebrows knitted together as he was trying to sort out the timelines as well.

"Is there a pass from Ashridge to the Grasslands? I don't see one indicated on the map." CJ asked.

"Not that low in the mountains," Mickel said. The room went quiet at the question.

CJ studied me for a moment.

"It will take him what five-six weeks then to make it to Morana? Depending on how fast he can move," I asked.

"Likely, Lady," Mickel said, gritting his teeth, knowing what I was thinking. "Only if he rides the Nocturnes, though, assuming there are more than what Clarice handled in Houndsmire."

"You mean to go through the Lost Plateau," Alexei said in understanding.

"I do," I said confidently. Surprising even myself. "The army can't go through there, or it could take months to get to the other side. There are just too many things that could go wrong."

"So, the family goes through the Plateau. The army goes around via the Grasslands," Owen said.

I nodded. "It could cut a couple weeks off the trip, and if we have five or six weeks until Ansel gets to Morana, then we need to cut as much time as we can. We just have to take our chances."

"Megan and I go through the Plateau," CJ said, and I closed my eyes. The tension that went through everyone in that room was potent as they looked at CJ.

It was Clarice who said, "Not happening, CJ."

"Clarice is right," Mickel said, putting his hand on CJ's shoulder. "Everyone in this room knows what is at stake, and we are here to ensure everyone's safety. All of us know this could be a one-way trip. All of us have agreed to take that chance."

"I'm not sugar coating this. Everyone is here ensuring that I get into a position to end my father." I looked up and met CJ's eyes. "The family goes through the Plateau. Armies skirt it and meet us in Morana."

Commander Kaiwan, Alexei, and Mickel all studied each other. "Do you wish to lead them, Mickel and Duke Alexei? Through the grasslands, I mean," Commander Kaiwan said.

They both looked at me, while Clarice studied Alexei, but I just stared at the map in front of us. One of them needed to head that army, and I couldn't stand the thought of pulling Alexei from

Clarice or letting Mickel go. It was a chickenshit move for me to stand there staring at the map, without making a direct order, but I couldn't do it.

"Once we make land, we will march and meet you in Morana," Alexei said. "If you don't arrive in five weeks, we will come after you."

I felt Mickel stiffen at Alexei's words, but he kept his mouth shut. My heart sank, but I just nodded.

It was Clarice who said, "Alexei will command the diverse soldier makeup. With it being Nalrin Guard, Obsecuritan soldiers, and Nalrin Soldiers, he has the ranking to ensure no orders are questioned. No offense Mickel, but some of the Obsecuritan soldiers would likely push back on orders from you. As Grand Duke, Nalrin will not question his authority."

"Understood." Mickel nodded. "I will order them to follow his commands anyway, just to prevent any problems."

"I want horses stocked and ready by the time we make land. I want to be on the Plateau before the rest of the boat has even disembarked. Whomever is feeding Ansel information will be watching the army. It's late. Go get some sleep. Alexei and Mickel, make the arrangements so that when we arrive in Millmore we can be on our way as soon as possible," I commanded, but there were a couple of confused looks that came from Commander Kaiwan.

"Hopefully, he will expect the army to be with us." CJ ran his hand through his hair. When the Commander gave him a look, I narrowed my eyes, but CJ said, "I believe that Lady Megan gave orders."

There was a salute from Commander Kaiwan, who turned and, with a short nod to Alexi and Mickel, walked out.

"Be safe, Megan," Alexei said, and then followed the Commander out as well. Mickel gave me a soft smile before he, too, left.

I let out a long breath before turning back toward the map. I leaned on the palms of my hands, my eyes flicking between Ashridge and Morana. Five or six weeks. That is all I could have left. A little over a month with my family, before...

"Logan, let's get some more practice in before we get the best night's sleep we will get for the foreseeable future," Owen said, clapping Logan on the back. Logan studied me a long moment before looking to CJ, who shook his head slightly, and indicated he should go.

As Owen, Jean and Logan left, Clarice stood on the other side of the table, looking at the map as well.

"I'm sorry, Clarice." I breathed.

"Why?"

"For getting Alexei here, and now you are going to be separated again."

"Megan, what I said was true. He is the best person for the job in this case," she said.

"But—"

"No buts. He is Grand Duke of Obsecuritan. This is his very job description. This is what he does, Megan. He runs the military," Clarice said, every inch of the Empress. "Do not apologize for having him do his job. He may be my Silnaree, but he still has responsibilities. Do not apologize for having him do it."

When I just looked at her sadly, she huffed a small laugh and the corner of her lip lifted. "My Silnaree and I have been putting our time to good use. Don't worry about that. We will have much more time to come. Now, you go and enjoy your last night of comfort. Captain Parro said we would be docking at sunrise, so it will be an early start. If you want to get going that quickly, then we better be packed and ready." With a quick glance and nod to CJ, she strode from the room.

CHAPTER 37

WE HAD BEEN OUT in the middle of this blasted Plateau for a week and a half already. The horses were mounted the moment we pulled up to Millmore and stood ready for when the ramp was secured. Once it was, the horses bolted as fast as they could and ran until they couldn't anymore. By then we had stopped and made lunch and continued to head as straight as we could to keep from getting lost. The night sky was different here. Where we would have normally been able to keep direction by the stars, they were non-existent over the Plateau. No wonder people got so lost.

"I don't know what is worse. The expanse of dry land or this field of stone." Logan grumbled. "You can see for miles in any direction."

"At least we can see any predators coming for us here," Mickel said.

"True. In that dry grass, I kept waiting for a rattlesnake to jump out at us," Logan said. I couldn't help but shiver at the thought.

"You okay?" I pushed to Clarice, and she nodded. She had been quiet since we hit the Plateau. At CJ's questioning look, he moved Tucker closer, and I said, "Just checking on Clarice. She's been pretty quiet."

"I suspect her power is telling her all sorts of things that could haunt her for the rest of her life," CJ said quietly, and I nodded in agreement. "I do not envy her that. She's always in thought, always contemplating. Reminds me of how Lindy... how Lindy was when we were trying to stop them from making the weapon of The Five Angels."

I nodded as I looked up at the sky, which was quickly darkening with sprawling clouds. "It's going to rain."

"I've been thinking the same thing. You can smell it in the air."

"Temperature is dropping, too," I said quieter.

CJ studied me again before saying, "Megan, what is going through that mind of yours? You are all kinds of antsy."

"Remember what the Cinder Queen said?" I pushed toward him. When he shook his head, I pushed, *"She is most powerful in the snow."*

He took only a moment before he took a deep breath. "We are still days or weeks away from Morana. Then we have to get to Morte Alta, back down the mountain, and find his army."

"I know," I said, my voice distant. It was hard not to fixate on the fact I didn't have more than a month of life left. I wasn't sure if that terrified me or if I found that comforting. I could truly be in the here and now when with CJ, enjoying each moment I had left with him. Truly, absorb the laughter of my family.

"Megan!" Owen called, pulling me from my thoughts. When I looked up, everyone had lined up almost in a line, and Clarice had even dismounted ahead of us.

The ground crunched slightly when I jumped off of Ziggy. I turned to look out far off in the distance, to the Black Mountains. They were covered in snow, and even the clouds made way for them. I jerked my head toward the mountains and pushed to CJ, *"In the snow."*

He looked off at the snow-capped range and sighed.

"I'm going to have to use Helena in the Black Mountains?"

CJ wrapped an arm around me and whispered in my ear, "It just means it will be snowing if we do have to use her. Doesn't mean we have to use it there. Not to mention, there will be a loophole where you don't have to." He kissed my cheek, and to anyone else, it could have been passed off, as CJ and I just having a moment. I smiled at him and looked back off at the mountains.

"Are we really going to hike that high up to Morte Alta?" I said, defeated.

"That isn't what I'm worried about," Owen said, pointing to the expanse between us and the mountains.

"That is going to be all kinds of fun to get across," Logan said as Mickel just groaned.

Ahead of us was a murky stretch of land and water. It was green and lush, but also had a mixture of swamp and bog. There was going to be no sure footing in any of it. Some sections appeared to have shadows, which made it look like there were sections of the water that were deeper than others. I cringed to think of the creatures that could be laying in there.

"What are the chances there are crocodiles or alligators in there?" Logan said, looking at CJ.

"Likely all sorts of creatures much worse than crocs and gators," I mumbled. Logan, to his credit, just chuckled.

"There is a path over there," Owen said, pointing to a spot about 30 feet to the north. "We should walk the horses down. It's a thin, narrow access point."

I didn't waste any time and led Ziggy to the path. I heard the others behind me, but I couldn't make myself look back toward them. The path was not really even wide enough for the horses. I took the stirrups and hung them over the horn to give Ziggy a couple more inches along the wall. Everyone moved slowly and watched their footing on the way down.

It took hours, and the sun was getting ready to set when we finally made it down. I half-wondered if maybe we shouldn't have stayed the night up on the cliff. At least there we could see all around us. Here, there were trees, and moss, and mud, and... we were going to be soaked as we crossed this. There was going to be nowhere dry to sleep, either.

Mickel found a denser, drier part of ground that we could lie on, so here we would stay. Clarice and Jean had set out into the deeper waters to find something to eat as we set up.

They returned an hour or so later with a giant Dassimze carried between them. I just stared wide-eyed. There was a single arrow that went through the feline eye, and a knife at the base of its smooth skull. Quick and clean.

"How? What?" Owen sputtered, rushing towards them. The cat was huge, easily the size of Mickel and Logan together.

"How are we going to cook all of that?" I asked. There was so much meat, and a fire was unlikely. "Everything is soaking wet, and we ran out of fire kits a few stops ago."

The nights had been cold without the fire, and I couldn't imagine how we were going to get through this without losing some limbs.

Clarice smirked and said, "I'll use my power to encourage a flame to continue to burn, if you can just get something started." She looked pointedly at the ground.

"Clean it away from camp. Don't want the blood and entrails to lead other predators to us. Downwind would be best, please," CJ said, jerking his head in the opposite direction.

Walking around, I pulled some branches and twigs off the trees that were low enough to reach. I dumped the armful of wood and twigs back where we had set up a little clearing and went in search of something I could use to light the fire. A flame would not get hot enough to get those logs burning. Even with Clarice's help, I could feel CJ watching me the entire time.

"Worry wort." I pushed to him. I knew that if I had turned around, there would have been one of two responses, *'Do you blame me?'* or *'Duh!'*. So instead, I roamed the area looking for anything that looked remotely dried up enough to take a flame.

Eventually, I found some purple moss growing just above eye level on one of the nearby trees. I reached up and pinched it between my fingers, sighing in relief as I realized it might actually burn. I took my syth out and cut some off, being careful not to cut too deep into the wood.

"I thought these only grew in the Seltic Marsh," Jean said, scaring the crap out of me.

I whirled around and had my syth positioned in front of me, and when I looked at her, she merely smirked and held her hands up. "Angels, Jean! Make a noise or something."

"Sorry. Soft ground equals quiet entrances?"

"Hence, make a noise. You almost made me need a new pair of pants, and I'm running low on ones that wouldn't stand on their own in a corner."

"Welcome to life on the road. The untraveled road," Jean said, smirking. "Maybe in Morana we can will have a chance to get cleaned up."

"It is pretty," I said, gesturing up the trunk that stretched about 25–30 feet into the air. The entire area here had a thick canopy.

"Good thing you didn't cut too deep into the bark. If you had, it would have emitted fumes that would have knocked you out for days." She said, looping her arm with mine as we headed back.

I shrugged and said, "I know, hence, why I didn't do it. I have learned a thing or two over the last few years, Jean."

By the time we got back, Clarice, Owen, and Mickel had butchered and cleaned the Dassimze and had it ready to be cooked for dinner. It took about twenty minutes of coaxing, both with skill and magic, to get a fire to light. Once we did, though, the meat was cooked, and the rest was laid over a makeshift bone rack, to dry and smoke overnight. With any luck, it would be enough to get us to Morana.

Once my stomach was full, exhaustion set in. I glanced around the camp and said, "I'm gonna lay down and get some sleep."

I was met with a bunch of weary gazes who just nodded, and it was Clarice who said, "I feel like I've been on the road for weeks without sleep." Then she just slid off the log she was sitting on and rested her head on it like a pillow. She was out in moments.

I huffed a small laugh, because she wasn't wrong. We all looked like we had been traveling with next to no sleep. I found a spot to lie down myself, and when CJ snuggled up next to me, I fell into a dreamless sleep.

CHAPTER 38

"ONE MORE NIGHT, YA think?" I asked Mickel and Owen.

"Likely, maybe two. There is still a lot of area to cover before we reach those mountains," Mickel said.

"They are so large it's hard to determine the distance," Owen said.

"I just want to be dry, warm, and..." Logan's statements were cut off by a deep growling sound from behind us.

We were walking the horses, since the ground was too muddy and slick for them to bear our weight and keep their footing. Ziggy had slipped several times before I just dismounted and led him through. I didn't want to chance him breaking a leg. The others followed suit soon after. We had all face planted in the slick, wet clay at some point, and were now mostly covered in mud.

Ziggy became restless and pulled at the reins. I rubbed his neck and tried to calm him while looking around for what had made the sound. I saw the other's trying to sooth their mounts as well, but when I turned toward Logan, there was a shadow lunging for Duchess. She jerked the reins out of Logan's hands and bucked, kicking in the head before running off toward flatter ground.

Logan took off behind her, and with the toss of his reins to me, CJ went after him. I took Ziggy and Tucker as quickly as I could in chase. I saw them through an opening in the trees near the water's edge, Duchess' eyes wide and pawing at the ground.

"Shhhh," Logan was saying, walking slowly toward her.

CJ moved closer and Duchess backed up closer to the water.

I broke through the tree line and tied Ziggy and Tucker to a nearby branch. Owen, Mickel, Jean, and Clarice were there a few moments later.

"Shhhh," Logan continued to say, trying to calm her. He had a carrot out trying to entice her.

Off to the right, there was movement in the water. Just a ripple that could have been dismissed just as the wind, if there had been any.

"Logan. Careful. Something is in the water. Off to the right," I pushed toward him and CJ.

Logan had just grabbed the reins when something lunged out of the water from the left, grabbed Duchess' back flank and pulled her into the water.

Duchess thrashed as Logan and CJ pulled on the reins. The creature's six stumpy legs had leveraged itself against the mud when its huge torso and lizard shaped head had speared out of the water and clamped down on her flank. I threw my power at it, but it hit the creature and flowed up and over it, as if I hadn't cast a thing.

I threw more and more stunning and slicing incantations at it as I made way to them, but each one, while it hit, did not do anything to deter its hold on Duchess. Her cry of pain was heart wrenching. Owen, Jean, and Clarice were throwing their power toward the creature in the water as well, but even Clarice's just flowed up and over them as if nothing was there.

Seeing movement from the right this time, I screamed as another one of those things jumped out of the water and grabbed onto Logan's leg and pulled him under.

I ran and dove into the water, CJ right beside me.

Dark. It was so dark under the water.

I flung my power out to light the way and saw Logan below us, struggling to get free.

"Down!" I pushed to CJ, who followed me as we swam further down.

My lungs were already burning, and I swam as fast as I could.

Logan reached for CJ. One more firm dolphin kick, and CJ reached for him, grasping forearms. They pulled against the hold the creature had on Logan's leg, causing red to bloom through the water. I took Logan's other hand and pulled. Logan's eyes were wide with terror.

CJ pulled his syths out and, after stabbing its jaw multiple times, one went to the hilt, and the creature finally released Logan. CJ grabbed him under the arms and swam up.

I turned to follow, closing my eyes to the shrieking that had started in my ears, when long, spiky fingers wrapped around my neck. My eyes flung open to find a scaled creature with large eyes holding me and staring into my eyes. There were spiky fins protruding from both cheeks, three on the top of its head, and many more all over its body.

It screamed at me again, and then everything went black. Flashes of lightning streaking throughout filled my vision, but then I saw a black crystal in my hands, and bright pulses of light again.

When it faded, the creature who had me by the throat was still staring at me. A moment later, in a screech of many voices at once, it said, *"Danger, Megan Mathewson. Darkness meets you in the Death. The eye will find your black. Black you must find first. The Darkness covers more light. Meet the Darkness in the Death and... explode."*

With a force a creature that appeared fragile should not have had, it flung me toward the surface, and out of the water. I gasped for air the second my head broke the surface and was in CJ's arms in an instant.

We both crashed to the ground in a heap. "Megs."

"What happened?" Clarice said, running up. Jean right behind her.

I turned my head and saw Owen working on Logan. Green light flowed around his hands against Logan's leg.

I laid there gasping for breath. CJ looked me up and down and brushed my hair back off my face. His eyes locked on my neck, and they flared in anger. "Jean, Clarice," he said, trying not to panic.

Clarice crouched down and ran her fingers carefully over my neck and I felt the small bite of her power. "She's wearing the Sa Ra. She will be fine in an hour. The cuts aren't deep. No signs of poison."

I sat up, coughing and sputtering, turned toward where Logan and Owen sat and asked, "Logan?"

"He'll be okay. He's more upset about losing Duchess," Jean said sadly and then jerked her head off to the side. "After you and CJ went in after him, his pack floated to the top. We grabbed his stuff, but knew Duchess wasn't coming back up."

I nodded.

"Megs, what happened down there?" Clarice asked.

"I got to the surface, and just when I got Logan to the shore, I felt..." CJ stopped and swallowed. "I knew something had happened to you. I was just about to dive back under when you came flying up."

"Something blue and spiny grabbed me. It had spikey fins all over its body," I said, rubbing my face.

"A Nelki maybe?" Jean said.

"It told me I had to meet the darkness in the death. The wording was strange." I shook my head again. "It said to meet the darkness in the death, then it paused and told me to explode. It stretched out the word."

"Nelki have been known to be seers in their own right," Clarice said, worry crossing her face. "But I thought they were extinct."

"If that is what it was, then apparently not," I said, getting to my feet and going to inspect Logan.

I squatted over him and studied the injury to his leg. It was pretty extensive. Skin and muscle were shredded to the bone, which poked through. Owen was keeping the bleeding down but was only making mild progress on healing the tissue.

"Lucky bastard," I said, a lump forming in my throat. "It missed the main artery. Which saved your life."

"I'm fine," He said through his teeth as Owen continued to work on his leg. Owen nodded his reassurance at the statement.

CJ came to stand behind me and pulled me close to him before saying, "Don't ever do that again, Logan. You scared the fucking hell out of me."

"No problem. Next time a creature just jumps out of nowhere and grabs me," He cringed at the pain as Owen sent a wave of his power into him, probably on purpose, "I'll just let them know they have to let me go because my brother and sister don't want me hurt."

"That would be much appreciated," I said, smiling. I could only let him joke about it, because he was going to be okay. That leg was going to take a while to heal, even with the Sa Ra, which I played with my fingers. It would take all of us to get him up and moving again. Plus, he would need time to rest.

"Let's just set up camp. We can take turns working on Logan's leg to make sure there is no infection, and we get it healed enough that he can ride tomorrow," I grumbled, but relieved.

There was total silence behind me.

I turned to face them. "What?"

"Megan," Mickel said, surprised.

"We all need to be at our best when we reach Morana. If my father is supposed to be heading in that direction, I want each of us as healthy as possible before we face him. If we have to lose one night, and rotate shifts to heal his leg, then we will. Logan can't travel like this." I said, trying to show every ounce of bravado I had left in me. "Not going to lie, Logan. You will be exhausted by morning, but if we all do a little battlefield healing, while you may have a wicked scar, you will be fine. When Owen wears out, Jean and Mickel can take over, then Clarice."

Everyone just looked at me.

I side-stepped out of CJ's arm that had a hold on me and headed into the tree line. When I thought I was far enough away that no one could hear me, I sat against a tree and cried.

We were so royally fucked.

CHAPTER 39

THAT NIGHT, AFTER I took over healing duty from Clarice, I used the Sa Ra to aid in healing it. With CJ's help, we continued working long after Logan drifted off to sleep. When I felt my power draining, I curled up with CJ and tried to work out how long we had been out here. It had only taken a little over two weeks by my count. It was better than the anticipated time frame.

The next morning, I told Logan to ride Tucker. CJ and I could ride two up on Ziggy. Logan had tried to fight us on it, but when I pointed out that he was going to have to ride someone's horse, he just glared at me with sad eyes.

"I know how much you loved Duchess," I said, putting my hand on his arm.

"I was going to ask if I could buy her when we returned to Nalrin." His eyes lowered, and I saw the tears line the ridge, but he kept them back.

"I was already planning on doing that as a minor thank you gift, anyway," I said, smiling. "Ride Tucker. Ceej can ride with me. Ziggy is already comfortable with him, so it should be fine."

Logan finally nodded, and with a little help from CJ and Mickel, he was sitting astride Tucker. We had wrapped his leg so stiffly; he wasn't able to move it much. I bound it to the stirrup and fender, just to help that little extra bit.

We rode all day, and that night, I spent a good portion of it working on Logan's leg again. Riding had split the leg open, and it was bleeding by the time we had stopped. CJ helped with the pain as I worked on it, and by the time I curled up with CJ to sleep, I collapsed into an exhausted heap. As we ate the following morning, Clarice and Owen worked on his leg, and Logan could actually bear some weight on it. He still needed help to mount Tucker but was able to rightly sit in a saddle again.

It was late in the afternoon when we could see the edge of the plateau. "Megan, do you see that?" Jean asked.

"Yes." An immense wave of relief washed over me. Two and a half weeks, including the extra couple of nights healing Logan. It only took us two and a half weeks to get through the Lost Plateau.

The horses begged to be let loose. We had been pushing them just as hard, if not harder, than we were pushing ourselves. They could very well fall from exhaustion, but the call of a stable was too much for them to resist. I could just see the top of buildings as we neared the edge of the plateau. I looked at Mickel, whose face lit up with what I assumed would be the opportunity for a warm bath.

I turned to look at Logan, who had a smirk on his face.

"Get ready to ride hard," I pushed to CJ. I felt him tense just slightly behind me, and he wrapped his arm tight around my waist and when I met Logan's eye that evil, sly smile crossed his face, I put my heels to Ziggy's sides, who bolted toward that ledge.

I vaguely heard Logan urge Tucker on, but even double up, Ziggy was just faster. It had to be a good half mile to the edge and when we got there, we skidded to a stop and looked out over the Town of Morana. There was a gentle slope down toward the town, and it took a moment to register what I was seeing.

Shouts went up in alarm, magical shields popped into place, and then there were shouts of "Stand down! Stand down!" from a familiar voice, Commander Kaiwan.

The army.

They beat us here!? How?

"Calm," CJ warned me as panic built up in my chest.

"Ceej. How? How did the soldiers beat us?" I asked. "I thought we had made good time. By my calculations, it had only been two and a half weeks. How are they here already?"

As Jean, Owen, Mickel and Clarice met up with us, they looked at us, just as confused.

"How?" Jean said.

Mickel was doing the calculations in his head, too. "Three weeks at most. And that's if I lost count of a couple of days."

Alexei came running through the lines. Clarice's face lit up, and she took off down the hill. Her horse was still running at a full gallop as she dismounted, and a soldier caught it. She ran the last few feet to Alexei and jumped into his arms.

"Very Empress like Clarice." I pushed to her. She gave me a vulgar gesture over her shoulder as Alexei kept her in his arms.

CJ nudged Ziggy, and he moved forward, almost in slow, hesitant steps. Soldiers were there to take the horses when we dismounted, and Alexei led us down to the tavern where he had already secured us rooms.

No one spoke. None of us knowing what to think of the fact they were already here, and Alexei likely gave us the space to sort out what had happened in the plateau.

We were sitting at a long wood table with long wood benches eating the first hot meal in what felt like ages, when Alexei said, "I was organizing a party to go in after you."

I froze, fork halfway to my mouth. We all looked at him. He had said he would wait five weeks. It had only been two and a half. Slowly lowering my fork, I said, "Just how long were we gone?"

"Five weeks, two days. We were going to leave tomorrow," He met my eyes with a determination I hadn't expected.

"WHAT?!" I said in a whispered shout.

"Megan, you left Millmore thirty-nine days ago. It's been over a month since we saw you last."

"Alexei, that can't be right," Owen said slowly.

"We arrived in Morana a little over a week ago. It took us four weeks to go around the Plateau. We even had some trouble with one of the supply wagons and we lost a couple of days having to get it fixed."

Alexei looked to each of us, noting the sheer confusion on our faces. Then looked at Clarice, "How long do you think you've been gone, my Silnaree?"

"By my count, we were out 17-18 days," Clarice said carefully, but firmly.

He scanned each of us as we nodded in confirmation. That sounded about right.

"Two and a half weeks is about all I can sort out," Jean said.

Logan was rubbing his leg as he said, "Does time work differently in the Plateau?"

"It must," Clarice said.

"Or... while on the rocky expanse, we lost more time than we thought. It never really gave a day / night cycle." Owen's voice was low but confused.

"Five weeks," CJ said in a long breath.

My heart raced when he said that, and his eyes jumped to me. He gave me a questioning look.

"One night. We stay one night. Tomorrow we leave for Morte Alta."

"Why can't we stay a couple of days?" Logan whined. "Two nights in a soft bed would be so nice."

It was CJ who realized what I was saying. "Because if we have been gone for five weeks, then Ansel could be here any day."

"You had estimated five to six weeks for him to get here, right?" Alexei asked. I just nodded, and he huffed out a breath. "Well, get a good night's rest. We will hold him off as long as we can until you get back."

Clarice was staring at Alexei, and my heart broke when I saw the tears in her eyes.

CHAPTER 40

WE HAD FINISHED EATING in silence, gotten our room assignments, and headed up to our rooms without much more discussion. Alexei said he would have hiking gear and supplies ready for us at dawn, then he took Clarice's hand and she followed him.

"Tell me what you're thinking," CJ said as we laid in bed. We had both taken a much-needed bath, and when we crawled into the soft bed, we just laid there staring at each other. He reached over and moved hair out of my eyes and tucked it around my ear. He didn't pull away, but instead left his hand on my neck and scooted closer to me.

"Everything," I said, trying to hold back the tears. "Feeling a bit overwhelmed, if you know what I mean."

He nodded.

"Ceej, what if we are at Morte Alta and Ansel barrels through the town?"

"I don't have an answer for you, babe," He mumbled.

"I know."

He didn't respond. He didn't need to.

"I thought... I thought for once we had the upper hand." I felt the fear rise in my chest, but CJ's thumb rubbed my cheek and it dissipated slightly. "I thought that since we made it through the Plateau so quickly, we could go meet him. Not have him chase us down, but we could go to him and stop him."

I felt his grip on my neck tighten just that bit that told me he knew what I meant. "I'm not giving up on a loophole, Megs. I can't accept that as the only option to stop your father."

I reached up and ran my hands across the scruff that had grown. "I kind of like the short scruff on you," I said, fingering it softly.

He raised an eyebrow. "Are you trying to change the subject?"

"No," I said. He huffed a snicker at that, so I conceded, "Yes. I don't want to fight with you about it. I don't want to die. I'm tired though, Ceej. I don't want to do any of this, but there isn't anyone else who *can* do it."

"I will continue to look for that loophole until the very last moment. I'm not giving up on us, Megs."

I ran my hand along his ear and slowly down his neck. His mouth opened slightly as I traced the muscles on his chest and placed my palm on his heart. "I love you Cory James Mathewson. No matter what else happens in the next few days, always remember that."

"Megs." My name was whisper of a prayer on his lips.

I rolled on top of him and kissed him gently as his hands wrapped around me tightly. When my tongue ran across his lips, he opened for me and kissed me. There was nothing hurried or demanding in any of our movements. Just us, holding each other.

He rolled me back onto my back and when he looked down at me, we were both breathless. His eyes burned with sadness, need but, most of all love. Slowly, he kissed my neck, my collarbone, and when he reached my breasts, he simply kissed each one. Tenderly, he put his head down against my heart, and when he heard it racing, I felt him smile against my skin.

Running my hands through his hair, we sat like that for moments or hours. When he lifted his head, he kissed my heart, and looked up at me, fiery need now burning in his eyes. He still didn't hurry or rush, but he slid my shorts off and kissed each side of my thighs.

"Ceej."

"Shh, baby," he said as he separated me and flicked his tongue over that bundle of nerves. I moaned and grabbed onto the sheets.

CJ slowly and methodically licked every inch of me. He circled my opening, and then slowly slid his tongue in to lick up every drop he could reach. His tongue left no part of me unexplored and by the time he clamped down on my clit, I was writhing. He licked and sucked as he slid two fingers deep inside me, and I grabbed onto the headboard to keep from flying into the skies. Moments later, CJ had me coming.

As I came down from that high, he raised his head, kissed my womb, and hovered over me a moment, looking down the length of our bodies.

"Spectacular," he said as he met my gaze. Kissing me softly, I felt him nudge himself against my opening, and I thrust my hips up to meet him as he filled me.

A soft purr of pleasure came from him, as he stilled, hovering over me. "I love you, Megan Isabel Mathewson."

"And I love you, Cory James Mathewson. In every lifetime," I whispered against his lips.

When our eyes met, he moved within me. Small, gentle strokes as we just stared into each other's eyes. We moved slowly, just enjoying the feel of each other. This wasn't a rage of emotions that needed to be released. This was just us. Slow and gentle, and when he hit that spot inside me, I moaned and softly raked my nails across his back.

I wrapped my legs around his waist as he moved slowly within me again. He'd slowly pull out, and I met him for each full joining and roll against him. His breath was a caress on my skin as we moved. My eyes rolled back and back arched as he hit that spot within me again.

"Like that, do you?" he whispered in my ear and nibbled it. A soft moan was my only reply as he did it again. Then again.

I raked my nails down his back a little harder as he nibbled my ear again. I could hear his breathing getting faster, and he rocked his hips again, rubbing that spot.

"Holy…" My words were cut off as he repeated the movements again and again. "Ceej," I moaned louder.

When he grabbed my breast, his hips rolled against me and I arched my back, feeling him twitch slightly within me. When he pinched my nipple as he rolled his hips, I moaned his name to the universe as I came so hard that my entire body shut down. My mind went completely black. He thrust long and hard one more time, and this time it was my name that filled the room.

He rested his forehead to mine as I held his face, eyes closed. He kissed me and whispered my name against my lips. There was nothing I could do but smile.

When we had caught our breath, he got up and brought back a washcloth. He cleaned me up and kissed either side of my legs, then my womb again before standing and smirking.

"What?" I asked, sitting up on my elbows.

"Just thinking about how happy you make me. Even with all that is going on. When I'm with you," he said as he tossed the washrag back into the pile of dirty towels and crawled back into bed, to lay next to me, "those things don't seem so bad. Well, most of them anyway."

I smiled at him. "I can do anything with you by my side. I will face the Darkness itself if you are there with me."

He kissed my forehead again, and then said, "Let's get some sleep. We have a long few days ahead of us."

He wrapped me up in his arms, and it didn't take long for me to get to sleep.

CHAPTER 41

THE NEXT MORNING, ALEXI indeed had a warm fur-lined jacket for each of us, along with gloves, hiking boots, and everything we needed for our trip up the mountain. We expected it to take two to three days to get there on foot, and then there was the trek back down. The terrain wasn't going to allow for us to take the horses, so while we got things together, I stared at the medallion that would be our guide. How it was going to be our guide, I had no idea, but the Cinder Fairies had said it would help me find Helena.

It had warmed when we got to Morana, and I tried to take that as a good sign that we were at least heading in the right direction. While we were packing a few of our belongings, I asked quietly, "Clarice, why don't you stay here with Alexei?"

She looked at me like I had lost my marbles. "What?"

"Why don't you stay here with Alexei?" I asked again.

"Are you ordering me to stay to help protect the town?" she asked. There was a twitch in her eye that made me think she might have been hurt by the question.

"Clarice, technically, you outrank me," I said, giving her a knowing look. "But no, of course not. I'm just asking if you'd like to stay with Alexei."

She stopped and then came around the table we were at and took my hands. "Megan, we are family. No one outranks anyone and I will not abandon you. Sure, once all of this is over, and should we live, Alexei and I will have to go back to Therth, but until then, I will not abandon you to face this on your own. It's what family does or is supposed to do. Be there for each other."

"But Alexei is your Silnaree," I said, emphatically.

"And he is doing his job as I am doing mine," She said proudly. "He is running the military we have here, and I am working with my family to save the world."

I met her gaze and there was not one ounce of sorrow or hesitation in her gaze.

"What if—" I started to say, but she interrupted me.

"He dies while we are at Morte Alta?" she asked quietly.

I nodded. "I would never forgive myself."

"While I will be devastated on the day that the Angels take him to the Underworld, I will also know that he loves me unconditionally. And if that day happens to be in the next week, I will also know he died trying to protect his family. What more can I ask for from my Silnaree?" Her eyes were lined with tears and there was a small catch in her voice as she said the last words.

I threw my arms around her. "I love you, Clarice."

"I love you too, Megan," She whispered against my head. "Now, I think just about everyone is ready to head out. It's going to be a long day."

I swung my pack on and buckled the straps. I had to adjust my syth belt slightly to still have access to them, but I did a couple of test jumps, and everything stayed secured. Walking out of the tavern, Owen, Jean, Logan, and Mickel were also ready to head out. Logan had even procured a sword from one of the soldiers and it was attached to his side. I stood there and just looked at my brother-in-law. He had changed so much in the last year. He quirked an eyebrow as if to say, *'Yes?'*

"Nothing. Just noting how much you've changed in the last year," I pushed to him.

He huffed a short laugh, played with the strap from his backpack and just whispered, "Love will do that to you."

I studied him, and while there was pain and heartbreak in his face, there was also a sense of purpose. How had I even considered leaving him in Nalrin? He needed to do this. I looked at CJ and noticed the look of pride on his face as he looked at his brother.

"I'm proud of you, Logan. Lindy would be too," I pushed toward him and he just gave me a sad smile. It hurt my heart so much, but Lindy would be very proud of him for stepping up to help protect his family.

"You two done having your own private conversation?" Owen teased.

"Should I be worried?" CJ laughed. I just leveled a look at him that had him smiling brightly.

"Ready?" I asked, rolling my eyes. Quick short nods from everyone, and CJ reached his hand out for mine as we headed up the mountain to find Helena.

CHAPTER 42

"THE PLATEAU LOOKS SO unassuming from here," I said, as we stopped for the second night. I had been staring at the eye medallion as it nudged us in the right direction. Mickel sat down on the edge of the cliff with me as Logan and Owen worked on making dinner. Just earlier today, we stood at a fork in the path, and when I laid it flat in the palm of my hand, the point of it moved to show the direction we needed to go. It did it again a couple hours later, when there were three paths that we could have taken, it still pointing the way toward Helena. Hopefully. I slid it back into the interior pocket of my jacket and zipped my jacket back up tight.

"Five weeks," Mickel said quietly. "We spent five weeks in there. I still can't wrap my head around it."

He fell quiet again. In fact, he had been pretty quiet since we had gotten to Morana. There were times I'd find him in deep contemplation, and others, he just quietly observed. I didn't know if it was the training, or what.

"You okay, Mickel?" I asked carefully.

"Yes. No." He sighed. "I've just got this pit in my stomach that something isn't right."

I gave him a look. "What in the last couple years has been right, Mickel?"

Mickel huffed a laugh and said, "That's true, but that isn't what I mean." He looked down at his lap. "Just a bad feeling is all. I feel like shit is going to hit the fan, as you say."

"It indeed is, but we knew it was coming eventually," I said with a deep sigh. "Can I tell you a secret?"

His eyes widened, but then became weary.

"I'm scared to fucking death. I don't want to die. I don't want to leave you, the family, and I definitely do not want to leave CJ, but I can't think of a way around it. CJ is still looking for a loophole, but no matter what way I look at it, there isn't one." I said and took a shaky deep breath.

Once I calmed myself again, I continued, "I will die, Mickel. I will do it to save you. I will do it to save Jean, Owen, Clarice, Alexei, Logan, and CJ. I will do it to save Julian and Nalsar. Even if I had known where my life would lead me, I wouldn't change the last few years. It led me to being able to finally be with CJ, meeting my family and you. I don't think I've ever told you how much I appreciate you. You protect us, worry for us."

His eyes flicked to where Jean was.

"It goes beyond that." I smiled. "Mickel, you are one of the most loyal, kindest, and bravest people I know. You did not have to go on this mission. You could have stayed in Nalrin to protect Julian. Yet you didn't. You came with us. Why?"

"I was assigned to protect Logan." Mickel said, not meeting my eye.

"Mickel." I drew out his name in reprimand.

He hung his head for a minute, sighed, and smiled. "Because you *are* family. Owen and Jean have been for as long as I have known them, but you, CJ, Clarice. Over the last year you have become irreplaceable family." He looked over at Logan, who was laughing with CJ, and it made my heart warm a little. "Now it has grown by two with Logan and Alexei."

There was a hidden meaning in there I didn't understand. I studied him for a moment before I asked, "Mickel, you don't talk about your own biological family. In all the time we have spent together, I can't think of a single instance where you have."

He took a deep breath, before turning back to look out over the Plateau. "That's because for one, they are all dead. Second, somewhere along the line, as I rose in the ranks in the Guard, they just stopped communicating with me."

"I'm sorry, what? Why?" I stammered.

"I tried, but they ignored all my letters. Once, I even tried going to the family property to see how they were doing, and it was spelled against me. I couldn't cross onto the land. I saw one of my brothers working the field, and when he saw me, he just turned his back on me and walked off. Didn't even tell me to go away. Just walked off."

I blinked. "Mickel..."

"A few years later, I found out that the entire property had burned and so I went to find out if they still lived. When I got there, the neighbor said he had torched the place after they had all died, as per my father's instructions. He wouldn't tell me how they died but handed me a letter from my father. It said that if the family had perished, that he was leaving me nothing. He instructed the neighbor to torch the land, so that I couldn't even have the house as a memento. He told Nalrin they could add it to the general Nalsar Forestry. The worst part? I don't even know what I did. I have no idea where I went wrong with them."

"You already had watched Jean and Owen get married by that point, right?" I asked. Not sure why that was an important distinction.

"Yeah. They had wed about a year after I had stopped hearing from them," Mickel said, looking over at Jean and Owen. "So, my biological family is dead. I continued to live my life, and now I sit here to protect my new family. For the family that I have chosen, and the family that has chosen me."

Tears were streaming down my face now, and I looked to where CJ and Logan were sitting and, while still talking to

Logan, CJ turned to me with a question on his face. *"I'm fine,"* I pushed to him. He nodded and turned back to Logan.

Sniffing, I asked, "So do I call you Uncle Mickel? Oh no, I got it. Uncle Mickey!" I said, laughing.

"No!" Mickel said, horrified. "Never. I might die if anyone ever calls me Uncle Mickey. And no. You are not to call me Uncle Mickel. If anything, I think of you as my baby sister."

Warmth filled my heart at that. "Gods, another brother. I have brothers coming out of my ears." I teased him but beamed at him. "I would be honored to have you as my brother."

"Good." He smiled back. "I love all of you, and I am terrified of the day when we have to face Ansel. I swear Megan, oath or no, I will do everything I can to protect each and every one of this family."

"I know." I looked back out over the Plateau, and murmured, "I just hope it doesn't cost any of us our lives."

We sat in silence, just watching the clouds roll over the Plateau in odd waves for another twenty minutes before Jean came over and told us dinner was ready.

That night, none of us talked about what was to come, but only talked about the happiness in our lives. We joked, reminisced, teased, and cherished each other. If I were to die soon, I would be glad to have had this as one of my last nights.

CHAPTER 43

BY NOON THE NEXT day, we were having to stop more often to rest. The air was getting so thin that I started to wonder if we should have asked for air tanks. I was fighting headaches, and I kept trying to sip on water to keep myself hydrated. It was helping, but the headaches persisted.

Two hours after our last stop, we were staring at a long stone stairway to what appeared to be an old gothic church. This high up, we hadn't seen much in the way of vegetation, but along the stairway there were green bushes with small white breathing flowers with bright blue tips. I blinked, looked to the rest of my family, and they were as well.

"Desmo Nitors," Clarice said, reaching toward one. As her fingers trailed along the thirteen-pointed petal, blue sparkles rose and dissipated into the air.

"What is it about the flowers?" Logan asked. Mickel had a small crunch to his eyebrows and clearly wanted to know as well.

"A couple years ago, when my parents were trying to build the weapon of The Five Angels, we attempted to stop them from getting this flower in the Angel of Beauty's garden in the Manusia."

CJ took my hand and rubbed his thumb over my wedding ring, and I smiled. He said, "I asked Megan to marry me there. Then her parents showed up, and we tried real hard to stop them, but we failed. They got the flower and Owen was pretty seriously hurt."

"They aren't supposed to bloom though unless it's the third Friday the 13th of a year, and between midnight and sunrise. There isn't one here in Nalrin for several years yet," Jean said in awe.

"So, how are these here and blooming?" Logan asked.

As we looked up to the main building, there was ivy growing all over the stone of the church, and I said, "I have no idea. Maybe it's an Angel's location."

I took out the medallion, laying it flat in the palm of my hand. The heat radiating off the medallion burned, but as it laid in my hand, it spun like a top for a moment and settled to point the way up the stairs. Closing my hand around it, gritting against the heat, I turned in circles and faced another direction. As I did, I felt it fight to stay pointing in the direction of the stairs in my hand. I opened my palm, and it sprung into place. Once again, indicating up the stairs.

"Stairs it is," Jean said.

"At least it will be a stable surface to walk on." Owen chuckled. "I've lost count how many times I've almost rolled my ankles."

So up we went. About halfway, Jean and Owen stopped, putting their hand up in front of them. Against a clear wall.

"It's warded," Clarice said, her face distant.

There was a small plaque just to our right that read, *"Morte Alta. Where the winged ones can fly and the Blessed can enter."*

"Umm, okay," Mickel said, confused.

I went to put my hand against the wall to see if I could use my power to coax it to allow us through, but my hand went straight through, right next to where Jean and Owen's hands were.

CJ took my hand and gave me a meaningful look. I took a step beyond that invisible barrier and walked right on through, CJ right behind me. We just looked at each other.

Mickel reached the wall, and his hand met with solidness as well. Logan tried, and it was the same. CJ took Logan's hand, but where Logan should have been able to cross the threshold, his fingers met the solidness of the barrier.

Clarice stepped up and walked right on through.

"I don't understand," I said to everyone.

"Clarice is the Gatekeeper to the Underworld. Her entire family line is Angels Blessed. We determined long ago that you were blessed by the Angels, and CJ is an Angels Blessed Vernadali, for goodness' sake." Jean said, shaking her head. "Guess they mean the blessed part of that statement literally."

"Show off." Logan said, smiling and rolling his eyes.

"But—" I started to say.

"No buts. Go. Get what you need. We will wait and make camp. It will be tight, but at least once you get her, you can rest. We can make our way back down in the morning." Owen said encouragingly.

"Besides, it will give Logan some time to rest." CJ whispered to me. "He's been limping on that leg the last couple of hours."

"Have not!" Logan said, glaring at his brother.

"You have," CJ said firmly, crossing his arms. "No one expected you to be perfectly fine. That was a serious injury that took the Sa Ra and most of this family to heal. The muscles are bound to be fatigued at the very least. Go. Put your leg up and stop bitching."

"Asshole," Logan said.

"Fuck-tard," CJ retorted.

"BOYS!" I said as they looked at me, their eyes wide with shock. "Logan, go help get camp set up and put that fucking leg up. Your brother isn't wrong, and you need to just admit that you have been seriously hurt. Now I'm going to say this one more time. Go put your fucking leg up and rest it, fucker."

Clarice chuckled next to me and finally said, "We shouldn't be more than a few hours." Then turned to head up the stairs, CJ close behind her.

I glared at Logan again before he stuck his tongue out at me. Owen smacked him upside the back of his head. As he rubbed the back of it, his shock at Owen actually smacking him, I laughed and headed up the stairs.

CHAPTER 44

WITH EACH STEP, THE air got thinner and heavier at the same time. By the time we reached the top of the stairs, where a path rounded around a rock formation that led to the massive entrance to the structure built into the mountain. We were all breathing in short, quick breaths. The entrance was made completely of stone with tall delicate windows open to the air around it. It was beautiful and eerie at the same time. With the passage of time, the vegetation was taking back the stone structure. Vines and flowers covered much of the ground, sprawling up the walls, to the arched ceiling spearing up into the sky.

CJ took my hand as we slowly walked through the entrance to the structure. We stopped a few feet in, and just stood there staring in awe. It was warmer once you were inside, and I could feel the humidity in the air. It almost felt tropical. We could breathe easier, and there was an easing calm that flowed through me, like this was where I needed to be. This was no mere building in the mountains. This place radiated power.

I unbuckled my pack and removed my jacket, letting them drop where they fell. CJ did the same, but when I looked at Clarice, she was just standing there, her head cocked to the side.

"Clarice?" I said, walking carefully up to her. Putting my hand on her shoulder, I heard her whispering low and fast in that tongue I did not know. Her eyes had that gray haze over them again, a clear sign she was talking with the dead.

"She okay?" CJ asked softly.

"I hope so. She's having a session." He nodded and looked around the room.

I went behind Clarice and just whispered, "I'm going to take your pack off, so you are more comfortable." Carefully, I unbuckled her pack and slid it off her back. Once the weight was off her, she half sighed, but continued to have her talk with the dead.

"So, what does the medallion say?" CJ asked.

I retrieved it out of my jacket pocket, moving it around in my fingers, as not to leave it in one place too long. "That it is close. It's almost too hot to hold. You have any scrap fabric I can use?"

He took his syth out and cut a piece of his t-shirt off. I gave him a smirk, and as he handed me the cloth, "No time for that right now, m'lady."

"Tease." I grinned. I grabbed the medallion, and it pointed to the right. "So deeper we go." There was a huffed cough behind me and I chucked, "You are such a child."

Centered on the back wall were two dual staircases that led to a narrow balcony surrounding the room. The closer I looked, the more corridors I saw stretching into the darkness. At the top, where the staircases met, there was a wide triple door entrance to an oversized corridor, bright with light.

I held the medallion flat in my hand as CJ followed behind me, leading Clarice with us. It twitched and moved continuously, indicating that we should head to the right. Turning down that hall, Clarice's voice became harsher and slightly louder, making me jump.

"I've got her," CJ assured me, and I nodded. The farther down the hallway we got, the warmer the medallion was in my hand. We were almost at the end of the corridor when a bright light pulsed from the last doorway on the right.

I drew my syths as CJ pulled one of his out, while guiding Clarice along with us. I slipped the medallion into my pocket, pulling on my power to be ready at a moment's notice. I felt the electricity buzz and pop in my ears. I quickly shook my head and took a deep breath to calm it. When we reached the doorway, it took everything I had not to drop the syths in my hand.

Before us was a massive, open room, twice the size of the first one we walked into. Sunlight streamed through the glassless windows at the other end, reflecting beams of light up to the arched ceilings. While it was much the same as the first room, it had a freaking creek running through the center of the room. It just randomly appeared out of a crack in the wall, near a bridge toward the back. Portions of the mountainside had crumbled into the room where ivy, ferns, grass, and flowers grew. If I closed my eyes, I could almost imagine myself back at the river near our home. The bubbling of the water as it flowed over the rocks to just below the balcony we were on was incredibly soothing.

"Prohibra!" Clarice shouted.

Turning to look at her, she was staring off toward the end of the room, where two winged creatures stood, swords in each hand on the bridge above the creek.

They leapt into the air, flying toward us, and as I threw a wall of my power up, Clarice's power barreled through my wall, and a dark wind pushed against the creatures. As they got closer to us, I saw that their bodies were humanoid, but their feet were that of a bird. The top of their head was covered in feathers, one blue, one red, and flowed down their backs to their feathered wings.

There were attempts at speech in various languages, before they reached one, Clarice understood. With a wave of her hand, CJ and I looked at each other as we understood what they were saying.

"Eta," Clarice said. "Auta tu."

"But yet you speak the language of the Underworld," The blue one said, cocking its head to the side.

"For I am the Gatekeeper of the Underworld," She said, black smoke covering her.

The red creature's eyes popped slightly at that.

"How did you find this place?" The blue one said.

"We were sent by Queen Seraphina, Queen of the Cinder Fairies," I said, standing tall.

They studied me for a moment. "The Cinder Fairy Queen." I nodded, and they continued. "For what did she send you here for? There are many things here we protect."

CJ and Clarice looked at me, letting me determine how much to tell them.

"Who are you? How do I know you are protectors, and not scavengers looking for a tasty meal?" I asked.

"We do not eat Sangra," The red one spat.

"We are the Colunt Alti," the blue one said. "May we land and speak as civil beings?"

I nodded, moving closer to the entrance in case we needed to make a run for it. They landed with smooth gracefulness and bowed toward Clarice. Sheathing their swords, they turned toward her as the blue one said carefully, "Pleasure to meet you, Gatekeeper of the Underworld. I assure you, we are no threat to you."

"The Colunt Alti were killed nearly to extinction in the 1,000 Years War," Clarice said in awe. "How did you find yourself here?"

"Helena and the Five Angels placed what was left of us here in these mountains to protect what needed it most," the blue one said.

"Yet, they didn't hide pieces for the weapon of the Five Angels here?" I asked incredulously. The Colunt Alti just shook their head.

"We do not know how they determine what to hide here and what not to hide here." The red one's voice was sad and solemn.

There was a long pause as we studied each other.

"What is it you seek, Sangra?" the blue one said as they both studied CJ carefully.

"Queen Seraphina sent us here to retrieve Helena, the Crystal of Pureness," they both snapped back to look at me.

"Helena," the red one said solemnly. "Do you know the cost of Helena? You willing to make that cost with no hesitation?"

"I do know the cost. And yes, I am willing to pay it." I stood tall as I made myself look them in the eye. CJ's hand was on my back, and I could feel his charge pulse over me.

"But he is not," The red one stated as fact, and not a question.

"I am not. I will always be looking for a loophole. Megan is my heart, and I do not want to lose her. Yet, I also understand this may be the only way to stop her father from destroying this world," CJ said, his voice filled with a determination that I didn't necessarily feel at this moment.

"But you have an... Angel's Blessed Vernadali, who was once... human and the Gatekeeper of the Underworld with you, and yet you are here to collect Helena," the red one said.

"I am." I felt my gut twist but continued to look them straight in the eye.

"Do you know why the Colunt Alti were placed here?" they said as one.

"You were some of the fairest and skilled warriors of the time," Clarice said.

"We were fair, because we could tell without a doubt whether there is truth in someone's words, or if they are bending their words to their will," the red one said, standing tall and fluffing its feathers.

"Living truth detectors," CJ said.

"Yes," the blue one said.

"And do you believe us?" CJ asked.

"There is truth in your words. While you are not telling us the complete of it, there are no false statements that have been made," the blue one said.

"Tell us your path to Helena. How did you get here?" The red one said.

So, I did. I told them of Matt, my parent's fake death, my happiness in finding my new family, Noctulanar, marrying CJ, and the death of Lindy. I told them of our realization this was the only way to stop Ansel, our way here, and when I was done, I said, "So now I stand before you, asking that you let me pass to obtain Helena so that I can stop Ansel. I am the only living being in any dimension that can stop him, and I can only do so with Helena."

When they said nothing, I looked up at them and their wings had both drooped slightly, their mouths both slightly slack jawed. They looked at each other, their own silent language between them, before they turned to us and said, "Queen Seraphina gave you the key?"

"The key?"

"The key," they said in unison. "Follow us."

They walked down the stairs, and we made our way along the creek. I couldn't help but bend down and run my hands through it. The water was warm like bathwater. I looked to Clarice, and she had a very strange look on her face, then said, "When I first passed through the entrance, I... I was swarmed with stories of the dead. Why did none of the Colunt Alti speak to me?"

The blue one stopped and turned toward her. "Because the Colunt Alti do not go to the Underworld, or the Five Angels. The Colunt Alti disappear into nothing upon our death."

"You aren't reborn or go anywhere after?" CJ said. "What about your soul?"

"As I said, our being disappears into nothingness. It is what keeps us from ruining the life that we have. Knowing that we go nowhere and that we do not have a life to do over again, we live our best lives in the here and now," the red one says with a small smile on its face.

As we reached the bridge, the medallion in my pocket went cold as ice.

"She is in here," the blue one said.

I looked under the bridge, beyond the bushes and flowers that bloomed. Just to the left there was a small altar about knee high. I glanced at CJ and Clarice.

"We will stay out here with the Colunt Alti," Clarice said.

Nodding, I pushed a little of the foliage away and walked toward the small alcove.

CHAPTER 45

I DROPPED TO MY knees before the small altar and ran my hands along the stone edge of it. It was simple. Just long irregular stones laid atop each other until there was a flat surface. Dirt and moss had grown within the cracks, and upon that surface a larger stone sat with a little alcove carved into it.

I sent my power into the back of the alcove, to light it up and saw six figures carved into the stone. The center figure was different from the other. A woman, hair flowing in every direction, sitting cross-legged, with her hands out to either side. Slightly behind her and on either side were five figures I would know in my sleep. The Five Angels.

"Helena," I breathed.

A small stone box sat in front of the carvings. I reached out and ran my fingers over it and my power reacted to it instinctively. Electricity arced from my fingers to the edges of the box, clearing away all dust and debris. Slowly, I pulled it closer and tried to lift the lid, but it did not budge.

I studied the box, looking for a button, a sliding mechanism, something to release the lid. Looking back to CJ and Clarice, I saw CJ talking fervently with the Colunt Alti, both of them looking deep in thought. Clarice looked back at me and smiled softly.

Turning my attention to the box again in front of me, I noticed the light etching on the top. I ran my fingers over it by memory now. The medallion. Slowly, I pulled it out of my pocket and looked at it, comparing the images. Mirrors. They were mirror images of each other. I looked back to the Colunt Alti and whispered, "The key."

Placing the eye shaped medallion carefully on the top of the box, it sat within the grooves. With a small click, light flared around the medallion as it spun, and the lid popped up. Air whooshed out of me in one quick breath.

Sitting there in the box, was a solid black sheet of paper with clear, elegant silver writing on it. The words had my heart stopping. "Megan Isabel Mathewson."

"Holy fuck," I whispered as I sat back on my heels, staring at the contents of the box.

CJ was there in an instant. When he noticed what I was staring at, he said, "How?"

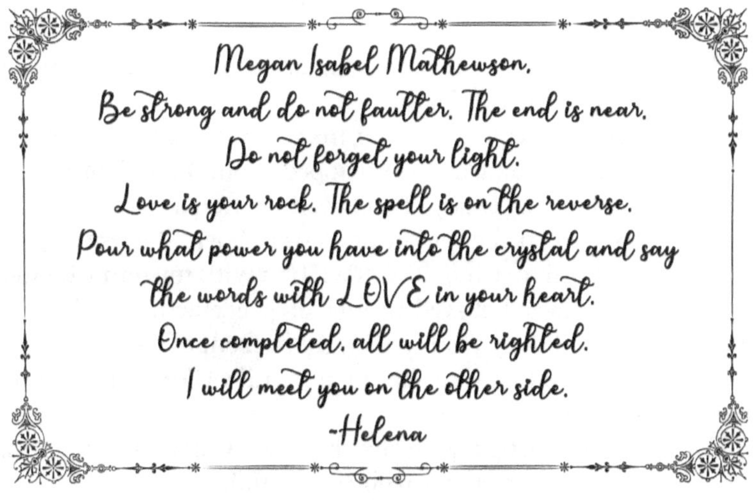

Slowly, with shaky hands, I pulled it out and when I opened it, there was a soft caress along my bones.

Flipping the page over, it simply gave me the incantation to read. There was a rock–hard lump in my throat as the last shred of any hope faded away. This was written long, long ago, and while I had accepted what I must do, there was that little sliver of hope that CJ would find a way to stop it.

That was well and truly gone now.

"She knew you would retrieve it," CJ said in awe, his hand on my back as a steady presence. I could do nothing but nod.

Hands shaking slightly, I picked up the parchment wrapped rectangle out of the box, and slowly unwrapped it. A solid black rough crystal sat there in the palm of my hand. I fingered the irregular grooved grains on the surface, and that soft caress whispered against my bones again. Only this time, there was a soft whisper to it that sounded like my name. CJ put his hands on my shoulders and a bright light surrounded us. It was warm and welcoming, but when it retreated, I felt empty and cold.

I quickly wrapped it back up and stuffed it into my pocket, taking a deep breath to solidify myself again.

I stood. Walking back out from behind the foliage, I turned to see CJ staring at the box. Feeling the weight of my stare, he turned toward me, and I saw tears flowing down his face.

"Ceej." I whispered.

He shook his head as if not to say anything, but as I walked back to him, I pushed, *"I know."*

"There has to be a way," He said, his voice cracking as I put my arms around his waist, as his wrapped around me tightly.

There was nothing to say. It had been written in silver elegant ink long ago. Long before either of us were born. It was written with the Ash'bani in mind. It was written with my name bound to him. I had never believed in fate, or predetermined destiny, but... how could I deny what was right in front of us?

We stood there like that for a long while, Clarice letting us have our moment.

The sun was getting low in the sky when Clarice finally said, "We need to get to the others before nightfall."

Only then did he release me and lead me out by my hand.

"Thank you both for your help," I said sadly to the Colunt Alti.

"May your Gods and Angels be with you." They bowed before taking to the sky and out one of the upper windows.

We put our jackets on, and I slid Helena into the inside pocket. Slowly zipping it so that it wouldn't accidentally fall out. It was a solid, weighted reminder of what waited for me when I met with my father. Once my pack was back on, CJ took my hand again, holding tight the entire way out of Morte Alta and down those stairs to where our family waited for us. It was only when Logan handed CJ a bowl of hot soup that he let go of my hand.

"So, by the look on CJ's face, I take it you have her?" Logan whispered. I felt CJ stiffen and the rest of my family looked at me.

"Yes." My voice was barely a whisper as I stared at the ground.

"Megan?" Jean asked. "What happened?"

"We met the guardians of Morte Alta. The Colunt Alti."

"What?" Mickel said. "They... haven't been seen for eons."

"Apparently, the Five Angels have them up there to protect relics," Clarice said. "Helena wasn't the only thing up there."

"Wow. What a sight that would have been. They were fascinating warriors. They are rumored to have felled entire fields in moments. Until they were nearly wiped out, then no one knew where they were," Mickel said.

"I suppose that we probably shouldn't mention that they are up there." Owen said sternly.

"Of course not." Mickel said with some wry amusement.

"What else, Megan." Jean asked.

I glanced at CJ, who took a deep breath and spat, "We got Helena and her fucking spell."

"Ceej," Logan said.

CJ got up and walked off. Logan narrowed his eyes at me in question, and I just looked away. Logan's stare weighed heavily on me for a long moment before he got up and said in a way that made it clear his heart was breaking, "Cor."

Logan caught up to him about thirty feet down the path and pulled him into a big hug. CJ resisted for a moment, but then he grabbed a hold of him tight and I saw his shoulders shake. CJ has always been so strong for me. To see him like this, it shattered my heart.

"Megan," Jean said again.

"Yeah?"

"Are you okay?" she asked.

"I don't even know anymore. I knew I would be giving my life for this. I thought I had accepted that fate, but the realization that there really is no other way is a bitter pill. There was this small shred of hope that CJ could find a way out. That was shattered today."

"How?" Mickel said carefully.

I just looked at him.

Then in his bodyguard voice, that big brother voice he said he was going to be to me, he said, "How Megan? How was that hope shattered today?"

"Because there was a note. From Helena. Written eons ago. It had my name on it. Not just Megan. Not Megan Keller, in anticipation of me killing my father, but Megan Isabel Mathewson. My name as given to me by the man I will shatter to pieces when I have to kill myself to save him and the rest of this world." My voice was hard and I was barely able to get the words out around the boulder that was in my throat.

I couldn't look at any of them. I stared at my bowl of stew, feeling the weight of their stares. When I heard Logan trying to comfort CJ and put my bowl down. "I'm going to lie down. I'll see you all in the morning."

I laid there shivering for two hours before CJ came and laid down next to me, pulling me close. I was instantly warm against him.

Neither of us said a word all night.

Neither of us got much sleep, either.

CHAPTER 46

AS WE ROUNDED ONE of the many switchbacks two and a half days after getting Helena, you could see far across the Vandrer Grasslands and into the Lost Plateau, Morana, just below us. The town was so small, but the soldier's camp seemed to be bigger than it was when we left. Movement out back into the grasslands caught my eye, and I froze.

"Megan, what is it?" CJ said, instantly on alert.

"CJ," I said, my heart racing. "Please tell me that isn't what I think it is."

"Oh, holy fuck," CJ said slowly and grabbed my arm. "We have to get moving." I planted my feet in place, and just stared out at the mass coming toward Morana.

"What is it?" Jean asked, Owen and Clarice joining her next to me.

I felt more than saw their horror and fear at the expanse of black that was heading straight for Morana. A quick look below us said that we had hours of hiking down the mountain still.

"Owen, we have what, maybe a day before Ansel's army arrives?" I asked.

"If we are lucky. They could arrive before nightfall. If we can see them move from this distance..." Owen said, trailing off.

"We have hours back to the town," Jean said, turning to him.

When I turned to Clarice, her eyes had gone distant. "Clarice?" I said carefully.

"Shhhhh," she said, and I cocked my head. What was she hearing?

"It's an army of Ja'Nee. Ansel *is* with them," she said, her voice throaty and distant. After another moment, her eyes cleared, and she looked at me eyes wide. "Rage. Anger. So much fury."

"Does he know?" CJ asked, pure Vernadali. "Does he know we are here?"

Her voice broke as tears were in her eyes, "I... I don't know. The dead are quiet now. They... they fear the Ja'Nee, and... him."

"We need to get down this mountain," CJ said, looking down the hill. He was wondering if we could survive just going straight down. "We have to evacuate the town. We have to get all the innocents out. Get to Alexei and have him prepare the soldiers."

"Megan, can you push a message to him from this distance?" Clarice said, fear lacing her voice. It was fear for Alexei, the fear for the fight that was coming.

I shook my head, pulling my fur-lined hood over my head and then whispered to the wind, "The creature in the water..." Didn't it say that Darkness would meet me in the Death? Not in death, but in *the* death.

"What does Morana mean?" I asked quietly. I was met with blank looks. "What is the meaning of the name of Morana?"

Realization crossed Jean's face, but then it fell into one of despair and dread. "The Death."

"What is it?" Owen asked.

I replayed the creature's words in my head over, and over, as my heart raced. *"Meet the Darkness in the Death and explode."*

I shook my head and pulled the fur-lined hood tighter around my face. All the warmth had drained from me. The weight of

Helena with the spell wrapped around it felt like a lead weight in my pocket. "I need to be closer before I can warn Alexei."

CJ was still looking over the edge and weighing the options. Owen and Jean stared at each other, and the shadows of that silent conversation broke my heart. Clarice just looked at me for a long moment until her eyes popped as she, too, realized what was likely going to happen down there. I just grabbed CJ's arm and said, "Let's move. No more breaks. We rest tonight."

Hopefully.

Four hours later, light was fading on the horizon, the temperature was dropping, and now it was sprinkling. When we could see the town off in the distance, I pushed toward Alexei, *"Ansel and his army are incoming. Evacuate the town."*

Two minutes later, the town bells cried, and I released a breath in relief he had received it. It took us another ten minutes to get to the town where Alexei stood with Commander Kaiwan and a few various other commanders.

After a quick reunion with Clarice, I said, "There are more soldiers?"

Alexei smiled and said, "Another five battalions arrived yesterday from the North. Most are from the Lankspur Islands. They got Julian's call for aid, and they sent what they had training on the ice fields of Nalsar south down along the Black Mountains. Scared us near to death."

"Five battalions?" Mickel said in shock.

"Little more than that, really. There were people who volunteered along the way that just joined them on their trek down here." Alexei said, still surprised at the reinforcements that arrived.

"That's another three thousand troops," Owen said in awe.

More and more people streamed by on their horses heading north.

Sighing, Alexei said, "I sent scouts out to see if they are stopping for the night, so we have more time to get people out." His eyes flicked to me. "To get *you* out."

CJ asked, "Do you have an exit plan? Do you have a way to get Megan out of here without having to go through the Plateau?"

"If you can ride hard and fast enough along the mountain range north," Alexei said, "You can ride to Jacquon Port. There a ship can take you to the Curtails of the North."

I just stared off toward that army and to where I hoped Ansel was. I could hear them discussing exactly how they were going to sweep me away during the night, but I didn't hear a word of it.

"No."

"Megs." Logan huffed out. Mickel stared at me stone faced, his eyes betraying the hurt he tried to hide. Yet there was understanding there as well. Owen, Jean and Clarice looked at me, wide eyed, but CJ and Alexei continued to talk and work out the escape route.

"No." I gritted through my teeth. "We take him out. Here. We end this."

CJ's face was frozen in horror as he stared at me.

"Lady Megan." Commander Kaiwan said, but clamped his mouth shut at the look I gave him.

"There are no towns for well over a day's ride in any direction. With the Plateau cliff face to the west and the mountains to the east, he has to filter into us. It's the best defensible position we are going to get." I turned to the Commanders, "Get the town people out. Make sure to spirit away anyone with Ash'bani blood in them immediately. Get them as far away as possible. Soldiers, too." They turned without another word to carry out my orders.

"Megan," Jean said, but her words got stuck in her throat.

"I know." My voice sounded small, even to my own ears.

"Megan," Jean said again, her voice cracking on the words. I stood up straight and stared her down.

"I know." I said more forcefully, refusing to look back at CJ. "We get everyone out. Verify that Ansel is here, and I get to the highest point in town. The belltower should work. "

"If we can lead Ansel to the tower, he will be at ground zero," Owen said methodically, but even his voice hitched slightly.

I looked at Clarice, whose eyes were filled with tears. She simply nodded. Streams of villagers barreled past us on horses. Not taking one small glance backwards at what they were leaving behind.

"Go. Help the Commanders get everyone out of town," I said, still avoiding CJ's eye. When Clarice moved to walk by me, I took her hand and said, "Please, if you can feel any Ash'bani in town, please ensure they get as far from here as possible." She nodded and strode off.

I watched them walk toward the town and let out a long sigh as I felt CJ come stand behind me, that Vernadali Charge rolling off him in desperate waves, and took my hand.

Pulling myself together, I turned to face him. "Cee—"

My voice was cut off as he took my face in his hands and kissed me.

CHAPTER 47

"No." CJ BREATHED, BARELY pulling back.

There was a lump in my throat so hard, it hurt to breathe, but I said, "It's time."

"Megs, please."

"It's time," I repeated. I cupped his face in my hands and made myself look into his eyes.

"No. I'm not ready," he begged. "There has to be another... I'm not ready."

Running my thumb across his cheek, I croaked, "I know."

His mouth opened and closed as tears filled his eyes.

"I will wait for you," I said, my voice cracking horribly. "I will wait with the Angels for you, and we will move on to our next lives together. You are my heart. In every lifetime. You are my heart, and we will have a happily ever after."

The sounds of shouting and orders were heard all around us. I heard someone call for me, but Owen pulled them away. I couldn't thank Owen enough for that.

"And you are mine." He cracked so hard at those words, I felt a shudder go through him. "I told you before, it has always been you. It will always be you. You are my heart Megan Isabel Mathewson."

I moved and kissed him as softly as I could. "I love you."

"I love you," he said in one final plea.

A scout on horseback came skidding to a halt next to us, making us jump back. CJ already had his syths in his hands and was standing in front of me. I put my hand on his shoulder, "It's okay. It's just the scout Alexei sent out." CJ relaxed slightly, but did not put the syths away.

Alexei came out from behind another building and said, "Report."

"They do not stop. They march on. The town will be under siege by nightfall, likely earlier."

"Is it just the Ja'Nee? Does he have the tar as well?" I asked carefully, trying to pull myself back together. "Did you see Ansel there?"

"I did not see Ansel, Lady Megan," he said and then lowered his voice, "but yes, there is a large mass at the front of the army."

"Spread the word," Alexei said.

CJ looked back at me, and I couldn't meet his eyes.

"How many are left to be evacuated?" I asked, facing Alexei.

"About 150," he said, looking at CJ, and the look on his face was one of understanding. "Clarice scanned the town and found one family with Ash'bani blood. They are loading their horses now. They live on the northern edge, so they should be able to clear the... spell zone," Alexei said, "Depending on time."

"Hopefully, we can hold off the army and Ansel long enough for them to get far enough away." I said, looking at the soldiers around us. How many of them would make it through the next few hours?

Commander Kaiwan asked tentatively, "How long do you need, Lady Megan?"

"I don't know," I said, my hand going to my pocket.

"Everyone who came from Obsecuritan, Lady Megan, is here as a volunteer. We all knew this could be a one-way trip," Alexei said, knowing what I thought.

"When we received orders from Head Julian to meet you, Lady Megan, they were given a choice. There was no dishonor in refusing to join the ranks," Commander Kaiwan said. "In fact, many from other battalions joined us. More than what was ordered came to defend you, Lady Megan."

"Any of them have Ash'bani blood?" I asked quietly and when no one answered, I growled through my teeth, "I am about to die to save everyone. The least you can do is give me the honor of fucking answering me."

"There are," Alexei said.

"Do they know? Do they know that if I use Helena that they will die?"

"They do, Lady Megan." Commander Kaiwan said. "Most of them have told stories of their families being taken by Ansel. Some come to join those families, others come to defend their memory, whether they make it out or not."

CJ took my hand and interlaced his fingers with mine, then brought them up to his lips. He didn't say anything, but there was nothing left to say, anyway. I turned back to them and said, "So we have what, two hours to sundown?"

They nodded and I let out a long breath. "I need verification that Ansel is with the army. I won't use Helena until we are sure he is here. Let's see if we can fight him first. I don't want any soldiers to die to Helena if he isn't even here. I will use her. Vernadali CJ will stay with me. We need to get Ansel to wherever I am. Understood?"

"Until then, we fight. We kill each and every Ja'Nee that shows up," CJ said. His voice steadier now. His Vernadali Charge gave him the strength to keep moving, to keep me alive. "The only way they die is to decapitate them. They pop into dust at that."

Commander Kaiwan turned and started yelling instructions. The last of which being to protect Lady Megan and Vernadali CJ at all costs. The thought of CJ being the only one standing by the end of this made my heart crack further.

CJ led me back to the tavern and up to our room. I know it wasn't right to let everyone else prepare the town while CJ and I hid away. I knew it was weak, but there was nothing I could do out in the town, anyway.

When we got to our room, he turned and softly closed the door, and without turning around, said, "We have said what needs to be said. I don't need to make love to you one last time. I just want to hold you."

I took my jacket off and took his hand, forcing him to turn to look at me. Tears were streaming down his face. "I'm your Angels Blessed Vernadali, and I'm supposed to be the one who is supposed to be strong for you. Yet, I can't help but fall apart inside at the mere thought..." he said the last word as a broken whisper.

"I know Ceej. I don't want to die," I said, letting out a short huff of a breath. "I'm just so tired."

His eyes cleared a little as he picked me up and carried me to the bed. He sat up against the headboard, pulled me over his lap, and held me tight.

"I'm tired of the running. I'm tired of the hate. I'm tired of my family being hurt. I'm tired of the fear of Ansel getting ahold of you again, or any of the family. I'm tired of everyone being Lady Megan this, Lady Megan that. I'm tired of the judgmental looks. I'm tired of going into a town and the people either being consumed by that tar, or the people staring at us wondering if we were going to bring Ansel there, just because we passed through. I hate knowing that could happen." I leaned my head on his shoulder and he squeezed me tighter.

"I just want this to be over," I whispered, but even that sounded too loud for the room. I ran my fingers over the tattoo on his forearm, committing it to memory.

"I know," CJ said. He took a shuddering deep breath, and I felt his charge wrap around me like a warm blanket.

A little over an hour later, there was a soft knock on the door.

"It's open." CJ called.

"Megs," Logan said, dripping wet, with a sword sheathed behind his back. He slowly stepped inside with Mickel behind him, looking much the same.

I pulled myself from on top of CJ, crawled to the edge of the bed and slid the black crystal and paper into my pant pocket.

"I just wanted to come and," Logan sniffed, and when he looked at his brother, then to me, the tears started falling. I ran to him and gave him a big hug.

"I love you, too, Logan." I said against his shoulder as he wept. "I love you too. Tell Mom and Dad I love them. Tell our friends in the Manusia that I loved them fiercely, and I wished I could have seen them one more time. Finally, take care of CJ for me. He will need you." I felt him nod and hold me tighter. When the shudders calmed, he pulled away from me, giving me a kiss on the cheek.

I looked him dead in the eyes and whispered so only he could hear, "I know it's not fair to ask, but promise me you will take care of CJ for me." A small nod. It was completely unfair to ask him to do this after everything he had endured, but CJ would need him. They would need each other.

I turned to Mickel. A small smile was on his lips, but his eyes were lined with tears. I just pulled him into a big hug. There was a shuddering hiccup from him, a long tight squeeze, and as we pulled apart, he stopped to whisper in my ear, "I vow to protect them both. Thank you, Megan. For being my friend. For being my little bratty sister. For everything."

"Okay. I'm not saying goodbye to everyone. I can't handle it," I said, wiping my tears with my sleeve as I pulled away from Mickel. CJ came over and gave me a rag to blow my nose.

There were loud shouts floating in from the window, but I couldn't make out what was being said. A moment later, the door blew open, Jean standing there syths out. "The army is at the town's edge. Ansel is with them."

"Are you sure?" Mickel said, any trace of emotion gone.

"Saw him myself," she nodded.

"Okay," I said, taking a deep breath. I closed my eyes, pulling all my power into my core. A moment later, the room was glowing from the electricity that was burning white hot at my hands.

CJ's hand touched my back in a simple gesture that made my electricity jump. I cringed slightly, and CJ smirked. "Megan has been reserving her power since we left Morte Alta. It's... a bit jumpy when she brings it all to the surface."

"All of it?" Jean asked, her eyes widening.

"Yeah. One of many reasons I've been a bit... more temperamental the last couple days," I said with a small smile. "I'm highly uncomfortable right now. I'll be fine once I use it. It will let some of the pressure out. Calm it, knowing that I'm not just bottling it up."

"Let's go kill some Ja'Nee," Logan said with a wicked gleam in his eye. I raised an eyebrow. "You knew they were working with me on fighting techniques. What did you think I was doing the entire time you were in Therth and tromping around the world? Origami?"

I smiled big at that. "Yes, actually. I figured Mickel would have you making little paper cranes all day. And if you had gotten really good at that, maybe rabbits."

CJ shook his head and actually chuckled as we filtered out of the room.

CHAPTER 48

NEAT ROWS OF NALRIN, Obsecuritan, Lankspur Island, and other soldiers stood at the edge of town as Ansel's army approached. With each step, the smell of that rotting tar brought memories back of what it did to Lindy. I could do nothing but stare at it. The vision of Lindy being consumed and then roaring at me was all I could see. My heart raced in both fear and anticipation.

CJ put his hand on my shoulder and whispered, "It's in the past."

Blinking, I saw the army in front of us.

The Ja'Nee outnumbered us two to one. More soldiers stood behind us, and I could hear the shifting of their feet.

"Hold the lines," One of the commanders said.

Clarice softly started chanting in an old language, and soon the Nalrin and Obsecuritan soldiers were all in sync. It flowed through the soldiers and melted into the sound of the rain. Soldiers stood taller and soon there was the sound of boots splashing the mud in time with the chant.

The Lankspur soldiers, who reminded me of Vikings with their elaborate braids, painted faces, shields, swords, spears, and pelts, grunted in time with the Obsecuritan soldiers. I looked out over the soldiers, men and women, standing tall, not showing an ounce of fear for what could come. The bravery of these people gave me strength.

Rain continued to come down as Mickel's voice rang out in front of us, "Decapitation kills them. Stay out of the tar."

Then silence.

Ansel's army just stopped.

Ten solid minutes of silence.

Ansel wasn't stupid. He was working the soldier's nerves. He knew the longer they had to stare them down, the longer they would let their imagination get a hold of them. They would start to visualize how they would die.

Everyone stood at attention, weapons out. Electricity flowed down each of my syths, and Clarice gave a quick twitch of her whips. Darkness coiled around her, and her eyes glowed with that black fire as she smiled at me.

A soft male laugh filled the space, and then, "So, my daughter is here."

"Show yourself, Ansel," I said, amplifying my voice with my power.

Slowly, the black tar retreated from the front lines of that army, and I saw him rise up from the back. He was so far away, but he looked thinner. Worn.

"Hello, my precious child," he said sweetly, but his fingers writhed with darkness.

"Hello, *Daddy*," I said mockingly, as I sheathed a syth and let electricity flow through my fingers. "Are you here to play with me?"

He smiled and showed those too many teeth. "Did you not like the game we played in Alnwick?"

CJ and Logan growled next to me. "You fucking bastard."

Ansel just raised his eyebrows at the two brothers. He sighed, and said mocking us, "Oh that's right, my darkness consumed one of you. I take it Logan was attached to her?" I saw red as he looked back at me. "I out number you Megan. You can't win this."

"I will kill you, Ansel," I said, strong and determined. "You will not live to see the sun rise tomorrow."

As if on silent command, the tar lowered my father, and the Ja'Nee advanced. The sound of our soldiers' swords and the Ja'Nee colliding was deafening. My family rushed for the Ja'Nee, all except CJ, who stayed at my side. His charge was rolling off him in waves, and I knew that if I looked at him, there would be lightning in his eyes.

The Ja'Nee burst through the center of the lines, splitting our army in two. Soldiers ran past and engaged, some with blasts of power to push them back, others just used that power to decapitate the closest Ja'Nee.

"I have to make it to Ansel, Ceej," I said as the clangs of syths and shields rang around us.

"We should stay here. Let him come to us."

"I have an idea. That little something I've been working on," I said, cocking my eyebrow up in meaning.

"I don't want you that close to him." he said, knowing what I was thinking. I had been working on it on and off for weeks now with him. If I could just get close enough.

"What if I can stop him without using Helena, though?"

"That isn't fair, Megan," CJ said, giving me a knowing look.

I shrugged at him and said, "True, but there are soldiers in this battle who have signed up to die if I use Helena. It was one thing when it was just me, but..." I looked out over the battle. Clarice's whips were encased in her power as she whipped them around and decapitated about five Ja'Nee in one go. Alexei was by her side, and I was momentarily mesmerized at how quick he could move.

CJ's hand was on my chin and turned me to face him. "So, it's okay for you to die, but not for others?"

"Yes," I said with every ounce of conviction I had in me. He studied every inch of my face, and then kissed me.

"Fuck it. We are out of options. I'll take the chance. Let's go kill your father," CJ said as a wave of that charge washed over me. "But I go with you. Every step of the way. I go with you."

I nodded, and we ran into the fight. Electricity flowed bright down my syths, and with every slash to the neck of one of those damn Ja'Nee, there was a sizzling sound and a pop. CJ stayed right on my back and killed just as many as I had.

The deeper we got into the fight, the closer the fighting became. Thanks to Clarice's training, and her absolute insistence on stretching and yoga, I easily moved around in the tight space. I felt out to see where my family was, and I half paused at what I saw. Jean and Owen fighting back-to-back, Clarice and Alexei doing the same. Mickel was between us and my father, and Logan was holding his own behind us.

But... the soldiers, I saw their embers, against negative space. I turned to where I thought my father was, and there was a vast, open blackness. Not an absence of embers where you thought you could walk through it, but it was as if there was a void in the world.

That is, until I saw the tar circling my father. That tar swirled and eddied with embers of power. All those people...

"Megan!" a voice from the distance shouted. Then I was sliding in the mud as I hit the ground. I shook my head and CJ was on top of me. Two Ja'Nee swung their blades for us. I fingered a string of lightning across their necks and their bodies went flying in separate directions than their heads before disappearing into dust.

"What the fuck, Megs," CJ said breathlessly.

"The tar. So many souls," I said, trying to keep half a view on the embers around us. The Ja'Nee are just a black void, but the tar. I thought it was consuming the souls back in Alnwick, but to see so many of them. The tar wasn't that dense in Alnwick. There were flickers and swirls before, but now... He's been collecting them for months from all over the Nalsar dimension. Nalrin, Ashridge, and everywhere in between.

"Come on. At least now you know where he is," CJ said, helping me up.

We ran straight for him, ducking each slice from the Ja'Nee. We both slid in the mud, and when we reached the battles edge, Ansel was just leaning back and picking at his nails on a lounge chair of that very tar.

"I would have thought you would have been here sooner." Ansel said coolly. "And you brought CJ with you. Hi, CJ. Miss our time together? I had such fun back in Noctulanar Castle."

To CJ's credit, twirling his syths in his hands, he just said, "Thought I could return the favor."

Ansel jumped down off the tar and stared CJ down. "You think you can tie me to a table, and slice me up like a Thanksgiving turkey?"

"I'd like to try," CJ said, a smirk crossed his face. One that reminded me of when he was working on the Governor at Bellstar.

A black whip of Ansel's power flew toward CJ. There was a loud sizzling thud as it hit the wall I had put up between us, my power was so much more settled and controlled than the last time I faced him. I could see the tar move closer to Ansel's feet behind him as Ansel threw blast after blast of power against that wall.

Pulling my power up from the deepest parts of me, and concentrating on the image in my head, I willed my power to comply. A moment later, there was a hard, solid weight in my right hand. Ansel glared at me.

"Been practicing, I see." Ansel said.

"I've had to be a quick study," I said panting, feeding that now 5-foot spear in my hand the electricity of my power.

I have to take the wall down. Get behind me. I have one shot to get this right." I pushed to CJ, who did exactly as he was told. When he was, I took three surging steps and threw the spear at Ansel. When it reached the wall he had put up, it smashed through.

Unfortunately, it caused the spear to change directions slightly and missed his chest. Instead, cutting right through his left arm. Gray blood sprayed from just above his elbow as he howled in pain. Where the spear landed in the tar behind him, it burst into electric blue flames and screamed mist rose into the sky.

"SHIT!" I panted.

"It worked," CJ said with a smirk.

"Except it takes so much of my power to do, I can't do it again, not if I need to continue to fight," I said through my teeth. "That damn wall of his re-routed it. I was aiming for his fucking chest." Before I could think more on it, I threw bolt after bolt at Ansel. Ansel's initial wall may have disappeared with the spear, but he had reconstructed another one against him. Each of my burst were absorbed by that shield.

I screamed in anger and rage. There was a small smirk as Ansel continued to patch himself up. Tears were flowing down my face now. "I was hoping I could end it."

CJ looked back at where the spear was still lodged in the ground. Where the tar touched it, it burned white blue and more and more screaming mist rose into the sky.

"The tar does not like your power," CJ said quietly. "Look. It burns *against* your power."

I glared at Ansel, who was clutching his arm and murmuring. From this distance, I could just see where he was trying to cauterize the wound to stop the bleeding.

"Do you think you could burn it away?" CJ said.

"I don't know. That would take a lot of power, and I don't think I have that much left in me." I looked at CJ and then back at the tar. I had minutes before Ansel would be back on his feet, but if his wall was not around the tar. I sent a small burst toward the far right. A small burst of blue-white light, and a screaming mist.

"How much *do* you have left?" CJ said.

"Does it matter whether it is dregs or everything? If we can get the tar out of the picture," I turned to look behind us, and while our forces were suffering casualties, we were holding our ground. I felt out for our family, and while I couldn't see Jean or Logan, everyone else was still fighting strong.

"It gives us that much more of a fighting chance," CJ said.

"Okay," I said, re-centering myself, and calling forth what I had left. CJ came and wrapped his arms around me to help hold me up and still. "The belltower is a hundred yards to the left. Once the tar is gone, and if this works, you have to get me there, okay?"

"Okay." CJ said in my ear after a short pause.

"Mickel and Owen are just in front of it. They can help," I said, gritting my teeth. The buzzing in my ears was overpowering and my skin felt like it had right after my Maltal ceremony, only so much stronger. My muscles were twitching at the strain of trying to contain it.

"Let it out in small, short bursts," CJ said in my ear.

"I love you," is all I said as I shot my power into the tar.

CHAPTER 49

THERE WAS NOTHING IN my head but the buzzing and humming of my power and screaming white light everywhere else. I opened my eyes, and I could see the embers in the tar turn all their attention on me. It flowed and shifted toward us.

CJ was screaming in my ear, but I couldn't make it out. He took half a step back, but I planted my feet into the ground, and I felt his Charge leap against my power. It simply bounced back. I dredged more and more up from the pit. I had no idea how far it would go, but if this would give us a fighting chance against Ansel, I was going to use every ounce of it.

One moment the tar was still a good twenty feet away, the next it surrounded us. My power bounced back into my body so violently, I lost my footing. CJ had me standing a moment later as we stared at skeletons bouncing and flowing in and out of the tar as it circled closer and closer to us.

I looked around. CJ doing the same. "Any ideas, babe?"

His Charge was bursting from him hard and fast, and when I twisted my head to look at his face, there was nothing but terror. "Can you burst a hole to run through?"

I tried, even though it felt like shards of glass were being pulled to the surface. While the area burned white hot, the screaming mist rose to the sky, the area was almost instantaneously filled again. My power snapped back into me, and every sound and defensive thought went out of my head. My power sat coiling up in the pit of my stomach, just like it used to when I had to create a cocoon for it.

A smooth male voice broke through my thoughts and said, "All that power, and you still can't save yourself... or CJ, for that matter." A wave of his hand and it circled in tighter still. My heart raced. If I tried to use Helena here, the tar would be on me before I could finish the spell.

The tar was now not three feet from us. I wrapped my arms around CJ and sighed as Ansel said, "Now that power will be mine to control."

The tar leaped atop us.

CHAPTER 50

NOTHING. I FELT NOTHING but CJ's arms tight around me. I cracked my eyes open and touched CJ's face. Real. He was real. I turned and slowly reached out my hand. My fingers tingled in recognition of the bubble that covered us. My power. My power had instinctively encircled us in a bubble of electric fire. White hot light surrounded us where the tar burned. I continued to run my hand along the interior, and it sang back to me. It was the only way I could explain it.

Tar swirled around us, but with every moment that it tried to get through that bubble, it burned away.

"Megan," CJ said awed. "How?"

"I didn't... I," I turned to face him and there was nothing but reverence on his face. "Ceej."

I reached up and kissed him, feeding my power the love that CJ and I have for each other. I could feel it burn brighter. When our kiss broke, we were both breathless. I turned back to face where my father had been earlier, and when the tar parted just in front of us, I saw my father's rage on full display. A burst of his power sent off toward the belltower and when he looked back at us, there was a toothy evil smile on his face.

As that tar burned, my power pulled back closer to me. The tar shrank with it, and soon there was only a 2 foot by six-foot section left. A full skeleton stepped out of it, surrounded by an ember facing Ansel. It turned to us, and there was a single nod. I knew that ember. I knew the pattern of the burning flames within it. Knew how its arms felt around my shoulders, and the sound of the laugh it would make.

"Lindy?" I choked.

"What?" CJ said, realization of what I had said hitting him. "How do you know it's her?"

"The ember." I reached for her. Tears now streaming down my face. "Lindy?"

The skeleton ember turned to look at Ansel, looked back at us, and burned brighter. Then, as the last shreds of that tar melted away under my power, my bubble contracted around us like a second skin, but did not break.

"I'm sorry I couldn't protect you. I love you. We all love you," I whispered. The ember burned hotter before it lifted a hand and caressed my cheek against my bubble, before it, too, burned away. Unlike the rest of the tar, it did not scream in agony and fly for the skies, but instead, there was a mournful sigh that filled our ears as it encircled us and shot into the fight. A moment later, we could barely see it shoot like a star across the sky.

We were so focused on that shred of our friend that we didn't see Ansel stalk closer. "You insolent child," He growled.

My eyes snapped back to him, just as he bound me and CJ in black ropes of his power and tossed us backwards. We flew over the fight in a matter of seconds, but I saw the whole battlefield in slow motion.

Clarice fighting against the Ja'Nee with Alexei.

Logan bleeding from his nose, with a long gash down his left arm.

Owen limping and trying to make his way to where Mickel was... where Mickel was... screaming to the heavens. In his arms was Jean, a hole through her chest.

I had no air. I couldn't breathe as CJ and I landed a few feet from Owen. I rolled and slid in the mud on my hands and knees, gasping for breath. I turned to CJ, who was doing the same, his eyes wide. He just mouthed, "Jean."

I nodded my head and tried to breathe. Just to the left of CJ was a Ja'Nee, and I tried to throw my power at him to push him away, but it only whispered out of me. I was drained. There was nothing but dregs left, and not really much of that.

Luckily, CJ saw it and rolled out of the way. Popping up on his feet, he unsheathed a sword from a fallen Nalrin Guard's body and swung, decapitating the Ja'Nee. Then he was helping me to my feet. Our eyes met, and the look in his eyes mirrored mine.

My eyes flickered to the top of the belltower and back down to him. Owen caught up with us then. "You two okay?"

"Not another member of my family is going to die today," I said through gritted teeth as rain turned to snow. When my eyes met Owen's, they were empty and hollow. "I need to get to the belltower. Ansel is close enough."

We fought our way to the base of the tower, and when we reached Mickel, my stomach hollowed out.

"Megan," he said, astonished. He looked at Jean, then at me, and carefully laid Jean down on the ground. I looked at Owen, whose eyes were fixed on Jean.

Nodding my head toward the belltower, I held my hand out as snow landed in my palm. "*She is most powerful during the snow,*" I pushed to what remained of my family.

I could feel CJ and Mickel's eyes on me, but it was Owen, his voice dead and empty as he stared at Jean, who said. "I'll hold off the Ja'Nee at the entrance. Mickel, you take the first level, and CJ the second. Megan set up on the third. There are no windows to that level, so they will have to go through us first."

"Owen!" Mickel and I said in unison.

"Mickel, I know you loved her. I can't blame you. She is so easy to love," he said, a small smile on his lips. He still had not stopped looking at Jean's body, but he looked up to Mickel now and said, "You are my brother, and we have fought as such our whole lives. You have always protected Jean and I."

He looked at each of us again, before meeting Mickel's eyes, "You never once backed down in protecting me. Now, I need you to protect Megan."

Mickel and Owen stared at each other, had a long silent conversation, nodded, and gave him a long hug as Logan came running up.

"I won't let any more of my family die today," I said through my teeth as tears streamed down my face. I would not accept anything less. "Owen, you are not dying."

Logan looked between us, then to Jean, and saw the look on our faces. I thought I saw CJ shake his head and Logan's shoulders drop.

"Logan. Fourth floor. Make sure no Ja'Nee get through from the top," Owen said as his eyes met mine and stared me down. Logan's throat bobbed, but he didn't say a word. He simply nodded and disappeared up the stairs.

"Owen," I said, my voice breaking. "No."

"Megan. You have to do, what you have to do. We have all stood by and watched you accept it, all while we were with CJ looking for a fucking loophole," he said, putting his hands on my shoulders, his eyes flicked to Jean and his shoulders shuddered a moment before he looked at me again. "My heart is gone. I will defend what she loved most. I will hold them off as long as I can."

"I love you, Owen." I pushed to him.

"I love you too. I'll see you on the other side," Owen said quietly in my ear as he pulled me into a tight hug. To his credit, his voice didn't crack. "Now go. We don't have much time."

I looked to Owen, Mickel and CJ, then up to where Logan was looking out of the window on the fourth floor. Words couldn't be voiced, so I just pushed to them all, hoping that Alexei and Clarice heard me, *"I love you all, so very much. Thank you for everything."*

I turned my back on everyone and walked into the belltower.

CHAPTER 51

MICKEL AND CJ FOLLOWED me up the stairs, and as we left Mickel on the first-floor landing, CJ twined our mud crusted hands together. This one last show of affection before he had to let me go. Slowly his thumb rubbed over the back of my hand and when we got to the second-floor landing, I made to just let go and keep walking, but he pulled me to a stop.

"In every lifetime," he whispered. The sounds of the battle coming through the windows.

I hiccup around my tears, "In every lifetime."

Only then did he loosen his grip and I made my way to the third-floor landing alone.

Each step felt like a mile.

Each step, heavy and lighter.

I pulled up any and all dregs of my power, only to find the smallest flicker there. I felt his eyes on me until I turned the corner up the next flight of stairs.

Step. Breathe.

Step. Breathe.

Around the next corner, I stepped into the only real room in the belltower.

Slowly, I removed my syth belt and let it drop to the floor.

Step.

Methodically, I stripped myself of every other piece of steel.

I pulled out Helena and the now worn piece of paper out of my pocket. Written in a long-forgotten language. I've read it enough times now that I didn't need to read it to cast the spell to save all of Nalrin.

I knelt in the middle of the room, and tried to block out the shouting from below, the ringing of steel, and a bellow from Mickel. My heart broke at the realization he was the next line of defense between me and my father. That bellow echoed through me, tearing off another piece of my heart. *Owen.*

In the stairwell, I could hear CJ unsheathing his weapons.

No one else. No one else was going to die today.

I would put an end to all of it. All of the pain.

I cradled Helena in my hands and pooled those dregs of my power around it. The last bits of electricity arcing from my fingers to the crystal.

Each word was heavy on my lips, but then there was a clarity that washed over me, and I said in my own language:

Be banished by the powers of the Five.

By the power of Helena and my blood, you shall not thrive.

To Stone you shall be for seven then to

Nothingness ye shall be.

Cleanse this world of thy Darkness,

Heal thy land destroyed by thy Darkness...

I bit down on the pull at my bones and gritted my teeth.

I screamed the words to the world, as I finished the spell.

I banish ye Ansel Keller by my own blood.

I banish ye Ash'bani

I banish ye Ash'bani to ni.

Light. Bright and painful, shot from Helena and into my chest.

CHAPTER 52

I WAS SHREDDING.

For what felt like eons, I was shredding.

I could feel the power of Helena's words shredding my heart. Shredding my mind, body, and soul.

My eyes flew open at the searing pain to see CJ running into the room and grab my hands just as another burst of light shot out from Helena and me to hit him in the chest. It bounced between the two of us, causing CJ and I to rock from the force of it.

There was this moment, only a moment, where our eyes met, and there was blissful silence. Complete, peaceful silence. I didn't dare take my eyes off him. In my death, he would be the last thing I saw.

Another, more powerful wave of bright white light burst between us. The warm heat from the light burned out the chill in my bones, and with each pulse, another wave of power went out to cleanse the evil from this place.

I felt it then. The loosening of my life from this body, the final shredding in my veins to end this. I smiled gently and loosened my grip on CJ's hand. He only gripped tighter.

"Don't you dare," he said through gritted teeth. There were lighting storms in his eyes, and I smiled softly at him.

"In every lifetime," I breathed, feeling myself slip away.

"Megan Isabel Mathewson. I command you, by the power of Vernadali, by power of an Angels Blessed Vernadali, you will not be separated from me. You will not go into the afterlife without me."

I froze.

Light burst again from between us and a soft voice said through the light. "The cost. The cost must be paid."

I looked toward that sound but saw nothing except for the shredding light flowing through my veins.

"Then we both pay it," CJ said, still staring at me. "Megan, look at me."

Slowly, I turned my head and met his gaze. Not registering the movement at all, CJ said, "I vowed to always be at your side, and I refuse to break that vow."

Six silhouetted figures surrounded us and that shredding white light gave one final burst.

CHAPTER 53

THAT SHREDDING LIGHT IN my veins was gone.

There was no pain.

My eyes popped open as I felt a gentle squeeze on my hands. They narrowed in confusion as it registered that CJ was sitting there on his knees, smiling at me. Our hands joined. Both of us neat and clean.

I cocked my head to the side and said, "Ceej?"

"Not *exactly* what we had envisioned when we worked together to have your spell able to be used again today." A male voice to the right of me said.

"Angel of Remembrance, please don't forget that the Five blessed *them*. *Those* laws obviously do not apply." That voice. It was the same voice I had heard moments, hours, eons ago, while I was shredding.

"Careful," a female voice chastised.

CJ and I looked around and only saw silhouettes.

"Where... where are we?" I said a little shakily.

Those silhouettes became fully corporeal now, and a woman who didn't look to be older than twenty-five years old, with long black hair swept back in a neat braid, kneeled next to us. Her clothing was simple, just a white loose billowy shirt and flowing cream pants. The medallion that sat between her breasts, though. I'd seen it before. It matched the medallion that the Cinder Fairies had given me... It was engraved on the top of that fucking box that... my eyes snapped up to meet hers.

"Helena Rowland," I whispered in awe.

"Yes, Megan. I am Helena." She smirked as she jerked her head to the others standing there. "These guys, you may know. They made a rather dramatic appearance at your wedding."

"The Five Angels," CJ said in awe. I could see him try to stand, but he looked down at his legs. I tried to get up as well but couldn't move. "I would bow, but apparently I am unable to move from this spot."

"You cannot move from how you are in the world," the Angel of Beauty said.

"Lindy? Jean?" I asked hopefully, then added tentatively, "Owen?"

A knowing smile from the Angel of Death before he purred, "All who perished fighting Ansel are safe."

A non-answer. No confirmation on whether Owen made it or not, and my chest tightened at the thought. I had heard Mickel's howl before I started that spell. I looked down into my lap and said, my voice so small, "And Ansel? My father, I mean."

"Eradicated from existence," the Angel of Love said calmly. "Just as Helena's spell was supposed to do."

"He is nowhere. His soul, his essence, his being doesn't exist anymore." Helena said. "You will not find him in any realm. That is why that spell requires so much from the caster."

A sharp glance at CJ who had the good sense to flinch, before she continued, more than a little peeved, "Until these five went and gave you an Angels Blessed Vernadali. Who then got it into his thick head to use those powers to keep you tethered to the world."

"Not the world," CJ said carefully. "Just not be separated from... me."

"Which is why you are here, Cory James Mathewson," she snapped.

"The legends said that when you cast the initial spell, that it severed you in two." I mumbled, looking at each of the Five Angels, "Is that happening to us?"

"AND there is the reason why we are here," Helena said as her head rolled toward CJ and she rolled her eyes at him. "The spell was meant to cleave you in two, so that the part you wish to destroy, the Ash'Bani part of you, to kill your father, would be separated from the rest of you."

"Only, you are already cleaved in two. Have been since the moment of your creation," the Angel of Healing said.

"I'm sorry?" I said, my eyes furrowing.

"Cory James Mathewson, is your other half," the Angel of Love said, her eyes flicking to the Angel of Death, who gave her a snide smile and a wink. When I still looked at her, confusion clear on my face, she smiled. "From the day you two met, has he not looked after you, protected you, and always had your best interest at heart?"

"Yes," I said, "but he's been a royal asshole too." He chuckled at that and gave my hand a small squeeze.

"Yet you still love him, care for him, and protect him," she said adoringly.

We had always looked out for each other. I looked at him and his eyes were on me, studying each of my reactions. "Of course, I protected him. That's what friends do. You care for and protect them. Even before he was mine."

"He has always been yours. You have always been his. Both of your souls go beyond that of being mates. They were made and carved from the same mold. I made that soul myself." The Angel of Love stood straighter, like she was indeed proud of herself.

CJ, with tears in his eyes, smiled. I returned it and said, "Not that I had any doubt, but at least I know I wasn't wrong about you."

He chuckled, "What was wrong with us that we waited so long for this?"

I just shook my head. Then I narrowed my eyes at him and said, with more bite than I had intended, "Why did you barge into the room at the last minute and grab my hands?"

His face fell at that. "I knew you were casting the spell. I felt it. I had prepared to let you do it." He sniffed and continued, "Then... then I felt you being clawed apart from the inside. It differed completely from the Vernadali bond. How it transmits feelings is weak and suggestive in comparison." His voice cracked at the end, and the pain in his eyes was almost unbearable.

"He could actually feel your life force being shredded, pulled, and separated from your body," Helena said softly.

He nodded, glanced at the Angel of Beauty who had a knowing smile on her face and continued, "I remembered that in the Garden, the Angel of Beauty said that I could numb the pain. Well, technically, for when you are healing with the Sa Ra, which you never take off. It was a fool's hope, even selfish I guess, but I thought that if I could at least take some of that pain away as you were taken from me, then I wanted to give you that."

"How, in any way, is that selfish?" I asked. "You were trying to give me a pain-free death."

"Instead, when that moment came, you used your Vernadali Charge," Helena said sharply, but turned to the Five Angels. A slow, wicked smirk crossed the Angel of Death's face. I could have sworn he even winked at CJ.

"So, where does that leave us? By right of the agreement originally made, she comes with me." She said, crossing her arms. "BUT, since *Death* has not claimed her, or him, and seems content to leave them in limbo in the world..."

"Do you wish to claim ownership of half a soul?" The Angel of Death said smoothly. There was more meaning to that statement that I didn't understand.

"Of course not." Helena said, flinching. She turned to face us, tapped her finger on her chin, and said, "I hereby release you to the Five Angels."

She stared them down for another moment, and with an extra-long look at the Angel of Death, he gave her a small nod. "Before you are released to them, though, I wish to bestow a gift."

Helena took my face in her hands and rested her forehead on mine as she whispered quietly and quickly. There was a warm feeling that settled into the pit of my stomach, lower even. She pulled away and smiled.

"You didn't know it yet, but you have been pregnant with twins. They have been restored and strengthened. You may wish to ensure *proper* Sangra and witch training for both of them."

"What?" CJ and I said in unison as she plucked the crystal from my palm.

Helena winked and nodded to the Five Angels, who in unison said, "Cory James and Megan Isabel Mathewson. You are hereby released from the tethers of the afterworld."

A blink and we were back in the belltower.

CHAPTER 54

"Ceej? Megs?" Logan's voice said tentatively.

I blinked.

CJ blinked.

"Did she really say what I think she said?"

"Twins!" he said, his eyebrows going to his hairline. His eyes flicked to my stomach, then back to meet my eyes.

"Megan?" Mickel said, worry in his voice. "CJ?"

I blinked again and realized we were not the only ones here. I turned my head and saw Logan and Mickel on our right, and Clarice and Alexei on our left. Relief flowed over each of their faces as I looked at them. I was acutely aware that Owen was not present, but I tried to remember that the Angel of Death said they were safe.

CJ took his hands from mine and rubbed his face before looking at them. We were caked with dried mud and it flaked off. Shaking his head, he was suddenly on his feet. "Did it work?"

"It... worked," Alexei said, cocking his head to the side as he studied us.

"Ansel was, is, about twenty feet from the belltower entrance. He was calling forth a lot of darkness." Clarice let out a long, long breath. "A lot of darkness, when it just popped out. Hollowed out my ears when it happened, too. Then he froze, hand still raised. Just froze in place. Then all the Ja'Nee just crumbled to dust in the wind."

Mickel chuckled. "Some of the soldiers were throwing snowballs in his face. Lower areas too."

A huffed laugh came out of me, but I said, "Owen?"

"He held off the Ja'Nee admirably," he said before taking a ragged deep breath. "When Ansel saw him at the door, Owen had his back to him fighting off a few Ja'Nee, and Ansel blasted a hole through his chest, just like Jean's."

My chest tightened, and I held back tears, muttering. "It was supposed to stop with me. No one else was supposed to die."

"Megan." I looked at her and swallowed the tears. "I have to ask you something. Well, I have lots of questions. The least of which being how are you not a vegetable or dead right now, but..." She looked to Logan, who had a small content smile on his face. "Do you know what you did to the tar?"

"I burned it away. Well, my power burned it away," I said, confused.

"You did more than that," she said, tears in her eyes. "As you destroyed it, the souls were released. I can hear them all now. All the voices of the dead. All the Vernadali and Guard who were lost in Nalrin. It was overwhelming, to say the least."

"She collapsed to the ground covering her ears, screaming at herself, as it happened. Once the last one, once Lindy was gone, she popped up and started fighting again," Alexei said quietly, putting his hand on her back. She leaned into him slightly.

I looked at CJ, then to Logan.

"There was this moment, right at the end, where there was a single skeleton, that had an ember that burned brighter than all the others." Tears filled my eyes as I remembered it. "That ember reminded me of Lindy's ember. It was her then?"

"Yes." Clarice's eyes were lined with tears as she smiled softly.

"Holy Gods and Angels," Logan said through a lump in his throat. "So, I *really* didn't imagine it?"

"What?" CJ asked.

"I was fighting, and I could have sworn that Lindy... that Lindy caressed my cheek and then there was a loving pressure over my heart. I felt lighter after it was gone. Like some of the pain of losing her was released." He said in awe.

I gave Clarice a questioning look.

"Lindy, Jean, and Owen are there. They are all so very proud of you," Clarice said, then pointed at me sternly. "No. We will not be having a family get together with the dead, Megan."

I couldn't help but huff a laugh. "You know me well, Clarice."

CJ reached down and helped me up but didn't let go of me.

"*Later. I'll grieve later,*" I pushed to him. He pulled me close and wrapped an arm around my waist as he said, "So, what do we do now?"

Mickel's eyes met mine. "We need to attend to the dead soldiers. Attend to Jean and Owen."

I nodded.

"Can we take them up the mountain, outside of town, and set a pyre?" CJ suggested.

"I think they would like that," Logan said. "A warrior's funeral."

He had been studying the ways of life here. Mickel's eyes had gone off into the distance and had nodded his agreement.

"We can set up mass pyre's outside of town for the soldiers. I'll work with the Commander's to get a list of the dead, so we can let their families know," Alexei said.

"Alexei?" I asked tentatively. "Are the soldiers who had Ash'bani blood in them..."

"The same as Ansel. Frozen in spot," he said sadly. "There were more of them than we had initially thought. Either they didn't know, or they didn't want others to know."

I nodded. "Seven days. They will be absorbed by the ground then."

"It took us about three months to get here from Nalrin, right?" CJ said. I looked at him, a little puzzled, as he pulled me tighter.

"Yes, but we lost a lot of time going through the Lost Plateau trying to avoid Ansel's army. We should be able to cut through the Vandrer Grasslands this time and save a couple of weeks," Mickel said. "Still won't be an easy trek."

"Okay. One week. We can stay for a week to help the town clean up after tonight's fight." CJ said with a heavy sigh and ran his hand through his hair. "I'd like to be back in Nalrin by the end of April."

"What's the rush?" Clarice said. "I mean, I realize that we all want to get home and start to relax, but why the timeline?"

I looked at CJ, and his eyes bore into mine.

"While we were, I'm not sure where we were, but after I cast the spell. CJ and I had a little sit down with the Five Angels," I looked to Clarice. "And Helena."

They blinked.

"What?" Logan and Mickel said, looking at each other and then back to us.

"We had a little chat. I won't go into all that was said, as it is still making my head spin," I said, taking a deep breath before continuing. "Apparently, I am pregnant. With twins."

Silence. Each of them just blinked, and Logan's mouth was hanging open. Clarice and Alexei looked at each other, then back at us.

"Congratulations. You are all about to be aunts and uncles," I said, crossing my arms daring them to say anything.

When my eyes met Mickel's they were lined with tears. "You said you wanted to be my big brother. Put up or shut up, Uncle Mickel—"

I didn't get to finish that sentence, as I was wrapped up in his arms and swung around in a circle.

"Careful," CJ said. "She is especially precious cargo."

"Shut the fuck up," Logan said, clapping him on the back. "She ain't gonna break. This is Megan."

"Twins," Clarice said. "That's what CJ said when you came back to us."

I nodded.

"Twins!" she said again, joy lighting her face as she jumped up and clapped. "Oh, we are going to have so much fun spoiling them!"

"We?" Alexei said with a raised eyebrow.

"Yes, we," she said lightly, smacking him on the chest. "If either one of those are boys, between you and Mickel, you two will make sure it will be the best warrior ever to walk the dimensions. If either of them are girls, you are going to spoil her with so many pretty dresses, *and* you and Mickel will still make sure she can whoop anyone's ass and be the best warrior in any dimension."

"And what if he wants all the pretty dresses, and she doesn't want anything to do with them?" I asked, my eyebrows raised.

"Doesn't matter. Whatever those kids want, we will be giving it to them, but they will be the best warriors to walk any dimension," Clarice said without a second's hesitation. "Good luck because they are going to be spoiled tyrants!"

"Mom and Dad are going to flip out." Logan chuckled. "I'm going to be an uncle. Shit! I'm with Clarice. Whatever those kids want, they get."

"Well, let's get some rest. It's been a long day, and the next week will be rough," Alexei said once everyone's head stopped spinning. "Emotionally and Physically."

CHAPTER 55

THE NEXT DAY, ALEXEI and Mickel gave orders to the remaining soldiers, only about half of what had marched into this town, to build the pyre's outside of town. We, however, went to work building one for Jean and Owen up the hillside. It took us two days to build one that would burn strong enough.

After carefully carrying their bodies out of town and up the hillside, we placed them next to each other and looped their arms together. Their bodies would go to the Angels in unison.

With tears streaming down my cheeks, I sparked a corner of the pyre with my power, Clarice encouraging the flames to burn brighter with hers, and Mickel blew a gentle wind of his power to help them spread.

My eyebrows knitted together, "I didn't know you could use your power," I said to Mickel.

"I... I don't rely on it. I use it enough to contain its ember within me, but I don't use it, except for very rare occasions. The fight down in town is the first time I've *really* touched it in over twenty years," He looked back toward Jean and Owen. "Story for another time."

I took his hand in mine, and as CJ wrapped his arm around my waist, Clarice and Alexei started humming. A few moments later, Mickel started singing. It was a beautiful mournful dirge in a language I did not understand. Tears flowed down his face, and he squeezed my hand tight. I had never heard him sing before, and it was beautiful, pure, and in this case, full of feeling he wouldn't be able to put into any words.

Mickel sang for hours as we stared into the flames. They burned and raged, carrying Jean and Owen, our family, to the Angels. Clarice and Alexei never stopped humming as he poured his despair into every note.

When the belltower rang midnight, he abruptly stopped, and the flames winked out. Mickel took a deep breath, and I felt, I actually felt Mickel's vast, potent power, as he let out a long breath and the ashes faded in the wind. Leaving nothing of the pyre left.

CHAPTER 56

SEVEN DAYS AFTER THE battle, just as the sun was setting over the horizon, a cloudless rain fell upon the town. Streetlamps lit the heavy unnatural drops as they fell. The 177 soldiers who had turned to stone, all 177 of them, melted away and were absorbed back into the earth.

I stood there staring at my father's face, my family behind me as I watched his physical being, which took much longer than the soldiers, melt away. It sizzled against the rain as if it were literally burning his essence away.

"Goodbye, Dad," I said, surprised to find my chest tight at the words.

The rain stopped when the last of my father dissolved into the ground. I continued to stare at the spot, drenched, and tears falling down my face as the realization of everything that had happened washed over me. A week ago, I was sure that I was going to have to give my life to save the world. I was willing to.

I had done everything that was required for me to do just that. Now, I have a future. A real future.

Three years ago, I had sat at Russo's having pizza with CJ as he asked me on our first real date. At the time, I was just so excited for the possibility of a future with him. He knew everything about me, and there was that *possibility* of a future with him. Never once did he complain as he left everything behind to be here with me. He had become a fierce warrior and protector and now... I let my hand go across my still flat stomach letting out a contented sigh and smiled. Now, I'm going to be having his children. Through all of this, I was going to bear CJ's children.

I must have been standing there for a while, because CJ took my hand and said, "Megs, let's go inside. It's the middle of February, it's freezing, and you are shivering. Everyone else went inside an hour ago. Let's get you in front of the fire."

I looked at him evenly. "Can I expect this kind of coddling until the babies are born?"

"Yes," he said firmly. "You are caring for the three most important things in my world. So, abso–fucking–lutly."

CHAPTER 57

THREE LONG MONTHS LATER

ONE OF THE BEST sights I had seen in a long time was the Nalrin docks as we stepped off the boat. They had indeed left shadows of war on the docks, but there were still remnants of the old and hopes for the future as well. Our horses were stabled, and we headed for the trains, but when we entered the train hall, everyone stopped and parted ways for us.

"Attention," a familiar voice bellowed across the chamber. Each and every one of the Guard stopped and stood at attention. I jumped closer to CJ. "Vernadali CJ, Lady Megan, Nalrin Head Guard Mickel de Seduisant, Sir Logan, and Empress Clarice with Grand Duke Alexei arriving."

Standing at the train to the center ring were three Vernadali, and the source of that voice. "Remi," I breathed.

I looked at CJ, who was smiling. I let go of him and ran to give Remi a huge hug.

"Lady Megan," Remi said as he wrapped his arms around me. "It is so good to see you safe."

I stepped back and CJ was there, greeting him formally. "Vernadali Remi."

"Vernadali CJ. Welcome home," Remi said before looking at me fully. His eyes widened when he saw my stomach. They snapped back up to CJ and a smile widened his face.

"Sorry for my attire, but I couldn't stay in those pants any longer. This was all they had on the boat," I said, gesturing to my black leggings and shirt. Luckily, I could loosen my syth belt to accommodate the extra room I needed now. It was only going to get worse, but for now, I could still dress the part.

All three Vernadali now bowed formally to us and said in unison, "Congratulations, Lady Megan and Vernadali CJ."

"Thank you. Now can we please get to the center? I have a meeting with Julian I need to get through, and I am already exhausted. I have been on horseback or on a boat for months." I whined.

They moved to the side and we took a seat. The last time we were on this track heading to the center, things were so different. Our lives were so different. I gazed out the window at the nature preserve that still showed the path the tar had taken to the city. Though grass was growing over it, it still marred the landscape. With the escort, we didn't slow through the various rings, but there were signs of rebuilding. Signs of a more equally distributed wealth as well.

As we entered the center ring, I saw much of the damage we had seen the last time we were here, still in place. "The repairs to the center are being delayed, to ensure that the people have somewhere to live first. Ensure the outer rings are repaired and in good condition," Remi said when he saw the confusion on my face.

The train stopped, and we were escorted out and onto a hovering platform. I eyed Remi and said, "I'm pregnant. Not an invalid. Not to mention the fact that for the last three months, I have been on a horse or on a boat. It feels great to stretch my legs."

CJ smirked at me, and I just pushed to him, *"Shut up, you horny bastard."*

"It's all your fault," he said, kissing my cheek.

"For the Angels," Logan said, exasperated, as he rolled his eyes.

Remi smirked and waved the platform off as we headed to the Council Buildings.

While they had not made repairs to the buildings, they had cleaned up the debris and closed off the damaged areas. The reflecting pools in front of the Council Buildings were clean, but not dancing, and as we entered the main building, the floors were clean, but not polished to a reflection. The halls were strangely absent of gossiping assistants and guards as well.

"Where is everyone?" Mickel asked.

"Julian ordered the government officials to return to their territories and concentrate on repairs at home after you left to go north," Remi said as we turned down the hall to Julian's office. "All meetings are being conducted by LightCall for now. The onsite assistants and remaining Guard are in the outer rings helping with rebuilding."

Remi opened the door and announced us.

I laid my hands in front of my stomach in hopes it would hide some of the growing babes within me.

"Thank you, Remi," Julian said, scanning us, his face softening as he said, "I am sorry for the loss of Owen and Jean."

When I said nothing, Julian looked at Mickel, who stood at attention behind me. "Mickel, you can relax. There will soon be no formalities here today. Except for this." He looked us over again, pushed a button on his desk, and multiple circular LightCall windows opened behind him. My eyes widened, and Julian smirked.

"Lady Megan. Please report what has occurred over the last six months," Julian ordered.

I eyed the fifty or so Heads of Territories, who were shining in their little circular windows behind him. A few of them rolled their eyes at me, and others looked at me like I was something

Angels sent. I noted the one from Bellstar was indeed a female, and I recognized her.

"Madam Strigas. Are things going well in Bellstar?" I asked, ignoring Julian's demand for a full report.

"They are, Lady Megan. Your message was well received here. Thank you." She smirked and the evil glint in her eye made me understand why the people of Bellstar would follow her and her husband.

I nodded to her then turned to Julian. "You really want me to give this report?"

"Yes."

"Even after the last three times I stood in front of this Council and mouthed off?"

"Yes." Julian smirked, and I heard Clarice chuckle behind me.

"Even after the regime change, I fostered?" I said, trying to keep my temper from rising. He couldn't have given me just a little bit of warning? Let me shower, get some sleep, and relax just for a day, before having to meet in front of the Council members again?

He just smirked at me, and I narrowed my eyes at him.

"Asshole," I pushed to him, and he snorted in an effort to keep from outright laughing.

So, I took a breath and gave them a basic rundown of what all we had been through, including a detailed report on why I fostered the regime change in Bellstar. As I did so, I scanned the faces of the various dignitaries, and there were faces of awe, surprise, and devastation on their faces.

I did not tell them about CJ and I's time with the Five Angels and Helena, nor did I tell them of my pregnancy, though I did not think that gossip would not meet their ears before long. Then, as my closing statement, I said a tad too snarky, "Now, I wish to take my family home and shy away for a year. I will be busy trying to put my life together and helping Empress Clarice and Grand Duke Alexei settle into their new roles in Therth. Please, do not need us."

As one, we all looked at Julian. He looked at each of us, and with a small smile said, "Vernadali CJ and Lady Megan, you are hereby released from all duties for one circle of the suns. Sir Logan, you are to advise the Council whether you wish to return to the Manusia or stay in Nalsar within three months' time, at which time, should you wish to stay in Nalsar, you will have one additional month to determine your vocation. Empress Clarice and Grand Duke Alexei, I will make the assumption that you are indeed heading back to Therth to oversee the Gate to the Underworld?"

"Yes," Clarice said, every bit the Empress she was. "The gate will be reopened, and there will be much healing that needs to happen in Obsecuritan." I noted she stared down a few of the dignitaries on the LightCall.

"Nalrin Head Guard Mickel de Suduisant." Mickel snapped to attention again and stood tall. "You are hereby permanently assigned to Lady Megan and her family." His eyes gave a quick flick to my stomach, which fluttered slightly at the touch of power I felt caress my stomach. I narrowed my eyes at Julian and pushed his power back with my own. Along with a little zap to the ass. A smirk, and Julian continued, "And any to come. For your bravery and utmost dedication to Nalsar and this Council, there will be no further assignments for you other than this. You will continue to hold the highest rank, highest clearance, and with Top Honor. You alone will decide any further jobs you wish to take as Enforcer."

I snapped my head back to look at Mickel, whose face was stone. There was no emotion there. He simply replied, "Yes, sir."

"You okay?" I pushed to him, and he grabbed my hand and squeezed. I looked back at him quickly as he smiled and nodded.

Julian turned to face those floating heads and said, "You are dismissed." He slapped the button on his desk and the LightCall was disengaged.

I glared at him and through my teeth I seethed, "Don't you ever use your power to touch me again." I felt CJ's charge flow over me as his hands were suddenly within easy reach of his syths.

"Twins even. Powerful ones too, if my magic tells me true," he said coolly. There was a meaningful look to Mickel before he said, "Why didn't you mention the pregnancy in your report?"

"It is none of their business, nor is it yours," I spat, feeling electricity jump to my fingers.

He raised his hands in supplication. "My apologies. I am sorry if I offended you. I meant what I said. Take the year off, Megan. Mickel can return with you."

"Why are you force retiring Mickel?" I asked, regardless of the fact that Mickel tried to tell me he was okay.

"He has served Nalsar well. He has also just suffered a great loss," Julian said sadly as he looked at Mickel.

"And because it is Nalrin procedure, that should you survive a situation such as this, you are recommissioned, so to say," Mickel said. "Owen and Jean used to be Guards as well. After what happened to her, they were recommissioned, and became Enforcers. She could choose the jobs she wanted to take for the Council. It is what I will now do. I won't have to be in Nalrin all the time. I can never work, or I can work as much as I like."

"On the books, he will be assigned to you and your family, but he won't be required to do anything other than what you command, which I suspect will just be to be happy," Julian said.

"I could use some time off, actually. Not that I know what to do, or where to go, but..." Mickel said and then he gave me a meaningful, sad look. "There are things to do."

"Julian, I would like to stay in my residence here for a few days. We need to sort some things out. Like, where we are going to live." I took CJ's hand. "Sort out what to do with Jean and Owen's estate."

"Megan," Julian said in a smooth fatherly voice, "The home you arrived in and have lived in for the last couple years is yours."

"I'm sorry?"

"Jean and Owen both provided me statements should they not return, that everything be left to you and CJ. Whether one or both of you returned, it would all go to you. The property is yours, along with their considerable funds." Then Julian turned to Mickel. "There was one exception in Owen's statement. He stated that should he not return, that Mickel would inherit the land of his fathers."

"I'm sorry?" Mickel choked.

"Owen inherited his father's land roughly two miles from Megan and CJ's, sixteen years ago. He stated you were to receive that property. He said you had never had any inclination to buy a property of your own, nor anything of your own, and should you decide to retire or step back for a while, he wanted you to have somewhere to go that was quiet. His words were, '*For rescuing me when all hope was lost.*' There has been a family who has been caretaking the land since Owen inherited it, and they are awaiting your instructions."

Mickel was crying then. "That, that was such a long time ago. I didn't think..." He just wiped his tears away and said, "Thank you."

"You are welcome to stay in your residences anytime you come to Nalrin City. They are yours forever," Julian said. "I'm sure that CJ would like to have the Physicians check on the babes, so I will let you be on your way."

We turned to leave, and just as I was about to, Julian said in a soft, painful voice I had never heard him use before, "I meant no disrespect to you or your family, Megan. I think of you as my own daughter. It is likely why I gave such lenience on the Council level." I turned to face him and there were indeed tears in his eyes as he said with a small sheepish smile on his face. "It was one of the hardest things I have ever done in my 200 years... to let you go north. To set up all that transportation, for you to go and give your life for Nalsar. I never want to feel that fear and hopelessness again. I hope you can forgive me for earlier."

"Julian, I appreciate everything you have done to help us along the way and everything you have done for my family. You took care of CJ and ensured his safety while in the Curtails of the North, and then when I shipped Mickel and Logan here..." I took a deep breath and I looked at CJ, who was standing in the doorway, waiting for me. "You allowed it and took care of him. Thank you for that."

I walked back toward the desk and said, "Your daughter?"

His face softened even more, and a tentative smile crossed his face. "As if you were my own flesh and blood. I cried and worried the entire time you were gone. I have never felt that massive amount of the relief as I felt when I received word you had used Helena and then still lived. Received word you were in route to Nalrin City," he reached out and took my hand and squeezed it softly before saying, "To know you were coming home."

"If that is how you really feel, then..." I looked back to CJ again who nodded, "Maybe after all this is settled, you could come visit for dinner one night. Life has been crazy since we met, and while I am thankful for you and everything you have done for us, I'm still pretty raw from losing so much family. I let Jean and Owen, Clarice and Alexei, Lindy and Mickel all in, and only half of them are left. In the last five years, I have lost my biological brother, my biological parents, Lindy, and now Jean and Owen. Underworlds being, one of them was by my own doing. I... dinner. Let's start with dinner, Julian."

"I would like that," he said with a light in his eyes. "And Megan, thank you for all you have done for this world. You had no reason to save us, yet you did so anyway. You have our... my eternal gratitude. Your sacrifice will be written in notable history for the ages."

"I never wanted it. None of the notoriety. Leave me out of history, and I won't lose a single moment of sleep,." I said, holding my head high. "I-"

"Just wanted to go home, marry CJ, and have a nice quiet life," he smiled. I smiled back, nodding. "Go. Start that quiet life. Please let me know what the physicians say about the babes. I want to be a part of your lives."

"We will talk soon, Julian," I said as I turned and walked out to start my new life.

CHAPTER 58

EPILOGUE

THREE AND A HALF YEARS LATER

"LINDY JEAN AND OWEN Matthew, stop throwing sand at each other." Mickel yelled at the twins. "If you are going to fight, at least do so with sticks, and practice what I showed you."

I rolled my eyes as I looked over at Aiden, who was fast asleep in the play pin. After returning to work two years ago, it seemed like we had done nothing but run. This was the first family vacation we had taken, and knowing I just wanted a quiet beach, CJ was able to arrange for us to come back into Hartwood Citadel.

"At least Aiden is being quiet." CJ adjusting the blanket over him. "That was the whole point of this trip, right? Quiet?"

"Ceej, we have two-and-a-half-year-old twins and an almost one-year-old." I smiled at him. "Quiet is not our life."

"When was the last time our life was quiet?" He stared out over the ocean.

"When I was pregnant with the twins and we were finally settled into the house. Mickel was working on his property, and Clarice and Alexei had just left?" I said without thinking as I saw Mickel head back up toward us. "That or when we were still in the Manusia and it was that first night that you asked me out at Russo's."

I looked up toward the estate and sighed. CJ said, "You would think that all these years later, we would look back at the estate and see something different. There are still Guards lining the staircase, and trying to give us privacy, yet they still hover. Just like our honeymoon. Mickel is even here."

One of those guards was making her way over and stopped short as Mickel reached us. "Kaitlin..." he blushed, "I mean, Sitgos. What can I do for you?"

The Guard blushed uncontrollably.

"Subtle, Mickel," CJ teased.

"What?"

"You and Kaitlin are adorable together. New order?" and he raised an eyebrow at me. Since that time in Julian's office, where he was permanently assigned to me and my family, I had given him two orders. The first of which was indeed to be happy, the second was three months later to check out his new property. The fact I was now giving him another one after so much time had passed, gave him pause. "If there are no other guards or pretenses that need to be given, fuck it. Just be yourselves. It's not like you both don't turn into puddles of goo around each other. There is not one person in this whole place that doesn't know of your... extracurricular activities," I said firmly, but smiling.

"Lady Megan." Kaitlin said, a little embarrassed.

"It's true. You two have officially been together for what, almost a year and a half now?" I said, sitting up. They had met while he was packing his things from Nalrin, and it did not take long for them to start down that romantic road. "You have helped him babysit, been on every holiday with us in the last two years, and you still insist on being formal?"

"Megan," Mickel growled.

"She isn't wrong, you know, Mickel." CJ chuckled.

"Before she so rudely embarrassed us," Mickel said, glaring at me, and I stuck my tongue out at him. "What can I do for you?"

Kaitlin once again blushed and gave him an evil eye when he responded, "You are not helping the situation, hun."

"And you calling me *hun* isn't helping either." I saw the heat rise in his eyes as he quickly looked her up and down. Then, in a voice that said exactly what he was thinking, "Now, what can I do for you?"

Kaitlin's cheeks reddened and, in a battle of wills, she turned and handed CJ a message. "Message from Sir... message from Logan. He said that the Vernadali want direction on how to move forward with the training grounds at Chantel Sprits."

"I'll respond to him after dinner," CJ said, stuffing the note in his pocket. Logan had indeed decided to stay in Nalsar after everything and was doing very well as the Project and Training Coordinator for the Vernadali and Nalrin Guard.

Just then, LJ ran up and said, "Uncle Mickey, Aunti Kait, lookie what I do," she opened her hand and a small ball of yellow light pooled in her hand.

I gave Kaitlin a meaningful look that she was indeed already part of the family. She just smiled and knelt down to take a closer look. She adored the kids. Spoiled them just as much as Mickel did.

"What do you have there, sweetie?" She asked LJ.

"Bright light. Be careful hot," she said as the light grew brighter, and said, "Owy said his water tricks are better. I like light, Aunti Kait."

"His water tricks?" I said, standing up, heart thundering, looking from the ball of light in her hand down to where Owen was down by the water's edge, moving his hands around.

"Yeah, Owy play with water. Got me wet." LJ pointed to her butt, which was indeed wet.

"Well, puberty should be interesting," Mickel said, scratching the back of his neck.

I gave Mickel a look to stay with LJ and went to talk to Owen. My heart raced as I reached him, crouched down, and I asked as carefully as I could, "What are you doing, Owen?"

"Play with water, Mama," Owen said, smiling. "I playing with LJ. She showed me light, and I make water splash."

"Where are you touching it?" I asked carefully.

"No, Mama," His eyes were wide in fear of getting trouble. "Uncle Mickey said not to get into the water because we eat soon."

"So, how did you make the water splash? Can you show me?"

His eyes were bright as he said, "Sure, Mama. Like dis." He raised his hand and the water from the ocean came up in a single thread. Turning his hand over, he said, "Water hand."

That single thread of water he had pulled up from the ocean balled up and hovered over his cupped hand.

"Very good, Owen," I said, rubbing his back. "Can you put the water back and we can go eat dinner? They are making your favorite."

"Dino Nuggies!" Owen yelled, flinging the water without a second thought into the ocean before turning and running up toward the others. My eyes widened slightly at the lack of thought Owen had to have at just throwing the water back into the ocean like that.

I stood up slowly and looked back to where my family stood. Mickel was picking up LJ and taking Owen by the hand, leading them up to dinner. The whole time screaming, "Yay! Dino Nuggies." Kaitlin reached down and picked up Aiden, who had woken up to Owen's screaming for said 'Dino Nuggies'. On the way up the stairs, she passed the guards and pointed to the play pin, giving them some instructions. He and another guard gathered up our belongings and took them up.

CJ was at my side now and let out a long, long breath, running his hand through his hair. I smiled at that. Every time he did that it melted my insides.

"Elementals," CJ said. "Strong elementals if they can do this already. Mickel's right, though. Puberty with a fire and water elemental?"

"He would know. Thank the Angels we have him." It had been a shock that he repressed his air elemental abilities. I looked back at CJ and said, "Helena did warn us to get proper witch and Sangra training for them."

"Do you think Aiden will, too?" CJ paused for a moment before he said, "or he could theoretically carry the Vernadali trait. Angels, what if they all end up being Elemental Vernadali?"

"Guess we just wait and see. Maybe LJ and Owen are Elementals because of Helena? Or because we were in that other realm? Maybe it's because we've been touched by the Angels? Maybe Aiden will be a normal Sangra? He was at least conceived under normal circumstances."

CJ chuckled. "LJ and Owen were conceived under *normal* means, too. We were just also under a lot of stress at the time."

"That isn't what I meant, and you know it." I said, but looked out over the ocean and took a deep inhale of the briny scent. "We *are* a normal family, right?"

CJ pulled me close, and I wrapped my arms around his shoulders. "Sure. The most powerful Sangra marries an Angels Blessed Vernadali, and they have two confirmed elemental children. Totally normal."

"Well, when you say it like that. I have nothing to worry about," I said against his lips, pressing my hips against him.

CJ moved his head to kiss down my neck and whispered, "The alcove is just there." A quick nip on my collarbone. The memory of our first moments there on our honeymoon, extraordinarily clear in my mind.

"The kids," I said, not putting up too much of a fight.

"They are with Mickel and Kait. They will be fine."

"Clarice and Alexei will be here soon with Karlo and Reka," I said, my breath catching as he ran a thumb over my nipple.

"They are coming to see the kids, not us. They can wait."

"Dinner?" I asked again, my resolve quickly failing with each press of his lips on my neck.

"I have my meal right here," He growled, slowly moving me toward that alcove.

I palmed him through his pants and there was a guttural moan that ended with us in that very alcove.

The End

Song Inspirations

<u>I'm Not Okay – Citizen Solider</u>
©2020 Citizen Soldier. All Rights Reserved.

<u>Climb – Adona</u>
⊠ Honeybee Music. All Rights Reserved.

Jump 40 Years in the Future

Duchess' Crown and Duchess' Throne is a duology about Megan and CJ's youngest son, Aiden Mathewson. While it is a standalone duology, it will contain characters and spoilers from The Five Angels trilogy.

DUCHESS' CROWN

EXERPT

CHAPTER I

JESSIKA

"Stop slouching." Amala said.

"I'm not slouching. I was resting against the wall. You know how much I hate wearing heels. Why can't I just wear what I normally do? Why do I have to stand here like I'm ready for this whole thing to turn into a formal celebration?" I said, smirking at her.

Amala slid her brown eyes to me and gave me a sideways look. "Because your mother, the Grand Duchess, required it."

"Is that my best friend talking, or my bodyguard?"

"Both," she elbowed me and smiled.

327

"Even the Nalrin Guard aren't in their formal attire. I've seen them wear more fancy outfits in Nalrin City." I pouted and then saw Janreka of the House of Heros standing about twenty feet away. I sighed, feeling a little better knowing that even one of my best friends, whose mother was Empress of Obsecuritan and Gatekeeper of the Underworld, had also been required to attend in formal wear. Why was she here, though? She couldn't be here to be assigned a Vernadali? Would she? Surely the Therth Guards could keep her safe.

"Jess..."

"Well, Mom just said head to the Curtails of the North, you are getting a Vernadali. No other explanation. There was no telling how many times I could come to these presentations every month for years, before the Angels grace me with a Vernadali." I growled. "Why do we have to be here again? They didn't use to make us come to these things."

"Things changed after The Keller War. So suck it up, Duchess." Amala's red lipstick smacked with the words. Even though our skin was a luxurious brown that never seemed to dull, she could always pull off the deep red color flawlessly, where I just looked like a cheap whore when I wore it. She had a deep maroon dress on that was so short, I wasn't sure how she could walk without it sliding up her hips, but she looked completely fuckable in it. Even the thigh syth belt didn't prevent at least four different guys giving her a double take as we passed by them in the last hour alone.

"Lots of things changed after Ansel Keller tore through Nalrin and Obsecuritan." I looked back at Janreka. "I know that better than anyone. Anyone who stayed in Ashridge died when he came through. We were lucky we were in Savanora on holiday when it happened. I still have nightmares about it. Luckily, Lemi wasn't old enough to remember what home looked like when we returned."

Angels, that was over forty years ago, and Ashridge, Obsecuritan, the Seltic Marsh, and much of Nalrin were *still* healing from it. There were parts of the Nalrin City center that had just finished renovations. Head Julian had waited until all the residential districts were rebuilt before repairing the main buildings. Decades later, it was only starting to look how it had over fifty years ago.

After defeating her father, Lady Megan Mathewson had dedicated her life to help to repair the damage. She still felt a responsibility to this world after what her parents did to try and destroy it. While she hated politics, she had taken a special interest in fixing laws that were archaic, and "just fucking stupid," as she called them. Her husband, Vernadali CJ had continued to work within the Vernadali ranks, but was never far from her side. They were *the* power couple of the ages, though it helped that Lady Megan Mathewson was one of the most powerful Sangra to have lived in memorable history. She was probably second only to Empress Clarice herself.

"The whole dimension is still healing." Amala chuckled. "Come on, I want to talk to Janreka. You haven't seen her in a while. I'm surprised you didn't run right to her."

We weaved through the crowd of dignitaries and royalty, but it was slow as more and more came into the main hall. It was almost the size of the courtyard in front of the main buildings in Nalrin City, and could easily hold a thousand people. The dark gray marble floors, tall, thin blue stained-glass windows were an impressive sight, but it was not what drew my eye. At the end of the room was a raised platform, where the Vernadali would be assigned their Charge. Etched into the light gray wall was the Vernadali herald.

It was made for the fancy ball that would be taking place tonight for all the Vernadali and their Charges to be celebrated. I did not want to attend, and would be spending the evening in my room, reading a good book. When Amala noticed I had gone silent, she looked at me and I sighed.

"Empress Clarice has done well in Obsecuritan, and yet Mom and I struggle just keeping the fishing ports open along the coast, and the farmers with water. There just wasn't enough snow in the Black Mountains the last couple of years to feed Ashridge's crops."

"The Grand Duchess is doing fine, regardless of the empty promises of Kaletta. You know that."

I shook my head at the thought of all those failed and empty promises. Later. I would worry about that later. That was so a future Jessika problem.

Janreka's eyes met mine and lit up when we finally reached her. "Jessika! Amala!" She hugged and kissed Amala, then pulled me into a warm hug before giving me Ashridge's customary kiss on each cheek.

"What are you doing here?" I said, holding her hands.

She rolled her eyes. "Mom says that if I'm going to be traveling the world as an emissary, I need protection, and I refused the Therth Guards. So, she pulled her weight with Head Julian, and here I stand, waiting to be assigned a Vernadali. Against my wishes, I might add. It's the third month that I've attended. I just wish the Angels would make the assignment so I can get started. Trade negotiations with the Seltic Marsh and Cinder have been slow, and will go so much faster once I'm able to travel. But Mom won't let me travel until I have a protection detail. Hence, my presence." She pulled her hand from mine and waved it around flippantly, rolling her eyes.

"Why?" I asked, genuinely concerned. "Why did you refuse your own guards?"

"Obsecuritan was decimated after the Keller War. It needs all the personnel we can afford to stay there. It's been forty years, but there are still limited resources. It's going to take a very long time before we can fully recover. Things are better. Crops are growing, and we aren't so reliant on outside goods, but it's still a slow process. I know you understand. Ashridge has been working just as hard as we have since it all happened." She said it like it was nothing, but looked me up and down and scrunched her nose. The small stud in her nose caught the light as she said, "Now, why did your mother make you wear a dress? She knows how much you loathe them."

"Because she is my mom. She can't control what comes out of my mouth, so she tries to control what I wear. There are enough people here that she would know if I didn't." I laughed.

It wasn't that the dress wasn't beautiful, because it was. The backless, floor length, deep green satin gown not only showed off my Maltal in the center of my back, the deep v-neck in the front beautifully accentuated my chest. While no one would ever describe my body type as athletic or toned by any stretch, I had learned to love every single one of my curves. It took my years to accept the body I had, and while I detested wearing dresses, I actually liked how stunning I looked in this one.

"Does Empress Clarice know you stole that dress from her closet? I know your mom, and that is something she would wear in a heartbeat. So, did you buy it and hide it or steal it from her closet?" I asked, motioning to her skin tight white chiffon dress. A silver metal snake gave the illusion of slithering up her back from the tailbone to the nape of her neck and was strategically held in place by silver chains. The contrast of the white fabric against her dark skin was nothing short of stunning. Her hair was up in a ponytail in small braids, with one larger thick braid circling the base of the ponytail. "You look absolutely amazing! Between you and Amala here, how am I supposed to get the eye of anyone?"

Janreka laughed. "First of all, you have no shame. I almost feel bad for Jayden."

I rolled my eyes and muttered under my breath, "He's one of my best friends and you know Jayden and I don't give two shits about each other like that."

"Second, Mom almost required me to wear this dress when she saw it on the hanger." She let out an amused breath, and smiled. "I'm so glad that Aunt Megan convinced her to change the dress code in Therth after the war. Can you just imagine me wearing those gaudy relics?"

"I bet Aunt Erida had a fit over that."

"Mom says she did, but Aunt Erida eventually gave in. She still looks at the heritage closets with longing, though. I think she just wants to honor my grandparents' tradition, but you know Aunt Megan."

"Fuck tradition." All three of us said in unison.

I did know her Aunt Megan, pretty well too. For six years I dated their son Aiden, that is, until he shattered my heart. Angels. That was almost five years ago. He broke it off saying he was a Vernadali, and there was no way he could be with me while I ran my territory. In addition to that, he was assigned to someone else. I understood the logic behind it, but my heart still ached at the thought of him. I had tried moving on, but no one could satisfy me in and out of the bedroom like Aiden could.

I knew there was a remote chance I could see him here, but the last I heard he was months away, somewhere near the Slumbering Expanse, so it was unlikely. Much to my relief and dismay. There were parts of me that wanted to see him again, but...

"So, how are things with Jadyen?" Janreka asked, nudging me with her elbow and bringing me out of my own thoughts.

"I don't know. He's in Cinder on some mission." I shrugged nonchalantly.

"What do you mean you don't know? Shouldn't you know where your betrothed is?" She was teasing me, and I just shook my head at her.

I snorted. "We are friends, but neither of us actually *want* the marriage. You know that. We keep trying to convince his father of that, not that he will listen to either of us. Mom told me she would sign off on the nullification, citing that Ashridge doesn't need the support anymore. We may be struggling, but we can manage without any of his help, not like he's given us much, if any, since the agreement."

"His father won't nullify?" Janreka said, her eyes bright with a million thoughts. She lifted her hand, looked to Amala, who met her smile before she looked back at me. I saw a gray smoke curl through her fingers. "I could help with that particular issue."

"No. No. No." I said, pointing a finger at her. "You are not..." I gave them both looks that meant that if either of them killed the Grand Lord of Kaletta, they would be sorry.

"Ahhh, you're no fun!" Amala chuckled beside me. "You know Princess Janreka could make it look like an accident." I saw

Janreka wince at the title, but I gave them both another stern look.

"Amala." Janreka warned.

"I know. I know. You hate honorifics." Amala looping her arm through hers. "Your Mom does, too."

Amala's eyes lit up a bit before she asked, "How is Karlo? I haven't seen him at the meetings in Nalrin as of late."

"My brother is fine. Been asking about *you* a lot, though." Janreka gave her a knowing smirk, and then poked her in the shoulder. "You need to step up. He's way too shy to make the first move."

"I know, but your brother is just..." Amela blushed, "He's your brother and Empress Clarice's son."

"And I'm her daughter. So? I'm to become her Suk'Natal, not him. He gets to live a relatively normal life. Privileged, but he's basically equal in status to you, Amala." Janreka said encouragingly. "I think I would like to have you as a sister."

Amela chewed on her bottom lip a bit, and nodded slowly.

"You two are great together. You've known each other since you finished schooling, took your testing, and received your Maltals. You deal with him constantly when you go to Nalrin City for me." I said, taking her hand. "Contact him. If you don't, once I'm crowned, I'll arrange your damn marriage."

"Jess! You wouldn't dare!" Amala gasped as Janreka laughed.

"I'll make my mom agree to that arrangement. Bind it in the Underworld's darkness and make you Silnaree." Janreka crossed her arms just as there was a loud drumming sound from the front of the room, commanding all attention to where Head Vernadali Samuel stood. We all put our fists over our hearts and bowed slightly in respect of the Vernadali who were strode into the room. These were the Vernadali that would be assigned their Charges today.

As I stood up straight, I couldn't help but scan the ten men and women who were coming into the room. My heart stopped as I watched a man with honey and chestnut locks that were just too long stride across the front of that room. I knew that the heat through those hazel-green eyes could burn through the ice

I had encased my heart in since the day he walked away. It took every ounce of my willpower to pull my attention from them, and I could instantly remember how that perfect amount scruff on his masculine jaw felt as it brushed against my cheek and he whispered in my ear.

Memories flooded my mind of him running that stubble down my jaw, and leaving sensuous kisses down my neck as he moved down to my shoulder. The deep rumble of his voice in my ear as he told me how I was a good girl. The feel of the calluses on his palms as they ran down my side, across my bare hips, and thighs. The way his fingers would dip between my legs... Angels, my knees almost gave out under me at the thought of it.

"Oh, the Angels are fucking with us, aren't they?" Amala said, bringing me out of the memories. She slowly slid her hand into mine and gripped it tight. She knew how hard this was going to be for me to see him. To see him tied to someone else for life.

"Amala!" Janreka hissed, but out of the corner of my eye, I saw her watching me for how I might react. She took a hold of my other hand and ran her thumb along the back of it for support. The well of emotion that sat at the base of my throat was thick, and I'm not sure I could have said a word, if I were required.

Each Vernadali stood at attention at the front of the room, and there was this tug for me to look at Aiden, but I stood looking straight, and kept my eyes on Vernadali Samuel. The problem was Aiden was standing only two down from him, and I could see Aiden's eyes flick to me repeatedly.

Not everyone in this room was being charged with a Vernadali this evening. For all he knew, I was here to support Janreka. I was standing right next to her. This was the third month in a row Janreka had been here and I could come every month for the next five years before I was assigned.

I squeezed on Janreka's hand and tried very hard not to think too much about it. She squeezed it back, and I swear I felt some of her power flow into me and help loosen my chest. I had to remind myself that not even the Vernadali standing there knew who was being assigned today, let alone to whom. The only one who knew who was receiving assignments tonight was

Vernadali Samuel. I could come to ten more of these before receiving my assigned Vernadali.

"It is with great honor I announce these Vernadali will be assigned their Charge this evening. Each of them graduated in the top five percent of their respective classes. Once their assignment has been given, they will immediately receive their name scroll. Full-time duties for each Vernadali upon their Charge will begin in the morning."

"Princess Janreka of the House of Heros." Vernadali Samuel stated as Janreka moved toward the front of the room. As her hand left mine, I felt that tightening in my chest return, and I struggled to keep my breathing normal. Vernadali Samuel bowed to her, as well as every Vernadali in the room. There could be a very clear argument she outranked everyone on this blasted island. The Curtails of the North may be a long way from Therth and the gate to the Underworld, but she still radiated power that could rival even the Mathewson family.

Vernadali Samuel reached over to a pile of envelopes and slowly lifted the seal, breaking the bright blue wax. Unfolding it, Vernadali Samuel said, "Vernadali Natasha Kapinov, will report to your quarters first thing in the morning and accompany you back to Therth. Please accompany Vernadali Kapinov for her to receive your name scroll." He said, bowing one last time.

"Thank you, sir." She turned toward Vernadali Kapinov, who had stepped forward and formally bowed to her. Vernadali Natasha Kapinov raised her arm, and as Janreka took it, she looked at me and gave me a reassuring smile.

As Janreka passed Aiden, I swore she narrowed his eyes at him, before she was led out of the room. Amala chuckled, and whispered, "Reka will handle him."

"Duchess Jessika Valenti of Ashridge." Vernadali Samuel said, and my heart thudded. I squeezed Amala's hand, before letting go. Slowly I moved toward the front of the room, my eyes flicked to Aiden, and I couldn't help but swish my hips, and lengthened my stride. For once in my life, I was grateful for the fucking ridiculous high heels I was wearing. I smirked when his attention traveled up the entire length of the thigh high slit in my dress. Aiden's hands clenched into a fist, and there was a sharp inhale as he fought to maintain his stoic composure. I resisted the urge not to smirk at him. I was more than happy to show him just what he walked away from.

When I bowed to Vernadali Samuel, my long white hair slid over my shoulder, thankfully creating a barrier in front of Aiden. I saw the blue wax crumbling to the floor and a moment later Vernadali Samuel's voice rang through the room, freezing me in place.

"Vernadali Aiden Mathewson will report to your quarters first thing in the morning, and accompany you back to Ashridge." Vernadali Samuel said.

It took entirely too long for my heart to start beating again. Remembering where I was, I slowly stood and my eyes flicked to Aiden's. His eyes flashed in surprise before returning neutral, but I saw how his jaw had slackened in shock. He stepped forward, and at least *he* remembered we were standing in front of a very large crowd, who had started to murmur.

I had to swallow a few times before I could say, "Thank you, sir." I turned toward Aiden, and when his eyes met mine, there were so many emotions going through them, I couldn't read them. He blinked, and I bowed toward him.

"Please accompany Vernadali Aiden Mathewson for him to receive your name scroll." Vernadali Samuel said, as if he hadn't just turned my insides to soup. He bowed to me, and turned to retrieve the next envelope.

Aiden lifted his arm, and I took it.

"Just breathe, Jess." He said, hardly moving his mouth.

"Aiden." I breathed his name. His hand tightened slightly around my fingers. The heat of his skin on mine sent a wave of all those old feelings through me, and I didn't know what to do with any of it. Fear and confusion were both very clearly present and battling for the top spot in my emotional turmoil.

When we cleared the room and the door shut so that we were the only two in there, I slowly lowered my arm, but he didn't release my fingers. No, instead, his thumb ran over my knuckles as he stared at where he held my hand.

"Aiden." I said, my voice stronger this time, but still shaking. My heart pounded so loud I wouldn't be surprised if he could hear it. "Does Vernadali Samuel know? About our history?"

"No. We did a really good job of hiding that aspect of it. Mom, Dad, and the Grand Duchess made sure of it." I took another step back from him, letting our hands drop, and he ran his hand through his hair, a habit he picked up from his dad.

"Angels. What are our parents going to say about this?" I said, as I started to pace. I felt a zap and a tug deep within my chest, and out of the corner of my eye, I saw him rub his chest.

"Our parents?" He said, half laughing in frustration. "Jess, what are we going to do?"

My eyes snapped to his. Anger fueled by all that hurt rose to the surface as I turned to him, my power rising to the surface, and my hand glowing purple. Aiden looked at it carefully, and winced. He had been on the receiving end of it many times. Anything I touched with my power would feel like being vibrated with hot spikes.

"Jess." He said carefully. "Calm down."

"You haven't learned a damn thing since you left, have you?" He winced at my words, but I continued. "First, I don't give a damn if you're my Vernadali, you *never* tell me to calm down. It is the one sure fire way to make me angrier. Second, you and I both know that once a Charge has been assigned, the only way out of it is death. Since I have no intention of dying, and even though there were times *I* have wanted to kill *you*, I don't want you to die either. Right now, it's probably out of respect for your mom and dad, more than anything, but," a lump formed in my throat, because the fact was, it hurt to even think about him dying. "I don't want you dead."

I took a few deep breaths, paced a few times across the room, his eyes trailing me the entire time. I faced him, held my head high, and crossed my arms, "So, we are going to be professionals about this."

"What about once you marry Jayden?" His voice was low, but there was something else there. I thought I might have imagined it, but I could swear his throat bobbed as he said it.

"We will do what Dad and Uncle Mickey did. You two will work it out." I would have to tell him eventually about how Jayden and I didn't want to marry, and that we were trying to get his father to agree to nullifying the agreement, but that was a future me problem. Right now, I had a very real drop dead gorgeous, six-foot three problem.

A door on the other side of the room opened and a small petite woman who looked to be about 35, though she was probably about a hundred, walked in and gestured for us to walk through the door. "Vernadali Aiden and Duchess Valenti, this way, please."

Like Chapter 1?
<u>You can get the rest here.</u>

Other Books by K.M. Ringer

Weekend Series

Weekend with Rylie
Weekend with Malcom
Weekend with Desiree
Weekend with Bethany
Angel's Shadow

The Ashstrike Sanctorum

The Ashstrike Sanctorum: Orgin Story
The Astral's Bonded
The Exorci's Touch
My Kismot Savior
The Kismot's Undesirable
My Kismot's Beloveds

Other Books

Ashes and Flame
Otter Be Saved
Under the Needle
Dedicated in Ink

Ashes and Flame

After working as an Advisor for the Roman Empire, Tiberius Maximus Vispania returned to Herculaneum in 79AD to start over. When he meets Sidonia Regilla, a fire instantly ignites between them. She would be allowed to choose her future husband. Could Sidonia be happy with Tiberius?

Just when happiness finds a way, an epic tragedy occurs and the entire village is wiped out. Only Tiberius and his best friend survive, courtesy of a curse that's provided them with immortality.

2,000 years later, Kelsey walks into his bar and lights a desire within him that only Sidonia had ever done. When their dark worlds collide, an overwhelming need to protect her takes over, and he realizes there may be more to Kelsey's ability to get under his skin than he thought. When Kelsey is kidnapped and tortured, unknown old rivals and secrets come to light.

When Max rushes in to save her, he vows that either all of them would come out alive, or none of them.

THE ASHSTRIKE SANCTORUM

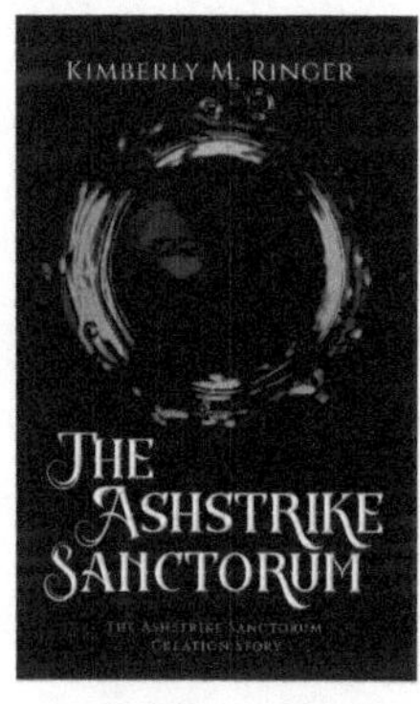

<u>THE ASHSTRIKE SANCTORUM:</u>
<u>CREATION STORY</u>

When the Dark Witches of Moesia go rogue, and start creating immortals, will the paranormal creatures allow the new beings to live, or will they be out to destroy them? They have tasked Benjamin, an Ovexa, with finding three of these immortals to be interrogated to determine if they can be trusted to keep the paranormal world a secret from the humans.

Jorgen Hegland has found himself newly made but quickly learns being an immortal isn't worth it. When Benjamin finds him and demands he meet with the other creatures of the world, he agrees, but it isn't until he finds his mate, that he decides he will fight for his right to live.

THE ASTRAL'S BONDED
THE ASHSTRIKE SANCTORUM:
BOOK I

EVEN ALPHAS HAVE TO ANSWER TO SOMEONE.

It was supposed to be a simple assignment. Astral Jade Romero was supposed to fix the werewolf problem at the Porter Ranch.

Only there was a problem, she hadn't prepared herself for, the human foreman Kolton Webster. He occupied all her thoughts and sucked her in like she never had been before.

When the wolves attack and Jade is injured will it be Kolton or the wolves that destroy her?

THE EXORCI'S TOUCH
THE ASHSTRIKE SANCTORUM:
BOOK 2
WHAT DO YOU DO WHEN YOUR ASSIGNMENT
DOESN'T DIE.

Exorci Jesse Westbrook can't touch anyone with his bare skin. If he does, they die. Such is the curse of an Exorci, the executioners for the Ashstrike Sanctorum.

His job is as simple and complicated as that. Receive the name and location of the person, and with a simple touch, the extermination is complete.

Jesse's life isn't all death and destruction. He has Maddie Taylor. The woman is his forever, but he's never dared to truly touch her. When her brother dies, her life spirals out of control, to the point she pushes Jesse from her life. Now... Now she's his next assignment.

MY KISMOT SAVIOR
THE ASHSTRIKE SANCTORUM:
BOOK 2.5

Angelica's life has been nothing but hiding from her parents and trying to make ends meet. It's been hard, but worth the freedom it afforded her from her family.

Morgan would have never guessed he would have found his queen just walking down the streets of Carmel, California, but there she was, arguing with the most despicable of women.

When Morgan intervenes, chaos ensues and Angelica and Morgan's secrets come to light quickly. Only Angelica seems to have one more...

Masen Cartwell was the son to the pride's king. It was his responsibility to ratify the treaty by marrying the Los Padres pride's undesirable, Veronica Aktins. There is something about her though. Something that pulls at his protective instincts and calls to his tom.

Ronni was the daughter of traders to her pride, an outcast, the Undesirable. Used and assaulted by the princes, the King has demanded that she marry the rival pride's prince and kill the Ventana Prides ruling family. Only, when she meets Prince Masen, his possessiveness over her and the adoration he showers her with sings to her heart.

When Prince Edwin steals Ronni, Masen will do anything to get her back. He had promised to protect her and keep her safe from her old pride.

Masen Cartwell won't let anything happen to what is his, and will stop at nothing to have his Queen back.

My Kismot's Beloveds
The Ashstrike Sanctorum:
Book 3.5

Leo Banks has watched his best friend and his prince find their mates. As hand to the crown prince, he was okay with that. They found their happiness and now his princess, and a woman he considered a sister, was pregnant with twins. He vowed to be her protector through the troubled pregnancy. He was happy with just being Uncle Leo.

Then when her pregnancy takes a turn for the worse, Dr. Marie Fuller and her nurse, Hadrian Fuller, come to Landow to care for her. When they arrived, Leo was not expecting to find his mate, let alone a queen and tom.

Can he balance the stress of protecting his princess, and welcoming his mates into his life?

Weekend Series

by K.M. Ringer

Weekend with Rylie
Book One

Luci's whole life changes in one weekend with her boyfriend, Rylie Allen.

Of course, there was the mind-blowingly good sex. It always was, but then there are secrets revealed, and a new job opportunity that would change everything between Luci and Rylie. When her ex-boyfriend comes back to haunt her, it threatens to throw their lives into further upheaval.

WEEKEND WITH MALCOM
Book Two

Malcom Henderson has been obsessed with his Project Foreman for months. When she's disrespected at a bar he steps in and after an enjoyable night, he hopes to have it turn into something more. The next morning, she's convinced that as much as she wants him, it was only a one-night stand, and tries to protect herself by kicking him out. A torturous week pulls between them when unexpected problems are occurring on the job site that ends up being tied to the Chicago mafia families, and it's not long before Malk and Raquel find themselves in the middle of a brewing war.

WEEKEND WITH DESIREE
Book Three
With threats against the Don Supreme and his family lurking around every corner, Jensen Maloy, the most feared man in all Chicago, has been working overtime to ensure everyone stays safe and alive. Desiree Hernandez loves and trusts Jensen with every fiber of her being, and while she understands the reason, they need to live in lockdown, it doesn't mean she's happy about it. Even if she

is living with her best friend and honorary sister, and her fiance.

Jensen and Desiree aren't used to being apart for such long stretches of time, and despite all the support from friends and coworkers, tensions rise, and morale drops to an all-time low. When the enemy takes drastic actions to finish the deal, they forget to factor in two very important things. Desi is not to be underestimated, and Jensen will stop at nothing to make sure his Princess is safe and in his arms. Who will still be standing when the dust settles?

WEEKEND WITH BETHANY
Book Four
Her strength will save them all.
Weekend with Bethany is the explosive conclusion to the Weekend Series. The war between Dallas and Vaux has become deadly, and no one is safe. When Beth is captured, she was shocked to learn that her Wes was the one and only Wesley Backnoff. Sure, she knew the name. Who didn't? Can she reconcile the compassionate man with whom she fell in love, with the killer who stands before her?

After rescuing Bethany, Wesley Backnoff, second to the Don Supreme of Chicago, can't hold back his feelings for her any longer and is bound and determined to keep her.

Old secrets come to light and threaten to destroy them all. Who will pay the price? Will Beth and Wes survive the night or has their time run out?

About the Author
K.M. Ringer

K.M. Ringer lives in California with her husband, little human, and two furballs, a Jack Russell mix and a Pomeranian Terrier mix. She loves providing some spice to her stories and showing that no matter what happens in your life, you are worthy of love.

Contact K.M. Ringer:

www.kmringer.com

Instagram: @kimberlymringer
Facebook: www.facebook.com/kim.m.ringer/
TikTok: @kmringer

Sign up for her newsletter on her website
and receive freebies, coupon codes, and stay up to date
on all things Kimberly M. Ringer and K.M. Ringer

www.ingramcontent.com/pod-product-compliance
Lightning Source LLC
Chambersburg PA
CBHW061044190726
48286CB00006B/1602